Books by Aimée & David Thurlo

Ella Clah Novels

Blackening Song
Death Walker
Bad Medicine
Enemy Way
Shooting Chant
Red Mesa
Changing Woman
Tracking Bear
Wind Spirit
White Thunder
Mourning Dove
Turquoise Girl

Lee Nez Novels

Second Sunrise
Blood Retribution
Pale Death
Surrogate Evil

Sister Agatha Novels

Bad Faith
Thief in Retreat
Prey for a Miracle
False Witness*

Plant Them Deep

*Forthcoming

MOURNING DOVE

✳ ✳ ✳ ✳ ✳

AN ELLA CLAH NOVEL

AIMÉE & DAVID THURLO

A Tom Doherty Associates Book
New York

This is a work of fiction. All the characters and events portrayed in this book are either products of the author's imagination or are used fictitiously.

MOURNING DOVE

A Forge Book
Published by Tom Doherty Associates, LLC
175 Fifth Avenue
New York, NY 10010

www.tor-forge.com

Forge® is a registered trademark of Tom Doherty Associates, LLC.

ISBN-13: 978-0-7653-7450-9

First Edition: April 2006
First Mass Market Edition: March 2007

Printed in the United States of America

0 9 8 7 6 5 4 3 2

To Monadita Berndes and Hortensia Martel—
for memories cherished in the pages of my mind

ACKNOWLEDGMENTS

We would like to express our gratitude to those members of the armed forces, particularly those of you in the various investigative divisions, who helped us out when we needed it. You wanted to remain anonymous, and we will respect that, but you all deserve a special thank-you.

A very special thank-you, too, to the Navajo Codetalkers and their relatives who helped us with our research.

MOURNING DOVE

ONE

✖ ✖ ✖

In all her years serving first with the FBI, and then the Navajo Tribal Police, Special Investigator Ella Clah had never had an office with a window—until now. Of course, back in her Bureau days, she'd never even had an office—just a desk. Progress.

Budgets had grown, not due to tribal prosperity but because of an increase in violent crimes across the Navajo Nation. That had forced an expansion of their existing station and Ella, as head of their Major Crimes Unit, had landed space in their new wing. The odor of fresh paint was a constant reminder of the changes taking place in the department as was the color scheme, a palette of soft aquas, designed to relieve stress and maximize efficiency.

Ella swiveled in her chair, took a sip of freshly brewed coffee, and gazed at Ship Rock, the rock formation that was their town's namesake. In actuality, the jagged rock outcropping was the eroded neck of a volcano that had formed three million years ago.

Ella recalled the old story about the huge flying monsters that had once lived there. The tale was part of every Navajo child's education from before the first grade—that is, if they attended reservation schools. The story was vibrant with the richness and rhythms of the *Dineh*, The People's, legends. She could almost hear her mother, Rose, telling her the tale, keeping the legends alive—a gift from one generation to the next.

The *Dineh* had lived in fear of the giant birds who'd made their home on the upper levels of Ship Rock, Rose had taught her. The birds would swoop down and smash their prey against the rocks, then feed on the remains. Monster Slayer, one of the Hero Twins, was chosen to do battle with them, but when he approached their hunting ground, one of the giant birds picked him up in his talons, flew high into the skies, and dropped him, leaving him to fall on the rocks below. Expecting nothing less, Monster Slayer had prepared well and landed gently because he'd possessed a life feather given to him by Spider Woman.

Then Monster Slayer discovered that the giant birds had young and, after he killed the male and the female, the young began to cry and plead for their lives. Monster Slayer took pity on them and, instead of killing them, he turned the older one into an eagle so he could furnish feathers for men, and the younger one into an owl so men would listen to the owl's voice and be able to discern the future.

Rabbit, who was below, took some feathers from the giant bird Monster Slayer had killed and stuck them in his fur. And that's why jackrabbits have large ears that look like giant feathers.

All the *Dinetah*, the land of the Navajos, was filled with stories about the ones who'd come before. Every sandstone formation, pass or valley, mountain peak, and rock formation within the Four Corners and beyond echoed with the tradition of the *Dineh*.

Ella sipped her coffee. It was still early, and she refused to rush as she made up for all those years of staring at painted cinder blocks and file cabinets instead of the blue sky and drifting white clouds. The wind was calm now, as it usually was during the early morning hours, and she intended to savor this moment of peace. By noon, or maybe even before, the gusts could start again, blowing sand and dust everywhere.

Gathering her thoughts, she watched the crows hop around

the parking lot outside, looking for crumbs and candy wrappers that still held a hint of flavor. Just beyond them she could see two support posts of a control gate built into the bank of the irrigation ditch. Last night some would-be comedian had slipped an old pair of khaki uniform pants onto the posts, then placed shoes on the ends. At first glance it looked like an officer was headfirst in the ditch. Everyone who'd driven past it on the way into the station had chuckled and commented about it, so it had remained in place for the moment. Later, the conservancy people would probably come by and return it to normal.

Finished with her coffee, she turned, hearing Justine step through the doorway. "Morning, partner," Ella greeted.

Justine nodded, a somber expression on her face. "Nothing's good about it now. Another possible carjacking went down late last night or earlier this morning. This time all hell has broken loose."

"What've we got?" Ella said, automatically reaching for her keys as she dropped the empty foam cup into the wastebasket.

"We've got a homicide, too—a soldier who just returned home from Iraq. The officer at the scene ID'd him."

"How'd he die?" Ella grabbed her jacket, and was out the door before Justine had answered.

"Multiple gunshot wounds, according to the officer."

"Do you have a 'twenty' on this?" she asked referring to the location of the crime as they hurried down the hall.

"Just off Highway 64 about three miles west of Rattlesnake," Justine answered. "And we'll have to take your unit. Mine's getting new tires."

Once in the parking lot, they hurried to Ella's unmarked vehicle, Justine taking the keys. As they pulled up to the highway and Justine braked, checking for traffic, they both heard an ominous high-pitched squeal. "It's the dust from yesterday's wind. Smell it in the air? It's starting early today, too. The breeze will turn into gusts before noon today for sure and sand will fly everywhere including the brake linings again," Ella said. "I read in the paper that the wind's been getting up to sixty in the afternoons. I hate this kind of weather. Waves and waves of sand, pitting the windshield, settling into the brake linings, even drifting into the gun barrels."

"Doesn't do much for your mood, does it, partner?" Justine observed with a wry smile.

"No, it doesn't. I can't stand the constant whistling through the slightest gap in the windows and doors, the sand blasting against your skin . . . not to mention evidence flying everywhere."

"Some say that Wind carries information. You just have to listen carefully," Justine said.

"Now you sound like my brother. Clifford knows all the stories. It's part of what makes him a good medicine man. He says that Wind has supporting power—that if I tune myself in to it, rather than become its adversary, I'd get farther. But I still hate the taste of sand in my mouth, and since Wind puts it there . . ."

Justine laughed.

Ella turned down the volume of the police radio. Today, it was mostly static and garbled transmissions. Another of Wind's side effects on obsolete equipment. The budget increases had targeted additional staff and facilities, not equipment, unfortunately. "What else did you get on this latest crime?"

"Officer Mark Lujan called it in just a few minutes before I came into your office," Justine answered. "He found the body down a side road near a cattle guard. It was visible from the highway. Most of the traffic this time of day goes toward town instead of away, so apparently nobody coming into work saw it across the road. Lujan was on his way west toward Beclabito."

Ella nodded. "I'm familiar with that stretch. It's pretty desolate out there past Rattlesnake. Just a few houses here and there down toward the river, and you really have to look for them. Most are earth-toned and they blend into the landscape, except for the generic red tar paper roofs."

They made a sweeping turn toward the northwest, and Ella

looked up at Ute Mountain over in Colorado. "What do you have on the victim?"

"The deceased lived on land that was allotted to his family. After his parents passed on, he and his brother leased sections of it. The victim's name is Jimmy Blacksheep," she added after a moment's hesitation. Although police officers, by and large, were modernists, most of them shared a reluctance to speak of the recently deceased by name. It wasn't so much fear of the *chindi*, the evil in a man that stayed earthbound after death. It had more to do with respect for the Navajo cultural practices they'd learned and followed most of their lives. Habits of a lifetime were hard to break.

"Officer Lujan have any help at the scene?" Ella asked, staring at the lonely stretch of highway before them.

"No, but he's doing what he can to protect the crime scene until we arrive. Lujan's a rookie, but he's good. He'll handle things. And it's not like there's going to be a crowd there. Most of our people will go out of their way to avoid a body," Justine said, then added, "Tache, Neskahi, and the M.E. should arrive at the scene shortly."

Ella nodded. Sergeant Joseph Neskahi and Officer Ralph Tache worked for her Special Investigations team and served as the Crime Scene Unit. Carolyn Roanhorse was a forensic pathologist, an M.D. who specialized in causes of death that related to court proceedings. Carolyn understood bullet trajectories, poisonings, and could differentiate between stab wounds and blunt injury ones. There were less than one thousand forensic pathologists in the country, but Carolyn worked exclusively for the tribe—an exception to the otherwise statewide authority of the N.M. Office of the Medical Investigators, headquartered in Albuquerque.

Carolyn had a thankless job. Since she worked with the bodies of the dead, she was virtually a pariah but, through her work, she continued to acknowledge her debt to the tribe who'd paid for her schooling.

As they approached the scene, Ella immediately spotted Officer Lujan standing ramrod straight in his tan uniform by the side of the road. He'd taken his post just outside the yellow crime-scene tape he'd used to cordon off the area around the body.

Officer Lujan was thin and lanky, unlike most Navajo males, and had large soulful eyes. Something about his posture, lack of expression, and the almost dogged determination not to look at the body behind him telegraphed far more than the officer realized.

"I bet you anything this is his first actual crime-scene body," Ella noted softly. "It's a toss-up what he wants to do more right now—puke or get into his cruiser and put some serious distance between him and this place. And, if my own experience is any guide, he's probably also wondering what other career choices he's overlooked."

They got out of the unit, and stepped over the yellow tape, which was flapping in the breeze. Office Lujan greeted them with a nod, but didn't say a word. Ella figured that he probably didn't trust his voice. She'd been there many times—when the need to erupt was kept just below the surface by sheer will. Even now, some crimes scenes still had the power to get to her.

"Justine," Ella called out, "put out some cones. We're going to expand the yellow tape perimeter out to the center stripe of the highway. Officer Lujan can redirect traffic through the far lane. I'll call for another officer to assist."

One look at the faceup, bullet-riddled corpse in the gravel along the shoulder of the road suggested that the shooter might have fired from a vehicle. That meant at least one lane, maybe both, could contain vital evidence. If necessary, they'd close the road completely and stop traffic for as long as necessary.

She made the call with her cell phone, standing about fifteen feet from two obvious and separate pools of blood. The largest was beneath and around the victim, a fit-looking Navajo male with a buzz cut. He appeared to be in his early to mid-twenties and had a dozen or more bullet holes in his torso and legs. The entire area, a good one hundred feet in every direction from the body, could contain evidence. They'd also have to check for footprints leading away from the victim, in case there was another body farther from the road, still undiscovered.

"I know . . . knew . . . the deceased," the officer said, his voice taut, as if someone had grabbed him by the throat. He was staring at the ground before his feet, his eyes narrowed, a sign Ella recognized. Part of him was fighting to shut out the images he'd carry with him for the rest of his life.

"Do you have any idea who might have done this to him?" Ella asked. "A local enemy?" Soon Officer Lujan would learn to push back the screaming in his head. They all learned to do the job by getting past the insanity that shadowed their world.

Lujan shook his head. "I don't know anyone here who may have wanted him dead. All I know is that he's been serving overseas with a New Mexico National Guard transportation and supply unit. They had a welcome home ceremony about two weeks ago at Fort Bliss, then most of them spent several days waiting for their heavy equipment to arrive so they could drive it back to the armory in Farmington. They couldn't step down until then. He was due back yesterday," he said, then added, "His brother is a Farmington police officer. Should I call him?"

"Got a phone?" Ella asked, and Lujan nodded, reaching for a cell phone clipped to his Sam Browne belt. "Get the FPD duty officer, and have him or her relay the news."

While Lujan called the Farmington PD, Justine placed some bright orange cones some distance up and down the road from the scene. Once finished, she came back to the site and crouched down by a set of tire tracks, notebook in hand. "We don't have usable footprints, at least not in the vicinity of the body because of the gravel, and probably nowhere else as well. The wind's already starting to gust. I'll check farther from the road, of course. We don't have shell casings either, assuming the victim was shot and bled out here. But there's always the chance the shooter or shooters had revolvers, not automatics, and reloaded. Later it would have been easy to pick up the casings."

"The rest of our crime scene team and the M.E. should be here by now. We need to expand our search," Ella muttered, checking her watch. "Where *is* everyone?"

Hearing traffic, Ella looked down the highway. "Never mind." A half minute later the tribe's medical examiner's vehicle pulled up, followed close behind by the even larger van used by the tribe's Crime Scene Unit. Ella nodded to Tache and Neskahi as they climbed out, then went to greet Carolyn Roanhorse, her longtime friend. As Carolyn walked, her baggy slacks and white medical jacket got whipped about by the wind, which had increased in intensity since Ella had first arrived on the scene.

Carolyn had always been a large woman, but she'd actually put on weight this past winter after her divorce. As she reached Officer Lujan, who was standing beside the yellow tape, she glared at him. "Large and in charge, and coming through. Get out of my way, son," she barked.

Carolyn stepped over the tape and went directly to the body, watching the ground for any obvious evidence in her path. "Some firefight," she said, crouching by the victim and looking closely at what appeared to be two blood trails. One led to the second pool Ella had noticed atop the asphalt. "Looks like he wasn't the only one who sprung a leak," she said.

"We'll photograph everything and take samples, but we still haven't got any shell casings or rounds, except what's probably in the victim's body," Ella said. "I'll need those slugs as soon as you can part with them. Also, I need an estimated time of death."

"Understood," Carolyn said, her eyes never leaving the corpse. "From the condition of the body, I'd say he died not more than a few hours ago—around seven in the morning, give or take. There are no obvious powder burns, so whatever happened here wasn't up close and personal." As she continued to study the body and the entry wounds in particular, she added, "Wait. Two shots were up close—execution style—so forget what I said before. Both went through his heart." Carolyn waited for Tache to take photos, then began the process of bagging the victim's hands.

Ella stepped away, letting Carolyn concentrate, and took in the scene. Justine was taking samples from the blood trail, and both larger pools of blood, labeling each according to location. There was a large amount of broken safety glass scattered in cubed little clumps along the edge of the road, presumably where the driver had been shot, but that was where the similarities between this and the other carjackings they'd had lately ended.

"This makes no sense. Why have the carjackers added murder to their M.O. all of a sudden?" Justine asked. "Until now, they've managed to pull off the heists by threatening their victims and manhandling them."

"The carjackers probably didn't know that their latest victim was a soldier who'd just come back from a combat zone—one from a unit that had been trained to be particularly wary of roadside attacks. Fighting would have come more naturally to him than surrendering, and it's easy to understand why he might have been wound a little too tight. But this wasn't a simple execution. Those heel marks on the shoulder of the road in the gravel suggest that the victim was dragged out of the vehicle to where he is now, and someone else was dragged several feet into the road, then disappeared."

"So there were at least two carjackers involved in the shooting, and the victim may have wounded one of them severely enough to prevent him from making it back to their vehicle without help," Justine said.

"If that perp couldn't walk, chances are he couldn't have driven the second car away either, which means we're talking three perps, at least," Ella said, "which is consistent with other reports of another vehicle nearby. We need to check with area hospitals and see if they've treated a gunshot victim. Also we need to look for that second car. Their M.O. so far has been to lure a person in by having a good-looking woman pretend to have car trouble, then having a big guy jump the good samaritan and strong-arm him or her. But this time they didn't leave the stolen junker behind, at least not in the immediate area."

Justine nodded. "I'll handle that right now. Should I also get a list of other returning soldiers from the victim's National Guard unit, particularly those who live around here?"

"Yeah. They were probably the last to see him before he drove north." Ella continued searching for ejected shell casings. Considering the victim's bullet-riddled body, it made no sense not to be able to find at least one. Most handguns produced and sold nowadays were semiautos and they ejected each spent casing.

The perps had taken the victim's vehicle—that had apparently been the point of the crime. But having the foresight to pick up a dozen or more shell casings as well as the victim's own weapon either meant that the shooters had been super cool and careful, or the murder itself had been premeditated and the victim's vehicle a bonus. Of course that presupposed the soldier had been the real target and the rest of the operation just window dressing. If that were true, he would have had to have been followed or maybe the perps had been waiting, knowing he'd be coming down this road at the right time. But all she had was speculation at this point and a dead soldier.

Neskahi was working a few feet away from her, scouring the ground adjacent to the road. "Based on the blood distribution and separate drag marks I get the idea that the victim shot at least one of the perps. There's also a small amount of shattered glass that could have come from a window on the perp's vehicle. But if the vic's gun isn't around, that means the perps must have taken it with them. Bad idea, if it's legal and registered," he said.

"I was just wondering about his weapon, too," Ella said.

"Maybe this started as one of the usual carjackings, but then the vic recognized one of the perps," Neskahi suggested, continuing his search pattern, his eyes still directed to the ground.

"That's another good theory," Ella said, then left him to his work.

Ella went to talk to Officer Luján next, who was watching for traffic. He was trying to look rock-steady, but Ella could see the jumble of emotions in his eyes. His face remained trained into neutrality—an attitude that he undoubtedly hoped would pass for the coldness of a seasoned professional.

"You okay?" Ella asked softly.

"Of course," he said, but his voice trailed off at the end.

"Your first homicide, right?"

"Yeah."

"And a friend as well. That's tough. I've called for help to direct traffic. When it arrives, you can return to the station and write up your report. Unwind a little, maybe."

"Not necessary. I can handle it." The answer came too quickly to be genuine.

"You mentioned that the deceased had a brother?" Ella said, directing the focus back to the investigation.

Luján nodded. "He lives in Farmington, but he's been keeping an eye on his brother's place. It's near here."

"Brother's name?"

"Samuel Blacksheep," he said, then after a pause, added, "Samuel's going to be out for blood when he hears about this."

"They were close?"

He hesitated. "When they were kids Samuel was always watching over his kid brother. That habit may end up creating problems for the department now. Samuel won't want to stand back and let our PD do all the legwork. You get me?"

Ella nodded, understanding precisely what he meant. An officer dedicated his life to protecting and serving the public. But when crime struck this close and involved a member of the family, the perspective twisted. Skills an officer used to protect himself and others and to make sure justice was served could easily become a tool to exact revenge.

"His house is over across," Luján said, pointing with his lips, Navajo style. "Family name's on the mailbox."

"Over across" could mean on the other side of a field, or in Albuquerque, hours away, but since he'd pointed to an area beyond the cattle guard that apparently contained only a few houses, she'd be able to narrow it down. "Thanks."

Ella checked with Carolyn, who was still by the body. "I'm going to check out the victim's home," she said, interrupting the M.E. "We don't know yet if the perps paid a visit there as well."

Carolyn nodded absently, then gestured toward the stretcher and body bag visible in the back of her open van. "I'll need help. Get Neskahi for me before you leave."

Ella gave her a bemused smile. "Still paying him back for that crack he made about you? That was ages ago." Contact with the dead was extremely difficult for any Navajo. Even the M.E. and the Crime Scene Unit used two sets of gloves as a precaution so that they wouldn't touch anything that had touched the dead. But the job *no one* wanted was helping the M.E. move the body. Knowing that, Carolyn always asked for Neskahi when the time came, no matter who else was around.

"Get him."

"Okay," Ella said, knowing the futility of arguing with Carolyn about anything like this. Several years back, Neskahi had made a half-hearted joke about Carolyn's weight and since that fateful day Carolyn had made it her mission in life to make Joseph as uncomfortable as possible at every crime scene.

Ella whistled, caught Neskahi's attention, then gestured to Carolyn. Neskahi's downcast expression as he approached spoke volumes.

As he walked past her, Neskahi muttered, "I even tried flowers. How long is she going to remember?"

"For the rest of your life, Joe," Ella said softly. "And don't *ever* send her candy."

"Come on, Sergeant," Carolyn said with a grim smile. "Quit dragging your feet!"

TWO

——— ✖ ✖ ✖ ———

Ella arrived at a crumbling gray stucco house less than five minutes later. As she stepped out of the SUV she studied the home, which seemed typical of the area. From the construction it was obvious that rooms had been added two or three different times. The roof was red, layered in rolls of mineral-covered fiberglass and sealed around the edges with black roofing compound and galvanized nails. There was probably no insulation anywhere, but, judging from the roof vents and a big LPG tank, the house had a furnace and cook stove. There was also electricity, thanks to the power lines along the paved highway less than a half mile away. Electricity and gas heating were a blessing still too rare on the Rez where the twenty-first century had yet to arrive. A small pump hose indicated a well. Running water was a luxury not everyone had on the Rez.

She stopped by the mailbox at the edge of the driveway and noted that the dirt road continued down toward the river and another house, barely visible beneath a willow. The mailbox, hand lettered with the name Blacksheep, was so full of mail that the door wouldn't close. If Samuel was stopping by to check on the house and take care of the mail, he hadn't been by for several days, maybe more.

Ella put on a pair of latex gloves, then took a closer look at the envelopes inside. Based upon some of the postmarks, the oldest mail had been there for at least two weeks. Along with the many advertisements there was an electric bill and two issues of a National Guard magazine. Then she noticed something peculiar. The mail, even the flyers, had been sorted according to size, unlike the jumbled mess that was normally rubber banded together and delivered to her home, and both sets of mail were delivered by the same post office in Shiprock.

Someone with a penchant for order had looked through the stack, leaving the rubber bands in a neat pile by the base of the mailbox before placing the mail back in the box. She doubted it was the carrier. Glancing down, Ella studied the four rubber bands, the kind the postal carriers in her community used. A barely discernible layer of dust covered them, suggesting they'd all been placed there at the same time, and probably recently.

Had Jimmy Blacksheep's assailants come here before or after attacking him and checked his mail? Jimmy had died less than two miles from his home after making it back from halfway around the world. That was either very bad luck or no coincidence at all.

Deep in thought, her senses alert for more clues, Ella noted a single set of fresh vehicle tracks that had been disturbed just enough by the wind to blur the tread pattern. Photos would have to be taken soon to preserve any record at all.

Ella climbed back into her vehicle and drove up to the house, avoiding the previous trail. The tire tracks left by the last visitor showed the vehicle had pulled up and turned around, probably facing back down the driveway to facilitate a quick exit. Vague imprints showed the driver had gotten out and walked to the house but, despite searching, she couldn't find any traces of blood. That told her one thing at least—the wounded perp hadn't been the one to walk around here afterward.

Dust had accumulated on the front porch, and she saw the vague footprints that went all the way up to the door. Looking closely, Ella then noted the absence of dust anywhere on the door-knob. Someone had come here recently, checked the mail, then gone inside the house, either using a key or, since there was no sign of a forced entry, maybe the door had been unlocked.

Ella knocked but no one answered. Gloves still on to avoid leaving fingerprints, she tried the knob. Many traditional Navajos didn't bother to lock their doors, though people in law enforcement, like Samuel Blacksheep, generally didn't share the public's illusions about safety on the Rez.

The door *was* locked. Ella looked around, searching the usual hiding places for keys. She checked atop the door frame first, then started looking under the four empty flower pots on the wooden floor. Her search was unsuccessful.

Ella listened but there were no sounds coming from inside at all, only the faint whistling of the breeze sweeping across the porch. She peered through a crack in the curtains and saw a sparsely decorated living room and beyond, in the next room, a kitchen table.

Ella heard the sound of an approaching vehicle and looked back toward the road. A Farmington police cruiser was racing down the side road trailing a rooster tail of dust. The vehicle turned sharply into the driveway, and a few seconds later slid to a stop beside her own, unmarked unit.

A stocky, barrel-chested Navajo man clad in the blue uniform of the Farmington Police Department stepped quickly out of the driver's side.

"Special Investigator Clah?" he called out, walking toward the porch.

"That's me," she said, going to meet him.

Navajos, even modernists like police officers, rarely shook hands, and today was no exception. "I'm Samuel Blacksheep. I've been appraised of the situation. What progress have you made so far?"

His tone was brisk but his eyes were wet and reddened and

there was pain etched in his features. Remembering her father's death, she felt a wave of sympathy. His brain was telling him *okay, get on with it,* but his heart was breaking into a million pieces.

"How you doing?" she asked him softly. But even as she spoke she knew that the last thing he wanted was her sympathy. Officer Blacksheep's eyes were lit by an inner—and dangerous—fire, and his hands were clenching and unclenching into fists. Anger was easier to release and let run free than was overwhelming grief. She'd seen this before. Everything in him demanded retribution—a life in exchange for a life. But those feelings would have to be reined in if he expected to remain a police officer.

"I'm coping," he answered. "But I need to know what happened."

She nodded. "How'd you get here so fast? We just called it in," she said, giving him a few moments to gather his thoughts.

He opened his mouth to speak, but there was a pause before he answered, as if his brain and his vocal cords weren't quite working in tandem. "I was on patrol on Farmington's west side when the desk sergeant notified me that there was a situation here involving my brother. He didn't have any details, but they took me off duty so I could come to the scene. When I arrived I was told my brother . . ." his voice wavered slightly. Pausing, he cleared his throat. "Officer Goodluck said you'd be here and would want to talk to me," he finished in a strangled tone.

Ella knew he'd gone way over the speed limit to make it here this fast—even if he'd been where he said he was. She watched Officer Blacksheep, trying to determine how much to tell him. He was already on the edge and trying like crazy to hold it all in.

"We *will* take down whoever's responsible for the death of your brother. You can count on it."

"I'll hold you to that. But I want to know what happened. Where's my brother's vehicle? Do you have a suspect yet?"

"We're still working, so all I can tell you right now is that his body was found by the road about an hour ago—no vehicle," Ella replied. "Right now I'd like to go inside his home and take a look around. I understand you've been taking care of the place. Do you happen to have a key on you?"

"How did you know . . . ? Oh, right. Lujan told you." Samuel nodded, searching his pocket. "My brother deserved a better homecoming than this."

"How long has it been since *you* were here?" Ella asked.

"About a week—give or take. Has someone been here since?"

"Someone stopped by after yesterday's dust storm, maybe earlier this morning, I know that. I found vehicle tracks and vague footprints that had to have been made since the dust began flying." She indicated the tracks. "I stopped at the mailbox. It looks like whoever it was checked the mail, sorted it all together, then stuck it back into the box. The rubber bands normally used to carry a day's mail are still on the ground, sitting atop yesterday's dust. Only that person knows if anything was taken. Any idea who it might have been?"

"No. Do you think that someone was waiting for my brother to show up, and came here first, before killing him and hijacking his car?"

"I can't say, not yet, though it would make more sense than coming here *afterwards*." She gestured to the door and waited.

Samuel went through the contents of his pockets, then cursed softly. "Damn. Must still be on my kitchen table. But step aside. Getting in is easy."

"It's locked," Ella warned.

"Yeah, but the lock isn't worth crap." He lifted the knob, jiggled the door, and it popped open. "I've been meaning to put in a deadbolt, but there's nothing of value inside. My brother's TV, radio, and electronics are all over at my place. Most of his good clothes, too."

Samuel took a few steps into the room, Ella behind him. It smelled dusty, which was natural, considering yesterday. But the dust was especially abundant. It probably hadn't been cleaned since Jimmy reported to his Guard unit, and that must have been more than a year, easily.

Ella stepped around him to get a clearer view of the living room. At a glance she could tell that the place had been searched— but not tossed—as burglars were prone to do. On the desk, which held mostly papers and old mail, she could see small, clean areas because the movement and replacement of letters hadn't been exact. A thick, worn spiral notebook was in another spot. It was virtually dust-free on top but not the edges. Something that had rested on top of it had been removed.

Without picking it up, she turned a few pages and saw it was a writing journal for James Blacksheep's English Four high school class. She crouched down, noting footprints on the vinyl floor leading to places farther into the house. "Someone has been here. They looked through things, and didn't put them back in exactly the same place, so the dust markings are off. And check out the floor."

Samuel saw what she was referring to, then added, "They looked behind the photos hung on the wall, too. They're slightly off-kilter." His voice reverberated with anger. "So they killed him, and then came here to see what else they could take from him?"

"Probably the other way around, but either way, this wasn't a regular burglary," she said. "Who else has a key?"

"No one."

"The intruder was here recently, or else the clear spots would have been covered by dust by now. And whoever was here wanted to hide their entry. But this may not be connected to the carjacking. Maybe a teen—they'd be prone to shake the door—or even a nosy neighbor," she said, thinking out loud.

"Yeah, you're right. A burglar would have trashed the place. Whoever did this was careful—just not careful enough." He turned around in a circle, then shrugged. "Nothing's missing that I can tell."

"Something was taken from on top of this old spiral note-book. Any idea what it could have been?" Ella indicated the spot.

He nodded. "Another spiral notebook. But that's weird. Why would anyone want it? My brother kept his stories—kid stories he wrote—in those. He wants . . . wanted to write children's books someday. Who'd take them?"

"Suppose he hid something valuable between the pages? Money or paychecks?"

"Maybe. But there were four or five notebooks there. It doesn't make sense."

"Could be we'll find them outside," Ella said. "Or do you think whoever sneaked in was a kid, or an old classmate planning on playing a trick on your brother?"

"He picked the wrong day for it then," Samuel said.

Ella led Samuel back outside. She wouldn't risk compromising the scene any more than they'd already done. With luck, Justine would be able to lift prints. She called her partner, filled her in, then turned her attention back to Samuel. "Tell me about your brother."

"He returned to Fort Bliss about three weeks ago and was released from service yesterday. He was going to drive home in a rental car since his pickup is at my home in Farmington."

"You said *car*. Do you know if he might have rented a pickup instead?" Ella asked, knowing that was the carjackers' vehicle of choice. No cars had been taken to date that they knew about.

"I have no idea."

"Where did Jimmy work locally before his unit shipped overseas?"

"At Jensen's Lumber in Farmington, out on east Main. But he was planning to quit after he returned. My brother was saving up to pay for some classes at the community college. Writing classes, mostly."

Samuel turned away from her, stared at the house for a few

seconds, then faced her again. "I want to be kept current on any progress you make. I need to make sure that we catch whoever did this and that he pays."

She'd expected nothing less. Ella met his gaze and held it. "I've been in a situation similar to yours, so I know what kind of things are racing through your mind. But *I'm* in charge of this investigation. I'll keep you informed as much as I can, but this is *my* case. If you start getting in my way, you'll mess up things for everyone—except your brother's killer or killers."

"What do you expect *me* to do? Sit on the sidelines?" he countered.

"Be a professional and make darned sure you *do* stay on the sidelines, Officer."

"I can help you," he insisted, walking back to her car, Ella beside him. "I'm on the team investigating the carjackings going down outside the Rez. And from what I saw, it's almost certain that the perps who've been running roughshod all over the Four Corners are the same ones who murdered my brother today. Our departments are supposed to be working together on this," Samuel said, his eyes flat and hooded—a cop's gaze that revealed nothing and spoke volumes. "That makes it my business— officially. And if someone had it in for my brother, I'm going to find out who, like it or not."

"Noted," Ella said. At this point it would make sense to suspect a strong connection to the carjacking ring. "Now tell me something I don't know. How come you didn't go pick up your brother?" Ella asked. "You knew when he was coming home, and it's only a six-hour-plus drive to Albuquerque and back."

"I was filling in for someone on the day shift and couldn't get off," he answered, then after a brief pause added, "But that wasn't the only reason. I probably could have found a way had I wanted to. You might as well find out now that my brother and I didn't see eye-to-eye on a lot of things. I've only spoken to him once on the phone since he got back to the States, and I wasn't planning on making the welcome-home parade in Farmington that was planned for tomorrow now that all the soldiers are finally back."

"What was the problem between you two?" Ella pressed.

He shrugged. "Except for politics, he and I disagreed on practically everything. We were brothers, but we haven't been friends for a very long time."

Samuel was in front of her, resting against the car door, but wouldn't look directly at her for more than a few seconds at a time. He was either distracted or holding out on her. Ella watched him carefully. Depending on where he'd been at the time of Jimmy Blacksheep's death, Samuel might soon become a suspect. "Where were you at around seven this morning?"

He stood up straight, the vein in his forehead bulging. "You think *I* killed my brother? Where the hell did that come from?" he said, then took a step forward, closing the distance between them.

Ella refused to be intimidated, and the fact that she was about an inch taller than him made it easier, though he outweighed her by fifty pounds, at least. "Come on, *Officer*. Give me a break. You're been a cop for how long? You know the drill." Her emphasis on the word "officer" and her dispassionate tone of voice got through to him, as Ella had hoped.

"Yeah, yeah. Assume nothing, don't rule out anyone automatically," he said with a curt nod. "I was home, getting ready for work," he answered in a calmer tone.

She'd known quite a few officers who were skilled game players and could lie with frightening ease. Unable to read him, she just nodded. "Okay."

He reached for the door handle, then took his hand away. "I forgot to ask. What's the drill at the morgue? I know the tribe has its own M.E. and that there'll be an autopsy. But how soon will my brother's body be released? I need to make burial arrangements."

"Call Dr. Roanhorse at her office and see where things stand. You can have the body picked up from the morgue once she releases it. And Samuel?"

His eyebrows went up.

"Me or one of my team will need to talk to you again, so I need your home address and phone number. And your cell?"

Samuel reached for his card, then scribbled a telephone number and his address on the back. "I don't have a cell, but leave a message on my answering machine or at the station if you can't reach me on duty. I'll call you back ASAP."

Ella watched as Samuel climbed into his unit, then drove off. Stepping away from the dust cloud his tires had churned up, she brought out her cell phone. She'd need everything the Farmington PD had on Samuel—but she wanted the background check kept under wraps. Mentally reviewing her options she realized that there was only one person who could pull that off—Shiprock Police Chief Atcitty—Big Ed.

THREE

✖ ✖ ✖

Ella sat across the desk from Shiprock's chief of police. Big Ed Atcitty was aptly named. What he lacked in stature, he made up for in bulk. He was a beefy man, broad shouldered and built like a fireplug, but he'd remained in shape over the years despite the fact that he rarely went out into the field anymore.

"Shorty, I'm trying to get what you wanted from the Farmington PD, but they're on the defensive."

Even though Ella was at least a head taller than he was, her boss insisted on calling her Shorty. Ella knew the nickname had stemmed from the easy relationship they shared, one based on trust and respect, and didn't mind. On the Rez, many people were given nicknames to avoid using their proper names which were considered the bearer's personal property.

"If one of their own is dirty, or even a potential suspect," Big Ed continued, "they want to handle it. It's that jurisdictional posturing again."

"Understandable," she said. "But I have nothing to give them in the form of physical evidence. All I've really got is a feeling that Officer Blacksheep is holding out on me. The thing is, Chief, I trust my instincts."

Big Ed rocked back and forth in his swivel chair, and stared pensively out the window at something Ella couldn't see from where she was sitting. Silence stretched out, but she knew better than to interrupt it. Pauses in conversation on the outside usually meant it was time for the other person to speak. Here on the Navajo Nation, more often than not, it just meant that someone was still thinking. Interrupting that process was considered extremely rude.

"Blacksheep has a good reputation with his department, so tread very, very carefully, Shorty." He leaned back in his chair and regarded her for a moment. "Any other suspects?"

"Too early to tell, though the carjacking ring is at the top of the list, for obvious reasons. But I'm not ruling out any other possible motives. We'll have more to go on after the crime-scene evidence is processed. Justine is also getting me a list of soldiers who served in the victim's unit and live in this area or may have passed through in the past twenty-four hours. After we find out what kind of vehicle the victim was driving, we can put out a statewide bulletin."

"At this point Farmington PD believes that the murder was the result of a carjacking gone wrong . . ." Big Ed said, letting the sentence hang.

"It's possible, I suppose, maybe even likely, but there're some reasons to believe otherwise. Not everything adds up right. For one, why would Jimmy put up a fight over a rental vehicle? And if it turns out he was driving a car instead of a pickup—I'm still trying to track down the rental agency—that'll be another discrepancy."

Big Ed considered it. "After you've been in battle—particularly the kind where there are no front lines—hostiles are everywhere and could be anyone—you're jazzed. It sometimes takes months to get your feet back on firm ground. The victim was carrying a weapon from what you could tell?"

"Yes, or else managed to grab one from his attackers. But we couldn't find shell casings or the weapon itself. The blood evidence is still being analyzed, but we know it came from two different individuals."

Big Ed leaned back in his chair. "Once the Tribal Council hears about this, it won't be long before they'll be on my back, pushing for a solution. One of our tribe's warriors goes to a foreign land, fights and survives while supplying our troops, and then dies here between the sacred mountains where he should have been safe from attack." He shook his head. "A hero like that deserved better. We have to balance the scales."

Ella nodded. At the core of the Navajo way was the belief that all things were connected, that nothing existed independent of its surroundings. To restore harmony, the scales had to be balanced—in this case, the scales of justice.

"Import manpower from other divisions if you need to. People—both on and off the Rez—will demand answers. Those carjackers have been running law enforcement in circles for months, but now a returning soldier has died. Their criminal operation will die next," he added flatly.

"I'm on it," she said.

"Your priority as of this moment is to catch the killer or killers," Big Ed said flatly. "Keep me posted."

Ella returned to her office, checked her watch, and sighed. She'd really hoped to go see her eight-year-old daughter, Dawn, star in her school play this afternoon, but it was out of the question now. Dawn was scheduled to play the part of a medicine woman who'd tended to The People after the Long March—when Kit Carson and the U.S. Army had forced the tribe to walk to an interment camp in Bosque Redondo.

Ella and Rose had been helping her rehearse for a month, and Dawn had been really excited. Although Ella knew that Dawn had been counting on her to attend, there was nothing she could do about that now. Ella called home and told her mother in general terms what had happened.

"We're under pressure to solve this case quickly, Mom. There's just no way I'll be able to take off work today to go to my daughter's play." Out of respect for Rose, who was a traditionalist, she avoided mentioning Dawn by name. Traditionalists believed that names had power that could be used by the bearer in emergencies if that power was kept fresh and strong. To use a person's name often depleted them of the one resource that was theirs alone.

"But your daughter has been looking forward to this for weeks! She's worked hard. It's *important* that you be there. Couldn't you at least stop by, let her see you, then leave?"

Hearing footsteps, Ella glanced up and waved Justine into her office. "Mom, I've made every event this year at school except for one. Besides, she knows what my job is like, and I warned her more than once that if an emergency came up—"

"Your child heard you with her ears, but not with her heart. She's young, and she thinks that if she just hopes hard enough, it'll happen."

"Mom, every parent has to make choices like this once in a while. But as soon as the case is closed I'll take her with me on a special outing. We can trailer the horses down to the *bosque* and go for a ride there. I know she'll love that."

"Do everyone a favor, daughter," Rose snapped. "Don't tell her your plans until you've got the horses inside the trailer, the phone turned off, and you're ready to go."

Rose's words coiled around her painfully, like barbed wire stretched over bare skin. Her mom was overreacting, but there was no sense in arguing with someone who'd already made up their mind. Before she could respond, Rose continued.

"Eventually you'll have to decide where your priorities lie, daughter. Just hope it won't be too late."

"Mom, that's *not* fair! You didn't attend every school event I had when I was growing up, remember? Conflicts are part of family life, and I never held them against *you*. If my daughter had an emergency, I'd turn the case over to Justine and be done with it," she said, hurt and doing what she did instinctively under those circumstances—fight back.

With that, Rose hung up.

Ella slammed the phone down, then, remembering she wasn't alone, looked sheepishly at Justine. "Mothers. With one hand you want to hug them close, and with another you'd cheerfully push them into the river."

Justine smiled. "Do you need to duck out this afternoon for a while? I can cover for you."

"No. I know you can handle things, but as head of this unit this is where I have to be right now. Dawn will understand that, even if my mother never will," Ella said, then taking a deep breath, gave her assistant a nod. "So what have you got for me?"

Justine glanced down at her notes. "As you know, we've got two blood types at the scene. One belongs to the victim. The other to someone else—one of the perps, or maybe Blacksheep had a companion—though the tracks and blood trails don't seem to fit in with that possibility. I did some checking and he rented a big two-door sedan in El Paso at a branch of Nationwide. The agent said Blacksheep was traveling alone—at least when he picked up the car."

"A sedan, not a pickup? That's interesting, considering that the carjacking ring has focused exclusively on pickups—and a flatbed or two."

"I've also got a list of local Guard soldiers who served in the victim's unit. There are eight of them, all male. The Navajos are Randy Billey, John Lee Charley, Jeremy Bitsillie, and Paul Curley. Jeremy's on our tribal force and the others work at various repair shops around Shiprock. Out of the Anglos, Calvin Sanders, Kent Miller, and Louis Smith are all FPD officers, and Ben Richardson is a mechanic in the PD's auto shop."

As her phone began to ring, Ella held up one hand. She half expected it to be Rose again. Her mother—who'd never worked outside the home when her own children had been at home—hadn't experienced the fine line every working mother had to walk.

On an intellectual level, Rose realized that Ella had to work to support Dawn, and that her law enforcement career was more demanding than a nine-to-five job. But emotionally, Rose expected her to be all things to everyone.

Ella picked up the phone and identified herself.

"This is Sergeant Calvin Sanders of the Farmington Police Department," came the voice at the other end. "I'd like to meet with you concerning the death of Jimmy Blacksheep. I'm on the carjacking investigative force, and I knew Jimmy. He served in my platoon. I'm—was—his lieutenant in the Army National Guard."

"Okay. Where do you want to meet—and when?" Ella asked.

"How about the Dry Hole? It's on Main here in Farmington, west of downtown."

"I've heard of it. How's forty-five minutes sound to you?"

"Good. It's a rough place, but I've got a good reason for wanting to meet there. I'll fill you in later."

Ella hung up and glanced at Justine. "I've stalled for time, so please find out what you can—off the record—about FPD Sergeant Calvin Sanders. And go easy. I just want some general information before meeting with him."

While Ella went over the physical evidence she already had from the scene, Justine left to get some background on Sanders. She returned ten minutes later. "Sergeant Sanders has served with the Farmington PD for eleven years. He's currently working days. He's not well-liked, based on what my source said, but he gets the job done. Sanders has served in the National Guard for the last six years, and was letting his enlistment expire when they extended his service another eighteen months."

Justine reached into the file folder she had in her hands. "Here's a photo. I printed it out from his records on the database. You want me to come with you?"

Ella glanced down to familiarize herself with the face, then shook her head. "Someone in law enforcement is always difficult to Q and A. I'll get more from him one-to-one." Ella started out the door, then glanced back at Justine. "Keep digging on everything you can about the victim. Anything on a weapon?"

"Nothing, not even a caliber on the perps' bullets yet either. Joe's going over the area one more time with a metal detector. He said that with the wind kicking up there was no telling what he'd find."

"Let me know if he manages to find something besides beer and soda cans," Ella said and stepped out the side door.

Ella reached the outskirts of Farmington twenty minutes later, and, coming in from the west, quickly found the Dry Hole. She'd heard about the tavern from other officers on the tribal PD. There was a huge TV over the bar, and half the time the games on screen led to fights below. The oil workers and gas workers in the county often met head-on with local cowboys and, more often than not, it became a free-for-all. She'd also heard that a few tribal officers had been arrested there—then released.

The Dry Hole was a testosterone den where the fights were real but the motivations vague. Like an elementary school playground, many egos went there to be tested, but it was a good training site for young officers needing to learn how to handle themselves in a hostile environment.

Fortunately, it was barely lunch time, so the mood inside would be far different than after the off-duty day shift drifted in around six. Not seeing anyone hanging around in the parking lot, she assumed her contact had already gone inside. Ella pushed her badge back on her belt and made sure it remained covered by her jacket. She wanted to stay low key. Just being female in this place was rumored to be a test of courage.

As she stepped inside the bar and grill, she stopped just past the door and stood, waiting for her eyes to adjust. There were no windows, which probably cut down on breakage considerably, and the lights were dim but probably legal. Then she saw Calvin

Sanders sitting at the bar, a cup of what looked like coffee in front of him.

He was out of uniform, but she recognized him instantly from the photo—buzz cut, tanned, and blue eyed. Sanders waved her over, having ostensibly checked out her photo as well. "Investigator Clah," he greeted. He started to hold out his hand, but then let it drop. "Sorry, been out of the country for too long. Forgot you people don't like to shake hands."

Ella nodded, not appreciating the "you people" comment that much, but having heard much worse in bars before. "No problem."

He grabbed his coffee and led the way to a table at the rear that offered a clear view of the room, then offered her some coffee from the pot the waitress had carried over. "Let me buy you a sandwich to go with it."

Ella shook her head. She'd planned to have lunch a little later with Carolyn. Though the morgue was scarcely the ideal setting, by the time she got there Carolyn would undoubtedly be needing a break, and they could both use downtime, though the topic would probably be the victim in the other room.

"Coffee's just fine," she said. "Now tell me why you chose this particular place," Ella said, looking around and noting gratefully that all was quiet. Even the sports program on TV was from some horse track in Florida.

"I was hoping to track down one of my men. He served in the Guard and was Jimmy Blacksheep's sergeant. He knew everyone in that section inside and out. Ever since I got the news about Jimmy, I've been trying to reach him, but I haven't had any luck."

"He hangs out here?"

"Yeah. It's his favorite joint. He likes mixing it up every once in a while."

"Is he Navajo?" Ella asked.

"No. His name is Kent Miller, and he's one of our patrol officers. He's a good cop, clean as they come, but he had some hairy experiences these past few months and mentioned needing to clear his head before reporting to work at the PD. I figure he's at the secret fishing spot he was always talking about over in Iraq. But once he's back in town, this is the first place he'll come. This is his haunt."

"Do you think Miller might have some pertinent information?"

"About the carjacking or the homicide, no, but he can help you get a better handle on Jimmy. All I can tell you is that Jimmy was a good soldier, the kind who could be counted on. Carried out his orders without any bellyaching."

Ella waited, trying to figure out where this was going.

"Okay, so let's cut to the chase," he said as if he'd read her mind. "PFC Blacksheep and I served in the same unit overseas for eighteen months, and before that we trained together. Everyone in our unit knew each other, and, on top of that, Jimmy's brother Samuel is with the PD. His death is family business as far as I'm concerned. So here's my card. If you need anything—backup, whatever—consider me on call."

She took the card and jammed it into her jacket pocket. "Thanks, I'll keep your offer in mind. But, so far, we've got it covered."

"Any idea why the carjacking turned deadly this time?"

"We're still checking all the angles." Big Ed had been right. Everyone wanted to help on this one, which meant all eyes would be on their investigation. "I do have one question you might be able to answer. Since everyone was coming home from the same place, how come more guys didn't ride back together?"

He shrugged. "Some of the enlisted men may have come back together, I don't know. I drove back alone because it's against regulations for enlisted personnel and officers to fraternize. I also came back a week earlier than some because my enlistment was up. It had been extended months ago, but I was due for my discharge."

She nodded. "Do you happen to know if Jimmy Blacksheep had a personal weapon?"

Calvin Sanders leaned back and considered her question. "All of the men in the unit are from New Mexico and a good percentage of them were born and raised here in the Four Corners. I'd be willing to bet that most of them owned handguns or rifles or both before shipping overseas," he said, then paused before continuing. "I've been told that some soldiers feel naked without a gun when they first leave the service. Overseas, your weapon becomes a part of you—your lifeline and your insurance. I wouldn't be surprised if Jimmy picked one up before making the drive back," he said. "But, to be fair, some soldiers go the other way. Once they're back and out of the service, they won't go within a hundred yards of a weapon."

"What's your best guess? Do you have any idea which way Jimmy would go?" Ella would normally avoid asking a Navajo to speak for another, but most Anglos didn't have that cultural restriction in their background.

Sanders thought about it, taking a sip of coffee. "I can't tell you for sure, but I remember hearing talk in the chow line. Private Blacksheep mentioned that he grew up hunting in Carson National Forest and down on the Jicarilla Reservation, places like that. If I had to make a guess, I'd say he might have bought himself a sidearm before making the trip home. But he would have had to have picked it up right before he left. He wouldn't have been allowed to bring it to his base quarters—unless he sneaked it in."

Sanders finished his coffee. "If Private Blacksheep bought himself a gun from a dealer, the Feds will have a record of it along with the rest of the paperwork."

"I'll be touching base with my FBI source later this morning. Right now I've got to get going."

"Something else," Sanders said as he stood up. "Once in a while a solder finds a way to smuggle a weapon back—a souvenir, you know—despite the new levels of security. So, if he had a weapon, you still might not find a record of it."

"Good to know. Thanks," Ella said.

Ella was walking toward the door when she heard a familiar voice yell out, "Hey, good looking, whatcha doing in a dump like this?"

Ella recognized Teeny's voice immediately. Turning, she walked to where he was sitting and, in the spirit of the game, crossed her arms across her chest, trying to appear indignant. "You talking to me, boy?"

Teeny laughed out loud, but before Ella could say anything else, Calvin suddenly appeared at her side.

"If you've got a problem, maybe you'd like to take it up with me instead of the lady," Calvin challenged.

Teeny, never one to back down, made a show of getting to his feet, which took some time. Calvin stood six feet tall, but Teeny was taller, and outweighed the Farmington cop by an easy hundred, at least. Teeny was as big as any National Football League defensive tackle, and probably a lot quicker on his feet. In comparison, Calvin suddenly looked puny and insignificant.

"Easy, guys. Sergeant Sanders, this is an old friend, Bruce Little."

Calvin still wouldn't take his eyes off Teeny. "Why don't I walk you to the door, Ella?"

Ella looked from one man to the other. This had started because of her, but it was developing into an ugly challenge that could pointlessly escalate unless she lightened things up. "Boys, boys," she said, trying to sound like a harried mother. "We'll take out a ruler and measure. Drop your drawers."

Surprised, Calvin chuckled, and Teeny burst out laughing.

"Bruce used to be a tribal police officer before he went into the private sector. We're all brothers here," she said, and introduced Calvin Sanders.

Teeny extended his hand and Sanders shook it. "Ella's an old, old friend."

"Hey, that was one 'old' too many, guy," she said.

Both men laughed again. "Well, I'm not needed here," Sanders said. "You two can catch up, but I'll be on my way."

"We'll talk again soon, Sergeant," Ella said.

Teeny watched Ella's expression as Calvin walked out of the bar. "I've seen that look. What's bugging you about Sanders?"

"Don't know, Teeny," she said softly, shaking her head. To this day, she was the only person who could call him Teeny and not end up gumming her food. "I'm working a really odd case."

"Yeah—the vet who got gunned down on the way home from the war. Heard about it."

It didn't surprise her. Teeny's network on and off the Rez was impressive. Perhaps part of it was that people didn't feel comfortable saying no to Teeny whenever he wanted information. In fact, they volunteered it just to keep him happy. And it usually did.

"You need help on that, call me in—on the house. Don't feel right having one of our servicemen go out that way, you know?"

"Yeah, I'm with you on that. I'll keep your offer in mind and let you know. Thanks."

"So, will you join me for lunch?" he asked, as the server brought him two full plates, one with a stuffed sopapilla that covered the dish, and another heaped with chicken fried steak, mashed potatoes, and thick gravy. Teeny's bulk demanded more meat than a college football team's training table, so he usually ordered two full meals just for himself.

"Wow, if I ate just one of those servings I'd explode." She'd had dinner with the big man before, and it was nothing short of impressive.

"Big boys gotta eat big," he said.

"Food looks good, though. Wish I could stay, but I've got someone to meet." With a wave she left Teeny to his banquet.

Once back inside her cruiser—an unmarked SUV—Ella pulled out into traffic heading west, then called Carolyn Roanhorse. Though Carolyn and she were good friends, thanks to their mutually busy schedules, they rarely managed to find time to get together. When they did, more often than not, it was on business. Despite that, their friendship continued strong, mostly because of the deep woman-to-woman understanding that existed between them.

Ella was considered *'alní* by many, a person who walked the line between two cultures—Anglo and Navajo. It was a hard road to travel, but Carolyn's path was even more difficult. She helped the tribe by serving them in a capacity that no one else would have willingly chosen. Belief in the *chindi* would forever make their M.E. a pariah on the reservation. Yet her job was crucial to the tribe. It gave them a good measure of autonomy over investigations that took place on the Navajo Nation.

Carolyn's marriage to the Anglo doctor, Michael Lavery, had seemed perfect at first. Both were forensic pathologists working with law enforcement, though out of different offices. Michael had retired, allowing them to be together, but, in the end, maybe they'd been too alike and too used to living alone. Michael was gone now, having taken up teaching, and Carolyn was alone again.

Ella finally connected with Carolyn on the phone. "Hey, I thought I'd come by, so we could have lunch."

"That's not going to get you the answers you want any sooner," Carolyn warned. "But a preliminary report is ready. The victim died of multiple bullet wounds to the heart and lungs from at least two different handgun-caliber weapons. The rounds I recovered are here waiting for you. They look like commercial ammo, nothing extraordinary. The man took multiple hits but those weren't immediately fatal," she said, then after a pause added, "He had a lot of bullet holes in him, Ella. I tested for powder burns on his hands, and got a positive on his right hand. He returned fire and it looks like he put up one heckuva fight, judging from the results of the powder residue. And I've verified the T.O.D. He died around seven in the morning as I suggested earlier."

"Except for the guns, that fits in with the M.O. of the carjackers. They strike early in the morning, trying to get people going to work on the less-traveled roads. Drivers are half asleep, not really thinking about anything except getting to where they're going."

"There are a lot of commendable reasons for dying, old friend, but protecting your car is a really bad one," Carolyn said.

"Yeah, and an insured rental at that," Ella agreed, lost in thought.

"So, I'll see you soon?" Carolyn asked, bringing her out of her thoughts.

"I'll be there in a half hour at most."

Ella was halfway back to Shiprock when her cell phone rang. Looking at the display she saw it was Rose. Dreading the call, she pressed the talk button.

"Your daughter is heartbroken that you can't come. Couldn't you at least stop by the school and wish her luck before she steps out onto the stage?"

The comment made Ella's chest tighten. She took a deep breath. Maybe a few minutes wouldn't hurt. "I'll do my best." Ella had just convinced herself that a small detour couldn't hurt, when her cell phone rang again.

"It's Justine," the caller said. "You have a package waiting for you here at the station. And, Ella—get this. It's from Jimmy Blacksheep."

"Open it carefully and find out what's in it." Mail from a dead man took priority. "I'll be there in a few minutes."

FOUR

—— ✖ ✖ ✖ ——

Ella called Carolyn, postponing lunch, then dialed her daughter's school and asked that Dawn be brought to the phone.

Hearing her daughter's excited hello, Ella smiled and the hard edges around her heart disappeared. "I just wanted to wish you luck, pumpkin," Ella said as she raced to the station.

"You can't come, can you?" Dawn said in a mournful voice.

"No, I'm sorry. But my heart's going to be right there with you."

"I know, and you were with my class all day when we went to Narbona Pass. But still . . ." a tiny voice replied.

Ella almost made the turn that would have taken her to Dawn's school. "I love you, sweetie. More than you'll ever know. But the tribe needs me. I'll be there next time, you'll see."

"Daddy's here," Dawn said. "He wants to talk to you."

Ella's grip tightened around the phone as Kevin got on. "Don't worry about anything, Ella. I'll be sitting in the front row along with our daughter's grandmother and we'll be clapping louder than anyone else."

His voice was cheerful and she knew he was speaking for Dawn's benefit. "I'm glad you're there," she said.

"She needed one of us."

He'd spoken in a matter-of-fact tone, but the words knotted her stomach until it hurt.

"So what kept you from coming this time?" he asked pleasantly in that same tone of voice that told her Dawn was still close by.

She imagined landing a solid punch in his midsection and found some satisfaction in that. Then she took a deep breath. "Certainly not the same excuse that kept you away the last *two* times. Just listen to the news and you'll understand. I'll talk to you later, but right now I have to get to the station."

"I've already told Dawn that you'll make it up to her by taking her on a special horseback ride. Maybe even this weekend?"

She would have shot him on the spot—had she been there. "*Why* did you say that without checking with me first?"

"I knew that horseback riding is something you two do together. And you can work out the timing yourself, right?"

The next voice she heard was Dawn's. "Mom, can we? Can we go for a picnic lunch? Or an early morning pancake breakfast?"

Ella swore that next time she saw Kevin, she'd reach down his throat and yank his tongue out. "We *will* go, I promise, but it may not be this weekend. I have to wrap up this case first. Your father will explain once he listens to the radio, or reads the newspaper."

"Oh."

Her daughter's small voice pierced her. "Pumpkin, you know I love you. As soon as this case is closed, we'll take off on the horses and stay out for as long as you want. Just the two of us."

"Breakfast *and* lunch?"

To Dawn, the ideal breakfast was pancakes and the perfect lunch, hot dogs, both over a campfire. "We can handle that," Ella answered, giving her daughter, the negotiator, a few points. "But I've got to go back to work now," Ella said as she pulled into the station and parked.

"Okay. Someday I'm going to be an officer, too," Dawn said, then promptly hung up.

The declaration stunned her. Ella sat in her cruiser staring at the wheel, trying to gather her thoughts. The *last* thing she wanted for her daughter was a career in law enforcement. She took a deep, steadying breath. She was taking it too seriously. Dawn had also mentioned wanting to be a basketball player and a rodeo star within the past six months. Two walls in her room, full of photos of two very different kinds of arenas, testified to those impulses.

As Ella walked into the station lobby, she started down the wrong hall before remembering her new office. Reversing directions and noting that if the duty officer behind the counter had seen her lapse, he wasn't showing it, she hurried on. The new wing still smelled of fresh paint, and seeing Ralph Tache in the hall, hoped he wouldn't get queasy from the odor. He'd been out sick yesterday.

Ralph nodded somberly as he joined her, his eyes filled with questions, not answers. As she went by Justine's office, her partner came out through a new doorway to the lab and followed them. "I left the padded envelope on your desk," she said. "What's inside is a real puzzle."

Ella saw the red and yellow envelope as soon as she entered her office. She studied the label. It had been mailed from an office supply store in El Paso with an express counter. She wasn't familiar with the streets in El Paso, but a glance at a map would probably indicate the big envelope had come from a store close to the military base. Jimmy Blacksheep listed his Shiprock area address, and a phone number she didn't recognize. She hadn't seen a phone at Jimmy's home; maybe the number was for his brother, Samuel.

Confirming it with a quick glance at Samuel's FPD business card, she returned the card to her pocket and put on a pair of latex gloves. Then she carefully reached inside the already opened thin cardboard envelope and extracted its contents while her team members watched.

A handwritten letter was stapled to an article about an earlier case Ella had solved. Below that was what, at first glance, appeared to be a short story using the animal characters that featured in the tribe's creation legends and other names of people and places she didn't recognize.

Ella read the letter, then looked up at Ralph and Justine, who were understandably curious. "The victim said he knew me by reputation and my honesty was what prompted him to contact me. He said he was in danger and that if anything happened to him, this information would help give me what was needed to restore balance and protect the citizens."

"Citizens *Dineh*, or people in general?" Ralph asked.

"Maybe the rest of the papers here will answer that question," Ella said. "He wanted to be a writer someday, according to his brother."

"His writing wasn't there yet," Justine muttered. "I couldn't make heads or tails out of it. "The obvious Navajo names like Trickster, sure. But not those like *Chopra*. Isn't he that guru guy?"

"Yeah." Ella studied the pages. Paper-clipped together was what appeared to be mostly a Navajo story, handwritten in inks of various shades and using more than one kind of paper. The pages were numbered, using ink that matched the last section. The narrative itself, from what Ella could tell, had been written over a period of time. She could see the evidence of coffee stains and greasy fingerprints on more than one page.

Justine stood and walked over beside Ella. "What do you think? It's obviously in code and very confusing."

"Did you both read it?" Seeing Tache shake his head, Ella read the story out loud. It was titled "What Mourning Dove Saw" and it was written in the first person, narrated by the animal character, Mourning Dove.

"'A terrible storm began in a distant valley, and a large hole appeared in the ground, trapping Big Monster. But when Big Monster disappeared from sight, smaller monsters appeared, preying upon the poor creatures still alive. Sun, who had caused the storm, sent the Proud Tribe from atop the local mesas of the *Diné Tah* into the distant valley to protect the poor creatures. This part of the tale began in the fall.

" 'The Proud Tribe brought their own food—and were expected to share their provisions, delivering firewood, food, and arrows among the worthy. The Proud Tribe also brought beasts of burden to carry the load. I did my part as well.

" 'Soon, I saw that, while most of the Proud Tribe was doing the work of Sun, a few from the Proud Tribe slipped into the shade, and became dark themselves. These Dark Ones decided that the rewards from Sun weren't enough, so they decided to trade for other things they coveted. As always, Trickster—Coyote—was with the Dark Ones, but he often went his own way. Others who became the Dark Ones were Gray Wolf, Stripes, and Gopher. As time passed, the Dark Ones found trading partners—Walpole, Mountbatten, Chopra, and Weigel were the ones that I saw and heard, and bartering was very profitable. The Dark Ones acquired Nails, Shoes, Umbrellas, and even Gumdrops, and this made them happy, and greedy for even more. Other goods exchanged hands out of my sight, however, but were said to consist of mother of pearl, shiny quartz, and turquoise.

" 'Konik and Bula, of the tribe, were told to make hiding places in the saddles and beneath the blankets of the beasts of burden for storing bartered goods, along with the shells and turquoise. After they did this, Konik and Bula unfortunately fell out of favor. A gray cloud came and they disappeared. I could not tell where they had gone, and why, though I suspected much.

" 'All the Dark Ones, and those in the Proud Tribe who also knew how Sun was being betrayed but did not themselves barter, kept their secrets from Talking God, their earthly leader. They feared his stern discipline.

" 'Coyote—Trickster to those who knew him well—watched and remembered everything he saw, though he did not see *I* was watching him. He took the bounty of turquoise and shiny quartz to a safe hiding place, hiding them behind his big eyes. One time when he came back, Talking God became suspicious. Trickster was sent away, his tail between his legs.

" 'But, alas, I was discovered as well. One day Gray Wolf saw my shadow as I flew overhead, and he warned me not to tell Talking God or Sun about the Dark Ones or their secrets.

" 'But now I am no longer afraid. I will tell my story and reveal many secrets to Talking God. I will show everyone that Mourning Dove has courage. (Continued on page five . . . ' "

Ella shuffled through the papers. "That's all of it, no page five, or six in here. Jimmy must have kept the rest with him, or never finished it."

"Maybe he had the rest of it in his car, and that was why he was stopped," Ralph suggested.

"And they took the car in order to do a thorough search in private. That's a possibility. Whatever it was, it was worth sending to me, and important enough to kill him for. Any thoughts?"

"Mourning Dove and Trickster are from our creation stories. Gray Wolf too. But I don't remember anything about Gopher or Stripes," said Justine.

Ralph shrugged. "Me, neither. And I've heard of Chopra and Mountbatten but not Walpole, Weigel, or the ones with the short names."

Ella looked down. "Konik and Bula?" Seeing him nod, she added, "Me, neither."

"I wonder if this is connected to the victim's experiences in Iraq?" Justine asked. "But if that's what it really is, there are some serious implications about the activities going on there, perhaps by some of the soldiers in his unit."

Ella started putting the papers together. "Could be. The only answer that makes sense is that the victim was trying to tell me something, but was forced to disguise it because he was afraid someone else might see what he was writing."

"Like maybe one of his buddies?" Ralph suggested. "Privacy is a luxury in a combat zone. Everyone is forced to keep watch virtually all the time. If he was trying to keep a journal of what was going on without tipping off the others, this was one way to do it. Even if they saw a page or so, he could always claim he was writing a children's book or something like that. After all, he wanted to be a writer someday, correct?"

"Exactly," Ella replied. "But if we're going to read between the lines, we need more information to go on. I'll start by verifying that there isn't anything even vaguely like this in our creation stories. My brother should be able to tell me that much."

Justine nodded. "That's a good idea. In the meantime, I'll get back to the lab. We're still processing evidence."

"So far, we've recovered one nine-millimeter round that went wide and lodged in a road sign about fifty yards from where we found the body," Tache added. "Also, there are some skid marks that show someone in a big van or truck made a quick stop, possibly when the attack went down, or just after. The location, near the broken glass, suggests it was beside the victim's car." Ralph paused, checking his notes, then continued. "I'm also trying to track down the sales rep at Nationwide who rented the victim his vehicle. Maybe the employee will remember something about Blacksheep that'll help."

Justine was looking at her own notes, and spoke as soon as Ralph was finished. "There was glass from two vehicles and also two types of blood at the scene. One's O positive and the other is

B. I'm sending samples of both to Dr. Roanhorse so she can confirm which belongs to the victim. There are very few American Indians with blood type B. That blood factor is common in Northeast Asians, Siberians, Japanese, and such. The usual theory for that is that our Indians entered the New World across the Bering Straits from Asia. Of course the races have mixed, so it's not impossible."

"Okay," Ella said. "Make sure all those details are in your reports. We also need to talk to Officer Lujan again. And Blalock. And we need to find the missing car."

"Justine, call FB-Eyes when you get back to the lab and see if the Feds can find a record of the victim buying a weapon after he was stateside. I'll be heading out to my brother's with a copy of this packet," Ella said. "And, Ralph, would you run some of the recovered blood over to the morgue while Justine continues working in the lab? Pick up the recovered slugs, too, and bring them back to her."

He nodded. "One more thing. The photos from the crime scene are ready. I'll put copies on your desk."

"And by the time you return, I should have more information for you on the bullets," Justine added.

"Good. Let's get to work," Ella said.

After making copies of the pages and leaving a set along with a preliminary report for Big Ed, she locked the originals up. Soon, Ella was heading south down the Gallup highway. Her brother's hogan was about twenty minutes' travel from the station at posted speeds. As a medicine man, Clifford spent most of his days there or out visiting a patient—which could be anyone within a hundred miles or more. Theirs was a big reservation.

Since Loretta worked these days and wasn't at home, and Clifford refused to carry a cell phone, there was only one way to get hold of him—start a search, beginning at his medicine hogan.

The drive was short and, when she arrived she parked by the

medicine hogan, well away from the small three-bedroom pitched-roof home Clifford and Loretta had built by themselves. The house had started as a two bedroom, but like most homes on the Rez, it had grown as the need arose. Rooms of different sizes had been added here and there with no thought taken to the overall design and resulting in what appeared to be a series of squares connected to a long rectangle.

In contrast to that, the big, six-sided medicine hogan had symmetry and elegance. Constructed of logs and chinked with mud, the traditional structure stood as a silent testament to the knowledge and wisdom that sustained the *Dineh*, the Navajo People. Clifford pulled back the blanket that covered the east-facing entrance to the hogan, and came out just as Ella took her keys out of the ignition. Seeing Clifford wave, she went to meet him.

Clifford was as tall as she was, but two years older, and a staunch traditionalist. Right now, with his white sash tied around his brow, he looked every inch the *hataalii*, medicine man, that he was. Clifford was as good a *hataalii* as she was a detective, and he was respected throughout the Navajo Nation for his skill and knowledge of *The Way*.

"What brings you here this afternoon, sister?" he asked. Clifford shared her high cheekbones and broad face. His black eyes were deeply set and his gaze was amplified with an inner fire that spoke of intelligence and hidden knowledge. "You have that look about you that tells me you're here on business, but I have a patient coming shortly, so I don't have a lot of time."

"Then let's go inside. I need to show you something related to a criminal investigation."

As they went in, Clifford gestured for her to take a seat on the sheepskin blanket spread on the north side of the hogan. He sat on the west side, the Singer's place. In the center, below the smoke hole, was a wood stove in place of the traditional fire. Two kerosene lanterns lit the interior when necessary, but, with the entrance open, no extra light was necessary this time of day.

Taking the copies of the pages she handed him, he leafed though them slowly, studying the story. "Mourning Dove was a good choice for the writer since the creature was said to report things reliably and quickly. Mourning Dove also understood the special war language of Box Turtle and Long Frog. But the details of this story don't match any that I've ever heard, so I find it puzzling. And there are a lot of non-Navajo names. Do you have the rest of it?"

"No, this is all I have."

"I don't think I can be much help. Do you have any ideas?"

"I suspect it's mostly a coded message but I wanted to check with you and verify there isn't a creation story like that one," Ella said. "But you mentioned that Mourning Dove knew a special war language? That's interesting because the person who wrote this was a soldier."

He looked at her curiously, but didn't comment. Clifford knew she only took the biggest cases, usually major crimes, so Ella figured that he'd already linked her questions to Jimmy Blacksheep's murder. But that wasn't a topic to be discussed in a medicine hogan, and they both knew that.

Glancing down at the papers again, he added, "As far as I know there's no story that's even close to this."

"Do you think this could be some kind of takeoff on the World War Two Codetalkers' system?"

Clifford considered it. "I have a patient coming by soon. His great grandfather *was* a Codetalker. If anyone can answer that question, he can. My patient was a soldier, too, and, because of his interest in history, he studied all of his grandfather's battles and the code that made our people famous."

"I'd like to talk to him myself."

Clifford took a deep breath. "I can ask him—that's all. I have to respect my patient's privacy much like an Anglo doctor should."

"I know. I could come back in, say, a couple of hours. Would that be enough time?"

"Probably—but when you come back, take your cue from me. If he thinks you're here to pressure him, he won't help you at all, and I'll lose a patient. He's a proud man, and one who won't approve of you."

"Me, why? Because I'm not a traditionalist?"

"No, it's much more complicated than that." Hearing a truck in the distance, he stood up. "Go now, and let me see what I can do. Do you want to leave the papers with me?"

"I can't let them out of my sight without Big Ed's permission. It's potential evidence. All I can do is show the pages to your patient, without giving him details of the investigation I'm working on, and then hope he can point me in the right direction. If he can't, I'll keep looking."

"Sister, this man, my patient . . . well, he has issues of his own. There's a good chance he won't be willing to help you at all. But we'll see what happens."

"Thanks. I'll be back." Ella returned to her unit. She'd had trouble with traditionalists before. They saw her tribal police job as just another arm of the Anglo world operating on their land. But if she was reading Clifford right, it was far more than that with this particular patient.

Ella fought the temptation to move slowly so she could catch a glimpse of the man, but then decided that it wouldn't be fair to Clifford. She passed his vehicle without looking, then called Carolyn while on the road to the main highway.

Like her, the good doctor still hadn't had lunch, so Ella continued past the station, once arriving in Shiprock, and headed up toward the hospital on the mesa. Carolyn worked in the basement, where the morgue was located. Noting a roadside vendor alongside the highway, she pulled over and stopped. The man had set up a temporary counter and serving area on the tailgate of his pickup.

Ella had bought from him before, though she couldn't recall his name. The middle-aged man, dressed in flannel shirt, jeans, and straw hat, sold Navajo-style sandwiches. In this case, the main fare was a homemade tortilla called a *naniscaada*, filled with ground beef, potatoes, sweet corn, and chile sauce, and individually wrapped in foil. The resulting burrito was mouthwatering. Getting an extra three for Carolyn, who was probably as hungry as she was, Ella was soon on her way, the big paper bag on the seat cushion beside her. The scent was so enticing her stomach was growling.

Ella looked at her watch. By now, her daughter's play had ended, assuming it had gone on as scheduled. The guilt failed to stave off her hunger, unfortunately, and she picked up speed.

After her arrival at the hospital, Ella took the elevator down to the basement and hurried straight to the morgue. Not many things could tempt her to eat in Carolyn's workplace—but the wonderful scent from the bag in her hand was motivation enough.

As she walked through the door, she saw Carolyn at her desk typing something on her computer. Carolyn glanced up as Ella came in, and sniffed the air. "I hope you brought plenty. I'm famished."

Carolyn moved a stack of papers, laid down a section of today's Farmington newspaper, and Ella emptied the contents of the bag onto the makeshift tablecloth. "Three for you, three for me. Let's not talk shop until after we've finished, okay? I need a break."

"Yeah, and so do I," Carolyn said, taking a huge mouthful and giving Ella a happy, grateful look. "Wonderful," she added, after swallowing. She turned around in her swivel chair and poured two cups of coffee from a pot atop a file drawer, handing one to Ella, who nodded, her mouth too full to speak.

"How are things going with you?" Ella asked as she finished her first *naniscaada*.

"So-so," Carolyn answered between bites. "The house seems impossibly large with all of Michael's things gone. He had more stuff than I did, and tons of reference books and journals."

"I'm sorry about the way things turned out, Carolyn. I really was hoping you two could make it work."

Carolyn nodded. "Me, too, and Michael really thought he was going to retire. But, after six months, he got bored and realized that he wanted to be free to pursue whatever interesting opportunities came his way. That meant being willing to travel at a moment's notice and even relocate. But I have responsibilities *here*, Ella, and a career I don't want to give up. The tribe needs me and the way I see it, they paid for my medical degree so I owe them."

"You've put in your time, girl," Ella said, starting on her next burrito. "That debt was paid years ago."

Carolyn shook her head slowly. "I belong here. Mind you, for a time there, I seriously considered going with Michael. But without my job, I'd end up just trying to get through an endless string of days and, pretty soon, I'd see no difference between January and June, except for the temperature outside. Here, I have a sense of purpose and . . . destiny, too. This is where I was meant to be. I love Michael, but if I have to stop being me just to be with him, then neither one of us will be very happy."

"I understand exactly what you're saying. I've had second thoughts about keeping my job since the day Dawn was born. But I'd be lost without my work. Being a police officer is in my blood. Yet there's nothing I love more than my daughter. I've spent years going through this tug-of-war with myself, trying to balance everything in my life. I've walked that in-between road all my life but this one was the hardest to follow until I came to terms with who I am—a mom *and* an investigator. If there ever was a crisis where my daughter needed me, I'd be there—no contest. In the meantime, I'll continue doing the work I was born to do."

"And you've got Rose and Boots helping you with Dawn, so you've got backup at home, too. I'm sure that's a huge help."

Ella leaned back in her chair and nodded pensively. "So far so good, but Mom has her own life. I've been getting the feeling that things are getting serious between her and Herman. It wouldn't surprise me if Mom decided to marry him one day," she said, then added, "In a lot of ways Mom's life is more black and white than mine."

"Do I hear a touch of envy?" Carolyn teased.

"Yeah, maybe a bit." Ella thought about how differently she and her mother had handled being widowed. While she had jumped into college, then a law enforcement career, Rose had gone back to mothering her, then Dawn, staying mostly at home. Now, Rose was working for the tribe as a plant consultant, dating, and looking forward to marriage. Since her breakup with Harry Ute, who was now married to an Albuquerque woman, Ella hadn't had an official date in, perhaps, two years.

"You're thinking about it, aren't you, Ella? Hey, you're still young. If you don't want to spend the rest of your life single, then you better start doing something about it. The older you get, the harder it is to adapt to someone else. And the more selfish you get, too," she added with a tiny smile. "I know firsthand. The more set in your ways you become, the less willing you are to sacrifice anything at the altar of love."

Ella nodded as she and Carolyn finished lunch and cleaned up the wrappers, tossing them into the trash along with the newspaper tablecloth. "I hear you. Thing is, I still have feelings for Kevin. But it's not really love, it's more like . . . echoes of what might have been."

"Do you want more children?" Carolyn asked.

Ella smiled. Carolyn always had a way of reading her unspoken thoughts. She took a deep breath before answering. "I love Dawn so much, it scares me sometimes. I can't imagine being able to love another child as much as I do her. But a part of me still wishes I had more kids, regular hours, a husband, the whole nine yards. The problem is everything in life carries a price. To have all that, I'd have to give up other things I love. The Navajo Way is right—everything has two sides. All things considered, I've decided to just hang on to what I've got."

Carolyn's eyes narrowed. "There's something else you're not saying. . . ."

Ella laughed. "If you get tired of being a pathologist, become a P.I. You'd be great."

"You haven't answered my question."

Ella stared at her hands for a moment. "The problem is time—it doesn't stand still. I can't keep Dawn with me forever. She'll leave me to chase her own dreams someday, probably a lot sooner than I'd like if her independent streak is any indication. When that time comes, it'll be just me and my work. That's a reality that makes me reassess my life a lot more than I should."

"Have you considered going out more—meeting new men—when you're not working a case?"

"I . . . yeah, I considered it—considered it crap," Ella said, laughing. "I'm closer to forty than thirty now, and there are still unattached men out there—good ones. But I refuse to go hunting for a mate like it's some kind of mission I have to complete. If it happens at all, let it be because fate or chance intervened, not because I was sorting through them like at a clothing rack full of cozy sweaters. That's my only illusion when it comes to romance, by the way. People who think that values, outlooks, and common goals don't matter, wake up to a mess as soon as the stars stop shining in their eyes."

"Where were you and your philosophy when I met Michael?" Carolyn muttered with a sad smile, then shook her head. "Enough of this. Let's talk shop. It's simpler and doesn't give us nearly as many headaches . . . or heartaches." Carolyn poured herself another cup of coffee, then wiggled the pot at Ella, who shook her head.

"I told you about the traces of gunpowder residue on the victim's hand. Judging from the amount, he got off several shots."

Ella shook her head in exasperation. "Why didn't he turn over the car keys! It was just a rental, for Pete's sake. What a waste."

"*You* would have fought back too—just on principle," Carolyn observed.

The thought made Ella pause. "Yeah, before I became a mom I probably would have. What the hay, even these days I would have had to force myself not to react. Reacting's easier in a lot of ways—more natural."

"For a warrior, not a civilian. I'd have given them the car, the keys, my credit cards, and my shoes just to get them out of my face."

Ella laughed. "Yeah, but listen to yourself. You would have *given* them your car. Ultimately, you would have made it your choice."

Carolyn smiled. "Different points of view but, you've got to admit, mine has definite advantages." She glanced down at her report and continued in a somber tone. "The victim went down hard. Most of his wounds weren't lethal, but once he was incapacitated—out of ammo, or whatever—his killer came up and fired twice at point-blank range."

Carolyn glanced up at Ella who nodded, then continued. "There's one curious thing. I found evidence that the victim had been in the water recently—probably less than a half hour prior to his death—but he used no soap. Didn't have any scent traces of that. And no scent or evidence of chlorine on his skin either, as in a public pool or with treated water. If anything, he smelled more like—river or ditch water, if that makes any sense."

"Well, he never made it home, so we can rule out the shower angle right away. Maybe he stopped somewhere beside the road earlier and fell in the river or a ditch, then dried off and put on a new set of clothes. But that sounds pretty unusual. I'm reaching here, obviously. Still, if you find anything else the least bit out of line once you finish the screens for drugs and the rest, call and let me know. Big Ed wants a quick wrap up on this, so don't wait for the paperwork. Pick up the phone."

"You've got it. And, Ella, I hate to eat and run, but today looks like it's going to be a long one for both of us. We've got to get back to it. But hey, let's get together for lunch sometime soon again. On me, next time. I can bring something from home."

Carolyn loved to cook—and she was very good at it. But because of what she did for a living, there weren't many who wanted to share a meal with her. "Call me anytime," Ella said.

As Ella walked out of the hospital and her friend's domain she thought about their lives. In certain ways they were vastly different, but they were kindred spirits when it came to their dedication to the work they'd chosen and the tribe they served.

Ella drove back to her brother's and pulled up in front of his hogan, noting the other vehicle by the corral, a flatbed truck with high wooden sides. She intended to wait in the SUV for an invitation to approach as was customary but, as she turned off the ignition, she heard a sharp whistle and saw her brother waving at her from the bed of the truck. Clifford and another man she didn't recognize appeared to be unloading metal fence sections.

Ella went over to join them, her eyes on the man working with Clifford. He walked with a very pronounced limp, but it didn't seem to keep him from doing his share of the unloading. Seeing a cane propped against the truck, she jogged forward.

"Let me take one end," she said, reaching for the opposite end of the eight-foot section of metal fencing he was carrying.

"I've got this one. Grab one off the truck if you want to help," he snapped. His tone was sharp.

Ella glanced at him quickly, surprised. He was a solid, muscular man with empty black eyes. It was the look she'd heard referred to before as the one-hundred-yard stare. A gaze that saw everything . . . and nothing, like an old man who knew he was dying and had stopped caring a long time ago.

"Sure. But I would have much rather shared a load than carry one on my own," she added with a grin.

He was impervious to her. "That's you, not me." Then as the

wind brushed back her jacket, he saw her sidearm. "Cop, huh? You need a pistol to unload a truck?"

"I'm on duty," she snapped back.

Clifford came back from where he was stacking the fencing beside the corral, sliding another length from the truck. "I see you've met," he said, after the other man moved away with is load.

"Rude jerk," she mumbled.

Although her voice had barely been above a whisper, somehow he'd managed to hear her. "I usually am," he called back at her. "I never get on well with people who think they deserve something simply because they carry a badge."

Ella clamped her jaw shut but, try as she did, she couldn't let it pass. "You mean like the right to defend themselves when confronting armed criminals?" She wanted to thump him on the head with his cane.

"I respect what you *try* to do—keep the peace. But you lose the second you strap on a gun. The Anglo way of meeting violence with violence does little to solve the problem."

"Most Navajos—cops included—are killed by other Navajos. What do you think we should do?"

"Let the tribe handle it. Word of mouth will identify the criminal and then we can take care of it the old way."

As her brother took the last fence section to where the others were stacked, Ella met the man's gaze, wondering what fairy tale he'd just escaped from. "I'm Ella Clah of the Navajo Tribal Police. And you are?"

"Lewis Water," he said, challenging her by holding the gaze. "What you do has some merit, don't get me wrong. I learned about meeting force with force in the Guard. But the old ways would work better here than Anglo-type law."

"If you're such a traditionalist, what on earth were you doing in the service?" she asked, intrigued.

"I was working several jobs trying to save enough money to

open my own trucking firm when I learned about the enlistment bonus the Guard offered. Signing up seemed like a good idea— until one day when the truck I was in hit a roadside bomb. After that, I was shipped stateside. The doctors did as much as they could, but I still lost my leg. That was a year ago. I used all my money to buy a modified truck with hand controls. I have my own company now and, when I raise enough cash, I'll buy a bigger rig and get that modified, too."

She nodded slowly, beginning to understand his distaste for weapons.

As Clifford joined them, Ella looked over at her brother. "Have you thought any more about the Navajo code the police informant sent me?" Ella had come up with a plan. The way she'd figured it, if she asked Lewis directly, he'd probably refuse to help her. But if she got him interested before he even realized that she needed his help, she'd have a better chance.

Clifford nodded, then guessing her plan, added, "I suspect it's a code where symbols are used to designate real things—a bit like the one our Codetalkers used in World War Two. They spoke in Navajo and assigned Navajo names for things like tanks, artillery, and so on. I think they gave the Navajo word for turtle to signify a tank—stuff like that. It's the reason the code couldn't be broken—except by another Navajo who was acquainted with the language and strategy."

"My great-grandfather was a Codetalker. We'd talk about his service now and then. Maybe I can help," Lewis said. Curiosity flickered in his eyes, and his voice had lost its attitude.

Ella had the papers folded in half longways, attached with a paper clip, and brought them out of her coat pocket. She looked at Clifford first, and waited for him to nod before handing them to Lewis—all part of showing a little phony reluctance, to further heighten his interest. "This came from a former GI who served in Iraq, but does this bear any resemblance to the code the World War Two guys used?"

He studied it for several long moments. "I don't see any parallel terms here, so it looks like the writer of the story invented his own code using everyday objects and even some Anglo names for the characters."

"If there was a code in here and you needed to break it, how would you go about it?"

"I'd talk to other Navajos who know him—try to figure out how his mind works and which characters, names, and symbols might have had double meanings for him. That's your best shot."

Ella nodded. He'd echoed the unspoken thought in her mind. Without the key, she had nothing.

FIVE
✖ ✖ ✖

Once she was on the road back to town, Ella called Justine. "Check any houses or businesses close to the river or near irrigation ditches on Jimmy's likely route and see if anyone remembers someone going into the water earlier this morning. Jimmy got wet, then dried off not long before he was attacked, so this may provide a clue to his whereabouts prior to his death."

"Maybe he took a late shower at a motel close by."

"If he did, there was no evidence of soap, and he smelled more like river water, according to the M.E. But check motels and hotels anyway."

"I'll get on it."

"Anything new I should know about?" Ella asked at last.

"No, nothing," Justine answered. "I'm looking over all the previous carjacking incident reports now and trying to figure out why this one escalated the way it did."

"This was the first incident where the victim was armed," Ella replied. "Bad timing for the carjackers—unless there's more to it than just a robbery."

"That's the thing, Ella, I think we're dealing with a crime that's getting more complex all the time. We have the carjackers we haven't been able to shut down, an armed ex-serviceman with part of a secret message he wanted delivered to the best known cop in the area, and we have a code we can't understand."

"What we need to do next is find out if the story code reveals anything pertinent to our case—like the motive for the murder of a serviceman during a carjacking—or if it's unrelated and involves some illegal activity the victim knew about or participated in while in the service."

"*If* the motive for his murder *is* linked to the story he sent you, then maybe the carjacking was just a convenient smokescreen for the killers."

"We can't make any assumptions either way right now. Keep at it. I'm going to go talk to Mom. She should be back home." *If she'll talk to me,* Ella added silently. Rose was very upset at the moment.

Ella drove home and saw Rose's old pickup parked in its usual place by the side of the house. Her mother had been in an accident several years ago and lost her first truck. The insurance settlement hadn't amounted to much, so Ella had offered to buy her a new truck, but Rose had flat-out refused. Instead, she'd bought another ancient truck, almost as old as the one that had been wrecked, with money she'd saved on her own.

As she went inside and crossed the living room, Ella saw her mother at the kitchen table, maps strewn around her. Rose had been documenting the locations of plants the *Dineh* used for medicinal and ceremonial purposes. The work was slow and painstaking, but her mother loved every minute of it. The initial report had been turned in to the tribe months ago, but Rose continued to update it periodically as new information came to light.

Ella realized she hadn't really focused on her mother in a long time, but frankly, she'd never seen Rose looking so young and alive. Rose was tall and slender for a woman in her sixties, with long salt-and-pepper hair. Her eyes were a penetrating black and she had the cheekbones of a model. One of the best compliments

Ella had ever been given was that she looked just like her mother at that age.

As Ella came into the kitchen her mother glanced up, gave her a slight frown, then continued what she was doing without saying a word.

"Mom, my daughter really *does* understand that I can't always be there. I've attended almost all of her school functions this year. That counts for something."

Rose glared at her, then looked back down at what she was writing.

"Her father was there, and you were there. That's more than most kids get."

"My granddaughter is not *most* kids. She's special."

Ella smiled. "I agree. That's why after this case is closed she and I are taking off for a day on horseback."

"An entire day on a horse?" Rose laughed. "When you come back you'll have to be put in traction for a month. It's been a long, long time since you rode more than an hour at one time, daughter."

Ella chuckled softly. "Gee, thanks for the vote of confidence."

"Just an observation."

"Mom, Dawn's a lucky kid. She's surrounded by love."

"Yes, but she needs *you* most of all now. Just remember, that in a few years she won't want you around at all. The minute they become teenagers . . ."

Ella suppressed a shudder, remembering her own teen years. She'd fought her mother and father tooth and nail on almost everything. If they zigged, she'd zag, and ultimately Ella left home and the Rez as soon as she got married, moving halfway across the country. "Dawn's pretty levelheaded," she said mostly for her own benefit.

Rose smiled. "Like you were?"

Annoyed, Ella turned the conversation back to business. "Mom, I need you to take a look at something connected to an investigation I'm working on. Tell me whatever pops into your head, keeping in mind that there's supposed to be a secret message here."

Rose read the pages Ella handed her, then finally looked up. "I don't know what to make of it. There's no ending and no obvious moral to this story other than the suggestion that the Dark Ones might end up paying for their betrayals of trust. Some of the animals, such as Trickster, we've all heard about in Navajo stories, but I've never heard of Gray Wolf and Coyote engaged in bartering or any Dark Ones created in the shade." She paused. "I can ask *Bizaadii*," she said using the nickname she'd given Herman Cloud as a joke—the gabby one. Herman was a quiet man of few words. "I'll see him tonight."

"That makes it every single night for two weeks, Mom. It sounds like things are getting hot between you two," Ella teased, expecting a protest or dismissal.

"He means a great deal to me, daughter," Rose replied without hesitating. "He and I may make permanent plans. . . ."

"You mean marriage?" Ella gave Rose a shaky smile. She hadn't expected this day to come so soon.

"Maybe . . . I haven't decided yet."

Ella nodded slowly. This was another sign that time was marching on, and the present was as fleeting as dust in the wind. "I'll see you later, Mom."

As she walked outside to her unit, Ella's thoughts weighed her down. Rose had enjoyed two lasting, serious relationships that had shaped who she was and had helped define her. She, on the other hand, had yet to find one that could stand the test of time.

Driving down the dirt road, surrounded by a cloud of dust, she continued to the main highway, then, once she reached the pavement and turned north, picked up speed. She'd traveled a few miles down the empty stretch of road, relatively straight at this point but with occasional low hills to climb and descend, when she spotted a vehicle keeping pace behind her.

Maybe it was because she was cruising at the speed limit and the vehicle following her was satisfied with that. Or maybe it was someone from Shiprock who'd recognized her unit as a tribal police vehicle despite its lack of department markings.

Yet faced with the reality that the carjackers were still out there, a murderer or two among them, Ella speeded up. The vehicle, an SUV, increased its velocity too and kept up—never narrowing the distance between them or allowing it to stretch out beyond visual range.

Ella glanced down at the envelope beside her containing what might have been a dead man's last written words. It was possible someone wanted to get their hands on those pages before she figured them out. Jimmy Blacksheep's house had been carefully searched, after all, and the only things known to be missing were stories he'd written before he shipped out.

As she came down a long hill just outside Shiprock, Ella turned at the last minute into a housing area that had grown around a middle school. The vehicle behind her turned as well, following. Ella slowed, as if looking for a house number among the inexpensive tribal development, and called for backup.

Going north, she headed down the street, noting that no children or people were outside in the streets and consequently in danger. When she reached the next intersection, she sped to the left quickly. As she reached the school parking lot, she noted with relief that classes were still in session at this hour and nobody was hanging around outside.

Ella pulled up beside an empty bus, blocked from the street, and waited, her window down, listening. The vehicle that had been following her slowed slightly, then drove on. Eyes still alert for children, she backed up, pulled out into the street, and saw the vehicle that had been following her now moving up the street slowly.

Switching on the sirens and emergency lights, she accelerated and narrowed the distance between them. If he tried to make it to the highway and turned south, she might have a race on her hands, but if he went north, he'd meet officers coming from the

Shiprock station. As it was, the driver pulled over to the curb beside one of the area homes and got out of the car.

Seeing Samuel Blacksheep, Ella slammed her hand hard against the steering wheel in anger. Taking a moment to cancel backup, she climbed out of the car.

"What do you think you're doing?" she demanded, going to meet him.

Samuel's eyes flashed with anger, and his fists were balled up. "Proving you're *not* doing your job. You've got to find my brother's killer before the trail goes cold. In murder cases each hour counts—every good cop knows that. Yet here you are on duty driving off to visit your brother and mother. Is that how the tribal PD works these days? Punch in, then go visit your relatives?"

Nothing was as guaranteed to make her lose her temper as having someone outside the department criticize their operation—particularly so unjustly. "Listen to me very carefully, Officer Blacksheep," she said, biting off the words. "I don't have to explain how I investigate my cases to anyone outside my department. What you've done so far is interfere with my job and behave unprofessionally by working *outside* your jurisdiction on a case you'd be forbidden to work on. This little stunt of yours has cost me time and manpower I can't afford to waste. But what really pisses me off is that you're following *me* in hopes of getting some leads *you* can follow up on your own. You're obviously clueless, because if you knew where to begin you wouldn't have to follow me, hoping I'd show you the way."

His face turned red, then redder, but Samuel managed to keep his temper—barely. "I'm working toward the same thing you are—solving my brother's murder."

"You're too close to this case, and you're going to end up muddying up the trail for me and my team. Back off *now*. If you bother any of my officers or get in my way, I *will* arrest you for obstruction of justice. I have no tolerance for this kind of garbage. You get me?"

"He was my *brother*. I'm not going to just sit back."

"You have to, and the very fact that you don't see why that's necessary, makes you a liability. Go back to your own department. Do the job you've been assigned. The carjackings seem to be at the heart of what's going on and at least half of those have happened over in your jurisdiction. If you want to do something, see what you get on that."

"All right. I'll see what I can do."

As he drove away, Ella followed. With one road leading into Shiprock, she'd be behind him for a few miles. Still ticked off about the stunt Samuel had pulled, she stormed into the station a short time later and nearly ran into Big Ed as she went around a corner.

"Sorry, Chief, I wasn't watching where I was going."

"Glad you weren't on the highway. My office," he said, then as soon as they reached it, waved her to a chair. "What's happening, Shorty?" He looked down at the report she'd left for him earlier.

Ella gave him the highlights. "If the victim wasn't singled out and the carjackers are now escalating to murder when it's expedient, then we have a huge problem on our hands. The thieves are well organized, and very tight-lipped. None of our usual sources seem to know anything about them. So far the gang's used an attractive woman who flags down a passing motorist—someone driving alone and always in a pickup. They strike in isolated areas, in the early morning hours. The carjackers leave behind the stolen, older sedan they used to lure in their victim and take the target vehicle. The leave-behind car, always an inexpensive sedan, is invariably wiped clean so we'll have nothing to go on. Intimidation and strong-arming have been part of their M.O., but there've been no deaths—until now."

"From your written report I gather that some of the circumstances were different this last time. No vehicle was left behind, and guns came into play, for instance," Big Ed said. "That leads me to believe that the murder wasn't so much a precedent or an indication of things to come, but rather an isolated instance where the violence got out of hand."

"You may be right," she said, "but there's also a possibility that Jimmy was their real target. Since I'm not sure, I've increased patrols in the areas the carjackers have worked in the past. *The Dineh Times* has also run a story cautioning people not to stop automatically. The Farmington paper ran a similar piece. But the carjackers are targeting rural areas where people may or may not get the paper. There are fewer witnesses there, too, and pickups are almost a given."

He nodded, lost in thought. "They've concentrated on trucks—so why a rental sedan this time?"

"That's another discrepancy," Ella said, "and I have no answer for you. Stealing an inexpensive sedan to set up as bait, but then stealing another inexpensive sedan—admittedly a newer model—still doesn't quite fit their established M.O. Since none of the stolen trucks have been found, we suspect that the ring takes them out of state—maybe even out of the country to Mexico where there's a thriving market for hot pickups and SUVs, particularly those that can carry a heavy load."

"And so far no informants?" Big Ed pressed.

She shook her head. "The ring is staying very much under the radar. I'll be meeting with Agent Blalock next. The FBI has been very interested in the carjackings because of the suspected south-of-the-border connection. That puts it into federal jurisdiction. But Blalock's working alone again these days, so he's swamped. None of the younger agents they send stick around for long. Look at the last one, what, six months?"

"Are you surprised? The Four Corners' beat isn't exactly a career-maker."

"True enough," she admitted. "When I first joined the Bureau I wanted to be on the fast track, too," she said, then remembered her father's death—the case that had brought her back for good. Sadness enveloped her as she recalled meeting up with his image again so recently when she'd had her near-death experience. But she pushed back the memory, knowing that the present, not the past, demanded her full attention now. The past couldn't be changed, the future was yet to be determined—the present was the only place where she could make a difference.

Big Ed looked down at the incomplete Navajo story Jimmy Blacksheep had sent Ella, skimming it for several minutes before looking up again. "He was trying to tell you something and you've got to figure out what that is."

"I'll keep digging," Ella said.

Big Ed nodded. "What about the other members of his Guard unit? What do they have to say?"

"I've only interviewed one so far, his platoon lieutenant—whose civilian job is with FPD. Justine got a list for me, and I'll be paying the others a visit starting with the Navajos living on the Rez. All were from his section, or at least his platoon, I believe."

"And his sergeant?"

"Name's Kent Miller, also an FPD officer. The man's supposedly unwinding—gone fishing—but Farmington PD has somebody trying to track him down. Miller's not with family, and nobody knows where he might be. There are a lot of places to fish around here."

"Especially when you include southern Colorado. Keep on it."

After leaving the chief's office, Ella went directly to Justine's lab. "Anything new for me?"

"Jimmy Blacksheep didn't check in at any area motels. Tache and I called every place in Farmington and on his route here within an hour of travel time. And we stopped at places next to river crossings and where ditches or ponds were close to the road. Nobody saw any impromptu bathers today or last night."

Ella nodded, frustrated, but tried not to show it.

"I've finished processing the evidence, but you've already got everything I have, Ella. I did find out that Randy Billey, one of the men who served with Blacksheep, got a hero's welcome at the Cudei Chapter House when he was well enough to return home, following recovery from his wounds. He's severely disabled now, and next week he's headed for a rehab program the Army has set up for GI's and Marines at Walter Reed Hospital in Washington. His wife is going with him."

Ella nodded. "I heard about Randy's return, but I can't remember what . . ."

"He saved three other soldiers who were trapped when their supply truck got hit by a rocket-propelled grenade. He got shot up in the process and lost use of his legs, and one of his arms. Randy's been home a month now, so he wasn't with the unit when they shipped back."

"But they spent months together in Iraq, and Randy was in Jimmy's section, so he might know something. I want to go see him today. Who else have we got in this area from that unit?"

"John Lee Charley."

Ella nodded. "Wasn't he one of the guys we hauled in on a drunk-and-disorderly over near the chapter house a few days ago?" Ella asked.

"Yeah. His enlistment was up a week ahead of most of the others, so, unlike Jimmy, he was discharged as soon as the unit returned. John sure ruffled some feathers at the chapter house. Always had a wild streak a mile long. Guess the military didn't settle him down any. Glad to be rid of him, probably."

"Do you know these men?"

"In passing. They're friends of Jayne's. She dated John Lee for quite a while," Justine said, with a sigh. Jayne was Justine's sister, and Justine's polar opposite. Jayne had her own wild streak, and it was no secret that the two sisters were often at odds. "I've got their addresses. Shall we go pay them a visit?"

"Yeah—but we're going to have to tread carefully. To the tribe, those men are heroes because of their service in a war zone. If any soldiers are involved in what happened to the deceased, we're going to have to get some very solid evidence before we make any waves," Ella said.

"Randy can be ruled out, I'd guess, because of his injuries. And I'm not sure what, if anything, he'll want to talk about. He got a silver star, by the way, but I'm told he left it in the box and never looks at it."

"That isn't unusual. Many vets do the same," Ella responded. The medals represented nightmares they'd relive for the rest of their lives—a time when they'd seen friends die. Medals were for the public, who often needed heroes. They were a symbol that was held up for others to see—a standard in an age where few ever rose to the level of courage and honor where special recognition was due. But the label of a hero could also demand that the recipient meet the expectations of others. The public wanted the larger-than-life fantasy of legendary deeds of war, but the reality was much more down to earth, stained with blood, pain, and the stench of death.

Justine nodded. "Soiling the reps of any returning soldiers will put the entire department on risky political ground, and it could hurt our community support."

"We'll be careful but we can't afford to let anything keep us from doing our jobs. If the killers are Navajos, I'm going to nail them to the wall—whether or not they were soldiers."

"Let's go talk to them," Justine said.

"I need to stop by Agent Blalock's office first," Ella said.

"Okay."

While Justine drove, Ella considered everything she'd learned. Instinct told her they'd barely scratched the surface, and there might be a dozen or more witnesses with important information still untapped. As usual, the pressure to find answers mounted with each passing hour.

Realizing that time was critical, she used her cell phone to call Tache and Sergeant Neskahi, giving them potential witnesses from Jimmy Blacksheep's unit to interview. They were to report their findings to her in writing, by phone if the information was more immediate and critical.

They arrived at Agent Dwayne Blalock's Bureau office, atop the mesa north of the river, a short time later. The generic brown brick-and-glass office was located in a row of several tribal agency buildings, part of a complex that once had held a boarding school.

Dwayne Blalock had earned her respect over the years. He worked hard and expected a lot from himself and any other resident agent assigned to his office—which partially explained why none of the younger agents who came ever stayed. The other half of the explanation, as Big Ed had pointed out earlier, was that no agent in the Bureau ever moved up the ladder by handling cases here. If you wanted advancement, you needed to be in the New York, Chicago, DC, or LA offices.

As they walked in, Ella saw the middle-aged but fit-looking Agent Blalock at his old metal desk, phone in hand. Blalock looked up at her and Justine, nodded, and waved them toward chairs. The office had held two agents, but even pared down to one again, it seemed small. At least he had a window.

As Blalock hung up and looked over at her, Ella was reminded of why the Navajos had nicknamed him FB-Eyes. A hard-edged but good-looking man with a tinge of gray around the temples, Blalock had one brown eye and one blue. "I've been cross-referencing the blood types Justine found on the scene," he said.

"Cross-referencing them against what?" Ella asked.

"I took a shot in the dark and decided to take a closer look at the other men in Jimmy Blacksheep's unit—at least in his platoon. I figured that was something I could do to get the ball rolling in another investigative direction, just in case the carjackers weren't in on this."

"And the Army gave you the men's records?" Justine asked, surprised.

"No, not 'gave', not exactly. I went around the usual roadblocks and got the information unofficially."

"How—" Ella started, then clamped her mouth shut when he

held up a hand. "Never mind. Forget I asked." She looked over at Justine, who rolled her eyes.

"Here's what I've got, though you two already know the first part. The deceased had blood type O, so that leaves the source for type B as unknown. Based on my information none of the men from his unit who live in this immediate area have type B blood."

Ella sat back and regarded him thoughtfully. "That brings us back to the carjacking ring. These perps are careful and they're savvy. I would have added cool under pressure, too, but the thing with Jimmy puts that under question."

"My gut feeling is that Jimmy Blacksheep was itching for a fight. Our guys go through some pretty rough times over in Afghanistan and Iraq. It was the same in 'Nam. Normal rules just don't apply. There's no front line—just bombing, sniping, quick and dirty firefights, and praying you come back in one piece."

"We've got a complicated case with lots of pressure coming down on us and more on the way," Ella said.

"It's going to get even worse pretty soon. I found out that the National Guard is sending someone from regular Army to investigate. A real hard-ass—Chief Warrant Officer Neil Carson. He's already working an internal investigation that may have direct tie-ins to what happened here. But my contact was very sketchy about the details."

"Can you get back in touch with him? I really need to see the whole picture. So far, all I'm catching are glimpses of Blacksheep's life here and overseas. And if it turns out the carjackers had nothing to do with the murder, I'm really going to need a much clearer idea of what I'm dealing with."

"What's your gut tell you?"

Ella's intuitions were legendary. Some ascribed esoteric explanations to it related to her ancestral background, but, to her, it was simply instinct based upon experience. "There're too many loose ends in this case. To find the big picture we're going to have to understand how things connect. Everything, even the details of a crime, form a pattern once you understand their relationship to each other. But without identifying that pattern we won't get anywhere."

He nodded slowly. "It's like that Navajo balance and harmony thing. Works more than I'd normally admit, at least in my experience here on the Rez. I'll try to get something for you, Clah."

Ella stood. "Will you be getting another agent anytime soon to help out?"

"I hear rumors—mostly no one wants the post. You know how it is. And priorities have shifted to fighting terrorism, something we don't see too much around here—at least lately."

Ella nodded, recalling a situation not too many years ago that preceded the 9-11 attacks. A group of armed activists had occupied one of the local coal power plants, threatening to put it out of commission during the dead of winter. "To Bureau agents on the way up, this may not be the end of the world—but they're pretty sure they can see it from here."

"Yeah. Like that."

Ella walked back out to the parking lot with Justine, then remained silent as they drove back south through Shiprock, crossed the river, then headed west on Highway 64. Ten minutes later, they turned north in the direction of the river, which at this location flowed northwest toward Colorado, then Utah. Off in the distance, silhouetted by the sun—now low in the sky—she could see Ute Mountain, which resembled a sleeping warrior from this position.

"What background do you have on Randy Billey? Do we avoid the use of names as much as possible, or is he a modernist?"

"Modernist. He was an okay guy according to my sister, who dated him before he got married, fortunately, and is on good terms with his wife. But his injuries have really made him reevaluate his life. Right now he's working hard to regain as much mobility as he can get and hopes that his upcoming trip to Walter Reed will help him learn to cope better around the house. He can still paint—he used to be an artist—only now he's selling his paintings on the

Internet and through a tribal cooperative that sells arts and crafts from all the Indian nations via catalog," Justine said, then in a somber tone, added, "Randy's paid such a high price. In a case like this, I wonder if dying's better," Justine mused.

"No, partner. I suppose it could be argued that things might have been easier for him then, but the fact that he's still alive means he's got unfinished business on this plane." Ella thought back to the time she'd been buried alive, and had stopped breathing. "I think we're each given a certain number of things to accomplish while we're here, though we may never know specifically what those are. After we complete them, then we can go on. But you also have to consent to die. Randy didn't. That's my personal opinion based on my own experiences."

Justine nodded, lost in thought. "Ella, someday I'd really like to hear more about what you went through down in that mine."

"Someday," Ella said. Truth was, she didn't like discussing it with anyone. They invariably tried to either discount it or take it as a new gospel—of sorts—and she wasn't comfortable with either. She still remembered every vivid detail of her own near-death experience but it was entirely possible that the answers to what a person found in the hereafter were as varied as the people who passed.

"So, how's your mom?" Justine asked, sensing Ella's change of mood.

Ella smiled slowly. "Sometimes I wish I were more like her. She's so together, partner, except for that tension-related episode this morning over Dawn's school play. I think it's just the pressure of making that big decision. It looks like things are getting serious between her and Herman. Marriage serious."

"That's serious. How do you feel about that?"

Ella considered it before answering. "I'm happy for her, but Dawn and I will have to do some heavy-duty adjusting if Mom decides to move out. I depend on Mom a lot, more than I care to admit sometimes."

"Rose depends on you, too," Justine answered. "Think about it. It's true."

"Maybe . . . I mean, I hope so," Ella said then added, "But you know what hurts? My mother has a more active love life than I do." She burst out laughing.

They arrived at Randy Billey's home, a wooden framed collection of added-on rooms like Clifford's, a short time later. Assured the family wasn't traditionalist, they didn't wait by the patrol unit to be invited to approach. Justine and Ella walked up to the front door, which now had a new concrete ramp instead of steps, and knocked.

Soon an elderly Navajo man came to the door. He was wearing jeans and a faded red sweatshirt. Though he looked to be in his seventies, he appeared to be remarkably strong and muscular. "Yes?"

Ella identified herself and Justine, holding up her badge. Justine nodded, not speaking. "We'd like to speak to Randy Billey."

"I'm his father. Come in. My son's just finished his nightly physical therapy session, so he's a bit tired. But visitors are welcome, even the police. Is this about the soldier from his unit who was killed?"

"Yes, it is," Ella said, without elaborating further.

"I think he wants to talk to you about that, too. The deceased was a friend of his."

Ella noticed that although he was clearly a modernist, Mr. Billey was still reluctant to call the dead by name. Fear of the *chindi* stayed with all of them, one way or another, much the way it was with Anglos who didn't consider themselves superstitious, yet would knock on wood or refuse to venture into a graveyard after dark.

As they waited in the small living room, Ella noticed that the house was nearly empty of furniture except for a couch, a low wooden table, and some strength exercise equipment in one corner. Overhead was a simple light fixture. Before long, they heard the hum of an electric motor and a specialized wheelchair carrying a young Navajo man appeared from down a short hallway.

He sat back against the cushion, his left arm manipulating a small joystick control. Cocking his head, he gestured them to sit.

"Please have a seat on the sofa. We got rid of most of the furniture because I need room to maneuver in my chair." As they sat down, he continued. "What can I do for you ladies—officers?"

"I understand that you knew the deceased man, that he was in your unit."

As Randy's father walked out of the room, giving them privacy, Randy nodded to Ella and Justine. "You can use his name now. After my tour in Iraq, the dead don't scare me anymore. The living do."

Ella smiled, understanding exactly where he was coming from. She'd had the same thoughts herself many times during tight situations. "I need you to tell me what you can about Jimmy. In your time together, was he involved in anything under the table?"

"There were a few under-the-table things going on over there. Many guys in the unit never dreamed they'd ever be fighting overseas, and then all of a sudden we got the call. Three months later we were in Iraq. One of the guys painted a sign on the bumper of his Humvee that said 'Weekends, my ass.' Even the lieutenant chuckled. Our platoon, and our section in particular, was made up mostly of guys like me who needed extra money so they could keep that tractor running, or just stay even with bills when the rains didn't come. Faced with long enlistments—longer than any we'd seriously considered—a few began helping themselves to whatever they could find. Not stealing from each other, but from the Iraqis. Anything of value they snagged and shipped home. But there were a lot of straight arrows, too, and Jimmy was one of them. He kept to himself when some of the guys started looting."

"Did he know about what was going on with the others?"

He nodded. "Sure. We all did. But nobody said a word. We had a common enemy, and had to keep the trust in order to stay in one piece. You learned to keep your nose out of where it didn't belong."

He paused, picked up his left leg and repositioned it slightly on the metal rests, then continued. "But Jimmy was different from us all in some ways—a real individual. He remembered the old ways, and would say prayers to the dawn and offer a pollen blessing to the gods, even when the dawn sky was full of smoke from last night's IEDs—improvised explosive devices. His little rituals put off some of the other guys. Medicine pouches seemed like voodoo to some. And what they didn't understand, they'd avoid, especially the Anglos and Chicanos in the unit. But that didn't bother Jimmy."

"And you?"

"I chose a different road. There weren't too many of us Navajos, even in a unit from the Four Corners, so I figured that the best way to get by was to become a *bilasaana*—an apple—red on the outside, white on the inside. I've never been a traditionalist, so it wasn't a stretch. It was the same way for the other Navajos in our platoon. Most of them are Catholic or Baptists anyway. Even a Mormon or two, I think."

"So you're saying that you, for example, were trusted more than Jimmy was?" Ella pressed.

"It wasn't like that, really. In a firefight, we could all depend on each other. But at least the Anglos didn't give me a wide berth during downtime, like they did Jimmy. I think they were afraid of him—creeped out. He was *too* different. I tried to tell him that it wasn't a good thing for the other soldiers to see him in that light—a soldier needs to know that he can count on his platoon without question if we start taking fire. But Jimmy was really trying to stay out of touch, remain a loner, and sometimes it seemed he'd go out of his way to piss people off. He played the part of the inscrutable Indian, you know?"

"Do you think that contributed in any way to what happened to him here? Some form of retaliation, maybe?"

"No," he answered resolutely, "unless something happened after I left the unit. That's why I wanted to talk to you. I would have called if you hadn't come by. The truth is that Jimmy couldn't have known much about anything that was going on because people didn't trust him enough to get personal. Jimmy made himself an outsider and outsiders stay out of the loop."

Ella didn't tell him about the package she'd received. Jimmy had his secrets, too, and he'd kept them, obviously, from Randy. "So what you wanted to tell me is that I should probably just concentrate on what happened once he got back here. There's no connection between the unit and his death. Is that right?" Ella asked.

"Yeah. I know for a fact that he had a major beef with someone here. He was coming home to fix that."

"What kind of beef?" Ella asked.

"I don't know."

"A woman?" Justine pressed.

"I doubt it. He had a girlfriend when he first shipped out, but she dumped him about halfway through the tour. He didn't talk about it, so that's all I know. But I think he was carrying a big grudge, because he shut down even more after that."

"Were you and Jimmy friends?" Ella asked.

He paused thoughtfully, before finally answering her. "Jimmy wasn't a team player, but I respected him. I think he felt the same about me, too. The deal is he was there for me when I needed him. Jimmy had been busy bolting a makeshift armor plate onto a Humvee, so I was asked to take over duty for him. I was riding in one of our supply trucks when we got hit by RPGs—it was like they knew we were coming. I got our wounded under cover but I went down while going back to the vehicle for ammo. I couldn't move or even feel my legs. Jimmy had been listening to radio traffic back at camp and made sure he was in the first unit to arrive. While security laid down covering fire, he pulled me out of the wrecked truck. He took a few hits himself on his vest. Luckily, the rounds didn't penetrate, and he got me to safety. If it hadn't been for him, I wouldn't have made it. He's dead now, so telling you what I know is the only way I've got to repay him."

Randy paused, and silence stretched out for a long time before he finally looked up at her again. "My life doesn't look like much to people who can't see beyond the chair. But when you come that close to death your perspective changes. I wanted to hang on to my life and I fought hard to stay alive. Now I'm getting a chance to do something I've always wanted—watercolors of the Southwest. I have a woman who loves me, my work is in demand, and I lead a comfortable life. I made it . . . but not Jimmy. Life doesn't make much sense sometimes. But despite what happened to Jimmy, I still owe him."

Ella nodded. She understood a debt of honor. Jimmy had risked his life for Randy, and Randy was now restoring harmony by repaying him in the only way he could. But there was more going on here than met the eye. Things just weren't adding up right. "If you think of anything else, call us," she said, giving him her card.

"Will do."

The sun had already set, and the moon was rising by the time they left Billey's home, heading back to Shiprock to see John Lee Charley. On the way, Justine glanced over at Ella. "That was an interesting conversation. Billey is sure Jimmy didn't know anything—yet Jimmy obviously did. He sent it to you in code. Do you think Billey was trying to B.S. us?"

"It's a possibility," Ella said. "I also found it interesting that Jimmy had been the one scheduled to ride in that truck. That may have been the first attempt to murder Jimmy—if the insurgents were tipped off. When we get back to the station, call the National Guard. If they have more details regarding the incident where Randy was wounded, we need to know as quickly as possible. Something just doesn't feel right about this case."

John Lee Charley lived in a modernist housing area on the

east side of Shiprock, above the river. The homes were small, three-bedroom units, each one virtually identical except for their condition, which was dependent on the resident. It was dark now, and there was a light on inside, but when they knocked on John Lee's door no one answered. His neighbor, an elderly Navajo woman having just arrived home, judging from the bag of groceries she was taking from her car, called out to them from her driveway. "His pickup's gone, so he's not home."

Ella recognized Miriam Tsosie. She'd been a member of her mother's Plant Watchers Group for many years, then dropped out. Rose claimed that Miriam had lost heart when her daughter and her family had moved away and was suffering from *ch'éénâ,* depression, or more literally, a sadness for what wouldn't return. Ella and Justine walked over to where she was.

"I know your mother," Miriam said looking directly at Ella, "so I won't waste your time by mincing my words and pretending to like or respect my neighbor. The only good thing about that man is that he was gone for over a year. When he came home again a few days ago, he started up with all his nasty habits again—gambling and drinking all day and night. Yesterday I had to wake him up when I found him in *my* driveway in his truck, surrounded by bottles. Passed out, is my guess, so that's where he spent the night. He said that they'll be shipping him back out again, and he just wants to have fun while he can."

"I know it's evening now, but do you have any idea where he might have gone?" Ella asked her.

She nodded. "I heard him talking to his friend when they left the house earlier this afternoon. They were going over to Amos Curtis's house to play cards and get drunk. Amos lets them use his place because it's in the middle of nowhere and the police can't sneak up on them there."

"Any idea where Amos lives?" Ella asked, knowing that the phrase "middle of nowhere" could describe many places on the Navajo Rez, depending on your point of view.

"Not exactly, but its southwest of Sanostee, not far from Old Sawmill Spring."

"I'm kind of familiar with that area," Justine said. "We can find it."

Ella gave her a surprised look, then nodded once. "All right then. Let's go." As soon as they were on their way south, Ella glanced over at Justine. "Okay, I've got to ask. How come you're familiar with that stretch? I didn't think there was anything even remotely interesting out that way until you get to Two Grey Hills or Toadlena."

"Jayne," Justine answered with a sigh. "Back in high school she used to ride up there on horseback from Toadlena so she could meet one of her boyfriends without Mom knowing. I was curious about where she went, so I followed her one time to an old abandoned sawmill. But I remember there was also a clapboard house close by and that's where Amos lived. At the time, the place was a wreck. Amos used to live alone with his sheep and his dog. He couldn't stand people but managed to make a living selling wool to the weavers. He must be in his seventies now, but I've heard he's changed his ways. He's decided that he has certain material needs, so he sold his sheep and started looking for some easier way to raise cash. I think he found it."

They'd only been on the road about fifteen minutes when Ella got a call from Joe Neskahi. "Ella, I managed to catch one of the victim's buddies, Ben Richardson, just before he was leaving to visit his parents in Pueblo. He'd heard about the crime, but wasn't able to tell me much. Richardson said that he and the victim barely knew each other, and were never on the same vehicle crew on a mission. He's going to be available again in a few days when he returns to New Mexico. Basically, I got squat."

"Thanks, Joe. Get to the others on the list as soon as you can, and write this up for me, will you? Just put it on my desk. You might be ready to call it a day," Ella added, then hung up. She shared the information with Justine, who just shrugged.

It took them forty-five minutes over dark, treacherous dirt tracks that were scarcely more than ruts, before they reached the spring. Only a few families lived there, most still raising sheep, and no lights were on. Large holes left by rains and water coming down from the hills made travel slow, and they were still a mile or two south of their destination.

"Jeez, they come through this just for a card game?" Ella mused after they traveled over a bump that made her slam her head against the roof of the unit.

"I'll bet you anything that to the guys this is fun," Justine answered, clenching her jaw. "My brothers used to think this kind of driving was a hoot, and you see those SUV and pickup ads on TV all the time, bouncing around places like this."

Justine paused, then when they hit a clearer stretch, continued. "How do you want to play this when we arrive? Like we're making a bust for gambling and maybe selling booze on the Rez?"

"No, they'll clam up then and we'll get nowhere. We'll go in looking for John Lee and haul him to the unit alone, if we can. Let the others continue what they were doing. With luck, John'll wonder why he's been singled out and start getting squirrely. That may give us a slight edge when we start with the questions. But this plan's flexible, so be ready to play it by ear."

"All right. Let's just hope nobody's so drunk they get violent—or worse, start puking."

As they crossed a small arroyo a hundred feet or so from the old building, Justine pointed to a spot illuminated at the edge of their headlight's coverage. "There's something going on behind the house. Just past that stand of junipers."

Ella leaned forward and tried to make use of the bright moonlight to get a clearer look. "It's a fight. Get as close as you can, then grab your stick. We need to break it up."

SIX

✖ ✖ ✖

Justine raced up and came to an abrupt stop just in front of a low juniper. Beyond, illuminated by their headlights, two men were rolling on the ground, wrestling furiously like bears at the zoo. Four others, one of them Amos Curtis, were standing together, cheering on the combatants like it was some kind of schoolyard entertainment. As Ella climbed out she spotted the pile of bills on the ground. The men were betting on the outcome.

Everyone must have been drinking because, despite the arrival of their vehicle, nobody even looked over until she and Justine closed their car doors. As they recognized Ella, one of the spectators squatted to grab the cash, but the others pulled him back. The pair on the ground kept fighting, still oblivious to their arrival.

As they walked past the spectators, one of the men grabbed Justine's arm but her response was swift. She jabbed the end of the baton into his stomach, and as he doubled up in pain, she pushed him to the ground. Seeing another man coming forward, Ella swung her baton at his feet, striking him on the shins. He stumbled back with a yell.

Ella brought out the Mace. "Not another move, or I'll spray you with something you're not going to enjoy. Your choice."

Justine came up behind her, Mace in one hand, baton ready in the other. "I've got them covered," she said.

Ella looked at the dusty pair still rolling around on the ground, grunting and groaning as they grappled. Though their faces were bloody and their shirts ripped apart, she could have sworn they were enjoying themselves.

Employing her baton once again, Ella struck the fighter currently on top on the side of his knee. He howled in pain, then rolled onto his back beside his opponent. The second man lunged for Ella's legs, trying to trip her but she dodged, then stepped on his hand. "Navajo Police, stay down!" she snapped.

Ignoring her order, he rolled, then scrambled to his knees. This time Ella struck him on the shoulder. "I said stay down."

He sat back, grimacing in pain.

Ella looked around, and noted that, finally, everyone was staying still. Nobody appeared to have a weapon, either, except Justine and her.

"You two on the ground. Facedown," she ordered. "And put your hands behind your back."

Two minutes later, both combatants were seated on the ground, their hands cuffed behind them.

"Hey, I didn't know you were a cop," the man who'd struck out at her said. "I just wanted to wrestle you next—in a friendly way. I never got a chance to wrestle with a woman over in Iraq."

"What's your name?" Ella asked, already knowing the likely answer.

"Not supposed to say our *real* names. Don't 'cha know anything about being Navajo?" he countered, his voice slurring just a bit.

Ella glared at him. He was in his mid-thirties—old enough to have matured beyond the nonsense he was involved with here. "You're no traditionalist. Stop the phony excuses."

"You want me to talk—then you want me to be quiet. What do you *really* want?"

Ella wanted to tape his mouth shut. Arguing with a man who was about half to three-quarters drunk was always a waste of time. "You're going to the police station in Shiprock. We can talk there."

"I'll bleed all over your car."

Ella stared at him. "I could cuff you to the door handle and let you walk until the blood cakes up. The dust will speed that up a bit, I'm sure. Or you can ride in the trunk."

"You're a mean woman," he said, shaking his head. "Abusing a soldier just back from the fighting. Where is your patriotism?"

Ella ignored him, then glared at the other wrestler and ordered him to go join the spectators Justine was guarding.

Hauling the drunken soldier toward the unit, Ella half shoved him into the backseat. "Turn away if you want those cuffs off." He scooted around, his back to her, and she unlocked his left hand, quickly attaching it around the extra seat belt latch so he couldn't escape from the backseat.

"Hey, how about my right hand?"

"If you don't quit complaining, you're going to find both hands behind your back again." She threw him a box of tissues they kept on the front seat. "Now shut up for a while," she said and read him his rights.

Ella went back to help Justine, but the men were denying that gambling had been going on. "You've all got liquor on your breath," Ella said, her gaze taking in the other fighter. He seemed bruised and scraped up, but otherwise in good condition. "We could haul all of you in, or you could save us the trouble and paperwork by just disappearing. Just give me your keys first. They stay here with Amos."

Within a few minutes the men had gone into the old man's house. Only Amos Curtis remained, the keys in his pocket. He stooped down and picked up the cash, which looked mostly like ones and fives, then started to hand them to her. "You gonna shut me down?"

Ella shook her head and waved away the money, which he quickly jammed into his pocket. "Probably not." One look at his shabby house told her that he needed the money and, in any case, the charges would get thrown out. The men who'd been fighting had obviously been doing it for the money, and assault charges would be hard to prove without a cooperative witness. In the end, it would only end up costing the system.

"I'll check on the prisoner," Justine said.

"Be with you in a minute," Ella called out.

Ella looked around, noting the very basic, simple life Amos lived, and wondering if someday the behavior of one of his guests would end up costing him his life. But then again maybe all the excitement helped keep him on his feet, too.

She took a step toward the department vehicle, then stopped and glanced back at Amos. "Why do you stay out here? There's modern housing closer to Shiprock, and you could probably get your rent subsidized. Electricity, reliable heat . . . you could have things there you can only dream about here."

Amos shook his head slowly. "When you look at me, you see someone with very little and maybe someone who's doing something that could be dangerous at times, especially living out here all alone. But that danger makes life sweeter. *You* should understand that."

Ella thought about what Amos Curtis had said as she went back to her unit. Like Amos, with his shadowy habits, she also needed the rush of uncertainty and the promise of a challenge that went past mere survival. But, unlike him, she also needed the clamor of voices and children's laughter. To her a rich life was filled with sound, vibrant and loud.

Ella climbed into the passenger side of the unit, aware that their cuffed prisoner had managed to clean himself up a bit. Ella gestured wordlessly for Justine, who was behind the wheel, to get underway.

"So you're really going to take me in? But for what? Disorderly conduct when no one was disturbed? Wrestling for money? Aw, come on!"

"Arresting you is a bonus, John. The reason we came here was to talk to you about Jimmy Blacksheep," Ella answered.

"So you know me," he commented, then nodded once, understanding. "I heard all about what happened to Jimmy, but that Navajo . . . well, he just didn't get it. He might as well have put a bull's-eye on his forehead, behaving the way he did. He was marked for death long before he got home."

"What do you mean?" Ella asked, shifting in her seat to look at him. What she was hearing was just the opposite of what she'd been told only an hour or so ago.

"I'll tell you—off the record—but I'll never sign off on any kind of statement. It wouldn't be right for me to talk badly of him."

"Are you worried about the *chindi?*" Justine asked, surprised.

"No—it's a different code. Soldier to soldier," he answered, then looked at Ella directly. "We have a deal?"

Ella gestured for Justine to pull to a stop, then shifted in her seat and faced John. "Deal. So now talk to me." Ella noticed that his cuts had stopped bleeding, though his face was puffy and bruised. A black eye was forming, suggesting that punches had been thrown, and landed, before they arrived, so it had been more than wrestling, at least at first.

"Going to war changes a person," he said slowly, bitterness tainting his words and giving them an edge. "You either learn to do whatever you have to in order to survive, or you die. But as you become what you need to be, something twists up inside you. Most of us adapted to what was happening around us by forming a tight brotherhood that went beyond skin color. It was one way to hang on to your humanity, but it was mostly about fear. You watched out for yourself and your buddies because you couldn't trust the Iraqis."

John paused for a long time before continuing. "But Jimmy didn't trust *anyone*. That kid was a loner from day one. Not like old man Curtis, either. Inside, Jimmy blocked himself off from the world. Even in a mess hall full of GIs, he'd go out of his way to stay by himself. He ate alone the entire time we were there."

"And you think he made enemies because of his attitude?"

"Oh, yeah. You could never be sure about him. Even when he said his prayers to the dawn, I always got the feeling that it wasn't out of devotion to culture. It was his way of pointing out to everyone that he wasn't like them. A real in-your-face attitude."

"So you think he got someone so pissed off they killed him?"

"Seems about right, but I don't think it was anyone in our unit. I think he probably pulled the same crap as a civilian and someone who had it in for him was waiting when he got back. Either that, or he brushed fenders with the wrong guy packing a gun."

"What makes you so sure it wasn't another soldier?" Ella pressed.

"If you managed to come out of that mess alive, you don't wish death on anyone, except the enemy."

"What about the moneymaking schemes that were going on?" Ella pressed. "Did Jimmy get involved in that?"

He gave her a long look, then shrugged. "I really doubt it. To get involved in stuff that got your hands dirty you had to be a team player and that's one thing Jimmy wasn't. But all I saw going on over there was kid stuff, nothing worth getting killed over. A few guys in our unit came up with some ways to make a few bucks on the side, but it was nothing, really."

"Give me an example."

"One of the guys grabbed a primo laptop he found in one of the palace stashes, and started burning music CDs for the other guys. He had somebody sending him the latest music from back home, then he'd sell the CDs for five bucks a pop. Made several hundred on it. Like I said—small stuff." He paused then, as if he'd just remembered something.

"Okay. What else?" Ella pressed.

"Yeah . . . well, it's probably nothing. . . ."

"Let me decide."

"One evening about five months ago, I was sent to find Jimmy. No one knew where he was, and we had to attend a briefing for a supply mission scheduled for the next day. I found him in the vehicle maintenance area with a crumpled letter in his hand. He was really pissed off, pacing back and forth and cussing in English and Navajo both. At first I figured his old lady had dumped him. You see a lot of that. When he looked up and saw me, I asked him if it was bad news from home but he didn't answer me right away. When he finally did, he looked me straight in the eyes and said that it was a good thing he'd learned how to kill, because when he got home, he had a score to settle. That surprised me because Jimmy never showed any emotion. It must have shown on my face, because he eased up then and told me to chill. He said he was just planning to shove some guy's teeth down his throat. But maybe whoever he was talking about got to him first."

"You're pretty sure his problem wasn't with another GI?"

"Positive. Jimmy didn't fraternize with anyone, not even with the guys he shared quarters with. Randy Billey suggested that maybe Jimmy didn't want to make friends with anyone who might end up dead. See, you get to know people in a different way over there—not only the names of their family members, but what problems they have, and what their dreams are for the future. When something happens to them, it really eats you up inside."

Ella nodded, understanding the sentiment. Had she served in the military, she would have also had to find a way to insulate herself—it would have been critical to her own survival.

"But why all the interest about what happened in our Guard unit? Shouldn't you be looking for the carjackers?"

Ella regarded him for a moment. "What have *you* heard about the carjackings?"

"They were the ones who took Jimmy down, weren't they?

I've only been back a short time, but I heard that those guys are well organized and they *don't* recruit."

"How do you know that?"

He gave her a cocky grin. "Is this off the record or can it be used against me?"

"Give. I'm not out to burn you, unless you know who killed Jimmy and aren't telling."

"I heard about their operation from reading *The Dineh Times* on the Net over in Iraq and I thought it might be a kick to work with them for a while. Piece of cake after driving around Iraq waiting for a bomb to go off under my ass. And it would keep my adrenalin going, you know? Things seem pretty tame around here now—well, I guess not for Jimmy."

She'd heard of similar stories before. After months and months of living on the edge, coming back to a routine life took some adjustment. "So what did you do?"

"I asked around pool halls, bars, auto shops, used car places. I figured that if I let word out that I'd be useful to them, after riding shotgun along the hottest highways in the world, they'd contact me."

"And did they?"

"Nah. Nothing. Just got blank stares and a few insults. Those doors aren't open. I heard a rumor from somebody who knows a cop that those guys are smooth. Nothing's left to chance."

She nodded slowly. That much she'd put together on her own.

"But I've got a theory 'bout what happened to Jimmy, if you're interested."

"Go for it," she said.

"When Jimmy got 'jacked he pulled his piece because he still wanted to mix it up—cap some bad guys. He had guts in a firefight, and the rougher it got the more he liked it. But this time he went down. Backup didn't arrive in time. It happens."

Ella nodded, glancing over at Justine, who'd been silent. Her partner shrugged almost imperceptibly.

"If you do happen to get contacted by the carjackers, try to set up a meet and get in touch with us immediately—*if* you really want to nail those who did this to him," Ella added.

"You've got it."

"Good. We're less than a mile from Curtis's place. You got transportation?"

"Yeah, my pickup."

"Think you can make it back?"

"No sweat," he said. "Don't have to worry about snipers anymore. I can walk wherever I want. Missed it more than women . . . almost."

"Okay," she said, then opened the back door and unlocked his other handcuff so he could climb out. "You're free to go, but stay in touch."

Her eyes adjusting to the darkness, Ella watched him walk off as she wiped off the dust and grime from her handcuffs with a tissue, then she got back into the SUV. "Do you recall how much cash Jimmy had in his wallet when we found him?"

"Two hundred and something. He wasn't robbed."

"Credit cards?"

"None with him, but I checked and found out he had a MasterCard account. He didn't have it with him overseas, so I guess he left it in a safety deposit box or with his brother. I put a watch out for any charges made in the past few days. So far nothing's turned up," Justine said. "Clue me in. What are you thinking?"

Ella stared down at her hands. "Everything in this case is just a little too off center to make it easy. We have one carjacking that doesn't quite fit the M.O. of all the others. The victim was attacked close to his home and in a more populated area than the ones they generally hit. The subjects took his car but not his money, though they might have taken his credit card or credit cards, if he has more we don't know about yet. And most important of all, why switch to a sedan when all they've been interested in are pickups?" Ella shook her head. "Nothing fits, and that generally means we're not looking at it in the right way."

"It's possible that Jimmy picked a fight with them—they were following too close or something like that—then everything went wrong. Road rage is a New Mexico specialty."

"Road rage, maybe, but road rage with the carjackers, that's a little too coincidental. And angry drivers that turn to violence because somebody cut them off never steal their target's vehicles. I'm not convinced," Ella answered. "We have to start digging deeper into Jimmy's life. I want to know who his girlfriend was and why she left him and who he wanted to strike back at when he returned. We need to know Jimmy like we'd know our own brothers. Once we do that, I think we'll have a better idea of what we're dealing with."

"Sure. Working past midnight is par for the course," Justine said, reaching over and turning on the headlights. "I'll start a background check as soon as we get back."

Ella sighed. "No, never mind. Let's call it a night as well. Drop me off at home on the way. But pick me up early tomorrow. I want to catch Sergeant Sanders in Farmington before he starts the morning shift. So plan on being at Mom's house no later than six-thirty."

"You've got it. But I'm still going back to the station tonight. I'm trying to get a fix on Paul Curley and Jeremy Bitsillie. Jeremy's in our department, and he came back the same day as Jimmy, supposedly, but hasn't reported back to us yet. I haven't been able to reach him. Paul came back a month ahead of the unit because his wife died in a traffic accident. He's taken his kids to visit relatives near Chinle, and no one knows when he'll be back. I've left phone and e-mail messages for both," she said. "I also want to continue my background check on the other men in Jimmy's section, both Navajo and Anglo."

"Good thinking," Ella said.

Justine dropped Ella off, and Ella walked into the house. It might not have been the longest day ever for her, but it had certainly been among the busiest. It was time to wind down and crash. As Ella crossed the kitchen and entered the living room, she saw Rose in her favorite chair, reading. Two, their mutt, came over, tail wiggling, and Ella bent down to scratch him between the ears.

"Did you have to fight Dawn at bedtime?" Ella whispered, knowing her daughter had enjoyed an exciting day and calming her down would have been a feat.

"Not really. She was exhausted. Her father took us all out to dinner at that pizza place your daughter loves. She played all those arcade games while the meal was being baked, then, once the pizza came, she sat across from her father and talked his ears off."

"About what?" she asked, surprised. Dawn was one of the most closed-mouthed kids she'd ever seen—except when she was talking about Wind—her pony, and her plans to enter him in competitions when she got older. Dawn was determined to compete in barrel racing, though she knew Ella disliked that idea and wouldn't allow it until Dawn was at least fourteen—and maybe not even then.

"The same as usual—horseback riding competitions. After listening to her for half an hour about barrel racing, her father suggested she look into competitive trail riding. He told her that the sport encouraged good horsemanship and that it also focused on caring for the horses before, during, and after the long rides. Apparently it requires getting the best travel time over a pre-set distance, rather than flat-out racing. She wouldn't be able to start yet since she's too young, but he thought she could start her training with Wind. Then, if she liked it, he'd see about getting a horse for her instead of a pony."

"Kevin needs to learn to consult with me before bringing up something like this," Ella said flatly.

"I agree. But your daughter really enjoys her time with him."

"Of course. She only sees him on weekends and a bit more on holidays and summer break. Once in a while he goes to a school event, or a parent-teacher conference. The rest of the time he's like a fairy godfather bringing gifts and providing entertainment, but never around quite long enough to have to resort to rules and discipline," she muttered.

"Daughter, be careful you don't convey that particular observation to your daughter. Competition between parents is *not* good."

"Mom, there's no way I could compete. He's always the good guy because he's not around her every day making sure she does her homework, cleans up her room, and all those things. It's a very convenient arrangement for him."

Rose shook her head. "Daughter, don't you know what's really going on? He's been spending more and more time with her lately, a good thing, usually, for a child with parents living apart. But I'm afraid that what he wants is for your daughter to look to *him* for everything—including the attention she craves. Your daughter's father now works almost all the time at *home*. He's built an entire new addition as his office, and had a big corral added to the back, along with a loafing shed, though he has no livestock to keep beneath it."

"I've seen all that. He just wants to be able to spend more time at home with his daughter. I'd do that, too, if I could."

"I've never seen a police officer so trusting!" Rose said, then made a show of going back to her reading.

Too tired to argue, and certain that Kevin's intent was directed toward Dawn's welfare, Ella went to her daughter's room. It was dark, except for a small night-light, and she didn't want to wake Dawn. She stood just inside the doorway and watched her daughter sleep for a while, listening to her slow, even breathing. It seemed like only yesterday when she'd stood in the same spot, watching her newborn baby sleep.

Ella touched the headband Dawn had hung from the doorknob, remembering the days when Dawn would rush up to her for help brushing her hair. Ella couldn't remember when Dawn had stopped doing that. Time was slipping through her fingers, like water in a cupped hand. More than anything she wanted to slow down that relentless march, to stretch her daughter's childhood, to lengthen the hours and days she'd have while Dawn was still young and needed her.

Her chest tightened as she crept up to Dawn's bed, gently brushed back some stray locks of black hair away from her face, and kissed her tenderly. Dawn filled her world with purpose and love. She'd never imagined love could be this total and all-consuming. When Ella saw her child she saw an affirmation of hope—the past, present, and future all in one tiny package.

"Mom?" Dawn stirred, then rubbed her eyes.

"Shh. I didn't mean to wake you," Ella said, taking her daughter's hand, pleased that Dawn had awakened, and feeling guilty that she'd been the cause.

"Dad said I could spend this summer with him when you're at work," she mumbled in a sleepy voice. "Long hikes and riding . . . that okay?"

"Summer is still months away. We'll talk about it and see."

Dawn rolled over onto her side, facing Ella. "I like being with Daddy. He's fun," she said, then yawned and buried her head into the pillow.

"Good night, daughter," Ella said, and slipped out of the room.

Rose was there when she stepped back into the hall. "Pay attention before it's too late," she whispered.

Ella shook her head and gave her mother a sad smile. "It'll be fine, Mom. Stop worrying," she said for her own benefit as well as Rose's.

"Don't ignore the signs, daughter. You'll regret it if you do." Rose walked down the hall, then disappeared into her room.

Ella passed through the living room into the kitchen, grabbed a soft drink from the fridge, then went back to her own room. Despite her brave words, she *was* concerned that Kevin's growing role in Dawn's life would take her away from her real home. And that would require a sacrifice Ella wasn't sure she was prepared to make.

But change was in the air, she could smell it in the March winds that flew across the mesas with the promise of spring. She could sense it in the air at home, even in the marrow of her bones. And that instinctive knowledge assured her that her little girl was growing up and the ties that bound them as a family would be tested soon.

Justine pulled up at the house at six-twenty-eight the following morning. Dawn was just getting out of bed when Ella stopped by her room, gave her daughter a quick kiss, and hurried past Rose in the narrow hall. They only had one bathroom and the morning rush was usually crunch time. Rose muttered a quick good morning and walked into the kitchen to fix Dawn's breakfast. Boots, Dawn's sitter, didn't come until after school ended these days.

Ella hurried to the living room door, grabbing her jacket on the way, then glanced back for one last look at her daughter and mother, wondering how long she could hold on to the present. Things were so right here at home—now. Pushing her personal life to a shelf in the corner of her mind, Ella hurried out the front door, and focused on the business at hand.

"Where do we start, boss?" Justine asked while Ella was fastening her seat belt.

"Farmington police station. We'll be visiting Sergeant Calvin Sanders first. See if anyone has a line on Kent Miller or Louis Smith, then pass it on to Tache or Neskahi to follow up. While we're on the way, I'm going to call Ralph and have him do some legwork for me. I have an idea I want him to follow up for me."

As they drove through Shiprock, which was on the route to

Farmington from Ella's home, she dialed Tache's cell number. To her surprise, he was already at the office. "I came in early. I've been trying to catch up on all the work that piled up when I went on vacation."

Ella noted how good the signal was this close to the station. "I need you to go talk to whoever you can from the area gangs—the Many Devils and the North Siders. See if they know who's involved in the carjackings. It obviously isn't them, so I have a feeling that an operation like this one, happening on their turf and right under their noses, is seriously ruffling their feathers. Play on that and push them hard so they'll get angry enough to talk to you. And take Joe Neskahi. Joey Neskahi, his cousin, is in the Many Devils, according to Joe."

"Okay. I'll let you know if we get anything useful."

Ella ended the call, then glanced at Justine, who was yawning. "You know, I hate vigilante groups like the Fierce Ones. Their motives are good, but their methods make me crazy. Yet, as much as I hate to admit it, they *have* suppressed most of the gang violence on this corner of the Rez. We don't have nearly the number of incidents we had a few years ago."

"But the Fierce Ones aren't active anymore, are they?"

"They've gone underground, but they're still there, according to a few of my sources. They're aware that they don't have the support of the police, so they stay out of cases under investigation, but The People still believe in them. Many feel that they're doing the job we should be doing but can't because of our limited numbers and all the rules we have to follow."

"They're a strange group but wanting to go back to the traditionalist way of dealing with lawlessness isn't all bad. They do get results."

"I wonder how often they go after the wrong person?" Ella said. "Mind you, our department isn't perfect either, but we have to answer for *our* screw-ups."

Silence stretched out between them as Ella watched a hawk

circling high above, swoop down and, at the last second, cut her speed and rip with talons and beak into some mouse or rabbit. The skill of the hunter was balanced by the watchfulness of its prey, and often the raptor went hungry, insuring survival of the fittest.

"When we get to the station, I'll go talk to Calvin. While I'm busy with that I want you to get me some information. We need to know what Sergeant Sanders was doing when Jimmy was killed, and see if the other officers—Miller and Smith—have alibis, too. Not just some vague 'they went fishing' response, either. We'll need to get the information through the back door, nothing official that'll set off alarms and generate gossip in their department. It'll be easier in the long run that way."

"No problem. I dated a guy in the administrative division, and I still see him from time to time. He'll help me out."

"Anglo?"

"Yeah," Justine said.

"Serious?"

Justine shook her head. "We had a lot in common but, as we got to know each other, we realized that there were no sparks. He's a nice guy, and despite the cliche, we really are still friends." She took a deep breath then let it out. "As a Navajo, I really don't think that passion is something to shoot for. By its very nature it's an undependable emotion. But I still like to feel that rush at the beginning of a relationship."

"For what it's worth, I agree with you on that. But Mom believes that half the reason things didn't work out between Kevin and me is because I counted too much on those sparks."

Justine nodded. "That's the problem with women like us. We want it *all*," she added with a wry smile.

"Heck, yeah, and we deserve it," Ella shot back, laughing.

As they drove into the Farmington police department's visitors' parking area beside the modern brick-and-glass structure, their thoughts focused on business again. "What if Sergeant Calvin

Sanders can't be accounted for or has an unverifiable alibi?" Justine asked.

"I'll have to change my tactics, so if that's what you find out, come and remind me about the meeting with Chief Atcitty in an hour. That'll be our code."

"Got it."

Ella and Justine went inside just as the morning shift was leaving the briefing room. Justine left to see her contact while Ella stood in the hall, waiting to catch Sergeant Sanders. Many of the street officers, in their blue FPD uniforms, had met Ella, and they nodded or said hello as they passed by. Sanders was one of the last to leave.

"Hey, you caught me just in time. I was about to hit the streets," Sanders said, a clipboard and zippered notebook in his hand.

"I'd like to ask you just a few more questions about Jimmy Blacksheep before you leave."

"Okay with me." Two officers brushed past him as they left the room, their eyes on Ella.

Sanders glanced into the room. "The place is clear, so we can talk in peace," he said, waving her into the room and toward one of the folding chairs in a row of empty seats.

She chose a chair and sat while Sanders put his clipboard and papers on the seat beside her, then took a seat in the next chair over.

"Sergeant, I'm trying to get a clearer handle on the deceased's last few weeks. I know he had friends in the unit—but who might have been his enemy?"

"I was his lieutenant—platoon leader—but orders came down the chain of command to his sergeant who was responsible for the men in Blacksheep's section. I worked with the sergeants, and that was the extent of my direct contact with the enlisted men. Like I said, the guy you need to talk to is Kent Miller, a patrolman in the department—sergeant in the Guard. Officer Miller's the man who'd know the details of Jimmy Blacksheep's service, his friends in the platoon, like that. But Miller's still fishing somewhere and I haven't been able to get in contact with him. I've left messages, but he obviously hasn't checked in."

"Could you do me a favor? FPD must have his blood type on file. Can you check it for me?"

"I suppose. Why?"

"Just following a hunch. Humor me?"

"All right. I'll find out what it is and get back to you."

Ella knew Sanders had seen Jimmy's service records, and had certainly written reports about the men under his command. She was about to ask him about that when she saw Justine walking into the briefing room.

"We gotta roll, boss," Justine said quickly. "Dispatch received a call about a suspicious vehicle—could be a carjacking in progress on the Rez."

SEVEN

✖ ✖ ✖

Ella welcomed the news, a rush
of excitement coursing through her. This could turn out to be
the break they'd needed. Ella nodded to Sergeant Sanders, who
grabbed his papers and stepped out into the aisle, allowing her to
pass. "Check back with you later, Sergeant," Ella called as she followed Justine from the room.

"Good hunting!" Sanders replied.

They were in the unit and in Farmington's western outskirts
less than three minutes later, full emergency lights and siren on.
"Fill me in," Ella yelled, having to speak over the wail of the siren.

Justine spoke, but her eyes never left the road. They were going fifty right now, with only one more traffic light to pass through
before open road. "We got lucky. Albert Tom was driving home—
he works graveyard as an orderly at the Farmington Medical Center and spotted what he said was a 'really awesome' blonde by the
side of the road just inside the Rez on the east side of Hogback. He
saw that she was having car problems so he thought about stopping, though she wasn't trying to flag him down. Then he remembered the carjackings and kept going. As soon as he got home,
which wasn't far, he ran into the house and called Dispatch."

"That's a pretty busy route this time of day, which doesn't fit
the carjackers' M.O. It could be legit."

"No, Albert lives just inside the Rez," Justine argued. "The Hogback is in his backyard, almost. This breakdown is on the old highway, you know, to the north of the new road. Nothing much back there but farmhouses and the abandoned trading post."

"Do we have any officers in the area?" Ella asked.

"Just us. If they're waiting for a particular target, then maybe we can get in on it."

"I'm going to see what else Albert Tom knows about the neighborhood and potential targets." Ella grabbed the radio, and, in two more minutes, had Albert Tom on the phone.

After a brief conversation, Ella hung up.

"What'd he say?" Justine asked, her voice clipped as she concentrated on her driving. They were back down in the river valley now, and at the speed they were going, would be closing in on the Navajo Rez within minutes.

"We've got a carjacking going down." Ella reached over and turned off the siren, then called for a roadblock leading into Shiprock from the east. Racking the mike, she turned to Justine. "You heard my report and request for backup. Keep your eyes peeled. Leroy Enoah was the target. Albert climbed up onto his roof and looked down the road to where the woman was standing beside the car. No binoculars, but he has a scope on his hunting rifle. As he was watching, Leroy—who lives farther north but has to take the turnoff east of Albert's place to get home—got sucked in and pulled over to help. When Leroy got close a big guy jumped out of the broken-down clunker and whacked Enoah with a big stick or axe handle. That's all Albert saw. He climbed off the roof to get to his phone, and that's when I got him on the line. Apparently Enoah has a big, brand new, white pickup with a long bed and extended cab."

Justine nodded, then Ella continued. "Albert saw the carjackers drive by his own home while he was still on the phone. The driver turned north, going down the same road Enoah lives on. If the carjackers don't get back on the main highway, or encounter the roadblock being set up outside Shiprock, that truck'll just disappear. Step on it, Justine. I want these guys."

They approached the steep sided walls of the giant rock formation of Hogback at high speed, with lights flashing but no sirens. As they took the old highway turnoff, to their right, they spotted a beat-up old sedan, brownish copper in color, parked on the shoulder of the road. Ahead, they could see Albert, standing beside Enoah, holding him steady.

Justine slowed as they reached him, but Albert yelled, urging them on, and pointed ahead, indicating where the truck had gone. Justine kept going and turned down the narrow farm road.

"Cut the emergency lights. When we finally spot them, I don't want to give ourselves away immediately," Ella said.

They'd only gone a quarter mile down the one-lane road, past a farm and orchard, when they saw a white truck that fit the description coming from their left, leaving a cloud of dust in its wake. The intersection coming up formed a T, which meant Justine had to go either right or left. The truck would have to continue straight, or make a left to get back to the highway.

"There's a one-lane wooden bridge ahead. Get there first and block the road. We'll pretend we picked up a nail on the bridge. If they want to go this way they'll have to stop and wait for us to let them by, and we'll have them," Ella said, reaching for the radio. "Worse case, they keep on going without making the turn toward the bridge and we'll be right behind them."

Justine slowed the car, then came to a stop just off the bridge at the far end, blocking access completely.

"Keep coming," Ella muttered, her eyes on the speeding pickup as she got out and pretended to check a tire, blocked by the engine compartment. Justine was using the partially open door for cover, her pistol in hand.

The white truck got close, slowed, then suddenly accelerated and raced on.

Within seconds they were in pursuit but, this time, they were chasing a vehicle, eating dust, and barely able to see, instead of trying to intercept it. The road felt like a washerboard in places where vehicles traveling too fast had bounced causing ripples across the road, and Justine had to slow to avoid losing control. Within a mile they dropped down into an arroyo. By then the dust had drifted away, and they had no idea where the pickup had gone.

"Keep going east," Ella urged. "They're trying to get off the Rez onto county land, but since we're in pursuit of a suspect I'm not going to worry about jurisdiction."

Ella called it in, requested backup from the county, but then the road curved back south, onto private land, and they encountered a pickup truck pulling a horse trailer stopped at a closed gate along the fence line. Ahead, beyond a rise, was the main highway, and they could see a cloud of dust. Although the rancher left the gate open for them, by the time they reached the highway, the pickup was gone.

Frustration, dark and crippling, washed over Ella, but she fought against it. Bad luck happened. She had to stay focused.

"We almost had them," Justine said through clenched teeth.

"Let's keep looking. They may have holed up, and, if they took off toward Shiprock, they'll encounter the roadblock," Ella said, then looked at the edge of the asphalt highway where the dirt road ended. "Look, dusty tracks coming from here turned left, back toward Farmington."

"But there are county units heading this way. The carjackers will have to turn off again," Justine pointed out as she eased onto the highway.

"If I were them, I'd get back off the highway as soon as possible. Keep a sharp eye on your side for a dust trail along one of these lanes."

They continued east, past farm houses, a few small, roadside businesses, and the inevitable cluster of new homes that had begun to pop up along the valley. Those belonged, by and large, to a new generation who'd inherited their parents' land but weren't interested in agriculture. Sections of old apple orchards remained, as did fields destined to become filled with new crops of alfalfa and corn once the danger of frost was gone.

Passing a large red barn close to the road, Ella caught a glint of light and a flash of white several hundred yards down a dirt road behind a cluster of cottonwood trees. "There's something back there. To my right."

Justine found a place to turn around about a quarter mile down the road, then came back up the highway, heading west. Crossing the median, she drove down the gravel lane. Up ahead was a solitary farmhouse about fifty yards from a large red barn and a shed with a shiny metal roof.

Ella immediately located the white truck. It was in the shade of the old cottonwood at the beginning of the driveway leading to the house, partially hidden by the tree trunk. "There."

"That the same one?"

"Yeah, I think so," Ella answered, then called it in and verified the vehicle plate number. "Block the drive," she said, noting that the only alternative direction of flight would be across a freshly plowed field. "We'll move in on foot."

Leaving the tribal unit in the middle of the small driveway, they approached in a crouch, covering each other and using the tree trunk to screen themselves from the vehicle cab. As they reached the tree, they could see that the vehicle appeared to be empty. The doors were open, and a closer look revealed the key was still inside the ignition. Ella grabbed the key while Justine kept watch.

They moved toward the house, which was shaded by two willows at opposite ends of the rectangular, shingle-covered frame building. Keeping a fifty-foot distance between them, they were able to watch the house and both sides. There was no cover, but they kept moving. As they got close, Ella saw a few chickens wallowing in the dirt in the shade of one of the willows. The birds rose up and started to scatter, all in the same direction, toward the shed, which lay closest to her side of the house.

Ella crossed over toward Justine. "If anyone else had come up, they'd have also spooked the chickens."

"Unless the chickens belong to them, maybe?"

Ella stood still and listened, watching the house and the yard at each end of the structure.

"Somebody's in the house," Justine mouthed, gesturing toward a window.

Ella didn't see any other vehicle around except for an old pickup with four flat tires and a missing hood. "You saw someone?"

She nodded once. "Curtain moved, and the window is closed."

Ella, with Justine alongside her, continued toward the door. They got within fifteen feet of the porch when a shot suddenly rang out.

There was a flurry of squawking from the frightened chickens, then a shaky voice. "Get off my property," a man ordered. The tip of a shotgun barrel was visible from the left corner of the building. It was pointing skyward.

"We're police officers looking for car thieves," Ella called out, crouching low and keeping her sights on the edge of the building. "Put your shotgun down."

A heartbeat later an elderly Anglo man with long white hair in a ponytail came around the corner of the building, hands in the air. "Don't shoot, Officers."

Ella moved toward the man, but stayed close enough to the building to keep from presenting a target to anyone inside. Passing a window, she ducked down while beneath it, not taking her eye off the owner. The last thing she wanted was to push an elderly man into a heart attack, but there was no way of knowing if he had someone else in the house—perhaps a son or grandson armed to the teeth.

As Justine watched the other side of the house, and the front door, Ella gestured for him to approach. "Are you all right, sir?" she asked, seeing fear in the man's eyes.

"I guess so. What's going on? Why are the Navajo Police here, off the reservation? Does it have to do with that pickup out by the road?"

"Is there anyone else in the house?" Ella pressed, sidestepping his question for now.

The man nodded. "My wife. She's bedridden." He turned his head and saw Justine peering in the windows.

"No one else is in there, so please don't upset my wife. If you want to come in and look around, do it, but if you want to check out our bedroom, I'll have to go in with you. Otherwise you'll scare my Margo. She's deaf, too, and if you just walk in carrying a gun . . ."

Ella went inside with him, and Justine followed, providing cover, alert to the slim chance that someone was being held hostage. They looked around the rooms quickly, but it was clear that everything was all right. The man's wife was asleep in bed, obviously alive.

Ella and Justine went outside into the backyard with the old man to make certain no one was hiding in the barn or shed. The old man showed them everything, explaining himself as he walked from his barn, which contained an old but serviceable-looking pickup, to the shed, which had been converted into a chicken coop. "I fired a warning shot because I'd seen a few people skulking around and figured they were up to no good. They roared up in that big new pickup, then jumped out and climbed into a beat-up old green van, which had followed them up the lane. I wasn't sure what was going on, so I went to grab my shotgun. By then, the green van was gone. I kept watch, then you came up and I saw you had guns. I didn't know you were with the police because you don't have a regular police car."

"Sir, I'm sorry. The people who drove up had just stolen that white truck. We were in pursuit—" Before Ella could finish the sentence, she heard sirens and two county sheriff's vehicles raced up the lane.

"I'll go fill them in," Justine said, holstering her weapon and bringing out her badge.

"Can you tell me anything more about the people you saw? A description?"

"A man and woman jumped out of the pickup and ran over to the van. There was a driver, of course, but from the angle and distance I couldn't tell if anyone else was in there. The man and woman jumped into the van through the side door and the driver backed up the lane to the highway. Then the van drove off toward Kirtland—east. It happened fast, like it was one of those reality TV stunts."

"Did you happen to notice if the van had any markings?"

"It was a Chevy, all beat up, like I said. The green was more olive than green, faded, like from the sun, and there were no windows in the back. I remember a lighter, rectangular spot on the side, like maybe a sign had been there at one time, then sanded off."

Ella gave him her card. "You'll be asked to give the county officers a statement, and they'll give you their names and numbers as well. But keep my card. I'd really appreciate a call, too, if you remember anything else once things calm down a little here. It happens that way sometimes."

"Okay, I'll do that."

After exchanging information with the county deputies, and making sure that the pickup would be held and processed for evidence, Ella and Justine headed west back toward the reservation.

"I want to talk to Albert Tom and Leroy Enoah. Call our PD and find out where they are right now."

Twenty minutes later, they met with both men at the station in Shiprock, where they'd been taken to make their statements. Leroy Enoah was in his forties and looked like he took bodybuilding seriously. If he'd been injured in the attack, he certainly didn't show any outward signs of it. He was sitting behind the table inside the nicer interview room reserved for victims of a crime, or those who'd witnessed a crime. The wooden chairs there had cushions on them, and the walls were painted a soft blue.

Ella joined Leroy and offered him something to drink, but he declined. "I can't believe that they set me up and *stole* my truck! I had to put in some serious overtime to get those wheels."

"We've already recovered your vehicle, but it'll have to be processed for evidence before you can pick it up at the sheriff's station," Ella assured him.

"Is it in one piece?" he asked quickly, leaning over.

"I think so. All I could see from a quick outside inspection is a little dust."

He exhaled, then leaned back. "Good. I have insurance, but it probably wouldn't have covered everything."

"Can you tell me what happened?" Ella asked.

"I got suckered, that's what happened. I've always had a soft spot for blondes."

She'd heard it before, but she'd never been able to figure out why some men turned into instant idiots over the color of someone's hair. "Okay, so you saw a blonde . . . did she flag you down?"

"Well, yeah," he answered. "She was waving her arms in the air, and that little halter top of hers was barely covering her breasts—which were large enough to pass for cantaloupes, if you have to know."

She nodded impatiently and tried to curb her temper. "Besides the abundant produce, what else did you notice?"

"Not much—my eyes just kind of hovered there," he said slowly. "Until I heard a noise and saw the guy with the baseball bat or whatever he was swinging. By then, it was too late to duck."

Ella was tempted to smack him in the head and knock some sense into him. "Okay. What about the guy who hit you? Was he big, small, short, fat? How about hair color? Was he Indian or Anglo?"

"Dunno. He was wearing a ski mask and leather gloves. Big, like me, wearing a stretchy black T-shirt. I don't think it was a bat he hit me with, come to think about it. Maybe an axe handle. At least there wasn't an axe on it. Caught me right across the back and knocked me down." Leroy squirmed slightly. "Gonna leave a bruise."

"Anything else about the guy?"

"Well, he had on shoes, lace-ups. When I went down I saw his feet. They were running shoes, I think. Black or blue, with white laces. That's it."

"Okay, I'm going to turn you over to a police artist. See if you can come up with a sketch that'll tell us something about the woman from the neck up."

Leroy gave her an embarrassed shrug. "Yeah, sure, I'll be glad to help."

As she left the room, Tache was approaching. "Ella, we've got the car they used to draw their victim in. And we now have a photo of the plaster cast made from the tracks of the van that picked up the car thieves—courtesy of Sheriff Taylor."

"They steal a piece-of-crap car, which they leave behind, and drive away in the stolen truck, while someone in a van keeps lookout. I think I remember seeing a van on the road when we first responded. All in all we have more than we had before. Progress."

"With luck, we'll get prints or hair samples this time that'll establish DNA," Tache said.

"I want you and Justine to get in touch with the county crime scene team and see if they'd like your help processing the truck and that decoy sedan. They know why it's a priority case for us now, but mention that anyway. In the meantime, I'll question Albert Tom."

Ella went into the next interview room and saw someone had already brought Albert some coffee. After exchanging a few pleasantries, she got right down to work. "I need you to think back and tell me exactly what you saw."

"I was driving home, and saw that blonde babe. I considered stopping but remembered the warnings about the carjackers from the paper. When I got home, I called the station, then climbed onto the roof of the house to take a look and see if she was still there. I have a ten-power scope on my Winchester, so I could even see the cleav—the woman—really well. Then Leroy stopped, and walked right up to the babe. The next thing I saw was this guy coming around from behind the car. He nailed Leroy across the back with that board or whatever. For a second, I thought maybe Leroy had made some kind of comment and the husband or boyfriend turned on him. But as soon as Leroy went down, the guy and the woman jumped into Leroy's truck and hauled ass. That's when I scrambled down from the roof and called you guys again. The truck whizzed by my house going sixty, at least. I ran over to check on Leroy, and you drove past me just about then."

"Tell me about the woman—what you saw through your scope. And the man who came out of the car."

"The woman had shoulder-length blonde hair, and boobs that would block out the sun. The guy was big-chested, too, but more like Popeye, with big arms and one of those muscle T-shirts. It was a smooth operation and they were out of there in ten seconds, like in the movies."

"Pros?"

"Had to be. You could almost hear the stopwatch counting down. Each second was planned."

"Okay. Thanks for your help." Seeing him yawn, and noting his drooping eyelids, she added. "You drive here on your own?"

He shook his head. "Naw, Sergeant Neskahi picked us up where it went down, and checked out Leroy. Anyone else would have needed an ambulance, but Leroy just shrugged it off, like just another bar fight. The sergeant said that when you were done, we should check in at the desk. They'd find someone to take Leroy and me home."

"Okay. You're free to go."

Ella went back to her office, and saw FBI Agent Dwayne Blalock waiting for her. "Nice digs. Beats that old closet you had before."

"That's for sure, but I haven't been able to spend much time in here lately." Ella sat behind her desk and looked out the window at the cloudless blue sky.

"I spoke to your partner a few minutes ago. I heard the clunker the thieves used as bait was stolen right outside the owner's home. It was left parked outside with the keys still in it. They didn't think anyone would steal it."

"Justine and Tache will go over it, along with county. If there's any evidence there they'll find it," Ella said.

"The carjackers have adjusted their M.O. just a bit. They're operating later in the morning. It was a blonde?"

"With top-heavy attributes," Ella said and explained. "It worked, I'll give them that much. The witnesses didn't take a careful look at anything else."

"At least this time no one's dead," Blalock said. "But the key may be that no one fought back."

"He was unarmed, and couldn't take his eyes off the woman long enough to see it coming," Ella answered.

"Think I'll stick around here until the car's processed. That okay?"

"Sure." She was about to say more, when she saw Samuel Blacksheep at her door.

"I got a call from Sanders, who said you might be having a run-in with the carjackers. How'd it go down?" he asked without preamble.

Blalock stood up. "I'll be with your crime-scene people," he told Ella, then ducked out the door.

"Sit down, Officer," Ella said. "We didn't get close enough to make an arrest, but we were able to recover the stolen vehicle this time. Add to that some new descriptions, a slight change in their M.O., and the possibility that we'll find something in the vehicles that'll help. But I'm glad you came by. I'm having a problem getting a clear handle on your brother. I need more to go on. You said he'd thought about taking some writing classes, but was there anything else? I understand he was a ladies' man, so who was he seeing? Anyone around here?"

"My brother had a lot of women in his life—off and on. Women loved to mother him for some reason. We'd laugh about that, but it was true," Samuel said seriously. "He spoke of getting married several times—but it was always just talk. My brother wanted to be a writer like I told you, but I don't think he knew he'd probably need a real job in case that didn't work out," Samuel said with a sad smile.

"I have witnesses that claim Jimmy said he had a score to settle with someone when he got back home."

Samuel's expression hardened. "Who told you that?" he shot back.

"I was hoping you'd tell me."

Samuel stood. "I think you're wasting time on useless speculation that has nothing to do with his death. Stick to the facts you have. My brother was murdered because he didn't want to relinquish anything to a man holding a gun. Considering where he'd come from, you can't blame him. Do you have any more information we don't already have that I can pass on to my PD?"

"The county will be sending your carjacking team copies of their reports, I'm sure, as will our department. But it'll have to go through channels," Ella said, forcing her tone to remain calm. "You said you'd spoken to Jimmy by phone once after he got back. Did he mention wanting to see anyone here on the Rez?" Ella pressed. It was a fishing expedition, but she caught the flicker in Samuel's otherwise steady gaze. He was holding something back.

"My brother and I weren't exactly drinking buddies, but I can tell you this much. Something happened to Jimmy over there that changed him. He wasn't the same. He was more focused, and . . . quieter. If he had an agenda once he got back here, he sure kept it to himself."

"Would it surprise you to learn that your brother bought a handgun once he was stateside?"

"Oh, hell no. He's had a deer rifle since he was fourteen. Both of us have always had a weapon of one kind or another. He probably got used to having a sidearm and felt naked without one—like it is for police officers. But if I had to lay odds, I'd say he wanted a weapon in case he had a problem on the road, or at a rest stop. Remember that he served in a transportation unit, and the roads over there are deadly. To stay alive he had to be on alert at all times, and there's a lot to be said for habits."

"Just one more question. Does Mourning Dove mean anything to you?"

"Morning Dove . . . a bird who flies before noon?"

"No, *Mourning*, like in sad."

He gave her a puzzled look. "Sounds like a character in one of our creation stories. You know, like Trickster, the Coyote. I remember some of those from grade school—but barely. My brother was the one who was interested in all that stuff, not me. Why do you ask?"

"It's just something that came up around here recently," Ella replied vaguely. But he wasn't convinced, she could see it on his face. When she didn't elaborate, he gave her a curt nod, and left.

Alone, Ella sat in her office, thinking. Samuel Blacksheep was holding something back about his brother, she was sure of that. But to learn what that was, she'd have to find a witness who'd known both Jimmy and Samuel.

Neskahi came into her office next. "Hey, Ella. I got some news from the Many Devils before the manhunt this afternoon took me away. Remember, you wanted me to make some inquiries about the carjackings?"

"Yeah. I knew that Joey, your cousin, is in that gang. What'd you get?"

"I gave it a shot and spoke to Joey first but, from what he said the kids really don't know much about it—and that's something that's really getting under their skins. The Many Devils think they deserve a cut of anything that goes down on their turf, but they haven't been able to find out who's behind the carjackings. Not enough adult informants, I guess. They've pressured everyone who's ever taken a joyride, since it's making them look bad. The thing is that most of the carjackings have happened on areas claimed by the Many Devils, as opposed to the turf claimed by the North Siders."

"Do you think this is somehow gang-related, but with some other gang in play we don't know about yet?"

"No. It's too . . . organized for youth gangs. Think about it. The operation goes down with almost military precision. They hit—they're gone. Later, we find the car they've used to lure the driver of the jacked vehicle, but there are never prints left behind or evidence of any sort. The gangs like to leave their calling cards for intimidation purposes and publicity. Besides, the witnesses have all insisted that the perps were adults."

Justine knocked on the door, then came in. "We have something this time. The blond hair? It came from a wig. A cheap one, too. And I found what looks like makeup, which probably won't be much help."

"Right, but check the places in this area that sell wigs," Ella said.

"Already on it," Justine said. "There are only a few retail outlets, but pages of mail-order places, which usually have better records because nothing is paid for in cash. I'll check those, too."

"See if Blalock can help you with that. Businesses outside our area might respond better to a request from him."

"Will do," Justine said. "I've also got other news. Officer Jeremy Bitsillie is back."

"The PD officer who served with Jimmy?"

Justine nodded. "He heard about what happened when he was in Arizona with his family. He's here at the station now. Do you want me to send him in?"

"Absolutely."

Justine and Neskahi left to get back to work and, less than five minutes later, a barrel-chested Navajo officer stopped by her door. "I understand you've been looking for me."

Ella nodded and offered him a chair. "I wanted to talk to you about the Guardsman who just died here on the Rez." Out of respect, since she wasn't sure how much of a new traditionalist he might be, she avoided mentioning Jimmy by name.

"Yeah, he and I grew up together. He was one of the good guys."

"Tell me about him."

"What do you want to know?"

"Anything that comes to mind that'll help me get a clearer picture of the deceased. To solve this case I'll need to know who he was and how his mind worked."

He studied her expression for several long moments, then said, "That makes me think you don't believe his murder was linked to the carjackings, do you?"

Bitsillie's eyes held hers, and Ella didn't look away. "We're still considering all the possibilities, so I need some feedback. What was his state of mind over in Iraq, and when he returned to the States?"

"That guy made enemies all too easily." Officer Bitsillie paused for several long moments before continuing. "All things considered, my guess is that someone was waiting for him when he got back . . . set him up, you know?"

"He's been gone for over a year. Do you think it might have been someone from his unit who followed him here?"

He considered it. "Maybe. But the way it shapes up, it would have had to have been someone familiar enough with the details of the carjackings to make it look like a busted heist . . . like a police officer. Someone he trusted and who knew he'd be back."

Ella nodded. Although he hadn't mentioned a name, she knew who he meant—Officer Samuel Blacksheep—Jimmy's brother.

EIGHT
✖ ✖ ✖

Ella reached for a pack of gum from her desk drawer and offered Officer Bitsillie a stick. "What was the deceased planning to do once he was back home? Do you happen to know?"

He remained quiet for a long time. "I know Jimmy had a score to settle with someone here, but I don't know who. He wasn't the talkative sort, and he only mentioned it once."

Ella knew now that Bitsillie was comfortable using the victim's name. "What do you know about his relationship with his brother?"

"Yeah, Samuel. I got the impression that they had their differences, and they got even further apart the past few months, but, deep down, Jimmy wanted the approval of his older brother. Jimmy mentioned going to the community college and maybe learning how to write stories and books. Navajo fiction, I think he said once."

Ella nodded, waiting for Jeremy to continue.

"He said that he'd been screwing around for too long, taking crappy jobs that didn't require anything except muscle power. He wanted more out of his life—a reason to feel good about himself when he got up every morning. A career."

Ella saw the flicker in his eyes—the hesitation created by a thought left unspoken. "And what else?" she pressed.

Jeremy smiled. "My grandmother is a traditionalist," he said. "She told me once that your clan has gifts—that you and your mother know things no one else does. And the other cops around here say you can read minds sometimes."

Ella shook her head. "No, I don't read minds. I've just learned to read people. And, right now, you're sending signals you're not even aware of. What else is there about the deceased you're not saying?"

Jeremy exhaled slowly. "He was a loner and never let on when something was eating at him. But whatever happened between him and the girl he left behind really set him off. For about a month, he was really on edge, mouthing off to other soldiers in the platoon. He ended up getting reamed out by the sergeant and pulling a lot of extra duty."

"What's this woman's name?"

"He never said, but he called her Bluebird once. I remember that. He was really into the old Navajo stories. According to him Bluebird was a symbol of peace and happiness and that's what she meant to him. Then he got a letter from home and went nuts for a while. We all figured she'd dumped him, but whenever anyone tried to bring him out, he'd just make some smart-ass comment and walk away. No one pushed it because, over there, you learn never to get somebody really angry—not when they're packing automatic weapons twenty-four/seven."

"I see your point. If you think of anything that might help, will you let me know?"

"Sure." Jeremy stood. "For what it's worth, my gut tells me that you should be looking for answers among the people who've been here at home the past eighteen or so months."

Lost in thought, Ella watched Officer Bitsillie walk out. Before she could consider the new information, Justine knocked on the door and walked in with two sandwiches from the machine.

"Have some lunch," Justine said, handing her one. "I've followed up on Calvin Sanders's whereabouts when Jimmy was murdered. According to my friend, Sergeant Sanders wasn't clocked in, but Calvin comes in at around seven A.M. regularly to catch up on paperwork. The day of the murder Calvin left some dated reports on his desk. My friend came in a little before eight A.M. and they were already there. Since they hadn't been there the night before, he assumes Calvin must have come in early that morning. He's got nothing on Louis Smith."

"Murky alibi. Those papers could have been placed there hours before," she said, eating the tasteless sandwich. It was either turkey or chicken. She couldn't tell.

"Yeah," Justine agreed. "We could use an eyewitness."

"Sit down, Justine. Let's do a little brainstorming here," Ella said, finishing her last bite, then waiting for her second cousin and assistant to make herself comfortable. "Here's what we got— Jimmy might have had an old enemy waiting for him to return, or was very quick to make an enemy *after* he got back. It's also possible he was the random victim of road rage, but the missing car doesn't support that theory. Jimmy might have also had an enemy in his unit who came home at the same time or earlier, knew when and where he was going, and was waiting on the road for him to show up."

"We have good reason to believe Jimmy was carrying a handgun, but there's still a problem," Justine said. "There's no record of Jimmy purchasing a gun, at least not one we've been able to find so far. It could have been bought under the radar, or from an acquaintance, like someone in his unit. It's also possible that Jimmy grabbed one of the carjacker's weapons and turned it against him before going down."

"True. But if he was packing then that means he was thinking trouble might be coming his way. Maybe that roadside bombing and shootout where Randy Billey was injured was more than just an insurgent attack. That may have been the first murder attempt. They botched it, and Jimmy began watching his back from then on."

"There's no way we'll ever prove that though, one way or the other," Justine said. "That's up to the Army investigators."

Ella nodded. "What might have ultimately sealed Jimmy's fate was the package he sent me. If anyone saw him do that . . ."

"You could be right. That means we need to break that code," Justine said. "Since the message might depend on Navajo knowledge, we have to find someone who knows the old Navajo creation stories like the back of his hand."

"I've already tried my brother," Ella said.

"There's someone else . . . but he and your brother have had some serious differences in the past. They're fundamentally poles apart."

"Clifford gets along with pretty much everyone—except me on occasion. He's pretty tolerant, too, about accepting other points of view, so I'm really curious. Who are you talking about?"

"Reverend Bilford Tome at our church."

"Never heard of him. What happened to Reverend Campbell?" Ella asked. She remembered talking to him after the accident in the mine. Though his perspective was clearly based on Christianity, he'd kept preaching out of it and helped her deal with the questions she'd had after her near-death experience.

"Oh, he's still there, but we have a new preacher who conducts an earlier service—in Navajo. Reverend Tome is Navajo, and he knows our creation stories because he wrote a book on the subject. He has a degree in anthropology, one in theology, and one in mathematics. He's super smart—some say brilliant."

Ella smiled slowly. "And you've got a thing for him?"

"Nah. I took my shot, but there wasn't any chemistry between us. Too bad for me," she added, laughing. "Anyway, he's someone to consider for help in breaking that code."

"Why haven't you mentioned this preacher to me before?"

Justine hesitated. "There's something strange about his background . . . and maybe him, too. I did a little curious checking on some of our databases, and discovered that he's got more security clearances than you, me, and FB-Eyes combined. When I tried to do a background check, all I got was access denied, then a blue screen. And I mean that literally. Everything just froze up on me," she said. "But the thing that made me really uncomfortable is that he somehow found out that I'd been . . . curious. He took me aside after last week's service, and told me that if I had any questions about him and his past, I should just ask him."

"Did you?"

"Yeah," she said with a smile. "Hey, it's me, remember?"

"You'll ask anyone anything, cuz. So, what did Reverend Tome say?"

"That some events in his life were classified because he used to work for the government."

"Doing what?"

"I don't know. All I really got out of him is that he used to live in Maryland, then Virginia. He gave me a name of an official at the State Department he said would vouch for him. But he wanted to know why I was checking. I didn't answer him. I figured he'd ducked my questions and well . . . quid pro quo and all that."

Ella nodded. "Hmm. The NSA is supposed to be located at Fort Meade, Maryland, and the CIA is in Virginia. He could be linked to some heavy hitters. I would have backpeddled, too. Do you think he has the kind of training that might help us crack Blacksheep's code?"

"Knowledge of our creation stories is a plus in this case, maybe the key. Ford—that's what he insists everyone call him outside of church—has got an entire library at the rectory—books and written accounts that he transcribed after talking to some of our tribe's elders and medicine men. It's really impressive. Our community college asked for copies of everything in his collection."

"Has he agreed?"

"He agreed to work on it—most of the stuff is copyrighted in his name—but he won't let anyone else handle the materials. He said that it's his personal collection and he doesn't want any of it out of his sight."

"Security-conscious. Interesting. Let's go pay him a visit. Maybe Ford can help us." Ella picked up the folder containing the copies she'd made of Jimmy's story, then headed out the door with Justine.

As they drove up the mesa, to the north side of Shiprock, Ella glanced across at Justine, who was behind the wheel, and began thinking out loud. "Here's what I don't get. Jimmy's brother is an officer. So why didn't Jimmy send *him* the story? If he was trying to tell law enforcement about criminal or illegal activities, wouldn't it have made more sense for him to contact Samuel?"

"Samuel's with the Farmington PD, not the tribe. Maybe that plays into it."

"Okay, but if that matters—why? Is something going on here on our land that ties in to what happened overseas? But what on earth could our carjackings have to do with anything going on in Iraq? Soldiers from his unit weren't here when the carjackings started."

"I don't have a clue. If there's a connection, I don't see it either."

Before long they arrived at the Christian church that Justine attended regularly. They parked in a large lot south of the main entrance, which faced west, and walked through a side door into a one-story wing containing meeting rooms for Sunday School classes. Reverend Campbell was on the phone in a small office and waved at them as they walked by.

Justine took Ella across the hall to the second office, but no one was inside. "Maybe Reverend Tome's out on a call," Justine said.

"I don't think so," Ella said. "I remember seeing two cars out there when we pulled up, and if I remember correctly, the custodian here drives a pickup."

Reverend Campbell came up to them from behind. The Anglo preacher was in his mid-fifties, with thick, bushy eyebrows that really contrasted against his baldness. "Are you looking for Reverend Tome?" Seeing Ella nod, he added, "We're having a problem with a water leak in the garden, and he's outside trying to fix it. Our custodian went to Farmington to get one of our pulpits repaired, and the soonest we'll be able to get a plumber in here is tomorrow, so Ford said he'd figure it out. He's in the garden on the southeast side of the chapel working on it now." He gave them a skeptical smile. "God help us all."

After thanking him, they walked around the building and found Reverend Tome trying to fix an outside faucet attached to the wall about two feet up from the ground.

As Ella approached, she heard him mutter something incomprehensible, then whack the open-end wrench he'd attached to the faucet with a monkey wrench. Suddenly water sprayed out in all directions like a sprinkler head.

"Tighten the nut, or turn off the handle!" Ella yelled, turning away from the spray.

"Water *is* off! But the nut's on crooked. If I pry it off, there's gonna be a flood!" he said, sputtering water.

"Where's the cut-off valve?" Ella asked, ducking and trying to avoid the main spray of water that was quickly turning the sand under her feet into a muddy soup.

"Down at the street where the water meter is? I'm not sure."

Ella crouched next to him and tried to turn the wrench. It must have been hammered into place because she couldn't budge it. The nut below was cracked and obviously cross-threaded. Soaked, Ella turned to Justine as she ducked to one side to keep the spray from shooting right up into her face. "Find Reverend Campbell. See if there's a water-cut off where the hot water heater is. If not, get the water key, run down to the street, and turn off all the water."

Ford wrapped his hand around the nut and wrench to block out the spray. "I can fix this. Just give me a minute to back the nut off a few turns."

Ella grabbed his arm. "The nut is *cracked*. When it breaks loose the faucet's going to fall off. Let's wrap an old towel or rag over the leak and slow it down until Justine gets the water turned off."

As soon as the reverend let go to find a towel, the collar nut dropped off in two pieces. The pressure pushed the faucet right off the pipe, and water shot straight out like a fire hose. Reverend Tome hugged the wall, trying to stem the flow with the palm of his hand, but water sprayed everywhere. Ella looked around, desperate to find somethi. g that would plug the pipe. She saw a big, flat rock, one of several positioned around a young tree, and ran over to grab it. Maybe they could hold it against the pipe hard enough to reduce the flow to a trickle.

"Hold this against the pipe," she yelled, returning with the rock. He looked up and smiled, his face soaked, hair dripping down over his eyes. Just then, the water stopped.

"Is it off?" Reverend Campbell shouted, sticking his head out an open window.

"Yes!" Ella answered, then glanced over at Tome, who was looking down at the muddy pool they were both squatting in. He might have been a genius with a computer or pencil and paper, but his IQ obviously took a hundred-point hit when he had a wrench in his hand.

As they both stood up, he gave her a sheepish smile and brushed droplets of water from his forehead. "Were you looking for me, Detective Clah?"

"I sure didn't come to try out for the mud wrestling team," she shot back, then smiled, taking the sting out of her words. "Well, what the heck. Haven't played in the water since I was a kid."

He gave her a relieved smile. "Forgive me, I'm not much of a plumber."

"Gee, you think?" she answered, laughing.

They went inside to warm up, wrapped in blankets Justine had brought and, after Reverend Campbell went to the rectory and ran their clothes through a quick dryer cycle, Ella met Tome again in his office. Justine remained behind to talk to Reverend Campbell.

Tome offered her a cup of herbal tea. "It's hot and will help you get the chill out."

Ella accepted the brew, which obviously contained some mint, judging from the enticing scent. "Thanks, Reverend Tome."

"My friends call me Ford. So, why did you come looking for me?"

"I need your help with a case we're working, but I'll need you to keep what I'm about to tell you in the strictest confidence," Ella said.

"I excel at keeping secrets," he said in a quiet, somber voice.

Something about the way he'd said it caught her attention and her eyes narrowed. She had a feeling he'd just uttered the understatement of the year. "I need help with something that's right up your alley," she said, explaining quickly about Jimmy's story and the circumstances surrounding its arrival on her desk.

He nodded, curiosity alive on his face. "I'll do my best to help you," he said. "But I'm puzzled about something. Why didn't you go to your brother, the *hataalii*?"

"I did, and, so far, he doesn't know what to make of it. Then I heard about your collection on the subject," Ella said. "Would you mind helping, too?"

"I'd be happy to give it a try, but it wouldn't be a good idea for your brother and me to try and figure it out together," he said in a quiet voice.

"It's that big of a problem?"

He shrugged. "A problem does exist, and trying to ignore it won't help anyone," he said slowly. "I respect your brother, but I think the type of work he does only ends up holding our people back. The time for medicine men has come and gone. Moving forward into the twenty-first century is our only choice if we want to survive as a nation."

Ella understood the problem now. Both were trying to help

the tribe—but their philosophies were diametrically opposed. It was the classic struggle between the traditionalists and the modernists—with religion and healing at the center. "But surely by hanging on to our culture—the beliefs that make us Navajo—we can only get stronger."

He shook his head. "I don't see it that way, and when your brother does a Sing that takes the place of medical science . . . or God . . . then we really have serious differences."

"Where does your faith in God come from? Were you raised Christian?"

He shook his head. "No, my family had no beliefs to speak of. Not Christian, not Navajo, not much of anything, really. But life experience quickly taught me that I needed something strong—something that could see me through anything. This is the path I chose."

"My brother came from a home with strong beliefs, and chose a different path than you, but you're both working for the benefit of others. When you get down to basic values, there's not as much separating you as you might think."

"It's what we choose to trust, to put our faith in, that's at the heart of what divides us. Wars have been fought for less, you know," he said, then met her gaze. "We have the same end goal—the preservation of our tribe—but our philosophies are totally incompatible."

"Your beliefs demand that you try and change him. Good thing his don't require the same thing."

"No, we're not that kind of church. Justine knows. We don't ram our beliefs down anyone's throats. We're here—that's all. We're a friendly presence, and we can offer a cold drink in the name of our Lord. . . ."

"In your case, Reverend, from the faucet!" Ella said, then laughed out loud.

He laughed hard, too. "I'm never going to live this down, am I?"

"A forced baptism? No, probably not," Ella said, smiling widely.

Twenty minutes later, Reverend Tome sat behind his desk, having read Jimmy's story. He looked down at the pages again, then spoke in a thoughtful voice. "With the exception of Mourning Dove and a few other characters like Trickster, nothing here belongs to any of the Navajo creation stories I know about. Without a frame of reference, it's going to be a tough code to break, especially with all those non-Navajo characters, like Chopra. And somehow I don't think Jimmy was talking about that self-help guru when he wrote this. Then there's supposed to be some kind of retribution or justice coming on page five. But there's no page five. Where's the rest of it?"

"We don't know. That's all I got. Maybe he sent me what he had on hand—getting rid of it fast to safeguard it, and the rest was taken from him when he was killed. I just don't know."

He nodded absently, his thoughts miles away. "The barter items—shoes, nails, umbrellas, even gumdrops, must have some other meaning. And Trickster, meanwhile, is probably a human with those devious qualities. But the only shot we've got to break this is to go deep into the head of the man who wrote it. Get me his bio and any intel you can provide or get from the military or any other government agency."

"We can interview people who knew him, but I don't know how forthcoming Army Intel is going to be," Ella said. "Getting information from them or other government agencies may take us months—or years."

"In that case, let me see what I can do," he said.

Ella nodded slowly. Somehow she didn't doubt that he'd get more information than they could—providing Justine's discoveries about him were on target. "If anything in the story jumps out at you, will you let me know right away?"

"Absolutely. And I'll keep the pages locked in my safe when

I'm not working on them. I'll also run some code-breaking encryptions on it to see if there is any structural significance or numerical relationships that could represent something else— longitude and latitude, Social Security numbers, whatever. If there's something like that in here, I'll find it."

It was the matter-of-fact way he spoke about it that assured Ella she'd come to the right place. Ford—Reverend Tome— obviously had been involved in some code breaking at one time or another.

"I've always liked puzzles," he added. "Do you?"

She nodded and smiled, knowing that such interests were always sought after by the intelligence services. "That's why I'm in the business I'm in. I like solving them, Reverend Tome."

"Call me Ford, remember? My friends do," he said with an easy smile. "By the way, since I'm helping you, will you reciprocate and help me with a problem *I've* been having?"

"I'll try," Ella said cautiously. "Not plumbing?"

He laughed. "Besides that. The women in this parish— particularly my neighbor, Lila Curtis—keep trying to fix me up with their daughters, nieces, you name it. I don't want to hurt anyone's feelings, but it's making me crazy. I need to find a reason for them to back off. Will you let them see us together a few times? Give me a few nice smiles, I'll do the same for you, and they'll fill in the rest." He paused. "But . . . never mind. You're probably dating someone, maybe even engaged. . . ."

"No, there's no one special in my life, and I'm in the same boat you are," Ella said, laughing. "With me, it's my mom." Outside the Rez she would have seen it as a deft way of finding out if she was available, but on the Rez getting paired up was as inevitable as the rising sun. And it could be annoying.

"I think it's a good idea, Ford, and it may work out really well for both of us. Lila Curtis will make sure the news spreads like wildfire, too. My mother will be pleased, needless to say, and won't have a complaint about your profession—after all, my father was a preacher. The best part is that it'll buy us both some breathing room."

"So you have to deal with it too—the type of logic that believes if you're single, you couldn't possibly be satisfied with your life, so you need to be rescued."

"And as quickly as possible," Ella added, with a smile. "It's all well-meaning, but it can make things awkward."

"Oh, speaking of awkward . . . your brother might have a problem with our plan. Remember that he's not exactly my biggest fan?"

"He won't comment. He never does."

"Okay. So we have a deal?" he asked.

"Absolutely."

"We'll be having the church rummage sale in a few weeks. How about if we kick it off then?"

"Perfect."

"Great," Ford said, walking her out. "Oh, one more question. Would you like me to try and find out more about Jimmy Blacksheep *unofficially*? People around here may feel more comfortable talking to the clergy than to an officer of the law."

Ella nodded slowly. "That's a good idea, but Jimmy was murdered, and it might not have been random, so we're dealing with extremely dangerous people. You'd have to watch your step."

"I can handle it. Don't worry," he answered without any particular inflection.

It wasn't bravado. It was a statement of fact, and the kind of confidence that came from a person who'd seen human nature at its worst too often to ever be taken by surprise. "Stay in touch."

"Will do," he said.

Ella walked out to the parking lot, experienced the pleasant warmth of the midafternoon sun for a moment, then climbed into her car. Reverend Bilford Tome interested her—and it had been a very long time since she had thought that about any man. And he made her laugh. It was a powerful combination.

Justine, who'd been talking to Reverend Campbell, saw her in their unit, and joined her. Seconds later, they were on their way. "I spoke to Reverend Campbell about Samuel Blacksheep," Justine said. "I remembered having seen him in church a few times. And here's a surprise. Reverend Campbell heard a rumor that Samuel stole Jimmy's girlfriend this past year while Jimmy was overseas, and *that's* what caused the recent falling out between them."

"Interesting news. That could explain a lot. Who's the woman? Did you get a name?"

"Only a first name—Juanita. And she's not a member of our church. Reverend Campbell's never met her."

"We need to ask around. Maybe Randy Billie or John Lee Charley will know more—especially if we give them a name."

"I found out something else that's interesting," Justine said. "Apparently Samuel's been out and about investigating his brother's death, mostly out of uniform. He's been interviewing everyone who knew Jimmy, and digging hard. Reverend Campbell heard him talking to a few parishioners outside the grocery store."

"We could probably use Samuel's help right now. Too bad I don't trust him," Ella said, telling Justine about the conversation she'd had with Officer Bitsillie. "I keep remembering that something was taken from Jimmy's house—his old stories, according to Samuel."

"Why the old stories, unless the thief is worried about what Jimmy was writing and believes there may be a clue in there to help figure it out, like we're trying to do now?" Justine asked.

"Samuel could have taken them himself, for all we know," Ella said.

"Could be. Did Reverend Tome help you any?"

"Yeah, he sure did." Ella recounted what she'd learned. "Ford's going to try to break the code—and he just might. If Samuel was the type who inspired more trust, I'd suggest that he get together with the Reverend. Let's face it, Jimmy's brother should be in the best position to tell us how Jimmy thought, and help crack that code. But my gut tells me that it's a mistake to get Samuel involved. As an officer, he could have easily set up his brother and made it look like a carjacking gone sour. He had all the details of the carjackings right at his fingertips. And what if the message in the code leads to him? That would explain why Jimmy sent it to me instead and why some of his stories are missing now."

"Even if he's innocent, the fact that Samuel's questioning people without even being attached to the case worries me," Justine said. "He's obviously working on his own and he could easily decide that revenge is better than justice." Justine paused for a moment then added, "He could deal with the killer in his own way and we'd never know—or worse, strike out at the wrong person or people."

"Okay—so we're in agreement. We need to keep an eye on Samuel. But he's on his guard around me, so why don't you try questioning him solo?" she suggested. Justine's petite good looks put men at ease, more often than not. "He may tell you more, especially if you don't play bad cop."

"You've got it, boss. I'll give it my best shot."

"Now let's go see my brother."

They arrived at Clifford's hogan a half hour later after a quick drive south and found him outside, chopping wood. Recognizing their vehicle, he waved, then set down his axe and walked over to meet them.

"What brings you both here?" he asked.

"Do you have a minute?" Ella said. "I need more information about the deceased's brother. Can you help?" she asked, knowing not to mention people by name here if at all possible.

"Not much. I've met him a few times, but that's about it."

"I heard that he and his brother were competing for a woman named Juanita. I don't have a last name, but I heard that she left the one who died while he was still overseas and took up with his brother. I'd like to track her down so I can question her."

"Jealousy can tear up families," he said with a slow nod. "I don't know who this woman is, but I'm sure there was a lot of gossip at the time among those who knew both men. I'll find out what I can."

"Anything that'll give me a lead will help."

He nodded. "I'll see what I can do."

Knowing how many people Clifford saw as part of his profession, his help was often invaluable. Her brother was a trusted member of the tribe and doors opened to him that would forever remain closed to her.

"Something else is bothering you," he added, walking with Ella to where he'd been chopping wood, while Justine remained behind on the telephone.

"I've been trying to piece together where the deceased went and what he did after he got back to our land. But some things just don't add up for me."

"Like what?" he asked, picking up an armful of split wood.

"According to the medical examiner he took a dunk someplace just before he died, but there was no soap residue on his skin. We checked motels—but got zip. I considered the river, but it would have been really *cold* this time of year. . . ."

"He'd just come home from war, so he probably stopped at his family's sweat lodge for a cleansing, then washed himself in the river before drying off. That's what our warriors do—even the ones who barely remember the old ways often cling to that custom. Find his family's sweat house. It's probably not far away—a good run maybe—from the river."

"Good thinking, big brother. I'm just surprised that I didn't think of that first," she answered with a trace of a smile.

"Remember to stay attuned to the Way. This awareness has helped you before," he said.

"You're right," Ella admitted. "Thanks for reminding me." Nodding good-bye, she headed back to the cruiser where Justine was waiting. The fastest way to find the Blacksheep family's sweat hogan would be to contact Samuel. Once they were underway, Ella filled Justine in.

"Shall I contact the Farmington PD and track him down?" Justine asked.

"I'll do it while you drive. I want to talk to him ASAP."

It took fifteen minutes, but Samuel finally contacted them just as they reached Shiprock. Ella asked him for directions to his family's sweat lodge, but Samuel insisted on meeting them at the highway, at a location they'd already driven past several minutes ago, to lead them in.

In a foul mood, Ella gave Justine the highlights, then added, "I want to make sure he doesn't tamper with any evidence. Don't let him touch anything. In fact, keep him back with you while I go ahead and take a look first. If he doesn't stay put, threaten to cuff him."

"Oh, that'll go over real well when his PD hears about it."

"I don't care," Ella said firmly. "There's something not right about Samuel. He says he cares about his brother, yet he had a relationship with his brother's girl while Jimmy was overseas in a combat zone. Now Samuel's investigating the crime on the sly, and isn't sharing any information with us. The whole thing just smells."

Justine didn't answer right away. "Part of the problem may be that he feels guilty about what happened between him and his brother and now it's too late to make amends—except by bringing in his brother's killer or killers. In the most basic of all ways, he may *need* to find whoever killed his brother—not for revenge necessarily, but to balance the scales again."

"Without balance, there's no harmony or walking in beauty," Ella replied thoughtfully. Anywhere else that wouldn't have made as much sense as it did here on the *Diné Tah*. Yet there was an inescapable rightness about it . . . *if* Samuel was innocent. "That's the problem with Samuel in a nutshell. He's a wild card. Make sure you keep an eye on him. If he's responsible for his brother's death, directly or indirectly, he could be a danger to us as well."

They headed back toward Shiprock's southwest quadrant, which was across the river, and on the way passed slowly through the traffic in Shiprock's tiny downtown area just east of the bridges. A fender bender had occurred just in front of a gas station, and Officer Lujan had stopped traffic while a wrecker was hooking up one of the damaged vehicles. They crept along slowly, then stopped, waiting for their turn to advance.

"How's Dawn doing these days? I haven't had a chance to visit with her. Is she still into riding?" Justine asked.

"Very much so, and though she adores Wind, it won't be long before she'll want to get a full-size quarter horse, too, and start competition riding of one kind or another. But for now, she's happy with the pony, which is good because keeping three animals in alfalfa and feed would be very expensive. Unfortunately for me, once my daughter gets a pet, it's for life. There's no way she'll ever let me sell Wind, even if I get her a horse."

"What about your horse, Chieftain? Can you two share him?"

"No way. He's too much horse for Dawn," Ella replied. "Too much for me, sometimes. I try to get up early on weekends and take him for a run, but he's hard to control and has almost gotten away from me a few times. Whenever he acts up, I run him uphill or in a tight circle until he gets tired."

"Good strategy," Justine said.

"It works, but his Saturday-morning workouts can be like a roller-coaster ride."

Finally, traffic opened up again as the wrecker pulled away with its load. As they crossed the old steel bridge, heading west, Ella's thoughts returned to the case at hand. "When we get back to the office I want you to try and do some more digging into Ford's background."

"Reverend Tome?"

Seeing the mischievous gleam in Justine's eyes, Ella continued before her partner could comment. "I still don't like unanswered questions about someone who's helping me with a case."

"In my limited experience, when you run into government fire-walls and screens that practically yell 'Access Denied' or 'Restricted Access,' the sensible option is to back off. Otherwise remember to smile when you look up 'cause there'll be a satellite watching you. Or they'll go cheap and just hack software onto your computer to record every keystroke from now on."

Ella considered it then shook her head. "No, I don't think that's how it's going to play out. In this case, if my hunch is right, the silence will be deafening."

They met with Samuel a short distance west of the junction of Highways 64 and 491, within sight of Shiprock High School. Samuel, who was in FPD uniform and in his departmental vehicle, had pulled off the road at the terminus of a narrow track leading north between alfalfa fields. She could see the edge of the bluff farther ahead and, beyond and below that, the *bosque*, the forest of willows, brush, and large and small cottonwoods that occupied the shoulders of the cold San Juan River.

Seeing them pulling off the shoulder of the highway, Samuel started his car and led the way. They bounced along on what optimists would call a road, over recent sets of tracks, for about five minutes before he finally pulled over. The dirt track they'd followed abruptly ended at the edge of the bluff.

Climbing out of their SUV, Ella glanced around. Behind them in both directions were fields, still dry and covered with the remnants of last year's alfalfa. In front of them, at the bottom of the low cliff, lay a strip of wooded area filled with willows that paralleled the river beyond both banks where the water table was close to the surface.

"We walk the rest of the way," Samuel said, pointing. The path down was narrow and rough, filled with rocks, roots, tumbleweeds, and deep arroyos large enough to swallow a person.

The hike itself wasn't long, however, and they were soon at the river. Willows in clumps often ten feet high or more grew all around. They looked like leaf-covered fishing poles and were great for roasting marshmallows, Ella recalled with a smile. The scent and ripple of water not far away took Ella back to her childhood and her father's many baptisms.

"Up ahead's where my brother went," Samuel said, cutting into Ella's thoughts. "It's halfway between the cliff and the water, right between those big willows, next to the uprooted salt cedar."

They hiked the rest of the way double-time. Then, at the outside edge of the bosque, Ella saw an old, traditional Navajo structure. Sweat houses, different from dwellings, were made to resemble a tripod at first. Then other sticks were added until the structure became airtight. Ella noted that the blanket that covered the front was tattered. Her best guess was that the small hogan had been standing since the mid 1900s.

"My great-grandfather built this. It was here for the ones who came back from World War Two, Korea, then Vietnam—and now Iraq. Blacksheeps have fought in all the wars. Our clan's returning soldiers would first come here, build a fire outside, then put heated rocks in the center and purify themselves before meeting their families," he said. "But unless Jimmy added several more blankets to that entrance, I'm not sure how much of a sweat bath he had the other day."

"Plunging into that cold river afterward must have been an exercise in willpower," Justine said and shuddered.

Samuel laughed. "Agreed, but it's a tradition with the warriors in our family."

He sang one of the verses of their sweat bath song, and it took Ella a while to understand his Navajo, which wasn't very good. But she got the last part which ended with, "An everlasting, peaceful world."

Ella still felt the power of the song—power that came from tradition as much as belief. She smiled, remembering her mother telling her once that the heart of a traditionalist often beat inside the most adamant modernist.

"Those look like Jimmy's tracks," Samuel said, pointing down as they reached softer ground. The tiny hogan was about thirty yards ahead now, just past a low ridge. The river was about fifty feet away, down a bank, and wouldn't rise even close to the hogan except at flood stage, which was rare.

Ella caught Justine's eye, and motioned toward Samuel, reminding her partner to stick close to him. They continued on, Ella leading the way when, without any warning, a sudden burst of gunfire erupted, kicking up tufts of sand all around them.

Ella dove into a thicket and, out of the corner of her eye, saw Justine and Samuel duck beneath the overhang of the bluff, into the shadows. Hidden among the brush, mounded by sand that provided some actual protection in addition to cover, she tried to determine the location of the sniper. But every time she raised her head, more shots whistled past her.

NINE

————— ✖ ✖ ✖ —————

Ella had her pistol out now, but from the sound, the sniper was using a semiauto rifle or assault weapon. They were outgunned. "Anyone spot him?" she called out, scrunching up against a fallen cottonwood for more protection.

Several rounds hit the sand just beyond, kicking dust up. Ella twisted around, watching for the sniper as she felt for her radio, then cell phone. Neither was working from their current location. "I can't get a call through," Ella hollered.

"Me, neither," Samuel yelled back. More gunfire erupted, breaking off chunks of hardened mud above where he and Justine had sought cover, but too high to do any damage.

"Either he's at the wrong angle to hit us, or he's just trying to pin us down," Ella yelled. "If we can zero in on his position, I want you two to cover me while I make a move."

Ella strained her neck, trying to peer from behind cover. Either their assailant was a bad shot, or he was just playing with them.

Four more shots struck, two in the sand between her and the two others, then two more into the overhang where they'd hit before. More chunks of dirt fell. "I think he's . . ." Samuel yelled but his voice was drowned out by an enormous thump that shook the ground like an earthquake.

Ella could feel the sudden rush of air strike her chest like a hand, then debris and dust dropped from the sky like an urban hailstorm. She kept her face down, covering her head with her arms as various objects bounced off of her and rattled all around. The air was hot and choked with dust, and she started to cough.

After about ten seconds, the shower of dust and debris finally stopped. Spitting dust, pieces of wood, and leaves from her mouth, Ella raised her head slightly, brushing away the long shreds of cottonwood fibers that had been ripped away by the force of the blast. Now that the dust was settling, she saw a small crater on the other side of the ridge. All that was left of the sweat hogan was rubble.

Aware that they were no longer being fired upon, Ella rose to her knees. Acrid white smoke was beginning to billow from the log fragments, now splintered and shattered, wood ablaze from the heat of whatever had just detonated inside the hogan.

As she stood, her phone signal reappeared. "I'm going to call it in," Ella said. "Samuel, Justine, keep an eye out for the sniper in case he reappears."

"Cover me so I can go back to my unit," Samuel said. "I've got a tactical radio that'll reach halfway across the state. I've also got some serious firepower stored in the trunk."

"Go," Ella said, then glancing at Justine as her partner came out of cover just enough to get a better field of view, she added, "Stay sharp."

Both remained low and among the brush, watching for movement around them as Samuel sprinted back up the trail toward their vehicles. "As soon as we can move freely, I want this area processed with a fine-toothed comb," Ella said. "I can still see Jimmy's footprints in places, though the explosion took care of everything close to the sweat house. But maybe we'll get lucky and some things were blown clear."

"The sniper's tracks will be obscured," Justine said.

"For the most part, yes, but some of his tracks should still remain," Ella answered. "It's unlikely that he managed to obliterate all of them. But we'll have to work hard."

Samuel came back up the trail carrying an assault rifle resembling an M-16. He positioned himself in a covering position, then signalled Ella. "I can cover both of you from here, but I don't see any movement in or around where the sweat lodge used to be."

"Just keep watch," Ella called back, "and every once in a while take a look behind yourself as well. We're going in from the flanks."

With Justine circling to the right, slightly, Ella edged to the left, then made her way over the low ridge that had shielded them from the main force of the blast and the flying debris. "I think the shooter's long gone," Ella said. "There are tracks leading west. His goal was to keep us from getting to the hogan—and he succeeded."

"This wasn't the kind of thing a nut job does for fun, so maybe there was evidence in there he didn't want us to see," Justine said.

They passed beyond the remnants of the smoldering hogan, and were able to see the ground clearly on the far side. Ella nodded as Justine crouched down and pointed to the ground.

"Three men were here," Ella noted.

"That explains the high rate of fire keeping us pinned, even when the charge was being set. What the heck are we dealing with?" Justine muttered, not expecting an answer.

Ella waved at Samuel. "Anyone around?"

"No. All clear. I'm coming in."

The call for emergency backup was quickly canceled, but soon Tache, Justine, and Neskahi, the tribe's crime scene team, were there processing the evidence.

Leaving them to their work, Ella motioned for Samuel to join her over by the river. "The presence of these three people, along with their weapons and explosives, wasn't coincidental. They made it here just ahead of us, obviously, or the sweat house would have been destroyed hours, maybe days, earlier. So my question is why now? Someone—maybe you—has been watching and monitoring us. Are you certain that you have *no idea* what we're dealing with?"

"No one outside my family knew about this place. And I haven't discussed it with *anyone*. I don't know why the perps struck now. And, for the record, I'm *not* holding out on you," he said firmly. "I want whoever killed my brother—more than you do."

"Did you tell anyone you were coming here?" Ella asked.

"Just Dispatch. And my sergeant," Samuel added. "Had to because it's out of my jurisdiction and I'm on duty."

"Include directions to this place?"

"In general, yes. But someone could have just followed us," Samuel pointed out.

Ella bent down, picked up a pebble, then threw it out into the river, watching the splash. Then she glanced over at him. "Tell me something—did your brother send you packages from Iraq, or once back in the States? Mail, boxes, luggage, clothes? Anything at all, even a postcard," she pressed, wondering, even hoping, that Jimmy had sent him a duplicate of the story he'd mailed her or the rest of it. That knowledge would go a long ways in establishing trust between them.

"No, there's been nothing," he said firmly. "Not even a damn postcard. Just a few e-mails or quick phone calls at the beginning, then the one I already told you about when he returned." He gazed at her, studying her expression, then added, "My brother's death is not just the result of some punk carjackers screwing up, is it?"

"I hadn't ruled it out completely—until now. Blowing up that economically worthless sweat lodge places what happened to your brother in an entirely new level of investigation. I think Jimmy made some serious enemies. They killed him, tried to make it look like a carjacking, and are now trying to obliterate any trail, even a hint of one, that might lead back to them. Jimmy came to this place before he died—and brought knowledge with him that they feared—maybe the identity of his killers. They couldn't risk the possibility that we'd find a message he'd left us, or evidence in that sweat hogan. So they blew it to hell."

He nodded slowly. "It makes sense and ties in. He wrote about the sweat lodge in one of his old stories, and maybe even had a drawing or two."

"And someone stole them from his house."

"It would explain how they were able to find it, and maybe if they knew we were coming here now. . . ."

"They had to make sure they got here first so we wouldn't find anything they'd overlooked," Ella concluded.

"I'll poke around and see what I can find out," Samuel suggested.

"No, that's *my* job. What I need from you now is information you've been holding back on. I want to know who Juanita is and what part she played in the rift between you and your brother."

Samuel averted his gaze, and stared off across the water, his jaw clenched. "That was a low point in my life."

"No more games, Samuel. I need answers," Ella pressed.

He nodded once, then began slowly. "My brother and I were close when we were kids but, by the time I graduated from high school, we'd stopped being friends and hanging out together. He went his way, me, mine. We had nothing in common."

Samuel cleared his throat, looking back for a moment at the officers working the crime scene. Then, he continued. "He'd been gone for about three months when Juanita Betoni came to see me. She wanted to break up with my brother, but wasn't sure if she should tell him while he was still over there. She was afraid he'd do something crazy and get himself killed, or get distracted and careless. My brother had been talking marriage in his e-mail letters and phone calls and making all kinds of plans for both of them. Juanita didn't want to lead him on, and wasn't sure how to handle things, so she asked for my advice."

"What did you tell her?"

"After seeing Jimmy's letters, I suggested she tell him that they needed to slow down and wait until he returned before discussing anything serious."

"Not break up, just slow down?"

He nodded. "I figured Jimmy would get the message without losing face. Juanita appreciated my help, so we kept in touch after that. She didn't really know any of the girlfriends or wives of the other soldiers in Jimmy's unit, so she started coming over to my house to visit and talk, and share the news. One thing led to another. . . ."

"How did your brother find out?"

"I still don't know, but he did. Maybe Juanita inadvertently told him. I got an e-mail from him a few months later where he called me a few choice names. He accused me of betraying him, and moving in on his woman. Turning her against him. I guess in his shoes I would have done the same. But the truth is what he had with Juanita was over before I came into the picture."

"Where can I find Juanita?"

"She lives in Kirtland, but works at the hospital in Shiprock. She's a nurse."

"Okay, thanks."

As Ella turned, he added, "Let me work with your crime team. Every extra set of eyes helps."

Ella shook her head. "No, thanks. My people are used to working as a team, and you'll just get in their way. Go home for now and try to write down anything and everything you know about your brother's activities overseas and his duties and associates in the Guard. Call me if you discover anything that seems important or out of place."

Samuel walked back to his own vehicle, and Ella joined Justine, who was studying a set of footprints. "There were three men here recently, but only two of them today," Justine said, "not three as we'd previously thought. The third set is older, and after comparing them with those we saw originally, I think they're a match to the deceased's. Now, after the explosion, we know why they pinned us down without really trying to kill us. There must have been something in the sweat house that they were afraid we might find. A hidden message?"

"That's exactly why we need to work this area slowly. I want every scrap of evidence we can find. One thing's clear—we're dealing with someone who can shoot quickly and accurately between two separate targets. That sounds more like someone with combat training than it does a hunter. A police officer, or a soldier."

"I'll know what caliber weapon was used soon enough, too. We're going to recover slugs from the embankment for sure. But Ella, before we really go after any of our former servicemen—which admittedly is a logical move based on the explosives and military tactics used by the perps—we'll need some solid evidence to back us up. Our people are very protective of our soldiers and the ill will that'll stir up may create some serious problems for our department."

"I know," Ella said somberly.

Ella worked alongside Justine up on the edge of the bluff where the sniper had sighted in on them. They quickly found several ejected nine-millimeter cases. Several autoloader rifles, most of them small and readily available, could be obtained in that caliber. Once they had the cases and some recovered slugs in the lab, Justine was confident she could determine from the rifling marks and other comparisons the kind of weapon used, possibly even a make or model.

Ella had just discovered what looked like an impression in the ground where the shooter had rested the butt of the weapon when her cell phone rang. It was Farmington Police Sergeant Calvin Sanders, Jimmy's former lieutenant in the Army.

"I've got some information for you. You'd asked me to get Officer Kent Miller's blood type. I checked with our department's doctor, but I've been told that kind of information can't be released without his permission, the proper paperwork, or unless he's been in a shooting incident and his blood must be identified and matched to evidence. And the Army—well, you'll have to deal with them directly."

"I understand. Have you been able to find or speak with Officer Miller?"

"No, but after some of the crap we've been through in Iraq, my guess is he's still someplace quiet where he can sort out all the images in his head. If you don't find a way to do that, you end up in a padded cell."

"Does Officer Miller have any relatives in town?"

There was a pause. "I believe his sister lives here in Farmington. But she's married, and I don't know her last name."

"Get it for me, and her address, if you can. I'd like to pay her a visit."

"I'll see what I can do," he answered.

Ella hung up, then went back to join Justine. The sun had begun to set, and with the wind still blowing, her team had asked for and received extra help, along with powerful lights and a generator. Ella recognized Officer Michael Cloud, who had a twin brother, also on the force. Herman was their uncle.

Seeing her approach, Michael smiled. "Hey, Ella. You think we're going to be related soon?"

"Mom and your uncle?" Ella answered, wondering if he'd heard something she hadn't.

He nodded. "I'm curious. I was wondering if your mom might have finally said yes."

Ella shrugged. "She's been thinking about it, but I don't know any more than that."

"Fair enough." Michael went back to work.

Forcing herself to concentrate on the work at hand, Ella pushed it out of mind for now. She'd have to ask her mom about that later on tonight. With meticulous precision, she processed the scene along with her team, bagging and tagging anything that may have been part of an explosive device or could have been inside the sweat house. She loved this—the gathering of evidence, the solving of a puzzle. It was an arena she understood.

They worked under the bright portable lights for another three-and-a-half hours. Then, assured there was nothing more to be found for now, they began to pack up.

Sergeant Neskahi, then Tache and Justine drove away. Ella was last to leave, in no rush to go home tonight. It was nine and her daughter would already be asleep. Ella would miss talking to Dawn, but her priority tonight would be speaking with her mother, Rose. Change was in the air and sweeping down on her like a cool breeze from the north.

Ella sat at the kitchen table as Rose fixed her a late-night snack. "You really have to start eating on a regular basis, daughter. You're as thin as a rail."

Ella glanced down at herself. "I'm as heavy as a railroad tie. I'm five pounds over where I should be."

"That's some Anglo health-nut measurement. Trust your mother. You're too thin," Rose said, scooping scrambled eggs into a homemade tortilla along with roasted green chile and warmed-over hash browns. "And this is *not* a proper dinner. Won't you let me make you something more substantial?"

"No, Mom. I've got a craving for this. It's fine," Ella said, enjoying the wonderful aroma of food. "But there's something else you can do. Sit down at the table with me. I think it's time we talked."

Rose exhaled softly, and joined her, a cup of herbal tea in her hands. "You want to know if I'm getting married, don't you?"

"I ran into *Bizaadii*'s nephew," Ella said. "We talked about it. But now I can see it in your eyes. You said yes, didn't you?"

Rose nodded slowly, a hesitant smile on her face. "I was hoping for a chance to tell you earlier today, but you've been so busy, and I was afraid that I'd need time to explain. I didn't want you to be upset." Taking a deep breath, she continued. "A part of me will always continue to love your father, but *Bizaadii* and I think alike and we're good companions. He and I . . . need each other. Can you understand?"

Ella nodded. Rose was a beautiful Navajo woman who deserved a chance to lead a life of her own. "Mom, you shouldn't have worried about how I'd react. I'm happy for you," she said but, unfortunately, her words came out sounding like an afterthought.

"You don't sound very happy," Rose observed instantly.

"I'm just trying to sort everything out now that it's really going to happen. Have you made plans? Will you live here?"

She shook her head. "We'll live in *Bizaadii*'s new house down by Hogback. It's close to the river, and he has irrigation there, so we can have a big garden. I'll no longer be here to give your daughter breakfast each morning, but you can work something out with Boots."

"Boots, yeah." The problem was that, now, Dawn wouldn't be with family a lot of the time. Her mother's influence on Dawn had shaped her daughter's view of everything, but Ella hadn't realized how much she'd taken Rose for granted until that very minute. "I can't imagine this household without you, Mom. We're going to miss you."

"It's time we all went on with our lives, daughter," she said gently. "You, too."

Without Rose around, Ella suddenly realized that Kevin, in a home office now, would probably make his move to get more time with Dawn. Though it wasn't necessarily a bad thing for their daughter, the possibility made her feel as if she were standing on quicksand.

"You'll have privacy, daughter, and for the first time you'll be able to raise your daughter without interference from anyone, including me," she said with a smile. "Think about it as an opportunity—to grow, to live life on your own terms."

As Ella listened to her mom, she wondered if Rose had come

to feel that Ella and Dawn had encroached on *her* life. "Mom, if anyone should move out of your house, it should be me and my daughter," she said at last. "We need to find a place of our own."

"This house has too many memories for me, and neither *Bizaadii* nor I would feel comfortable here. The best thing I can do is give it to you and my granddaughter." She placed her hand over Ella's. "But, daughter, *you* also need to go forward with your life. Find another man. Add to your family if that's what you decide. Or not."

Ella smiled ruefully. "Mom, my life is complicated enough as is. Like it or not, I'm probably going to have to give my daughter's father more time with her now." She stopped abruptly, closed her eyes, and shook her head. She wanted Rose to stay—for things to be the same—but she wasn't being fair. "You have your own life, Mom, I respect that. My daughter and I will be fine," she said.

"I know what you're afraid of, daughter, but he's not going to take her from you, not in the ways that really count," Rose said in a resolute and convincing tone. "The bonds between you and your child are very strong, and the reality of having a child around during the week will finally waken her father up to the real challenges of being a parent. Remember that he *works* from home. That means that the constant noise of having his daughter and her friends around will be a distraction. He's not really used to that. And wait till summer. . . ."

Ella looked at her mother. "I hope you're right, Mom."

Ella wondered about the road ahead. Her life was about to take another surprising turn and there was nothing she could do except wait and let things develop at their own speed.

The following morning, Ella helped Dawn get ready for school. Her daughter chattered a mile a minute about the new hand-tooled Western saddle she wanted. Kevin had offered to get it for her and she was delighted. She had already made drawings of Wind and the new saddle, and was waving them around at every step.

Getting her daughter to sit still in the mornings was difficult, but once she'd examined the drawings to Dawn's satisfaction, Ella somehow managed to get to work braiding Dawn's long, ebony hair.

"Your *shimasání* is getting married, daughter," Ella tossed out casually, not wanting to be too dramatic.

Dawn nodded. "I know. I heard *Shimasání* talking on the phone yesterday. I didn't think I was supposed to know yet, so I didn't say anything."

Ella finished Dawn's hair, but remained sitting with her on the edge of the bed. "That means it'll be just you and me here at home. And Boots, of course, in the afternoon. How do you feel about that?"

"Can I visit *Shimasání*?"

"Of course. She'd be hurt if you didn't," Ella assured Dawn.

"Then it's okay. It'll be like it is with Daddy, kind of. I'll visit him lots, too." Dawn picked up her backpack. "Hurry up, Mom! I"m meeting Beth Ann before school!"

"Beth Ann again?"

"She's my *best* friend, Mom!" she said, rushing out of the room toward the kitchen.

Rose, who'd been standing in the doorway, jumped back as Dawn ran by. "Is that the same girl who went with you and your daughter to the rodeo last month?"

"Yes, Mom, don't you remember? She's the granddaughter of one of your Plant Watcher friends. The children do everything together. Notice she's wearing a turquoise and red sweatshirt this morning? Her little friend will probably be wearing the identical thing."

"Some things never change. You did the same at her age," Rose said.

Ella laughed, then followed her mother into the kitchen. Rose had already laid out breakfast for Dawn. Seeing it, Ella wondered what they'd do without her mother around the house, and not just for helping with the meals and Dawn. Having Rose at home had made Ella feel as if a part of her had also remained home . . . maybe the best part of her. No matter how competent Boots was, it wouldn't be the same without Rose.

As they sat down at the table for breakfast, Ella watched Dawn eat the homemade breakfast burrito that was her mother's specialty. She'd miss the familiar routines. Yet life was about moving forward. Navajos, in fact, defined death as lack of growth.

Her life as a single mom had been a good one, and Ella had been fortunate to have her own mother around. But she realized now how complacent she'd grown with the arrangements. It was time to take a closer look at her life.

As a car pulled up outside, Dawn kissed them both good-bye, and rushed out the door. The car pool, too, had worked because Rose drove every other week. Maybe Boots would do the same.

Rose's gaze rested on Ella. "There'll be changes in this household, that's inevitable. But they'll be for the good."

Ella smiled, but didn't say anything.

"Daughter, believe me, *you* need this. It's your chance to deal with your daughter without me around, interfering. I've stood in for you at times and I loved doing that, but it's time for you to connect with her around the clock. Settle the issues with her father once and for all so you can look to your future."

"Kevin is my daughter's father. He'll never be out of my life," she said.

"You love your daughter and your work and those are very good things. But you need to open your eyes to the other opportunities life is offering."

"Is that what you've done?"

Rose nodded. "My time has come to move on—and so has yours."

Ella finished her breakfast without another word, then washed the dishes silently. Her mother was right. After nearly dying, buried in a mine cave-in two years ago, she'd promised herself never to get so bogged down with work that she overlooked the important things life had to offer. And, in her own defense, she *had* become a better parent. These days, it was herself she tended to neglect most of all.

Though still young, she couldn't remember the last time *she'd* been on a special date, or even if she had any date clothes for anything fancier than a trail ride or cookout. Even after the death of her husband, the man Rose had shared most of her lifetime with, her mother had found the courage to rebuild her life. Ella had known love, too, but only fleetingly, and a part of her yearned for the everyday commitment that her mother had found—twice.

Ella left for the station in her tribal vehicle five minutes later. It was time to put all those thoughts aside. Duty called.

She was almost at the station when her cell phone rang. It was Ford. "Good morning," she said. "I hope you're calling to tell me you've already deciphered the story. This case is really bearing down on me."

"I wish I had better news but I haven't got anything on that yet. What I do have is someone here at the church I think you'll want to talk to. He's painting our tool shed out back now. He and I started talking, and it turns out he served overseas with Jimmy Blacksheep. He shipped back when his wife died because of their children."

"Paul Curley?"

"Yeah, you know him?"

"No, but we've been hoping to interview him. Expect me there in twenty minutes."

Ella called Justine at the station, told her where she was headed and why, then added, "Have you turned up anything from the crime scene last night?"

"I'm still working on it. The nine-millimeter slugs all came from a Ruger carbine, a weapon that's been widely produced, so that isn't much help. But at least if we find the weapon, we should be able to match it to the bullets. By the time you come to the station I hope to have something more."

Ella arrived at the Christian church atop the mesa on the north side of the river a short while later. Reverend Tome stepped outside just as she pulled to a stop.

"I saw you coming up the road from my office window," Ford said, "and I wanted to speak to you for a moment before we go talk to Paul."

"What's up?"

"I've been studying the code from the point of view of a soldier trying to get a message out. He speaks of the fall, and the Dark Ones trading with the locals to get their hands on nails, shoes, and so on—which probably represents something else entirely. I'm wondering if he's trying to tell you about something that began last fall, maybe involving someone buying or trading for jewelry, stolen money, or some kind of contraband such as drugs, liquor, or weapons, represented in code as shoes and nails, for example. There's that mention of Big Monster being trapped in a large hole. It's got to mean Saddam Hussein, don't you think?"

"I thought that, too, but those everyday items to be bartered can't be anything too dangerous like explosives or the mysterious weapons of mass destruction. Something like that would have been way too hot to handle. I'm thinking that maybe the bartered goods Jimmy had in mind are more like rifles, pistols, fighting knives, and maybe even stolen gold or jewelry, stuff like that."

"Could be. Jimmy wasn't a polished writer or a trained cryptographer either, and this is an unfinished story. It's more like a rough draft, really, and not just because the ending isn't there. Notice how many places there are where he scratched out a word or paragraph and reworded it." He paused suddenly, then spoke quickly. "A thought just occurred to me. Maybe that mention of hiding places is Mourning Dove's way of telling the reader how the contraband was hidden or smuggled back home. Inside their beasts of burden—their vehicles. Or not," he added, running an exasperated hand through his hair. "We really need more to go on. If there's a chance that the second half of the story still exists, you've got to get your hands on it. Reading the entire narrative could give us the answers you need."

"No more pages have shown up anywhere, and every location Jimmy went, we've searched. I didn't mention this before but Samuel says his brother's old stories, written before his tour in Iraq, are missing, too. But I think that maybe the rest of this story was with him when he was killed and was lost along with the car and apparently his luggage. Or could be someone else got their hands on it and destroyed it." Ella thought about the explosion at the sweat hogan. They hadn't found any traces of paper that she knew about, but it might have been burned up completely, or taken by the sniper and his companion when they fled.

"What about the military? Can they help out at all?"

She shrugged. "So far they haven't been very helpful. I'll try to find out if they had any incidents in Jimmy's unit last winter, but the military has its own way of doing things, so I doubt I'll get answers. Last I heard, the Army was dispatching their own guy here but, so far, he hasn't shown up and I have no idea what kind of leads he's following."

"The Dark Ones are deadly when someone goes against them. Remember that part about Konik and Bula disappearing because they fell out of favor?" he asked. "My advice is to watch your back."

"Yeah, I hear you," she said. "Just keep working on that code, okay?"

"Don't worry, I will. When I get into a puzzle I solve it or go crazy trying," he added with a laugh.

Ella smiled. "I'm the same way. That's why I'm a cop. But how does that fit in with you being a preacher?"

"Life's a puzzle, Ella. Everyone has to figure out how to make all the pieces fit in a way that'll help them find happiness. When people come to me for help, I try to make the pieces of their puzzle come together in a way that makes sense to them and allows them to cope."

"You mean by steering them to God?"

"The ones who come to me are already in the palm of God. All I do is listen, try to advise, and know that God's taking care of them."

"My father was a preacher. His beliefs were similar to yours. But he believed in trying to convert people."

Ford smiled and shook his head. "Sounds like one of the old evangelists, but I'm not one of them. I don't try to convert anyone, so rest easy," he said, accurately guessing what was on her mind. "God calls whomever he wants; he doesn't need my help. My job is to be ready to help the ones He brings to us."

"You walk your talk, Reverend," Ella said with a smile.

Seeing two other parishioners approaching, Reverend Tome waved at them, then looked back at Ella. "One more thing about Paul before we go. I understand that he and Jimmy were close."

"Good. With luck he'll be able to shed some light on what happened."

"A word of caution, Ella. Paul has had a rough time of it, and not just because of the loss of his wife. Since he came home, he's been working two jobs, and he's having a truckload of problems with the kids. One got busted for drugs recently and sent to a detention home for evaluation. If Paul's short with you, keep in mind that part of it could be 'cause he's exhausted."

Paul was climbing down a ladder propped against the side of the shed as they approached, paint can and brush in hand. "Hey, Reverend," he greeted, seeing them. "I've made good progress, so I decided to take a break."

"Perfect timing. This is the tribal police investigator who has been looking into your friend's death."

Ella noticed Ford had avoided mentioning names. Bilford Tome might have been a modernist, and a Christian, but he was also a man who knew how to respect the customs of the majority, and his own tribe.

"Good morning," Ella greeted. "I'd like to ask you a few questions, if it's okay."

"Sure," Paul said. "Let me put the brush into some water and wash my hands while we talk."

"That's fine." Ella followed him to the nearby faucet, where there were a few tools, a drop cloth, old rags, and two empty coffee cans.

Hearing someone calling out to him from the door at the rear of the chapel, Ford excused himself. "I better go see what's going on."

As he hurried off, Paul Curley looked up from where he was crouched down, filling a coffee can with water. "The Rev mentioned earlier that you might want to talk to me. Something about what went down with our unit in Iraq, especially with an old buddy of mine. But I'm not sure how much I can help you. My family had a tragedy of our own and I came back early. I hadn't seen him for months."

"You served in the same platoon as the deceased, right?"

"Yeah, same section, actually, but usually in a different vehicle. For a while we were good friends. He wasn't an easy man to know, and he didn't socialize much, but I understood part of what was going on inside his head."

"Understood? How so?"

"A lot of things were happening over there—not just the war. You needed to know and trust the men and women you served with. Your life could depend on them when things got hot. For the same reason it was also important to avoid making enemies. My friend couldn't seem to manage any of that."

"How come?"

"It wasn't so much what was going on around him, but what he carried inside, if you know what I mean? He had problems back here—and they ate at him. As the time to go home drew near, most of us were making plans, talking about what we were going to do. Not him. He didn't say much of anything. All I know for sure is that he hated working at that lumber yard in Farmington, and he wanted to be a writer," he said, then paused for a long moment before continuing. "He was also expecting to have some major hassle with his brother. I remember him saying something about that in passing once."

"Do you remember what that was about?"

"There was bad blood between those two. A problem with a woman." He finished rinsing off the paintbrush, dried his hands with a rag, then brought out a chocolate bar from his shirt pocket and began eating. "My friend was kinda strange, and creeped out a lot of the guys, which was a job in itself, considering all the nasty things going on in that country."

"Creeped out? For example?"

"He'd come right up to people without any sound or warning. You'd look around and suddenly there he was. He wasn't eavesdropping. It was just a game he played, like he was stalking you. I told him he was being stupid, asking to get shot, but he just laughed. More than once, he did have a gun drawn on him before he was recognized. It pissed off the men in our section, especially when we were on alert, or had just come back from a mission or guard duty. I kept telling him to cut the crap, but he thought it was funny. Lucky he didn't get himself killed over there. Come to think of it, his luck ran out."

Ella carefully considered what he'd told her. Maybe Jimmy's habit of sneaking around had resulted in him overhearing something that had placed him in harm's way and he'd tried to convey that to her in the partial story he'd sent.

"What kind of things went on under the radar over there? Any contraband, black-market stuff, drugs, or things of that nature?"

Paul gave her a long look before answering. "Stuff like that is always going on in a war zone, but it's not forced on anyone. If you didn't want to take part, you made it clear that you couldn't be approached, or you didn't want to deal. That's all."

"What exactly *was* going on?" Ella pressed. "I need details."

"It's out of your jurisdiction, and it's already over, at least for the unit we were in. Why do you care?"

"It may have something to do with your friend's murder."

"It wasn't just a carjacking?"

"I don't think so, and I could use your help," Ella said.

Paul nodded slowly. "All right, but I think you'll be disappointed. All I know about was penny-ante stuff—burning CDs, software, booze, cigarettes, stuff like that. A little pot. I stayed away from it, myself, but it wasn't hard to see what was going on sometimes. It was harmless stuff, really."

"Give me the name of someone who might know more."

"Will you keep me out of it?"

"I'll do my best, and my best is usually pretty good," she answered.

"Try talking to an Anglo by the name of Louis Smith. He's a cop over in Farmington."

"Tell me more about Louis Smith," Ella asked.

"He was an enlisted man, like me, but I heard rumors that he had his fingers in a lot of pies. The little I know comes from here and there, people I can't or won't name, but I understand that Louis had a knack for finding ways to make extra cash. He called himself an 'entrepreneur' and said that was the real spirit of America."

"Modest son-of-a-gun," Ella said.

"A real pain in the ass, if you want to know. My friend hated his guts—but the feeling was mutual." Paul fished a key chain out of his faded jeans pocket, and gestured toward a beat-up old sedan half covered in gray primer. "I'm going to get a soft drink from the cooler in my car. You want one?"

"No, thanks." Ella immediately noticed the bullet attached to the key chain. "Souvenir?"

"Yeah," he said with a grim nod. "Not one of these Hollywood bullet-that-almost-killed-me stories, either. Just a full metal jacket reminder to myself, that so long as I've got my wits about me, I can deal with anything."

Ella remembered what Ford had told her about Paul's family problems and nodded somberly. "Thanks for your help," she said, and walked back around the building to her car. When she got there, Ford came out to meet her.

"Did you get anything you can use?" he asked.

"Several promising leads," she answered. "Thanks for calling me, Ford."

"I'll keep working on that story," he said. "But watch your step. I have a bad feeling about all of this. The series of clues Blacksheep sent you took time to figure out and write up. He wouldn't have expended all that energy without a good reason."

"Yeah," Ella agreed. "Let me know when you've got a handle on it."

Ford smiled, noting she'd said "when" not "if." "I'm glad we finally met, Ella," he said simply.

In his eyes, Ella saw interest and . . . more. Pleased, and annoyed with herself for getting sidetracked, she mumbled a quick good-bye. She didn't breathe normally again until she was in her unit, on the road. Farmington was her next stop. She had to find Officer Louis Smith.

TEN

—— ✖ ✖ ✖ ——

Less than forty minutes later, Ella stood across from Louis Smith's cluttered desk. It hadn't taken long to find him today. He'd recently been transferred to this small office at the back of the building and, from here, handled hit-and-run cases exclusively. Louis had just placed the phone back on the hook as she walked in.

Seeing the badge pinned at her belt, he waved her to a seat. "What can I do for you, Officer . . ."

Ella introduced herself. "No doubt you've heard all about the homicide. I'm looking into Jimmy Blacksheep's death."

"Yes, ma'am, I have. Blacksheep was a strange kid, but a good soldier who did his job when it mattered," he said. "How can I help? You thinking that the carjacking and my hit-and-run cases intersect somehow?"

"No, I'm just looking for answers to some incidental questions that have cropped up during our investigation," she answered, not wanting to give out any unnecessary information. Officer Smith was a dark-haired Anglo with hazel eyes. In his late thirties, she thought him a bit old for the National Guard. Perhaps Officer Smith had needed the extra income. His smile was wooden, and he seemed ill at ease with her. She wasn't sure if that was because of the usual jurisdictional turf thing that often cropped up between departments, or something more.

"I'm not sure how much help I can be to you, Detective Clah. I look into hit-and-runs, track down witnesses, follow up on reports, and that's pretty much it. I worked traffic before my tour in Iraq, but this is where I want to be now."

"There's plenty to do here from what I see," she said, glancing at the stack of files on his desk.

"Yeah, and providing my luck holds, I'll never have to shoot another person again," Smith added.

"That's what we all want," she said quietly.

"In a hit-and-run, an officer has more control over what situations he's walking into than in a patrol car," Louis answered. "But enough of that. How can I help you? Jimmy and I weren't buddies, though I shared quarters with him and the rest of the section for a while."

"I'm thinking that if I can get inside his head I may be able to figure out what went down the other day."

"That's a tough one even for those who knew him. Jimmy was hard to get a handle on. He could have made it a lot easier on himself if he'd played his cards right. But he liked keeping everyone at arm's length—standoffish, you get me? He was a good soldier though. Completed his missions and helped keep us all alive. That was enough," Smith said.

"What do you mean about making things easier on himself and playing his cards right?" Ella pressed.

"His brother, FPD Officer Samuel Blacksheep, was Sergeant Sanders's partner on the force for several years. Sanders was the lieutenant of our platoon, and also had the responsibility for the company's base security while we were overseas. Lieutenant—well, here, Sergeant Sanders—was willing, at first, to cut Samuel's brother a little slack, but Jimmy wouldn't have it. Took his turn with every crap assignment just like the rest of us, though he was given the opportunity to pull some lighter duty. That earned everyone's respect, even his sergeant's. I don't know why Jimmy didn't go for it, but maybe he didn't want to owe anyone."

"How well do Sanders and Blacksheep get along now?"

Officer Smith shrugged. "Naturally Blacksheep got another partner when Sanders shipped out, and Sanders is working with somebody else now. But I've heard that the two are still good friends and get together after duty hours."

"Getting back to the Guard—in Iraq. How often did equipment, supplies, and stuff like that go missing over there?" Ella said.

"War's messy," he answered flatly. "Things went missing all the time—including people."

"I understand a few of the soldiers found inventive ways to make up for lost income from their civilian jobs."

"Yeah, some did." He leaned back and gave her a long, calculating look. "But what happened overseas stays there as far as I'm concerned. It's up to the Army to deal with those issues, so I don't think you'll find many who'll talk to you about that."

"Is there anyone else around here who might be able to tell me more about Jimmy and his life leading up to the events of the other day? Especially for the time he spent in the Guard?"

Officer Smith lapsed into a long silence, and she was about to press him when she heard footsteps behind her. Smith looked up, and Ella turned her head. Sergeant Calvin Sanders was standing in the doorway. "Clah, will you come with me, please?"

It hadn't been a request, but she wasn't his subordinate, so she took her time responding. "Any place where I can get a cup of coffee first, Sanders?" she asked casually.

He didn't answer, but cocked his head down the hall. They reached his office a short time later. Though they'd walked down several corridors, Sanders hadn't said a word. Finally, after she entered his office, he kicked the door shut with the tip of his boot.

"You do *not* walk into *my* department and talk to *my* people without *my* permission—particularly men that I served with over-seas," he said, glowering at her.

"I didn't see Chief of Police on *your* door, Sergeant, and you don't sign my paycheck. My investigation is none of your business—unless you have something to hide," Ella countered. His face started getting red, but she continued. "My investigation points to events that happened before Jimmy came home, so I'm going to keep digging."

Considering the vein on his forehead was bulging, Ella was surprised when he waited so long before responding. "Your investigation points to *carjackings* that have been going on for months. The evidence is there in front of all our faces. Why don't we stop trying to pee on each other's street corner and join forces so we can shut those jerks down? Our department has doubled our early morning patrols and has questioned all the perps in our area who've been previously convicted of car theft. What is your PD doing?"

"Our job," she said, and stood up. "Right now I'm investigating a murder, and *that's* my priority."

"Let us help," Sanders countered.

"Good idea. You can start by not getting in my way."

"You were talking to one of my men about things that went on overseas. You overstepped your bounds," he snapped.

"We disagree on that," Ella said. "And you should know not to interfere in a murder investigation."

"Why are you complicating things, Clah? It's all right there in front of you. Jimmy Blacksheep, less than three weeks out of a war zone, blew his cool and reacted instead of thinking. In the armed forces, reacting can save your butt because the bad guys *are* after you. But in civilian life, resisting a simple robbery is stupid. In this case, it got him killed."

"I don't think that's what happened," she said.

"Why do you insist on making this about Iraq?"

"I'm not *making* it about anything. What I'm doing is following the evidence." She had no intention of telling Sanders about the story Jimmy had mailed her. The sergeant was still a suspect.

"Look at it logically—the guy felt squirrely enough to want to buy a gun for his return trip," Sanders insisted. "When the carjackers stopped him, fighting was the first thing on his mind. Jimmy wasn't about to put his life in somebody else's hands, not so soon after Iraq. Don't you get that?"

"That's one explanation. We just can't prove it yet. But keep in mind that it's equally possible that he had something in his car he didn't want anyone to take from him."

"Like what?" Sanders pressed.

"Makes you wonder. It's an interesting theory, don't you think?"

"You were asking Smith about missing supplies and equipment overseas. How's that tie into anything?"

Things were starting to get sticky. Sanders obviously had no idea that Jimmy had sent her a package—which, of course, raised other interesting questions, like why hadn't Jimmy sent the package to his brother or spoken to Sanders about whatever had been worrying him. Ultimately, had he considered one or both a threat? He obviously hadn't trusted them.

"I'd better be going," Ella said.

"Listen, we're on the same side," he said in a more conciliatory tone. "Private Blacksheep served in my platoon, and I want to catch whoever killed him. Unfortunately, I've just been assigned to desk duty to catch up on paperwork for a few days. But I'll be consulting with the officer taking my place in the field. I'll still be in the loop so if you need support from our department, like backup or technical assistance, all you have to do is ask and I'll make sure it goes through channels quickly."

"Who's covering for you?"

"Officer Samuel Blacksheep."

Ella stared at him. "How the heck did that happen?"

"It wasn't my idea, but he was putting a lot of heat on the supervisor and the rest of the higher-ups. They came to the conclusion that it was better to channel his energy for a while, and, as a Navajo, Officer Blacksheep was the ideal choice as short-term liaison between our department and yours. He's got a rep for being a good officer and a team player. Between you and me, this is a workable solution. We know he would have been involved anyway, but at least this way he'll have plenty of others keeping an eye on him. And, after a few days, I'll be back with the unit and Blacksheep will return to the traffic unit."

"It's their call," Ella said dubiously, "not mine or yours. How do *you* feel about Samuel being given your assignment right now?"

Sanders gave Ella a long look. "Samuel Blacksheep and I were friends for many years, but things have changed between him and me since I got back. He expected me to keep an eye on Jimmy, and the kid got back in one piece, but first thing back, he gets himself killed. I think Samuel feels that I somehow missed seeing a threat that was following his brother home. He'll bring that viewpoint into the investigation. Maybe he needs that now in order to deal with his own issues."

"So Samuel doesn't buy the carjacking thing?"

"He believes that it's just one aspect of a much larger case, and for the next day or two, he'll be working to prove those theories."

Before long, Ella pulled out of the station, questions swirling in her mind like snow flurries caught in the wind. Trying to figure out who was manipulating who, on and off the police force, was certainly getting to be a puzzle in itself. Knowing that answers always came more easily when she didn't force them, she allowed her thoughts to drift.

Her next step would be to find out more about Juanita Betoni. The woman probably knew more about both brothers than anyone else around, at least concerning the nature of their relationship and their attitude toward each other. Ella called Justine and had her look up Juanita's whereabouts, then report back with the information.

A short time later Ella arrived at the hospital in Shiprock where Juanita Betoni worked as a geriatric nurse. Ella turned her cell phone off in accordance with hospital restrictions, then went inside. Justine had called and arranged for a meeting, so Ella followed the directions she'd been given and took the elevator upstairs to the nurse's station.

"Can I help you?" a young Navajo woman with big, soulful eyes asked, looking up from her filing.

"I'm looking for Juanita Betoni," Ella said, identifying herself, then noted the nurse's name tag, and smiled. "Guess I found you."

"I've been expecting you, Investigator Clah," Juanita said with a quirky half smile, then added, "You've got perfect timing. It's time for my break. You want to go to the snack room? I'm a quart low on coffee at the moment. It's almost eleven-thirty now, and I need a sandwich and coffee."

As they walked down the hall, Ella studied Juanita. She was in her late twenties and slim, with an abundance of charisma that transcended her looks. Juanita appeared to be both confident and vulnerable—a combination she suspected men found very appealing.

They entered a small lounge equipped with vending machines and Juanita bought herself and Ella a cup of coffee and a sandwich. "I've been expecting you to come by, Officer Clah. I knew that, sooner or later, you'd track me down. I'm so sorry about what happened to Jimmy."

"I need to talk to you about Jimmy *and* Samuel," Ella said, taking a large bite out of the stale sandwich. It was better than nothing, but not by much.

Juanita nodded. "Jimmy and I dated for a few months before

he went overseas. We were really just friends. But, as we corresponded, his letters began to change. He got very intense, telling me he wanted to settle down after he got back and how much I meant to him. He was going way beyond what I wanted our relationship to be."

Ella waited as Juanita lapsed into a thoughtful silence and finished her sandwich. She was just about to press her to continue, when Juanita did so on her own.

"All things considered, I think his perspective changed because of where he was, but I'd been happy with the way things were. So I decided it was time to call it quits. I didn't want to lead him on. But knowing Jimmy was in a war zone, I started getting worried that he'd go nuts and end up doing something stupid and dangerous. That would have been just like Jimmy. That's why I went to talk to Samuel. I was hoping he could give me some advice on how to handle things."

"So what happened?" Ella asked.

"At first we just talked, going out for coffee. He was kind and we got along, right from the beginning—more so than Jimmy and I ever had. Samuel was so much more mature. Then one thing led to another and our stops for coffee became more . . . involved. We were careful, but somehow Jimmy found out, maybe from a girlfriend of another soldier in his unit who knew me. We'd been in contact off and on—you know, mutual support for the guys. After that, Jimmy started sending me really abusive e-mails. Samuel got a look at them, and told Jimmy to grow up, and to take it up with him if he had a problem."

Juanita took a sip of coffee, then looked down at her hands before speaking again. "I'm not sure what happened after that. I stopped hearing from Jimmy and Samuel wouldn't discuss it. I was really afraid that when Jimmy got back he'd find Samuel and they'd square off someplace. Now Jimmy's dead, and Samuel's determined to catch whoever did it. It's one thing for them to be at odds with each other—they were family, and that's what happens to brothers sometimes. But the way things stand, there's no way Samuel will rest until his brother's killer is behind bars."

Unless he'd done it himself. It was possible the men had found themselves locked in a standoff, and one of them had started shooting. As a police officer, Samuel would have known the details of the carjackings and could have manipulated the murder in a way that would mislead the investigation. But he probably hadn't expected his brother to come in armed and ready to fight. Somebody had been shot in addition to Jimmy, too. It wasn't Samuel, so if there had been a confrontation, someone else had been there as well.

"I can see it in your eyes," Juanita said softly. "You're thinking Samuel might have killed his brother because of me, but that's *not* what happened. If Samuel and Jimmy had met, there would have been busted noses and a black eye or two, but that's about it. No guns, no knives, no sticks and stones, just fists and words. Deep down they loved each other. They were brothers."

Ella didn't comment. She knew brotherly love could go sour and turn into hate. Stories of it abounded, dating all the way back to Cain and Abel. Times changed, but people did not.

As Ella drove back to the station, she reviewed what she'd learned, but the puzzle still refused to come together. What she needed most of all was evidence—hard facts that would point her conclusively in the right direction. The rest of Jimmy Blacksheep's story might give her some direction, or even make sense out of the part she had. But until she found it, she'd have to continue digging hard into Jimmy's life—the last months of it, in particular.

The ringing cell phone interrupted her thoughts. Ella identified herself and heard Rose's taut voice. "Can you come home?"

"Why? What's wrong?"

"Your daughter. She's been suspended."

"I'm sorry, Mom. Can you repeat that?" Ella asked, sure she'd heard wrong.

"Your daughter punched another child in the nose."

"Then she must have had a very good reason," Ella said flatly. She knew her kid. Dawn wouldn't have done something like that without being provoked. "I'll be right there."

Ella considered switching on the sirens but, because it wasn't an official emergency, decided against it. She hurried home as quickly as the speed limit allowed.

When she stepped into the living room, Dawn and Rose were waiting. Kevin was around, too; she'd seen his pickup in the driveway. When he stepped into sight from the kitchen, she directed her first question at him.

"What—" she began.

"Mom, it wasn't my fault!" Dawn interrupted and launched herself into Ella's arms. "He kept pushing me!"

Ella hugged Dawn, then led her over to the couch. "Okay, what's up?" Ella asked, looking at Rose.

"Apparently she just started having a problem with a boy at school. He pushes her whenever the teachers aren't looking. A real bully," Rose said. "I didn't tell you because I thought it had already been handled at school."

"*Shimasáni*, I told you he wouldn't leave me alone, but you said not to worry about it. When you told my teacher, she talked to him. But that just made him sneakier. Today he pushed me so hard I nearly fell. My books and notebooks were all over the hall. When I tried to pick them up, he pushed me again. That's when I punched him in the nose and Mrs. Perkins came out."

"Anytime anyone at school gives you a hard time, I want to hear about it. Understand?"

Dawn nodded.

"You shouldn't have been suspended for defending yourself," Ella said flatly. "I'll go talk to the principal."

"I've already done that, explaining our daughter's side of it," Kevin said. "But the school has adopted a zero-tolerance policy on violence. When our daughter punched the boy, he fell back and bumped his head on a locker. He's all right, but the two-day suspension stands. The boy was suspended, too."

Kevin motioned for Ella to come outside, so they went out onto the front porch, alone. "What are you doing here?" she demanded. "How did you get involved in all of this?"

"Dawn's principal tried to call you at the station, then she tried your mother. But neither one of you were available. I was her third choice, and her principal reached me immediately."

"Why didn't Dawn tell her to call me on my cell?" Ella asked, bringing out her phone and then realizing that she'd shut it off at the hospital for a while to comply with their rules. "Never mind. It's my fault." Ella checked, but there were no messages. "So she didn't?"

Kevin shook his head. "Dawn said she didn't want to interrupt you at work. She'd heard about the dead soldier from other classmates, and knew you'd have the case. But it's okay, I went down to the school and handled it. So far, your mom has been here, ready to step in when you're unreachable, but now that Rose is getting married, we'll need to make some changes."

"What do you mean, *changes?*" she countered.

"You can't wish it away," Kevin said quietly. "Face reality. Things are different now and Dawn needs a parent available full time. I've got my office at home. I handle the tribal legal affairs from there. I'm on-call for trials, but we're talking a few hours away at most, and my schedule is set days ahead, allowing for adjustments to be made."

"What exactly are you saying?"

"I want you to consider granting me equal custody of Dawn. Half time."

"That's a bad idea," Ella said flatly.

"Our daughter needs someone who's *available*. I can give her that—and consistency. She needs a schedule and a parent around when she's at home."

"You show up this one time, and all of a sudden *you're* the responsible parent? Really, Kevin, what have you been smoking?"

"Ella, had Dawn been under *my* care, what happened today might have never occurred at all. I would have been at home to listen and offer help that might have kept things from escalating at school. Your mother can't continue to do your share of the parenting anymore. She's not going to be around."

"If you're so convinced Dawn should be with *you* right now, why did you bring her home instead of to your office?"

"Well, I didn't want to get you upset."

"That worked out well, didn't it? But there's more, isn't there, Kevin?" Ella saw the hesitation in his eyes.

"Yeah, well. I've got a lunch appointment in a while over at the tribal offices. Dawn had to come here today."

"But if it was *my* appointment, I'd be neglecting our daughter. Is that how it works?"

"We need to come to terms on stuff like this, Ella, before things get blown out of proportion. I'm serious."

"So am I. Leave now."

"This isn't over," he said, then strode off to his truck.

When Ella went back inside the house, Rose was the only one in the living room. Sounds in the kitchen told her where Dawn had gone. "Mom, what happened today to bring all this on?" Ella whispered.

"I'd just come home from a Plant Watchers meeting when the phone rang. It was your child's father. He was already at school and told me what had happened. So I asked him to bring her home—here. I instructed him to give the phone to the principal so I could make that clear."

"Good!" Ella wondered how big of a fight Kevin would have started if he hadn't had the meeting.

Rose sighed. "I think this incident will carry a price. I hadn't realized until we talked about it awhile ago just how serious he was about getting more time with your daughter. He's a smart, powerful man and he *is* the father. That spells trouble."

"He might be able to bring some pressure down, but he can't have her half the time. I'm not the only working mother in the world, and just because I wasn't available today—"

"He didn't tell you about the rest?"

Ella held her breath, then with great effort added, "Tell me what?"

"He's been called in before on discipline issues. When she got into trouble for talking in class, she gave the teacher her father's number and said they were supposed to talk to him."

Ella's eyes narrowed. "The oldest kid trick in the book—choosing the parent who's easier on them." Without hesitation Ella stormed into the kitchen. Dawn was at the table, eating cookies.

"I understand that your father's been called to school before because of your behavior. And you didn't tell me. I want an explanation—now," Ella demanded, her eyes blazing.

"Oh, that. My teacher wanted to talk to *someone* right then, so I told her to talk to Daddy. I knew he would be at home, but you were working and *Shimasání* was on a day trip looking for plants. The teacher didn't care."

"And you didn't remember to tell me?"

"It was just the one time, and I was already in trouble with Daddy. I didn't want to be in trouble with you, too. I promised Daddy I wouldn't do it again. I was going to tell you . . . but then I forgot."

"You *forgot?*"

"Mom, you got home late that night. It happens a lot of times! By then I was probably asleep!"

It might have been true, but it was obvious that Dawn was using it as a convenient excuse. Ella felt the familiar conflict hemming her in again. She had a job she loved and a child she adored, but there *were* times when a workday lasted twenty-four hours or more.

"Do you think we're too busy for you? Is that really the way you feel?" Ella asked, sitting down out of necessity, not choice.

"Sometimes . . . I guess." Dawn shrugged, looked away, then absently took a sip of milk. "We still get to spend time together. It's no big deal, Mom."

But it was. She was about to answer Dawn, when her cell phone rang. "Hold that thought." Ella took a deep unsteady breath, changing from mother to police investigator in the blink of an eye, and answered.

Justine's voice came through clearly. "The New Mexico State Police pulled over a pickup on the hot sheet—it was one that was carjacked a few weeks ago on the Rez up by Four Corners," Justine said.

"Arrange for us to interview the driver."

"Already done. They made the arrest south of Albuquerque on the interstate, so they're taking their prisoner and the vehicle there. We can meet them when we're ready. But you're going to have to come to the station first. We have someone from CID here waiting to talk to you."

Ella knew the initials from her days in the Bureau. She'd been expecting someone from the Army's Criminal Investigative Division to show up sooner or later. "Does he have any information for us concerning the victim?"

"I couldn't tell you. All I know is that he met with Big Ed first, then was told to wait for you."

"Is Big Ed in now?"

"No, he had to attend a tribal meeting in Window Rock."

"All right, I'll be there as soon as possible—maybe twenty minutes."

Ella hung up, and looked back at Dawn. "We'll have to pick this up later. But I want you to think about the decisions you've made, not telling me what's going on at school, or about things that bother you. If you feel I'm not around enough, then we need to set aside time for us to talk each day. You have my telephone number and, unless I'm involved in an emergency situation, you can speak to me at *any* time."

"I know, Mom," Dawn said softly. "It's just easier to get Daddy. He's at home more than you now."

The words stung. As a consulting attorney, Kevin could schedule his day far more easily than she could. "I'm only a phone call away, and you know that." As she looked at her daughter's face, she suddenly remembered what had occurred to her before she'd come into the kitchen. "Your father's an easier touch, isn't he? Lets you get away with things."

Dawn winced, then added, "Well, he doesn't always get as mad as you do."

"We *will* talk later," Ella said, knowing she was going to have to deal with being manipulated by not only Kevin, but by her own daughter.

One glance at Rose's face as she came into the kitchen told Ella that her mom understood precisely what was going on. As Ella walked outside to her SUV, Rose accompanied her.

"Her father's laying down bribes and using strategies that play on her emotions, but he doesn't realize she's way ahead of him."

"You and I both know my daughter is playing him, Mom. Taking advantage because he's soft on her. But even if I told him that, he'd never see it. Not yet, anyway, because he *hasn't* been a full-time father."

"He wants her to love him, so he forgives her bad behavior too easily. All reward and no punishment or rules. He also buys her anything she wants, because it's easier to win her over with bribes than tough love," Rose said quietly.

"I can't allow this to become a tug-of-war between him and me, with my daughter in the middle. If it does, we'll all lose." She thought of what she'd said, calling Dawn "her" daughter, not "our" daughter. But that's the way it was on the Navajo Nation. Children were considered the property of their mother. Unfortunately, Kevin was a lawyer, and he knew the Navajo Nation was part of a larger nation, one where Anglo law ruled.

"You need to sit down and talk to him. And you might also remind him that although I'll be living with *Bizaadii* once I'm married, I won't be more than fifteen minutes away," Rose said.

Ella's gut tightened. Part of her felt like screaming "Mommy!" and running into her mother's arms. But the adult inside assured her that the time had come for all of them to carve out new paths. Kevin had been right about the need for changes.

"You and he will have to come to terms with the fact that neither one of you can be there for your daughter *all* the time. If you could work something out . . ."

"Mom, my daughter's father is a tough lawyer. He's used to manipulating situations and people. I've got to watch my step around him," Ella replied, slipping behind the wheel and putting the key in the ignition, then fastening her seat belt.

"If you take no action, you'll remain at a standstill, and your daughter will continue to play you against each other." Not giving Ella a chance to respond, Rose turned and went back into the house.

Ella muttered a short explicit curse under her breath, then started the engine. If Herman ever got into an argument with Rose, she'd reduce him to cinders with just a few soft-spoken words.

Come to think of it, Ella had never heard Herman arguing with her mother. Maybe he'd found it easier just to keep his mouth shut. Too bad she'd never been able to do that.

As she drove north toward Shiprock and the station, Ella pushed her problems with Dawn into a corner of her mind, while the case and its ramifications came to the forefront of her thoughts. Sometimes she felt like two separate people—the cop her mother had described to near perfection—afraid to show weakness, or to even admit that she had any—and the mom who was ruled by the fear that she'd botch the most important job of all.

Reaching for her cell phone, she concentrated on the task at hand. "Justine, I'm on my way. Have you gotten anything useful from our visitor?"

"I tried to make small talk, hoping he'd relax a bit, but he's not exactly friendly. He's . . . self-contained. He's sitting in your office right now, and, Ella, he's so still he could pass for a statue. I've got a feeling his mind is a million miles away. I offered him a cup of coffee, but he declined."

"I'm surprised he came to us at all—some of these guys would have kept a low profile and investigated on their own."

Several minutes later, Ella walked into her office and introduced herself to one of the most imposing men she'd ever met. Dressed in a casual-looking sports jacket, slacks, and no tie, her visitor was at least six foot five and built like Arnold Schwarzenegger in his early bodybuilding years. In deference to the big Anglo with short, blond hair and intense gray eyes, she shook hands, her hand engulfed by his. "Have a seat . . ." she said.

"Chief Warrant Officer Neil Carson, ma'am." Almost automatically, he answered her unspoken question. "We operate in civilian clothes, but we're FBI-trained investigators."

"Then we have something in common," Ella said. "I was an FBI agent for a half dozen years." His gaze was flat—she'd seen that in the military men she'd dealt with lately, even those who were back in civilian roles.

"You made inquiries concerning the possibility of missing supplies or thefts from Specialist Blacksheep's company," Carson said, getting right down to business. "But you weren't specific. Exactly what are you looking for?"

Ella leaned back in her chair and considered her answer carefully. She could have told him about the half-completed story Jimmy had sent her full of clues concerning his recent military experiences, but that begged the question—why hadn't Jimmy turned the matter over to the CID in the first place, or at least his commanding officer? If he hadn't trusted the military, then perhaps she shouldn't either.

"Are you aware of how Jimmy Blacksheep died?" she asked and when he nodded, added, "What we're still looking for is a motive that makes sense."

"I've spoken to his brother, Samuel, and I've learned about the carjackings—and the inconsistencies that suggest his death was not a botched robbery."

"There are a lot of inconsistences, like why the victim would get into a firefight over a rental car," she said. "I believe we're missing something important."

Carson smiled slowly. "You've redirected my attention, but you haven't answered my question. What do you think was stolen from us and what connection does that have to Specialist Blacksheep's death?"

Ella regarded Carson speculatively. The man had a sharp mind—something that would serve an investigator well. "Look, here's the bottom line. I've got one dead former soldier who refused to hand over his rental car—for no apparent reason. I've also spoken to some other soldiers in his unit, and I've noticed them carrying souvenirs of one kind or another," she said, overstating it to gauge his reaction. Point of fact was that she'd only noticed one ex-soldier with a souvenir—of sorts. "That led me to believe there might have been other, more substantial items taken."

"What kind of souvenirs did you see in the men's possession?"

"Nothing dramatic—a piece of Iraqi military ammo, that kind of thing. But I'm considering the possibility that maybe it didn't stop there. Rifles, pistols, money, gold, jewelry . . . maybe more. What do you think?"

"No way. If there'd been anything going on that involved more than one or two soldiers taking a knife or pistol as a souvenir, there would have been an investigation months ago. I've interviewed the unit commander, and his second in command, and they would have heard about it for sure. The reason I'm investigating this unit is because two of their soldiers died under suspicious noncombat circumstances at their Iraqi base. It's possible that others in that unit were responsible, and for that reason, my superiors have assigned me to look into the matter."

"Just to clarify—you do mean people in Jimmy Blacksheep's unit?" Ella asked.

"Yes, his National Guard company and his platoon in particular. But I don't have proof one way or another at this point. That's why I'm here. I've been in the area since yesterday, questioning soldiers from his unit, trying to find out what happened to the two men who died. And now that another soldier from that unit has also died under suspicious circumstances, I'm expanding my investigation, searching for any possible connection to the first two deaths."

Ella remembered Jimmy's story and the segment about two men disappearing after "falling out of favor" with the Dark Ones. Maybe this was the first solid connection between the story and real events. If only they could break more of the code.

"What were the names of the victims?" Ella asked.

"Jonathan Parks and Micah Hawkins."

She'd hoped to hear names that sounded like Konik and Bula, but that hadn't happened. "I wish I could tell you why Jimmy Blacksheep was murdered, but the truth is I don't know. Not yet."

"Who are your suspects? Other members of his section?"

"Among a few others. Tell me, Chief Carson, what's your theory? Something tells me you've got one," Ella added.

"Just call me Carson. Officially, I'm not at liberty to share that information with you at this time. But unofficially . . . ?" he added, then seeing her nod, continued. "Unless we work fast, we may never find out what's going on."

"How so?"

"Earlier today, I was notified that some of the units involved in the rotation overseas have been reassigned or reactivated due to training and equipment problems. There are shortages in manpower, so that means that the members of Blacksheep's National Guard company are going to be recalled soon, even those whose enlistments are up. They won't be going back into a war zone, but they'll be sent to Germany to replace another transportation unit being transferred to Afghanistan. It'll be a six-month deployment this time. The soldiers will receive official notices soon, maybe within a day or two, and will have to report in a couple of weeks."

Ella pursed her lips, the implication sinking in. It explained why Carson, who'd obviously been working his own case here for at least a day, had finally showed up at the station. "So what you're telling me is that if I need to conduct any interviews, I'd better do it fast. A big chunk of my suspect list is going to be out of the country this time next month?"

"That's the way it shapes up, yes, ma'am," he answered, then stood. "I'll be staying at the Thunder Inn on Farmington's west side if you need me," he said, giving her his card. "I'll keep in touch."

Ella watched him go, deep in thought. So now the pressure was really on—not only at home, but here at work as well. She needed a clone—or a miracle.

ELEVEN
✖ ✖ ✖

Ella was quiet as they drove east on I-40, headed toward a state police facility in Albuquerque's northeast heights. The three-hour drive, including a quick stop to pick up hamburgers and sodas, had given her plenty of time to think while Justine drove. The new deadline for military personnel was bearing down on her. She couldn't afford to keep going in circles.

"I'm your partner, you know. Something's bugging you, and has been for the past two hundred miles. What are you waiting for, talk to me," Justine said.

Ella smiled. It wasn't a surprise that Justine could read her so easily. For many years they'd been close as partners, friends, and second cousins. "I feel like I'm under siege," Ella said, telling her about the military's deadline, then explaining about the problem she was facing with Kevin over Dawn. "I always wanted to give my daughter the freedom to be herself. While I was growing up, I was always torn between Mom, the traditionalist, and Dad, the preacher. Even before I was in the first grade I was caught between them, and it was a no-win situation. Whenever I went in one direction I'd get a smile from one parent, and a frown from the other. More than anything I'd hoped to give Dawn the freedom to choose her own path in life, never feeling pressured by either

Kevin or me to do or be anything other than herself. But Dawn's a fast learner and has started using the differences between Kevin and me to her own advantage. She approaches whichever parent is more likely to give her what she wants. Kevin's easier on her because he wants her to choose to live with him, at least fifty-fifty, and that really worries me, Justine."

"Do you honestly think Dawn will want to split the time between you and Kevin, particularly if he forces the issue and makes that decision for her?" Justine asked, reading between the lines.

"Under those circumstances, no. But Kevin's far from stupid. He knows Dawn has to be the one to make that choice, and he's campaigning pretty hard, from what I've seen. The one thing in my favor is that my daughter's a bright kid and she's already figured out how to play his game. When push comes to shove, I don't think Kevin will get what he wants."

"But you're still worried," Justine observed, then, after a moment, added, "Ella, do *you* feel Kevin will be a better parent—or at least better for Dawn—because he'll be at home more?"

Ella sighed softly. "That's the real bottom line, isn't it? I'm honestly not sure. Being at home is a plus, but a daughter needs her mother in ways that are hard to put into words. If I'm working on a case and Kevin wants to take her for a few days, I don't see any problem with that. But Dawn belongs with me. The ties between us are stronger than Kevin realizes—or Dawn, for that matter."

"Do you mind a piece of advice?"

"Go ahead," Ella said.

"Take it one step at a time. Dawn's a very smart little girl. It's a given that she's going to love it when Kevin showers her with toys and attention. But to leave the home she's always known and live at his house every other week, or whatever? No way. It won't happen."

"Even if her grandmother moves out?" Ella countered, then told Justine about Rose's plans to live in Herman's new home.

"That'll be a big change for Dawn, but *you're* the focus of her life. And, for the record, I think you're being too hard on yourself. You're a *great* mom. You're not always on a case, Ella. You're supervising with her homework and reading with her at home. What about those horseback rides you and Dawn take on weekends, and the evening ice cream parties whenever Dawn gets an A on her report card? That grade-level trip to the mountains? Those add texture and form the framework of your lives together. Sure, there are days like now, when a big case takes over your life for a while. But what you two share goes beyond 'stuff' and Dawn knows it. Don't underestimate her."

Ella nodded thoughtfully. "I suppose you have a point. But even facing the possibility that my daughter might move out even part time is making me a little crazy. Don't get me wrong, I know she'd be in good hands with Kevin. He loves his daughter and Dawn adores him. I would never want that to stop, or to hurt their relationship. But I also want Dawn to grow up with me there to guide and take care of her. I need to be part of her day-to-day life, and Dawn needs that from me, too, even if she's not aware of it."

"Have you reconsidered your relationship with Kevin, Ella? You can't tell me you don't have any feelings for him," Justine said, changing into the right-hand lane to take the next freeway exit.

"I *do* care for him. And when I'm around him—and not furious about something he just did—I can certainly understand what drew me to him in the first place. But our differences would split us apart, no matter how hard we tried to make a go of it for Dawn's sake. What binds us—and always will—is the beautiful child we created together."

"I don't get it. If you know your relationship with Kevin isn't strong enough to base a relationship upon, why have you taken yourself off the market? You don't even date anymore, do you?"

"It's been a year or so, that's true, but I haven't been looking because my life was pretty much complete as it is, and I didn't want anything else."

"Past tense? What's changed?" Justine asked quickly, entering the left-hand lane of traffic, and waiting for an opening to pull into the row of one-story offices where the New Mexico State Police had a regional facility.

Ella watched the cars on the interstate below the overpass they'd just crossed. "Mom's finding a whole new direction for herself and that made me think and face a few facts. Truth is, Justine, I'd like another child someday, but time has a way of slipping by. I'd like to find someone who wants what I do—a home, career, and family, with all its ups and downs."

What she wasn't quite ready to tell Justine was that she'd already met someone who intrigued her—a man who honored his highest sense of right—a man who walked his talk. And she wanted to get to know him better.

Once inside the small facility, Ella met with State Patrolman Lex Harvey, the New Mexico State Police officer who'd arrested the suspect.

"I pulled the vehicle over at one-thirty this morning after the driver started sending me the wrong kind of signals. I'd come up behind him and noted that the vehicle was going just over the speed limit. When the driver slowed way down, and kept watching me in the rearview mirror, squirrely-like, I pulled him over and had a look at his operator's permit and registration. We get a lot of drug traffic along this corridor running into Colorado, and hundreds of undocumented workers coming in for the spring planting. You learn to spot trouble after a while."

Ella nodded, noting that, although Officer Harvey appeared to be around twenty-five, there was a weariness in his gaze that went beyond mere fatigue. She'd seen that look before on the faces of those who'd grown up knowing only hardship on the Rez, especially those who'd become police officers. "His papers were bogus?" she asked.

"His N.M. operator's license is valid—name's Benjamin Luna—but the registration looked too new to be authentic. The ink was barely dry, and the paper was watermarked with a common discount-store brand name. I called it in, and of course it's a phony. The suspect said he bought the truck cheap at one of these weekend flea markets at the fairgrounds, and was on his way to visit relatives in Juarez. Benji claims he didn't know the pickup was stolen, but told me the seller—one Joe Montoya, address and phone number not given—had printed up the registration. This was so Benji wouldn't get in trouble if he got pulled over. Of course Benji doesn't have any bill of sale, and there's nothing but dust in that truck. There must be a thousand Joe Montoyas in the Rio Grande valley, so even if Benji didn't make it up, checking it out would take days. The bottom line is that the vehicle's VIN numbers matched my hot sheet. It was stolen last month by the carjackers working your jurisdiction, ma'am."

"Can I speak to your prisoner?" Ella asked, trying not to smile after realizing that Justine was checking out Officer Harvey's behind.

"Knock yourself out," he said with a wave of his hand, handing her a set of keys and nodding toward a solid-looking door to his left. "Just leave your service weapon outside." Then he turned around and offered Justine a cup of coffee.

As Justine waited outside with Officer Harvey, Ella set her pistol on the counter, then looked through the observation window of the holding cell to confirm the location of the prisoner. A moment later she unlocked the door and went inside. She sat across the table from the suspect, who was shackled by his leg irons to the anchored table itself, though his hands were free to sip from a cup of water.

The prisoner, probably nineteen, wore a long-sleeved flannel shirt, several sizes too large, and had baggy black pants with about five hundred zippers. His hair was so short it was almost invisible, and his chubby face held a day's stubble of beard. There was a scar on his eyebrow, barely healed and still looking pink against his skin. He gave her the once-over, then either winked, or had a sudden muscle spasm. Both would have been equally enticing to her at the moment.

"Mr. Luna, you're in a world of trouble, you know?" she said, then when he didn't respond, continued. "This is more than a stolen vehicle case, my friend. Someone has been murdered and you just moved to the top of my list of suspects. You're an adult now, and I don't think you want to spend the next thirty years pumping iron at the state pen no matter how buff you end up. Talk to me."

"Like I'm scared now. I never killed nobody," he said flatly. "I don't know what you're talking about, and you can't prove squat."

"You really expect me to believe that you bought a truck with a fake registration and you didn't think it might be stolen?"

"Hey, the guy said he'd bought a new one, and the dealer had told him he could get more money for his trade-in by selling it on his own. He cut me a good deal, so I took it."

"Describe this man, Mr. . . . . ?" Ella shot back.

"His name was Montoya. Dark hair, my height, about thirty. Dark eyes. That's about it."

"We *could* call your possession of a stolen vehicle joyriding and you'd probably get a minimum of jail time, if any, but murder means life—unless of course, the jury goes for the death penalty. Lots of people get really upset when a returning vet is gunned down. Are you willing to take a chance in court once the press gets hold of this?"

"I know *nothing* about a murder," he said, then shrugged.

"That's a dumb move. Who are you trying to protect?"

He gave her a thin, grim smile. "You have a murder and you want to blame it on me—but that's not going to happen. I'm not guilty. All the speeches in the world can't prove something that isn't true."

"And once you get to prison, you can tell that to the rest of the lifers. They'll believe you." Ella gave him her bad-cop grin, then waited as he squirmed a while.

"Listen, Benji, you were driving a truck that was carjacked on the Rez. You have phony papers for the vehicle. You add grand theft, possession of stolen property, fraud, and whatever else we can come up with, and you'll lose twenty years of your life if we get a good judge," Ella warned. "And then we add on murder to the list . . ."

"You're not thinking right, *chica*. Carjackers make their living stealing cars and robbing people. Murdering the drivers, well, it's not good for business. Gets way too much attention. Next thing you know, people who'd otherwise give up their car and walk away are scared and fighting back even though their insurance covers it. I mean they've got to—why not fight back if you thought you were going to die anyway? Carjackers and murderers . . . not the same animal. *Comprendes?*"

"A murder took place during a carjacking," Ella answered flatly. "Somebody screwed up. Overreacted. It happens."

"I hear you, but that's not the way things are done. If you want to keep me locked up for buying a stolen car—okay—give it your best shot. Fraud, that's weak. I just had the paper in the glove compartment. I didn't know it wasn't for real. But killing someone over a car—it don't even make sense."

Ella nodded thoughtfully, then left the room. Officer Harvey looked up as she stepped out and relocked the door. "You believe him?"

"He believes it," she said firmly, handing back the keys, then retrieving her weapon. "Which means he knows for a fact that the M.O. of the carjackers doesn't include murder, or he wasn't there, or he's one heckuva liar."

"Benjamin Luna may have just been a courier—delivering the vehicle to a buyer. You mentioned checking out the truck for evidence?" Justine asked Harvey.

He nodded. "Wiped clean, according to the Albuquerque PD crime lab that processed it for us. The only prints there were the driver's. And they found one hair—from a blond wig."

"Have them send me what you've got. I may have a match to the wig hair," Justine answered.

"And see if you can get Luna to offer up the buyer, or maybe the person who's going to sell it out-of-state or out of the country. If you do, we might be able to make some headway, at least with the carjacking ring," Ella said to Officer Harvey.

After a few more minutes spent exchanging details, Ella and Justine left the facility, getting back on the interstate. They were on their way back to the main reservation, northwest of New Mexico's largest city, less than an hour after their arrival.

Ella gave Justine the highlights of her interview with Benji Luna, then Justine reminded her of the meager evidence they'd retrieved on the aborted carjacking the other day.

"I've checked the wig hair we found but it's just a cheap synthetic that several mail-order catalogs offer. I contacted them and asked for a list of customers living in New Mexico and I got over two hundred names—none of them in our immediate area," Justine said.

The ride back to Shiprock would be time consuming, but Ella's thoughts were racing, and she couldn't wait to get back to a more productive activity. "If Luna was telling me the truth, then our suspicions have been right on the mark. Jimmy Blacksheep's murder was a setup, made to look like a carjacking gone wrong."

"But if Jimmy brought contraband with him, and that was a motive for his death, the military's going to be reluctant to share what they know about that with us," Justine said.

"Yeah, but the capital crime was committed on our turf and, for now, the players are all pretty much at home. That'll change soon, so we've got to push forward hard or the killer may slip through our fingers. Clifford struck out, but I'm still hoping Ford can break that blasted code. He's one smart cookie."

"You're really interested in him, aren't you? Nah, don't answer. I already know. It's kinda hard to miss, actually," she teased with a grin. "I saw that look in your eyes the other day after you two spent all that time in his office. That was after you hosed each other off, I might add."

"Speaking of interest, I saw you checking out Officer Harvey's butt, Justine. He's about your age, too. You gonna make a move or are you just window shopping?"

"Changing the subject? You've confirmed my suspicions," Justine said, laughing. "You *are* interested in 'ole Ford, aren't you?"

"I've only seen him on departmental business," she protested.

"But next time it'll be personal. Am I right?" She grinned widely. "Come on, 'fess up!"

Ella laughed. "If you must know, we cut a deal," Ella said, still chuckling. "Apparently, Lila Curtis keeps trying to fix the Reverend up. When I told him I get that from Mom and *her* friends, Ford came up with a plan. I'll pose as his girlfriend at the church rummage sale. Once the gossip takes over, he'll get some breathing room and so will I."

Justine burst out laughing. "How perfect! Now you can take him out for a test drive and see if he's really what you want. And it was *his* idea!"

"It's just a way of getting some people to back off," Ella said, giving Justine her best glare.

"You can give me all the dirty looks you want, but I know sparks when I see them," she said. "You're interested."

"You're *so* irritating," Ella said flatly.

"It's a pain when someone knows you as well as I do, isn't it?" Justine asked happily, not really expecting an answer. "Get ready because it'll be even worse for you when Rose hears."

Ella groaned. "Of that, I have no doubt."

"But on second thought, your father was a preacher, so she can't come at you for that," Justine said. "And, who knows, she might even be relieved."

Ella smiled. "I think Mom'll approve of anyone at this stage, providing he's not currently under indictment. She thinks I've sworn off men."

"Well you have—had."

They lapsed into a thoughtful silence and Ella gazed at the area around them. A few hours later, now late afternoon, she recognized one of her favorite locations off the Rez. They were ten minutes outside Bloomfield, in the very scenic area where the highway wove down and around a series of foothills descending from the high mesa behind them onto the river valley still ahead. The road dropped down, straddling a wide arroyo—more of a narrow valley—crossed a long, low bridge, then rose up onto another hill.

Ella caught a glimpse of a car behind them, flying around the curve they'd just navigated. Monitoring it from the passenger's side mirror, she noted it was speeding up.

Almost intuitively Justine slowed down. "I see him."

There were no other cars on this stretch, at least for now, but as the beige sedan accelerated, Ella glanced at Justine. "Maybe it's a government car, or a gas company honcho late for a meeting. He's doing twenty over the speed limit easy."

As the car came up close, and whipped around to pass them, Ella caught a flurry of movement from the passenger's side and a window being rolled down. "Gun," she yelled, ducking down.

Justine hit the brakes and steered away toward the shoulder, simultaneously crunching into the seat and trying to lower her profile. The sedan flew past, loud pops rattling off in rapid succession.

Glass shattered, and Ella heard several hard thumps and a groan.

"Hang on!" Justine yelled, running off the road onto the shoulder, then onto the dirt. The emergency braking system slowed them down without flipping over the vehicle, and, though they bounced along madly for a hundred yards or more, the vehicle remained upright and didn't careen into the cattle fence enclosing the right-of-way. By the time they came to a full stop, the sedan had disappeared over the hill, no longer a threat at the moment.

Remembering that at one point she'd heard Justine groan, Ella shifted to look at her. "Are you hit, cuz?"

"No, just really short of breath," Justine whispered, sounding like she'd just run ten miles. "Something knocked the wind out of me."

"Check again. *Are you hit!?*"

"I don't . . . think so. Let's go after them!"

Justine tried to urge the car back toward the road, but it just dragged along in the soft earth. "Crap, feels like we've got a flat."

"I'll call it in. *You* check yourself out, just in case." Ella picked up the radio mike and called the county sheriff's dispatch, reporting the incident and the shooter's vehicle description.

Justine unfastened her seat belt, wincing as she shifted to move the seat cushion back. Attuned to her partner, Ella gave Justine a long look. "Feel around your vest for holes or blood. Are you sure you're not hit? He had two pistols, and got off at least six shots, maybe more."

"It hurts . . . ow, here. Okay, I feel it now, beneath my blouse. The vest stopped a round, and it feels like I've been kicked by a horse," she answered, her voice unsteady. "Wait till I catch their sorry asses."

Ella sighed loudly. Blunt-force trauma was sometimes enough all by itself to disable or kill but, overall, vests saved lives. It sure beat being dead, but Justine would be bruised for weeks even if no ribs had been broken.

It was deathly quiet now, except for the *tic tic* of the cooling engine. Suddenly it felt stifling inside the car, and Ella opened her door to let in some fresh air. Ella's gaze passed over the interior of the car, noting the fist-sized hole in Justine's window. She turned to look, and saw another hole in the rear window behind her. One bullet had passed between them.

The drive-by had seemed to take an eternity but, in reality, it had lasted less than five seconds. Of course five seconds was a long, long time, particularly when you didn't know if that last breath would be your last.

Justine was looking around, and pointed to a hole in the door panel just below the window trim. "Where did this one go?"

Ella estimated the position of the shooter, then looked around in the vehicle. She found an impact location just above where her feet had been during the attack, in the right side, forward of the passenger door. "Here it is. I don't see light, so it's probably still around somewhere."

"There's the one that struck my vest, the one that passed between us, and the round down by your feet that came through my door. That makes three. I wonder where the others hit?"

"We'd better check before we get out and make sure we're not going to dump anything important on the ground," Ella said.

"I've already pulled the slug from my vest." Justine held the bullet up, then put it into her jacket pocket. "But what was this all about? Teen gangbangers hitting the wrong car?" Justine asked, checking the door panel and interior within her vision.

"I don't think so. I only got a fast glimpse, but the driver was wearing a ski mask so I couldn't make an ID and the shooter looked big and fit. He was firing those two handguns like some Hollywood perp," Ella answered.

"Good thing you saw it coming in time. If I hadn't hit the brakes and veered off . . ." Justine pointed to the hole in her window. "That might have hit one of us in the throat. Or the one that hit my vest could have gone under my arm instead—and into my spine."

"The sedan was new . . . maybe a Ford, but I can't be sure. The color will help us narrow it down. And there were two men, the driver and the shooter," Ella said.

"Let's see if we can change the tire," Justine said.

"No," Ella said quietly. "It's evidence and county will want things intact. We can get out, though, and look around."

Together, they searched the unit and found another bullet strike, which had clipped the windshield on Ella's side and ricocheted off, but the remaining rounds were still unaccounted for. "Let's see the slug that's going to be leaving the mother of all bruises in your side."

Justine pulled the round back out of her pocket, and held it up again. "That looks like a nine-millimeter, but jacketed. Not a hunting round—maybe military? County might be able to narrow down the weapon a bit once the rifling marks are compared in the lab. It would also help if we could find some shell casings."

"I got the impression the pistols were semiautos, which means the casings were ejected. Chances are that at least a few went out the shooter's window and onto the highway."

Ella looked up as an eighteen wheeler rumbled by, the driver checking them out but not slowing. "If there are any shells in the road, we need to find a few before they get flattened. Set up a perimeter," she called to Justine, then jogged back up the road.

Five minutes later, she found two nine-millimeter shell casings. Picking them up by the rims, wearing latex gloves, she replaced them with quarters over business cards, so the crime team would know where they'd been recovered. With traffic still flowing and no way to stop it without help, it seemed the best move at the time.

Suspecting there were probably more shell casings around, but anxious to check out the vehicle more closely now that she'd recovered at least two, Ella hurried back. They inspected the SUV inside and out, but were unable to find any more bullet strikes or slugs without beginning the process of taking parts off the vehicle.

"Someone followed us—maybe all the way to Albuquerque and back—or at least was watching for our vehicle once we got close. There are only two even remotely reasonable routes into Shiprock from Albuquerque, so it wouldn't have been difficult to do either. But the fact that they came from behind suggests they were with us most of the way," Justine said, her eyes on the rocky soil. "We're still off the Rez, but in the general area where all our suspects live."

"Someone wanted us dead," Ella answered. "Maybe we're getting too close."

"To what? We have nothing," Justine said. "As far as the carjackers go, we don't have any suspects except for the guy Officer Harvey picked up. The carjackers would have nothing to gain by taking us out at this point. And what we have against the local Guard is shaky at best."

"We must be making too many waves then, by asking questions about missing supplies and what went on overseas—things that might lead to much more than the identity of Jimmy Blacksheep's killer or killers."

"So they've upped the stakes," Justine said thoughtfully.

"Exactly."

The county sheriff's deputies showed up in two cruisers, and the county's crime scene unit followed. Ella and Justine assisted, handing over what they'd already collected, and helping recover the slug that had wedged in the car body and one more shell casing, which, unfortunately, had been flattened.

"What do you make of the rounds used?" Ella asked the tech examining the slugs and shell casings.

"They're nine-millimeter, but the one fished from the side panel doesn't match the one that struck Officer Goodluck. The rifling marks are wrong. The same with the ejection marks on the casings. Three we found don't match the fourth." He paused as if lost in thought.

"Tell me what's on your mind?"

"I think the bullet imbedded in the vest was fired from an Astra, but I haven't seen one of those since my service in the first Gulf war. These weapons usually go to low-level Iraqi officers because there aren't enough of the higher-end weapons to go around. The higher ranks, including Saddam himself, usually carried Browning HiPowers—also nine-millimeter. Of course, Astra has imported handguns into the U.S., so we can't be sure until we examine the weapon itself."

"Thanks." Ella reached for her cell phone. Now she had a lead. By trying to kill her and Justine using a weapon obtained in Iraq, the perps might have sealed their fates.

Ella telephoned Blalock and gave him the highlights of what had gone down. "Can you search the databases and see if any weapons issued to the Iraqi military have shown up anywhere in-state?"

"You've got it. How are you getting back, Ella?"

"Neskahi or Tache. I sent word out and whoever can get here first will come get us."

"I'll have something for you as soon as possible," Blalock said, and hung up.

Ella called their own station and, learning Sergeant Neskahi was coming to pick them up, called and updated him. "I need a ride, Joseph, but I'd like to take your wheels and have you stay and work with County. They're about done, I think, and when they're finished I'd like you to bring the car back to our own garage, along with a copy of everything they've learned."

"I'm on it. I'm passing through Farmington now, and should be at your location in a half hour or less," he said.

While they waited, Ella joined Justine, who was helping search for more shells. "I wish I'd seen their license plate," Justine said. "Even if it was stolen, we would have had something else."

"I know, but at the time, you were a little busy saving our lives with your driving skills," Ella said. "It took a lot of courage, staying in control after getting thumped with that bullet. I've felt it before. It's like getting hit with a hammer."

Justine shrugged. "Experience and good training. By the time you think, it's already half over. You know how instincts kick in."

Ella nodded. "But you put something more into it than that, Justine. It's going into my report to Big Ed."

Justine smiled. "Think I'll get a raise?"

"No. Maybe a new vest."

They both started laughing, the pressure finally easing off as it always did once the danger was past.

By the time Neskahi showed up in his squad car, Ella was getting impatient, though it had only been twenty minutes since they'd spoken. The sun had set, and darkness was slowly creeping over the land as Ella and Justine got under way. Justine insisted on driving, giving Ella time to think.

When they reached the outskirts of Shiprock, Ella finally spoke again. "I need to go by Blalock's office, Justine. Are you up to it, or do you want to make a quick stop at the station? You can stay there while I continue on."

"I'm fine. I'll be sore, but I've gone through worse."

Ella's cell phone rang, interrupting Justine. Ella answered it on the first ring.

It was Agent Blalock. "Something important's going down, Ella. How soon before you get back to Shiprock?"

"I'm already here, with Officer Goodluck. We'll be at your office in five."

Just as Ella finished filling Justine in, they spotted a squad car's flashing emergency lights behind them. "Farmington PD," Justine said.

"Then they're way out of their jurisdiction," Ella said, then added, "Pull over. I've got a feeling I know who it is, but he'd better have a good reason. . . ."

They parked on the shoulder, and before they'd even come to a full stop, they saw the officer get out of his unit. Officer Samuel Blacksheep, illuminated by his own headlights, approached.

"I was on my way to a briefing when I heard what went down south of Bloomfield. Guess the shooter missed, huh? You two look okay. But I was wondering, do you think the incident is connected to the carjackings?"

"I doubt it, but we don't know anything for sure yet," Ella

said. "Look we've got to run. We've got a meeting coming up. Is there something you wanted?"

"I've been assigned temporarily to the joint task force that's investigating the carjackings, so we're working together on those cases. I just wanted to let you know right away because, in a pinch, I can cut through all kinds of red tape for you with my department."

All of a sudden she realized that he'd also have access to whatever progress *they* made on the carjacking investigation—the very thing Calvin Sanders had wanted. Since the men were former partners, it made things complicated. She still had persistent doubts about the innocence of either man.

"If you need background information, or anything else, just give me a call," Blacksheep continued. "I've got access to all the files."

"Okay, we'll be in touch," she answered, then leaned back in her seat and nodded to Justine. "Thanks."

Justine drove off quickly, then, after they were a quarter of a mile away, she glanced at Ella. "Is he really trying to be helpful, or was this his way of getting in his jabs—letting us know that he was going to have access to most of what we'd been uncovering?"

"I wish I knew."

The remaining drive took only a few minutes. As they walked down the main hall of the building where Blalock's office was located, they saw Teeny unlocking his own office door. As they waited for him to move out of their way—he practically blocked the narrow hall all by himself—he turned and gave Ella a worried look.

"Hey, ladies. What happened? I was talking to Blalock a while ago, and he said you'd seen some action." His voice was harsh. It was often that way whenever he was really worried about something. Although nothing had ever been said, she'd known since high school that Teeny cared for her.

"Drive-by on the open road," she said. "Poked some holes in my department car."

"With you two inside?" Teeny said in a low baritone, his eyes glazing over with anger.

"Yeah. One of the weapons used is believed to be a nine-millimeter Astra."

"Rare around here, I'd think. If I remember correctly, they look a lot like Walther PPKs, the one James Bond carried in the later books. A small auto."

Justine nodded. "That's the one."

Ella continued. "One of the crime scene unit people said he'd seen a lot of them in Iraq. Reliable, but not fancy enough for higher-ranking officers. I'm wondering if this particular pistol might have come from the Middle East via a G.I. If you hear of anyone trafficking in those, let me know."

"I'll ask around and see what I can get for you."

Hearing her voice, Blalock popped his head out of his office. "Ella, get in here. We're running late," he said and ducked back inside.

As Ella walked in, Justine a step behind, Blalock looked up from his desk, which held two Bureau-issue vests and raid jackets. "You and I are taking a chopper to Albuquerque, courtesy of the Bureau. Do you have a vest handy?"

"I'm wearing it," Ella answered. "Are we going dancing?"

"Oh, yeah. From one party to another tonight, you lucky girl," Blalock said, then glanced at Justine. "I couldn't get clearance for you, too. Big Ed said you were needed here . . . and he thought you might still be a little stiff . . . not to mention jumpy? I don't know about you, but I'm always in a bad mood after getting shot."

"You got that right. And I've got a ton of work waiting at the lab, so I'll leave you two to your . . . business," she said, then looked at Ella, managing a smile. "Call me as soon as you get back."

Ella said good-bye, then heard the sound of a helicopter close by, a relatively uncommon event away from the local hospital. Turning, she saw Blalock pull out his holstered SIG forty-five from the top drawer, along with two extra magazines. He hooked the holster to his belt and slipped the extra ammo into a jacket pocket. "We'll have additional weapons available to us when we land. Our ride's here, so let's go. I'll fill you in on the way."

Ella followed Blalock outside, where the whooshing sound of the rotor blades greeted them, along with a cloud of dust. A state police helicopter had landed less than a hundred feet from the building in an empty parking lot. Ducking low, they ran over and climbed up into their seats behind the pilot and crewman. They were airborne with a stomach-dropping lurch ten seconds after buckling themselves in.

"How about filling me in now?" Ella asked, having to shout a little over the sound of the engine. She was still queasy and trying to look at Blalock, not outside into the empty sky and receding lights far below.

"A sporting-goods shop owner in Albuquerque sold an undercover ATF agent an Astra with Iraqi military markings. There's reason to believe that there are other weapons of interest in there as well, including AK-47s, AKMs, and other variants of the original design. Considering the case you're investigating, and the connection to an Astra, I thought you'd be interested in taking part in this raid."

"Absolutely." Ella thought about the bartered "goods" mentioned in Jimmy's story, obviously not really nails and shoes. If this was a coded reference to illegal weapons trade, they were getting closer. She already knew how high the stakes were after nearly getting killed just a few hours ago.

Ella struggled to sit still and conserve her energy, but adrenalin was coursing freely through her now and her body screamed for action. As the helicopter hurtled through the air at over a hundred miles per hour, she could feel her heart racing nearly as fast. It was a curious fact, but nothing made you appreciate life more than facing the possibility of death.

TWELVE
—— ✖ ✖ ✖ ——

Ella met with a dozen FBI and ATF agents at their office. Everyone was equipped with compatible radios, vests, raid jackets, and caps. Pistols, MP-5 submachine guns, and Armalite M-15 rifles with night vision scopes were the most common weapons in hand. A two-officer sniper team from the state police was burdened with an enormous fifty-caliber autoloading rifle on a bipod.

"The firepower the perps have inside that store is impressive," the senior ATF agent, Jerry Murbach, told them. "I've been inside and, near as I can figure, that place sees action twenty-four/seven. Employees work late into the night after the place is locked up, and someone sleeps in a back room. They also have security cameras set up covering the front and rear exits of the building. Surprise will be difficult to achieve. Expect resistance, and be aware that the perps may be wearing vests, maybe even better than ours. That's what the fifty caliber is for."

Ella checked her own weapons, aware that the others on the team were doing the same. She trusted her pistol in close-range combat more than anything else they'd offered her, and knew a head shot would take anyone down despite body armor. But she'd also qualified with other tactical weapons, including submachine guns. If required, she could handle an MP-5. But it was a room-clearing weapon that allowed for little finesse in selecting targets. It did, on the other hand, provide excellent firepower when clearing out a sniper's nest at close range or encountering a roomful of armed perps.

A half hour later they moved in silently, using a variety of unmarked vehicles, and the teams got into standby position, backed up by APD's SWAT team. The shop was located in the city's north valley, with a major street at the front and a small alley in back. Another row of warehouses lined the street behind the business, most of them closed at this hour, then came the railroad tracks. They'd make their moves simultaneously from front and rear, giving the people inside only a few seconds' notice. Any delays in making an entry would only endanger lives. A city garbage truck coming down the alley would provide walking cover so the rear assault team could get close before being seen. The front assault group was using a city bus to screen them in a similar manner. With a bus stop at the curb right outside, it was the perfect answer.

The first move front and rear would be against the video cameras. A sharpshooter on each team would take out the lenses with a silenced twenty-two using special rounds. Then they would attempt a simultaneous break-in with battering rams. The garbage truck was scheduled to go out of service, so, if it became necessary, they'd use it to crash the back door, which had been reinforced.

Ella crouched next to Blalock. "I hope taking part in the raid will give us dibs on questioning the suspects."

"It'll get you that chance a lot faster than if we'd shown up tomorrow morning with a formal request. ATF doesn't have to cooperate—they're after the guns and they're taking point on this. But I thought you'd want to see this up close and personal, and your own training qualifies you as an expert here. These weapons are now making their way into some big-time gangs working out of Mexico and California, and I think the pipeline starts with your suspects."

"Snipers, take out the cameras!" Ella heard through her radio earphone. She was half jogging, keeping up with the garbage truck as it eased down the alley, screening her and the rest of Team Two from the flat-roofed, one-story brick sporting-goods store to her left. Blalock was a few steps ahead, his MP-5 ready. His weapon could have carried a noise suppressor, but, because the doors would have to be broken down anyway, stealth wasn't going to be an issue except at the beginning. Ella had the submachine gun slung to her right at the waist, ready, but had already decided on her familiar nine-millimeter pistol loaded with armor-piercing rounds.

A low pop from the suppressed twenty-two pistol in the two-handed grip of an ATF sharpshooter was barely discernible over the engine noise from the garbage truck. "Two out," Ella heard, followed instantly by a similar message from the shooter out front. With both cameras down, anyone inside watching a monitor at the moment would react. But until they looked out, whoever was inside had just been blinded. "Execute!" came the order over the earphone.

The truck stopped, and two helmeted men in bulky flak jackets, carrying the heavy battering ram by handholds on both sides, ran up to the back door. Ella and Blalock followed, covering them. Two more officers, with assault rifles, watched the windows and rooftop.

"ATF! Open up!" one of the men yelled.

The ram, basically heavy pipe filled with concrete, came back and hurtled forward, striking the door right above the lock. The door gave an inch, but no more.

"Again!" Blalock yelled, and the big men with the ram swung once more. The door flew open like it was on springs.

"Gun!" Ella yelled, yanking the man in front of her by the back of his vest as a rifle barrel appeared from behind a big wooden box.

Bullets flew from inside, striking the doorjamb and ram, which had suddenly become unmanned as the agents scattered.

When the ram struck the ground the officers behind the truck returned fire, splintering wood from the box that the man inside was using for cover. An assault weapon fell to the floor next to the box, but the shooter had either ducked back or gone down.

"Cover!" Blalock yelled. He paused a second to make sure everyone understood then ducked inside to his right, crouched low. Ella saw a face appear around the corner of the doorway leading into an adjacent room, and fired. The person ducked back, but Ella heard a yelp. She hadn't fired at the face, instead aiming for the wall a foot back from the trim.

"Cover!" Ella yelled. Blalock nodded, his submachine gun covering the passageway beyond. She stepped in, swung around the back of the door, and saw a man flat on his back on the floor, a big bruise on his head. Spotting a pistol near his hand, she kicked it away. "Target down! Storeroom clear!" she called into the radio mike at her throat.

Blalock fired a short burst into the doorway, and Ella turned, seeing a man raising a weapon in the other room. He ducked away, and so did she and Blalock. Ella pulled the door inward, realizing it served as good cover as well as giving those outside a better field of fire. She then holstered the pistol and brought up the submachine gun. Someone out of view sprayed the room with automatic fire, but the angle was wrong and all the rounds hit were the wooden boxes lining the wall. Sand began to pour out from the holes, and she realized the owners had reinforced the walls like a bunker.

Gunfire erupted from elsewhere in the store, and she kept low, aiming toward the door leading into the interior. No targets presented themselves, but it sounded like a real firefight was taking place at the front.

"Team Two, hold position," the call came over the radio. "Flashbangs in five."

Ella started counting, and at four covered her ears and lowered her head. There was a tremendous flash, then an enormous explosion that shook the building. She looked up, weapon up, as two men stumbled into the storeroom, their hands empty.

"Down on the floor," Blalock yelled, aiming at their chests. The men, shaken and dusty, one with blood on his arms, went to their knees, then down on the floor. Ella covered him as Blalock moved forward. Once he was in position and guarding the prisoners she was able to advance.

From her new vantage point, Ella could see into the next room, the main display area of the store. The air was hazy and the stench of cordite, strong. She could see a leg sticking out from behind a counter, but the person was faceup, probably wounded or dead, and the leg wasn't moving. Ella realized it was probably the person who'd stuck his head around the corner to look. Silently, she hoped to find a gun in his hand, or nearby, when she finally made it into the room. Killing an unarmed man would make her upcoming nightmares even worse.

Suddenly there was a shout, a short burst from an automatic weapon, then a loud bang. Ten seconds went by. Ella and Blalock remained in position, ready to engage anyone from the front who might still be mobile and thinking of moving in their direction.

"Front room clear! Take the prisoners into custody, then get the medics in the building," Ella heard Murbach say over the radio.

Blalock stood, his weapon on the two prisoners as their backup came in from the alley. "You take any hits, Clah?"

"No."

"Something bothering you?" Blalock motioned for the ATF guys to cuff the prisoners, then came over to where she was standing.

Ella realized she still had the submachine gun facing forward, so she lowered it on the sling until the barrel was facing down. "Yeah. But I gotta see something for myself."

She stepped around the men on the floor, brushed by the closest ATF man, who nodded grimly, then looked into the front room. Officers wearing raid jackets were all around the room, talking and searching for weapons. She could see two perps down, dead or dying. They'd been armed to the teeth, judging from the assault rifles close by and dozens of rounds of spent brass scattered over the floor. A third man, wearing a helmet, tattered and bulky vest, and some kind of metal thigh protection, was on his back beside the shattered door, a bloody hole in his chest. What appeared to be an AK-47 was close to his lifeless hands. He'd tried to rush the front, apparently, and had come face-to-face with the state police team and their big rifle. Finally she walked back to the spot by the storeroom passageway she'd been avoiding, but there was no body there.

"You looking for the guy on the floor?" an FBI agent Ella vaguely recognized said, coming across the room.

"Yeah. He still alive?" Ella managed, not seeing any blood on the floor.

"Lucky SOB. He's outside, in custody. Nearly peed his pants. According to him, one of you Team Two guys shot the pistol right out of his hand . . . through the wall! That wasn't you, was it?"

Ella nodded, a stupid grin forming on her face. Now, the nightmare would be a lot easier to take.

"Ella?" Blalock called from the doorway. "You ready to meet with Murbach?"

She followed Blalock back into the storeroom, where the ATF man who'd led the raid was examining the boxes stacked around the room. "I know they've got what we're looking for in here someplace, but all that's in these crates so far is sand. They had Iraqi-stamped Astras, Brownings, various models of AK assault rifles—fully auto, and more. My guess is they stashed them inside heating ducts, vaults in the floor, behind cabinets, or in the ceiling. Check everywhere you can think of. We've got three wounded men, and one of them might not make it to the hospital. I'm not leaving this hellhole until I find the cache."

Two hours passed, and the evidence had all been processed and the wounded and dead removed from the scene. Officers were still searching, but except for the weapons the perps had used in the firefight, nothing had turned up yet that wasn't part of the legal inventory of the business.

As the search teams met at the doorway between the display area and storeroom, frustration was evident on everyone's face. The adrenalin was wearing down, and everyone seemed dead tired.

"We've searched everywhere," one ATF agent grumbled. "It's obvious they moved the stuff."

"One more pass," Murbach ordered. "It's here. Why else make a stand like that?"

Ella watched a few heads shaking. They'd already searched the obvious and less obvious. But if ATF Agent Murbach was right, the guns were here—somewhere. She looked around the room, trying to see if anything looked out of place, and, as her gaze strayed over the new-looking, very large refrigerator, she decided to take a closer look. Officers had looked inside several times, directed a light beneath and behind, and always walked away. But she had to see for herself. Inside were several cans of beer, and what looked to be a leftover sandwich.

"Clah, whatcha got?" Blalock said, coming up to her. "You're not thirsty, and I can hear the little wheels in your brain working overtime."

"Look at the size of this thing, and it must be brand new. Why would anyone put this large of a fridge in here for just a few cans of beer? There's a diner at the end of the block. Help me move this thing out."

Blalock grasped one side and tried to move it forward while she pushed from the opposite side. "Ya couldn't have picked a desk, Clah?"

Seeing them struggle, two other agents came to help. "What are we looking for?" the taller one asked.

"The reason why this thing is really here," Ella answered.

"There's no hidden space behind the refrigerator," he pointed out. "I checked with a flashlight an hour ago. No secret panels either."

"Humor me," she said, putting her shoulder against it. The problem was that the fridge was wedged between two built-in counters. And wedged was the word. It seemed to have been glued in place.

"Is this thing stuck in cement?" muttered the younger Hispanic agent.

"We need to wriggle it back and forth, loosen up the space, then walk it out," Ella said.

Another agent came over to help and, working in tandem, they finally managed to move it forward. As it came away from the wall, only a large, empty space remained.

"Oh, yeah, this was a brilliant idea," an ATF agent behind her muttered.

Ella climbed up over the counter and slipped past the fridge into the area they'd just uncovered. "The space beneath a refrigerator is usually grungy and dirty as hell."

"My wife would say something like that," one of the agents cracked.

"Maybe you should help her clean the house instead of sitting around making wise-ass comments," Ella shot back, crouching down.

"I hear a voice, but I don't see anyone," the agent responded, and a few officers laughed.

Ella ran her hand over the floor. The outline of the press-on tiles had obscured it, but she could see things more clearly from this close-up position. "This floor was recently redone. I bet there's a trapdoor beneath me," Ella said, standing up into view again.

She'd spoken softly but there was an instant flurry of activity and several agents came over. Everyone was suddenly wide awake again.

"Move that fridge completely out of the way. Now!" Agent Murbach barked.

Five minutes later, an expertly designed trapdoor was uncovered beneath a layer of tiles. It had been glued into place, but the work was so recent the glue was still pliable, and agents were able to pry the door open. A wooden ladder led to a large area below. Covering each other, Agent Murbach and one of his men descended, followed by Ella and Blalock. Locating a cord with his flashlight, Murbach turned on an overhead lightbulb. The large, carved-out, earthen basement held at least fifty weapons inside plastic storage boxes of every size. There were pistols, automatic weapons—mostly assault rifles of foreign manufacture—and even several Russian-made sniper rifles. A few boxes contained military-issue ammunition.

A quick search revealed no additional hiding places or possible exits, and an old trapdoor with a handle attached was standing in the corner.

"Welcome, Hole-Mart shoppers. Here in our basement complex, you can find weapons for everyone on your shopping list," Ella said in a familiar singsong voice.

"If you have the cash," Blalock added, matching her tone, "you can equip the entire gang with more firepower than the average police force."

"Most of these weapons aren't U.S. made, which tends to narrow down the source, doesn't it?" Murbach said.

"Some of the markings have been filed down, but you're right," one of the ATF agents commented. "Most still have the country of origin—Iraq."

Ella and Blalock exchanged quick glances. "Was the owner of this shop in the military, say, within the past few years?" Ella asked Blalock.

"No, but all these arms were in somebody's army recently. I'd be interested in finding out how they got here."

"You and me both, Blalock," ATF Agent Murbach added, holding up a plastic storage box containing several ornately carved pistols. Ella could see Arabic markings on most of them.

Another two hours went by before Ella and Blalock were finally allowed a turn at questioning the store owner—and that was mostly because no one else had been able to get anything out of him. He'd played dead, apparently, when the shooting started, and it was his foot Ella had seen earlier behind the counter.

Ella sat across from the suspect. "Remaining silent is only going to ensure you end up in prison. If the wounded ATF agent dies, it'll be capital murder, too. If that happens, no one is going to offer you a lifeline. You realize that, right?"

"I have no idea what you're talking about."

"Those guns were there in *your* shop. You can't deny that."

"I'm as surprised as you are about that. I knew about the cellar, of course, but I never realized someone had hidden guns in there. I only deal in legal weapons sales and service."

"Right, so why did you resist arrest?" Ella pressed.

"Our security cameras went out, then somebody broke in armed to the teeth. We thought we were being robbed. That's why we defended ourselves. Our lives were on the line. Nobody ever heard anyone identify themselves as the police, so we just reacted to the threat."

"*That's* your story?" Ella said, staring at him.

"It's the truth, ma'am," he said with a smug smile. "When my lawyer comes in tomorrow morning, he'll make sure I'm vindicated."

"Several officers were wired for sound. The warning and notification of our identity comes out quite clear when you play it back," Blalock pointed out, holding up his own digital recorder.

"Recorded somewhere else, obviously at another time, to cover your butts while you storm troopers trampled over the Constitution."

"Bet we can find some fingerprints, Ella," Blalock said. "It would be hard to place all those weapons and boxes down there without leaving any. And what about that old trapdoor?"

The store owner shrugged.

"Just one more question. It's an easy yes or no. Or you can just nod. Did you serve in the Army, Reserves, or National Guard?" Ella asked.

"Me? No way. Put my life on the line for somebody else's political agenda? Do I look stupid?"

This time Ella was the one who shrugged. Shaking her head, she turned, heading for the door. Suddenly she stopped, and glanced back at him. "I bet we'll get some answers when we learn where you went to school, who your friends were, and when you graduated."

His expression suddenly became guarded. "I'm not saying anything else until my lawyer gets here," he said in a flat voice.

Once they were out of the room, Blalock gave her a thumbs-up. "You scored a hit on that last one. But what were you after?"

"I think we should cross-reference him against our local suspects who just returned from Iraq and see if we can find a link between him and them."

After reporting what they'd learned to the ATF, Ella paced in the hall, sipping coffee. "It's almost five in the morning, I haven't had any sleep, but I'm still too jazzed to wind down."

"I hear you. But my bones are older than yours," Blalock said. "I'm better off sitting than pacing. So what do you say we head home? I know a helicopter pilot . . ."

They ended up catching a red-eye commercial flight back to Farmington, and, by the time they landed, Ella could feel the first twinges of exhaustion despite having caught a half hour catnap. "I think I'm going to need a ride home. You renting a car?"

Blalock nodded. "Yeah, but Justine is waiting for you. I sent word ahead."

Ella saw the cruiser Neskahi had provided for them hours ago parked in the lot reserved for service vehicles, Justine at the wheel. "Some partners are worth their weight in gold."

It was barely six-thirty and the sun was perched on the horizon, bathing the desert in a rose-tinted glow as Ella left the Shiprock station. The barren, rocky landscape shimmered in that early light. It was at dawn that the desert was at its most beautiful. Her mother would be outside now, saying prayers to Sun and offering pollen as a blessing.

As Ella drove home, now in her own vehicle, the bluish purple of the sky and the presence of the sacred mountains that guarded the *Diné Tah* filled her with peace. People and animals all came and left, but the earth remained, giving life and waiting to welcome in death.

She was less than a mile from home when her cell phone rang. Ella muttered a curse, wishing she'd failed to replace the battery back in Albuquerque. She'd been feeling decidedly mellow, but now that was undoubtedly about to end. Early morning phone calls usually meant trouble.

This time, her instincts were off the mark. Hearing Ford's voice at the other end made her smile. "Did you break the code?" she asked, quickly dispensing with amenities. Surely there was no other reason he would have called so early in the day.

"I've got some ideas, Ella, but I need to talk some things over with you first. Can we meet at the Totah Cafe for breakfast?"

"Sure," she said, turning the cruiser around. "But I should warn you I haven't gone to bed yet, and I smell like gunpowder."

"Wonderful," he said, laughing. "The scent of danger and a beautiful female all in one. Who can resist?"

"Then I'll see you at the Totah."

As she hung up, she smiled for the second time in a minute.

She liked Bilford Tome's style. But she had to stay focused. The important thing now was breaking Jimmy Blacksheep's code and finding out what secrets he'd hidden in his story. She wondered if Ford had managed to make some sense out of it, or if all he'd come up with was more theories.

By the time she arrived at the Totah, it was six forty-five, but the 24/7 diner was already primed for breakfast customers. Ella parked the cruiser and was just getting out when an old green pickup came up the road, slowed, then picked up speed again and continued down the street.

Ella recognized the young men inside immediately. Tony Henderson and Winston Brownhat were in the Many Devils, and although out of high school now, they were too lost to know what to do with their lives. They'd probably been out partying, drinking, or up to no good all night and hadn't been to bed yet today . . . or was that yesterday?

She was still watching the truck when Reverend Tome drove up in his sedan, parking beside her. Ella smiled for the umpteenth time, and stepped up onto the sidewalk beside the door to wait.

"Good morning again, Ella," Ford called. "You thinking of going back to traffic duty?"

"Huh? Oh, no, I was just watching that pickup. Couple of gang members in there, probably looking for trouble."

"I know who you're talking about. North Siders, right?"

"No, and don't say that around them. That was Winston Brownhat and Tony Henderson. Many Devils—hardcore."

"Good to know. By the way, I've heard that the gangs are starting the turf battles again, leaning on people in the neighborhoods, trying to impress and intimidate."

"I'll have to pass that along. Maybe all the attention the carjackings have been getting has hurt their image." Ella turned around, hearing a vehicle coming up the road at high speed.

"Here they come again," Ford said. "Whatever happened to low, slow riding?"

The green truck with the young men inside pulled up on the other side of Ella's department unit, sliding to a halt in the gravel.

"Hey, guys, slow it down in the parking lot, will you?" Ella said, tired and not in the mood to babysit nineteen-year-old hoods.

"Hey, Clah. We need to talk. Wanna go for a ride?" Tony yelled out.

Ella didn't move, but she waved. "I'm too hungry for a road trip. How about here?"

The young men exchanged glances, then got out of the pickup and walked over.

"What's up, guys?" Ella asked.

"Not in front of the Rev, okay, Clah? And not in public. What about taking a walk with us down toward the river if you're not in the mood for a drive?" Tony reached for her arm.

Ella remained still.

"Boys, don't worry about me. You can talk here, or inside. I'll give you some privacy," Ford said.

"Butt out, Rev. We've got it covered," Tony said, motioning to Winston, who stepped around to the other side of Ella.

"What's your problem, Tony?" Ella demanded. "You can trust Reverend Tome not to put your business on the street."

"We need to talk to you *alone*," Winston answered. "Maybe you can get in the truck and the Rev can go inside a while. We'll stay in the lot."

Ella considered the strategy that would work best without a fight, but she wasn't going anywhere with these guys alone, and once she got in the truck, she'd be cornered. As she was trying to figure out her next move, Tony grabbed her arm.

Ford reacted instantly, executing a painful nerve pinch that sent Tony to the ground, squealing like a pig on a hot wire. Winston stepped up with a roundhouse punch, but before Ella could run interference, Ford spun around ninety degrees and landed a solid kick into Winston's groin.

Ella quickly handcuffed both disoriented teens to the door handles of their own pickup. "Hey, guys, now your reputation is clean. Nobody will accuse you of sucking up to the cop."

Looking over at Ford, she smiled and said, "Let me guess—you took personal defense at divinity school."

He shrugged, saying nothing, which didn't come as a great shock.

After frisking the two frustrated gangbangers, removing two knives and a set of handmade brass knuckles, then calling in for backup, Ella glanced at Ford. "These boys aren't going anywhere, Reverend, and I doubt they're going to be vandalizing their own pickup while waiting for a ride to jail. So why don't we grab a quick breakfast?"

The boys began yelling at her in unison, and Ella gave a thought to the patrons inside the restaurant, who were probably hoping to eat breakfast in peace. But just then, a patrol unit with Officer Michael Cloud arrived. "Book them for assault on a police officer," Ella told him. "I'll be in later this morning to do the paperwork."

Ella helped him transfer the suspects, then went inside the Totah with Ford. They'd just sat down and had reached for their menus when Lila Curtis came rushing over.

"I saw what happened!" said the middle-aged Navajo woman. Ella knew Lila was an incurable gossip, and that the story would be all over the Four Corners by noon. If the M.D.'s were looking for publicity, they'd get it now.

Remembering that this was also the person who'd kept fixing Ford up, and the one he'd hoped to convince that she and he were an item, Ella gave Ford an extra sweet smile, then reached over and patted him innocently on the hand. "The Reverend certainly moves fast in a crisis."

Lila gave her a curious look, then shifted her gaze back to Ford. "But Reverend, resorting to violence?" she asked. "Is that the *Christian* thing to do?"

"I prayed first, of course, and that was what I was led to do. The boys were attempting to use force and intimidate two innocent people, maybe even kidnap someone. I couldn't allow that and remain true to my faith. I won't attack someone, but when someone else begins an attack I *am* allowed to defend others to the best of my abilities."

"Of course." Lila looked at Ella, then back at him and smiled. "So I guess I won't have to find you a date anymore?" Wordlessly, Ford reached for Ella's hand, and Lila gave him a sad smile. "Too bad. I have a niece who's visiting from Gallup, and I would have loved to have you over for dinner. Maybe some other time."

As she moved away, Ford sighed with relief. "I just dodged a seriously large bullet. Lila is a good woman, but her mutton stew is just plain awful and that's all she ever fixes."

Ella laughed softly. "Actually this works for me, too. Mom will hear about us in an hour or so, if Lila's communication skills are up to par. Of course Mom'll be convinced that there's something going on—particularly if I deny it," she added, laughing. As their eyes met, Ella felt the powerful current of attraction between them. It was almost a physical pull—the electric rush that happened between the right man and woman. But there was more at play now than a physical attraction. She actually enjoyed Ford's company a great deal.

They kept their topic neutral until Lila left the Totah, knowing how sharp her hearing was reputed to be. Breathing a sigh of relief as she strode out the door, Ella gave Ford a nod. "Now we can talk freely, so tell me what you've learned about the code."

"I haven't broken it, but I think I've got the key. Our Navajo Codetalkers made up their own terms for objects such as fighters, bombers, machine guns, and tanks, because there was no Navajo equivalent. I think that's what Jimmy did with the nails, umbrellas, and such. We already suspect that the animals represent real people. So we need to find out who within his Army section or platoon, or associates, might have Trickster's attributes—someone who appears to be one thing but is another. Unless Jimmy picked some less obvious link between real person and animal. The story has a pattern—maybe more than one. In my opinion, he's used more than one code to conceal the message from the casual reader."

"A modernist who searches for the pattern," she teased. "You and my brother have more in common than you think."

He shook his head. "Patterns are in every discipline—math, physics, politics. What separates your brother and me is rooted in incompatible ideologies and theologies. Common ground is not possible, not even at the most basic level. The most we can hope for is respect and tolerance."

She remembered her father, and how he'd felt about her mom's beliefs. In some ways, Ford and her father were cut from the same cloth. The thought disturbed her on some deep, visceral level. She wasn't about to repeat the mistakes of the past, especially not those of her own parents.

They ate breakfast slowly and, by the time they finished, Ella was aware of the intense weariness creeping over her. It was always that way after a night of action. When the adrenaline stopped flowing, total exhaustion set in. "I'm going to have to go home and get some sleep. I'm winding down fast."

"You look beat," he agreed with a nod.

"Gee, thanks so much for the flattery. I'll try not to let it go to my head," she teased.

He laughed, then, after insisting on paying for breakfast, walked her to her cruiser.

"You'll need to give a statement about what happened here," Ella told him.

"My pleasure. I'll go to the station next. It's on my way, so it's no problem."

"Justine should be there. Ask her to help you," Ella said.

Ella got underway soon, driving a bit slower than usual because she knew her responses and senses were reduced. It took her an extra five minutes to make the journey south from Shiprock and by the time she got home, she found Rose cleaning up in the kitchen.

Rose glanced up and saw Ella walk wearily toward the fridge and pour herself a glass of juice. "I've been so worried about you!" Rose said. "I was about to send out a search party. Why didn't you call?"

"Mom, it's been one thing after another," she said, giving her the general highlights, but no details. "Where's my daughter?" she asked, looking around. "Wasn't there a teacher in-service today? No school for the kids."

"Yes, but your daughter wanted to spend the day with her father, so she called him last night and he came over to pick her up."

Ella rubbed the back of her neck with one hand. "Was there a special reason she was so eager to go over there?"

"He has a very fancy computer and a color printer. She wanted to use it to make up a chart she needs for her science class." Rose took a deep breath. "That's the bad news. But there's good news. It seems she's doing a paper on Navajo medicine plants. She even asked me for a medicine bundle she can carry with her."

Ella smiled. Dawn was interested in almost everything these days, and her moods fluctuated as often as the weather. Despite that, she could understand why Rose was pleased. Her mother had great hopes that Dawn would become a member of the Plant Watchers someday. But, in her gut, Ella knew that Dawn would never follow in anyone's footsteps. She'd be blazing her own trail. Watching her daughter grow up was like seeing a beautiful, unique flower develop and blossom. Ella hated to miss even one day of her daughter's path to adulthood. She looked around the room, missing Dawn's presence.

"You're worried she'll continue drifting more toward her father and less toward you," Rose observed.

"I'm a little worried," she admitted. "Kevin's legal hold on her is tenuous. Since we never married, he can't claim the rights of fatherhood in a court of law without making a big, public noise and I don't think it's in him to do that. But I'm sure he's hoping that Dawn will decide on her own that she wants to live with him at least part time. If that happens, my trying to stop her is only going to make an already impossible situation even worse."

"So what's your plan?" Rose asked.

"I can be flexible. He could take her for a few days here and there when I'm working a case, particularly once you're not here, and longer times during the summer. But I want her the rest of the time. I'm prepared to fight for that."

"Your daughter's father has always thought in terms of black and white. Mine or not mine. Legal or illegal. Convincing him to do what's best for all—to adapt and flow with the rhythms of life—is going to be a tough sell. He's just not that flexible."

"Yeah, Mom, I know." Ella yawned. She couldn't think straight anymore. She had to go to bed, or she'd fall asleep standing up.

"Go get some rest, daughter. Then, when you wake up, you can tell me all about Reverend Tome."

Ella's eyes popped wide open. To think she'd believed that it would take hours for her mom to find out. She'd vastly underestimated Lila's broadcasting system.

THIRTEEN

— ✖ ✖ ✖ —

Ella woke up a little after 2 P.M. even though the house was quiet. Truly sound, restful sleep wouldn't come until a day or so after the case was over and all the questions still roaming through her mind were settled.

After washing up, she went into the kitchen in search of something to eat, and saw her mother working at the table. "What's that?" Ella asked, peering over her shoulder.

"My wedding list, but the more I think about it, the less I like the idea of making this into a big event—or an event at all. *Bizaadii* and I are both on limited incomes, and we're not young people embarking on a new life. The end of our life's walk is nearer now than the beginning, so one looks at things differently, I suppose. To spend truckloads of money on a wedding . . . well, it doesn't seem right. We're too old for all that nonsense."

"So what's on your mind? Do you want to elope?"

"You almost did." Rose smiled.

"And you and Dad waited until the last moment to decide to come, remember? He was offended because I didn't get married in his church, and you were annoyed that my husband and I chose to have the ceremony at his cousin's house with the military chaplain."

Rose was still smiling. "A Navajo wedding *would* have been

nice. But you were still a vision of beauty in that white Irish lace dress."

Ella couldn't help but blush. "A borrowed dress, actually. I never told you, did I? You were just pleased that Dad said it was hard to decide which of us looked the most beautiful that day."

Rose grinned even wider. "All true."

Ella sighed. "Well, if you do decide to elope, at least give me a heads-up so I'll know it's coming."

"The only thing holding me back is your daughter and my son's son. I know I already have the blessing of you and your brother no matter what I choose to do, but I'm thinking that my two grandchildren should see a ceremony. It'll help them accept *Bizaadii* as their grandfather." She paused. "And I'd like you and your brother there, too." Rose stood and went to the refrigerator.

"Mom, if you want a small ceremony, go for it. You're calling the shots. It's *your* wedding."

"Do you *really* feel that way?" Rose asked, holding her gaze and searching her daughter's heart.

"Sure, Mom. This is *your* day. But as long you're asking me what I want . . . I sure wish *Bizaadii* would just move in with us. This house is large enough to accommodate one more person. And, best of all, we'd still be together. My daughter's lived with you all her life. She's really going to miss you."

"I know. I've already spoken to her about this. And it'll be hard on me, too, you know. Having her around keeps me feeling young."

"Then stay," Ella said.

Rose, filling a tortilla with food taken from the fridge, shook her head. "*Bizaadii* doesn't feel comfortable being here since your father lived here with me once." She paused, then added, "I wouldn't feel comfortable either."

Ella nodded slowly. "I understand, Mom. I just wish . . ."

"I know."

While Rose sipped herbal tea, Ella ate the burrito her mom had prepared for her. Once finished, Ella took her plate to the sink and washed it off. "I have to go back to work now, but if my daughter returns, give me a call. I need to have a talk with her."

"About staying with her father?" Seeing Ella nod, Rose added, "Would you like me to explain that she should get our permission first *before* calling her father and asking him to pick her up?"

Ella considered it for a moment then shook her head. "No, let me talk to her about this myself. I want to make sure she understands that last-minute plans only put added pressure on *all* the adults in her life."

"The problem is that she's learned her father will buy her whatever she wants. She goes over there in search of *things*. There are feelings involved all around, mind you, but I don't think she looks that deeply into the consequences. She just goes with the moment."

"I'll handle it," Ella said.

"Oh, one more thing. Remember that Boots will be leaving for a two-week vacation in a day or so. She's decided to go to Albuquerque instead of Denver. But we'll still keep the schedule we worked out earlier. I'll be able to take care of my granddaughter."

"I know we discussed this, but are you sure, I mean with the wedding and all . . ."

"It'll be fine."

In transit to the station, Ella called in and Justine answered and updated her. "Reverend Tome came in and gave us his statement. But Winston and Tony are still insisting on talking to you— and you alone."

"What about?"

"I don't know. Joe questioned them, but could only get scraps of information before they shut down completely. All I can tell you for sure is that they want you to get in contact with the leaders of the Many Devils. We're not sure if that's because they have information about carjackings or if they're making a move to assert themselves in the community. Joe followed up by trying to question Joey Neskahi, his nephew, but the kid has taken off. Joe's sister told him that he'd called, telling her he wouldn't be home for another day or so."

"What are the gangs up to now?" Ella said thoughtfully, not expecting an answer.

"Hopefully, we'll know more after you get here. I've already got the guys staring at the walls in the interview rooms."

Ella arrived at the station less than ten minutes later. As she walked in, she saw Justine slapping the side of the vending machine.

"Give me my candy bar!" Justine roared, and then kicked the machine on the side. A second later, the candy bar fell down with a thud. "That's better."

"Talking to machines now, partner?"

Justine gave her a sheepish smile. "It always takes my money, but after that it gets snarky about giving me what I paid for. A good, swift kick works wonders."

"How do you eat so many candy bars and not gain an ounce?" Ella asked, wishing the same could have been said about her. Gaining weight was becoming too easy these days, probably because she hadn't been out jogging in forever.

"I burn it up in our weight room and by running the high school track at night. Well, that, and I've switched over to the low-cal bars."

Ella pointed to the chocolate-and-almond bar Justine was unwrapping. "In what planet is that considered low cal?"

"I'm not a fanatic, Ella. Everyone needs a perk once in a while," she answered with a sheepish grin.

"You're hopeless," Ella said, then walked with her to the interrogation rooms. Standing by the one-way glass, she looked in on each and made her choice. "This one first, Tony. He looks like he's crawling out of his skin."

"We put him in there an hour ago."

"Good." Ella was reaching for the doorknob when Blalock came down the hall.

"I heard about the incident and picked up some vibes from Sergeant Neskahi. Mind if I go in with you? You never know what these kids have managed to uncover by way of information. With luck, we may get a lead or two about either the carjackings or the case involving Jimmy Blacksheep."

"Sure, come on," she said. "Let's see how the Many Devils fit into the big picture."

They walked inside while Justine remained behind, watching through the one-way glass. At first Ella said nothing, studying the kid. He was still wearing the gang's colors and standard-issue dress—long-sleeved T-shirt and baggy pants. "Okay, Tony," she said at last. "I get it. You don't want to talk to anyone but me. So here I am. What's going down?"

"Who're you, Anglo?" he challenged, looking at Blalock. "I'm talking to Clah—not you."

"This is Agent Blalock with the FBI. And in case you haven't noticed, this is *my* turf. If I say he's in, he's in." Ella sat down across the small table from Tony and leaned back in her chair. Blalock remained standing by the door. "You want out of this jail someday, don't you?" Ella added. "Give me a reason to get the charges reduced."

Tony scowled, stared at the handmade tatoos on his arm for about a minute, then finally nodded. "I've heard that your cops were thinking we had something to do with these carjackings. But that's crap. Those guys are poaching on our turf and disrespecting us. One way or another, we're going to shut 'em down. That puts you and me on the same team."

"Convince us," Blalock said.

Tony looked through Blalock as if he wasn't there, then turned to Ella. "You know we can't have these guys operating on our turf. The other gangs will think we're weak, and make a move on us. Without respect, you're nothing."

Ella made a show of yawning. "Get to the point."

"You need help finding them, right?"

"So you came to get my attention by trying to push me and Reverend Tome around?" she said, giving him an open look of skepticism.

"Don't look right sucking up to a cop."

"Of course," Ella said with a straight face.

"Forget about all that now, Clah. Just think of what we have to offer you. We've got contacts everywhere. We *knew* when you left the Rez and when you came back. Some of our people were keeping an eye out. How do you think I found you at the Totah?"

"Chance?"

He shook his head. "I drove by the place to check out the scene, then came back to talk. I already knew where to find you. If our guys start looking around for the carjackers, we can spot them too and get you on the scene while it's still going down—if you move fast. Then you can take care of them. And to show our good faith we've come with something to trade."

"If you had been up front with me this morning, you could have been sipping a cold one right now and kicking back instead of sitting in a cell."

"Yeah, well. We have business with the Reverend, too. He's got to learn not to be messing with us. He's been screwing us over by talking to the Fierce Ones."

Ella nodded. The Fierce Ones were a bunch of adults—essentially a vigilante group—who'd banded together to take parts of the reservation back from the youth gangs. They were an impressive power and, though they worked outside the law, they managed to accomplish more than the police sometimes. Pressure on the parents of troubled kids, along with more direct action, had led to violence being curtailed and the reduction of crimes against the general public, especially vandalism and theft. These days, the gangs mostly strutted around and talked big, which, as far as Ella was concerned, they were welcome to do.

"So you wanted to lean on Reverend Tome?" Ella pressed.

"Yeah. But who knew he was the Navajo Jackie Chan?"

"Okay, enough chitchat. What's your good-faith offer?" Blalock said, this time getting well inside Tony's space.

"Word's come down that the carjackers are feeling the heat from all the cops, so they're switching tactics."

"Where'd you get this?" Blalock shot back.

Tony shook his head.

"We need to know," Ella insisted. "Is one of the Many Devils in with the carjackers?"

"No way. We tried and got word out onto the street, but . . . nada."

"So, how do you know they've changed tactics?" Blalock repeated. "If you want our trust you're going to have to give us more."

"Whatever," he muttered. "No names, but one of the Many Devils got nailed by the Farmington cops for DWI and while in lock-up heard some stuff."

"Are you saying that one of the carjackers was in jail for a separate offense?" Ella pressed him.

He shook his head. "Word just gets around. The 'jackers have everyone's respect. They've been making fools out of the police, and they don't rat out their people. The one the state cop nailed over by Albuquerque? He still hasn't told you jack, has he?"

Ella stood up. "You better be playing it straight with me, Tony."

"Winston'll tell you the same thing. Ask him."

"I intend to," Ella said. Then she knocked on the door and Justine let her and Blalock out. "You heard?" Ella asked.

"Yeah. So what are you going to do?" Justine said.

"Talk to Winston. Then, if the stories match, I've got an idea."

"Tell me that doesn't include accepting their help," Blalock said.

"Call it recruiting an informant, then. The way I see it, Tony had a point. They have lookouts and contacts everywhere, and our department can't cover all the roads. The fact that they knew where I was impresses me, since I made the decision to go to the Totah at the last minute. That's good intel."

"Unless they just got lucky," Blalock said, shaking his head. "But we do need to make some headway on this, that's for sure."

Winston told them basically the same story. Since Tony had already managed to find an adult to bail him out, they released him so he could carry the news to the other gang members. Winston, whose relative was still trying to raise the cash, would have to wait.

"I hope you know what you're doing," Blalock said, as they watched Tony drive off with his neighbor. "I wouldn't trust any of those punks for a bleeping second."

"It's not about trust, it's about opportunity. We have to cut some corners, remember? If any of the National Guard soldiers are tied up in this, we've got to nail them before the Army ships them to Germany," Ella reminded him.

After Blalock strode off, still skeptical, Ella turned to Justine. "Time to reorganize the hunt. Call the team. We meet in my office in a half hour."

Once Neskahi and Tache joined them, Ella filled everyone in on what had transpired since their last contact. "So here's the deal. We have a ticking clock running with the Nation Guard suspects. Jimmy's killer may soon be out of the country if he's a soldier with that transportation company. According to Chief Warrant Officer Carson, those men are all going to be recalled, so we have to speed up this investigation. Unfortunately, all we have on motive is what's in the partially written story we got from the victim himself. Jimmy was obviously trying to tell us something, but, so far, we haven't been able to break his code. And either he never finished the story, planning to tell us the rest in person, or the other half is already in the hands of the bad guys. If so, it's probably lost forever. What I need now is your feedback. Anyone have any ideas on where to go from here?"

"We've done everything by the book, taken each logical step, and processed and followed up on every piece of evidence we've managed to track down," Justine said. "Maybe we need to start thinking outside the box."

Ella nodded slowly, then met her gaze. "You've just given me an idea. You know the package that came from Jimmy?" Seeing her nod, she continued. "That came overnight express. The box is in the evidence room. Get me the tracking label number."

Five minutes later, Ella was at her computer, the other three officers looking over her shoulders as she logged on to the delivery services Web site. By subtracting one digit from the tracking number, searching, and then by adding one digit and searching again, she hoped to find out if Jimmy had sent out another package to someone else at the same time and place. The forms used were probably sequential if he'd sent more than one at the same time.

Subtracting a number only got her information about a package sent from the El Paso mailing address to an office-supply place in Denver, Colorado. But when she added one digit, she got the answer she wanted.

"Here it is. Jimmy *did* mail a second package. It went to the Farmington Police Station, and the recipient was his brother—Officer Samuel Blacksheep."

"But Samuel told us he hadn't been in touch with his brother in months, except for e-mails and a phone call or two," Justine recalled.

"So either he's lying, or someone intercepted the package—which would mean we've got another player at the station. I haven't scratched Sergeant Sanders off the suspect list, and he was Jimmy's lieutenant. This news also doesn't rule out the possibility of woman problems between the brothers. If what we're dealing with is a group of crooked cops, some of them also soldiers in the Guard, it's possible Samuel's been in on it from the start and Jimmy didn't know about his brother's participation. In sending this story, or part of it to Samuel, Jimmy may have made a fatal mistake. Brothers have been killed over money as well as women."

"Agreed," Neskahi said. "But I think the real bottom line is that we have to be careful who we trust outside our own PD. If the Farmington police have some of their own personnel involved in carjackings, or a smuggling op of some sort involving local soldiers, there's no telling who we can trust."

"The carjacking that resulted in Jimmy's death was simply a copycat crime, a way to take advantage of what was already happening, to muddy up the trail to the killer. So the circle we've been following leads us back to the question of motive. Why was Jimmy Blacksheep really killed?" Justine said.

"We have to put a tail on Samuel," Ella said. "But this has to be done without the Farmington's PD's knowledge, so we'll need Big Ed's permission. And we'll have to handle it ourselves. Anyone have any objections?" She looked around the room, but no one spoke up. "Okay, then give me a half hour to run this past Big Ed, then we'll get this show started."

Ella walked around the U-shaped hall to Big Ed's office in the older part of the building, then gave him the broad strokes of what they'd uncovered so far. "Samuel Blacksheep is involved somehow, and is either a part of this, or an unknowing victim, too. I can't guarantee results, but I think a tail would pay off. Maybe we can rule out his guilt, at least. The people involved in this are getting scared and moving to cover their butts. We need to move fast before we lose our opportunity."

"I agree. But if word gets out and we're wrong about this, a ton of grief will come down on this department," Big Ed warned. "Count on it."

"I know. That's why it's got to be very low profile and a limited scope type of thing. Just my team will be involved, and we'll rotate shifts after Blacksheep goes off duty. Trying to follow him at work could just get somebody shot."

"How are you going to find out when his shift is over?"

"Justine has a contact I think we can use," she answered.

"Okay, but watch yourselves. Police officers can be paranoid, even the innocent ones."

Ella met again with her team and set a tentative plan in motion. "Next, we need to find out what Samuel's hours are," Ella said.

Justine stood up. "Give me a few moments," she said, and stepped out of Ella's office.

"We'll be specifically looking for other players—people Samuel meets, especially anyone who might be connected to the Army, or gunrunning. I don't think we've got the whole picture yet," Ella told the others. Just then, Justine returned.

"He's got the day shift for the rest of this month, not including any overtime he may clock in. Samuel is temporarily assigned to the carjacking strike team, of course, and spends a lot of time meeting and conferencing with the other officers on the operation," Justine said.

"So Officer Blacksheep'll be on his own at night," Ella concluded with a nod. "Good. Justine and I will cover him tonight until he turns in. You two can take it tomorrow. And—a word of warning. We do *not* want to get caught. Big Ed has enough problems dealing with tribal officials without getting embroiled in some interagency stink. He wasn't thrilled with this idea to begin with."

After her team dispersed, Ella and Justine headed to Farmington, Justine at the wheel. "I've got his plates and a description of the pickup he drives off-hours in case we need to look around," she told Ella. "But my contact said that he has a meeting with his sergeant at the station this afternoon, so he'll be there until his shift ends."

"If he's already left, then we'll go to his residence and see if he's there," Ella said. "And if not, there are some bars where cops hang that we can check out."

"Or we can go to the house of the woman he's seeing these days."

Ella gave Justine an approving look. "Good work! I'm impressed, partner! You need to take your contact out to dinner—my treat."

Once they reached the Farmington Police Station, they cruised around until they found Samuel's unit, then waited at a visitor's parking slot, keeping watch.

"How's it going at home with Rose and Herman?" Justine asked after about five minutes. "I've heard that they're really getting serious."

Ella nodded. "As serious as it gets. They're getting married. Mom doesn't want a fancy affair, so I think it's going to happen soon."

"Are you and Dawn moving out?"

Before Ella could reply, Samuel came out of the station, jacket in hand, moving in the direction of his unit. "Here we go."

They tailed him across Farmington to a two-story-high warehouse just north of the river. Blacksheep parked face-in beside a loading dock next to three other vehicles, one of them also a police car, then walked up a flight of steps to a metal door with a sign that said OFFICE. He knocked, the door opened almost immediately, then Samuel disappeared inside.

"I wonder if this place is connected to the carjackings," Justine said. "It looks like a great place to strip a vehicle for parts, or let it cool down before moving it south to Mexico."

"If it is, two cops are involved. Park around the corner at the curb, and I'll go in for a closer look," Ella said. "It's dusk so the entire side of the building will be covered in long shadows. There are no windows except the two in the office so if I stick close to the wall, I won't get spotted unless somebody steps outside."

"But if they do, they're going to nail you."

Over Justine's protests, Ella inched around the corner, staying low to the ground. The building's exterior wasn't well lighted, and it was past day-shift business hours, so the chances of anyone coming along in what was essentially an industrial park was unlikely.

Stepping lightly on the gravel after noting that the closest window was open several inches, she forced herself to concentrate solely on a silent approach as she moved up to listen. Comments about flushes and a full house, king high, beer, and pizza made her realize immediately that she'd followed Samuel to a night of poker with the good ole boys. Cursing her luck, she decided to return to the car. Then she overheard something that made her freeze in her tracks.

"I think the carjackers have moved on," a male voice said. "Or gone to ground. We haven't even had a bad tip since that incident over by Hogback. It sucks. We've got to take them down, hard."

"They're playing it smart, laying low until the heat dies down, Bobby," Samuel answered. "With the focus on them, they have to be careful. In a few weeks, a month, they'll hit again."

"Too bad the Navajo cops didn't nail them. I would have liked to have been in on it. Maybe with a few more units on the scene, we'd have done more than recover the vehicle," another voice said.

"Ben, any action you see around here must be like kid stuff after your tour in Iraq. And I've heard there's lots of black market crap going down over there. Bet it wasn't easy keeping your mitts clean," Samuel commented offhandedly.

"Nothing's clean over there," he muttered. "The sand's as fine as powdered sugar. Hard keeping the vehicles from grinding into junk. I used up all my rubbers keeping the muzzle of my weapon clear. Shocked my mom, asking for more in a care-package. Impressed my dad for a moment, though, until I explained."

At least three men laughed.

"Seriously. There must have been a lot of ways a guy could

have made himself some serious cash over there," Samuel said casually. "Lots of G.I.'s risk losing their homes 'cause they can't make the payments on Army pay, and that's just plain wrong. As long as no one gets hurt, I figure a soldier's entitled to show the American entrepenurial spirit."

"Hey. Quit using words you can't spell," a fourth voice said.

"Forgot to dumb it down for you, Jake. Got a crayon?" Samuel shot back.

Ella stayed where she was. Maybe this was about to pay off. Samuel was obviously angling for information, and if he got it, she would, too.

"A couple of the guys in the platoon found an angle or two and made some extra scratch," the one called Jake said. "Can't say I blame 'em. Serving your country is expensive in more ways than one."

"So much crap is going on over there, it's a full-time job keeping your butt out of a sling," Bobby answered. "After a while, you learn how to play the game."

"I'm sure glad to be back in the motor pool here doing brake jobs and tune-ups instead of retrieving broken-down fuel trucks north of Samara. RPGs, IEDs, snipers, sergeants on my ass—I've seen enough action to last me a lifetime. But I learned my lessons over there and I've got plans. I'm tired of working for someone else. I'll be leaving the department to open my own shop as soon as possible," Ben said.

"That'll take a bucket of money, won't it?" Samuel asked.

"Hey, the U. S. of A. has been taking care of my basics for over a year now, and I've been saving every dime. My credit's solid. Hell, if I don't do it now, when?" Ben said. "Of course, since we're shipping back out again in a few weeks, my plans are on hold. But this should be a short tour, and no hostiles, unless you include the pissed-off boyfriends of the German ladies I'm going to be spending time with. Once I'm back, I'm going into business full time—for me."

"I guess it's easier to save money when you're overseas. No groceries, no rent, no new clothes," Samuel said.

"You still have to play it smart with your bucks," Ben said. "Date cheap, and save your money for beer."

"Beer!" Ella heard two men yell at once, then a clink of glass, like two bottles being touched together.

Samuel laughed, but stayed on the subject. "I don't think I could have made much of a soldier. I can handle the department, but that's because I run my own life off duty. But the Army owns you when you're, like, in Iraq or Afghanistan. I'd question some dumbass order, and get thrown in the stockade. These days you can't defend a wrong action by saying your captain told you to do it, you know?" Samuel said.

"True, but you gotta know not to fight the small stuff," Bobby said. "Like in the department. You don't narc on your own guys."

"Yeah," Ben piped in.

"Most of the guys over there, maybe eighty percent, are righteous," the one called Jake said. "They just want to get the job done and come back home in one piece. But like you said, there's always some kind of black market action. In countries where it's forbidden, you can still get your girlie magazines, DVDs, pirated CDs, looted merchandise—all kinds of contraband from local merchants, for a price. Sometimes you go along with it, because the guy who's selling Johnny Walker out of his Humvee may be the one working the fifty the next day, covering your butt in a firefight. The lines between right and wrong start to fade when it comes to the little crap."

"Yeah," Bobby said. "I served in 'Nam, not in the Gulf, but I hear you. Hell, there were times when we had to buy flares on the black market. Now *that* pissed me off."

"Yeah. You liberate more than people," Ben added, then they all laughed. "Now shut up, give me another beer, and deal."

"Here you go, Richardson. Light beer. Gotta watch your figure," the one called Jake said, then laughed.

The talk switched to poker and sports. Ella crept silently back to the unit where Justine was waiting, then quickly conveyed what she'd learned. "Get hold of Neil Carson, the CID guy, and apprise him. Ask him to get us more information on Ben Richardson, one of the men in Jimmy's Guard unit—the one who's the mechanic at FPD. While you're getting Carson, I'll call Blalock."

Moments later, after Ella finished her conversation with Blalock, Justine glanced over at her. "I've left voice mail for Neil Carson. He's unavailable."

"I'm not surprised. But Blalock's already working on what we need," Ella replied.

"So what next?" Justine asked.

"We need someone who can get us some fast information on Richardson—someone who's not afraid to cut corners."

They looked at each other, both already smiling. "Teeny!"

FOURTEEN

— ✷ ✷ ✷ —

Ella called her old friend at home, then, not getting an answer, tried his cell, with the same results. "Teeny must have turned off his voice mail for some reason. Let's go by his office. Sometimes he's there late but won't answer the phone unless he's actively working for a client."

"I know he loves to tinker with computers—adding memory, tweaking the operating system, anything to make them faster or more efficient," Justine said with a nod. "I remember when he'd fix the ones at the station. He'd concentrate so totally on what he was doing he wouldn't have heard a nuclear blast one desk over. When his special assignment for the department got swept up by the budget cuts and he quit, we ended up losing a good cop and our best tech."

It took just five minutes to reach the stone-and-metal office building where Teeny and Blalock both had their offices. Blalock's office door was closed, but Teeny's door was wide open and beyond it they could hear country-western music.

Ella knocked on the door as they walked inside, and predictably, Teeny, who was sitting before one of the computers, didn't stir or take his eyes off the screen.

"Earth calling," Justine muttered.

Ella stepped around Teeny's chair—which was like circling

a major appliance—and stood in front of him. Noticing her at last, he glanced up and smiled.

"Hey, good to see ya. I didn't hear you come in," he said, then turning his chair and seeing Justine, added, "You, too, girl."

"I wanted to make sure I didn't startle you," Ella said, remembering one instance when Teeny had been on a stakeout and another officer had come up from behind him. He'd bounced the two-hundred-pound rookie against a wall before realizing the man was a fellow officer.

"You two want something to eat?" He pointed to a plate half full of his favorite apple-filled doughnuts. "The cinnamon helps you think."

"And the sugar rush helps you work?" Ella added with a grin. His computer screen was split into two windows, one with some kind of codes related to computerese, and the other with a colorful graphic display that responded to the music coming from the computer speakers.

Teeny touched a button on his keyboard twice and the music went down about half in volume. "Go on. Help yourselves. Neither of you have to worry about calories, so enjoy," he said, noting that Justine had already picked one up.

Ella did the same. They'd be here for a while. "I need your help. I want anything and everything I can get on Ben Richardson, a mechanic working for the Farmington Police Department in their motor pool. He's also in the same National Guard transportation unit as our recent murder victim. He was interviewed initially after Jimmy's death, but didn't add anything we didn't already know. Richardson said he knew Jimmy only in passing and hadn't seen him for several days because he'd come back earlier at his department's request. There are some additional questions I have for him now, but I'd like more background on the guy before I go talk to him."

"I can't go through channels—don't have official authorization or current passwords. But I do service their network and . . ."

His words trailed off then he shook his head. "Why don't you two wait for me in the outer office? You can't be held accountable for something you never saw or heard."

Ella took him at his word, and they left the room, closing the door behind them. As they waited, she glanced at Justine, who'd just finished the doughnut.

"These are great. Look homemade," Justine said.

Ella nodded. "They are. Teeny bakes them himself. He's a great cook."

"You should have married him. In fact, I may ask him if you don't," Justine said. "I wonder if he likes to shop. . . ."

It took a full fifteen minutes before Teeny opened the door again, which, overall, wasn't very much time at all.

"Okay, some of this you probably already know, but here's what I've got," Teeny said, gesturing for them to join him. "Your white boy worked as a mechanic overseas, keeping the heavy equipment running and going on some dangerous missions to recover broken-down vehicles. He and Blacksheep shared quarters for a while at their base north of Baghdad."

Justine and Ella exchanged glances. "I don't remember reading that in Joe's report. He's the one who spoke to Richardson."

"I don't either. Maybe it was in his notes and we missed it," Justine answered. "But I was under the impression that Richardson barely knew Jimmy."

"Either way, we should follow it up some more. Ben might have some insight into what was going on inside Jimmy's head. I want to have a real sit-down talk with this guy. You don't happen to have an address, do you?" Ella asked, looking at Teeny.

He smiled slowly. "Have some faith, little girl."

Ella was tall for a Navajo, but next to Teeny she was practically a hobbit. "I owe you dinner," she said, taking the slip of paper he handed her.

"Someday, I'd like to get your recipe for these doughnuts," Justine said, licking her fingers. "They're really top of the line."

"All I could give you would be an estimate," Teeny answered with a proud smile. "All my recipes are spur of the moment. Gut instinct, if you'll pardon the comparison. I like it that way," he answered, then growing serious once more, added, "Ella, can I have a word with you in private?"

Ella looked at him in surprise.

"I'll meet you outside," Justine said, then walked out the door, giving them some privacy.

Ella followed him back into his office. "What's up? I'd trust Justine with my life, you know."

"Yeah, yeah, but this is personal. I heard about what happened at the Totah. Gossip from those who saw the action from inside, report that the Reverend has some well honed-fighting skills. That got me curious, so I did a little checking."

"What'd you find out?" Ella asked quickly.

"It's not what I found out—it's that I couldn't, and didn't. Usually, given enough time, I can dig up information on just about anyone. But when I looked into the Reverend's past I ran into a firewall that just screamed Fed. That he'd worked for a government agency quickly became obvious, but he's being protected, and in a big way. My background search resulted in an all-out attack on my own system. It would have nailed me for sure if I hadn't been protected by the best hacker-proof stuff available. Of course I intend to make breaking through all those barriers my new mission in life—unless the Feds come knocking at my door."

"If I said you didn't have to do that, would it stop you?"

Teeny grinned—a truly frightening gesture that only passed as a smile to the ones who knew him. "What do you think?"

"Okay—if you get anything I should know about . . ." she said, letting it hang.

"You've got it. Ella, are you serious about this guy? Serious, serious?"

Ella smiled. "I wouldn't say that. At the moment, we both have something in common, and it's in our benefit to be seen together. It seems that everyone who knows the Reverend isn't married wants to fix him up. That's a nuisance I can relate to personally, and I think it might make my life easier as well, if people make the assumption that we're dating. So we're taking advantage of the gossip, that's all."

"You doing this so Kevin'll back off? I hear that your mom's getting married soon. Without her at home, Kevin might just make a move for joint custody. Everyone knows he's crazy about Dawn and, with no adult at home and the long hours you put in at work . . . Of course, if he plays his cards right, he'll get to fix two problems at once. If he's got Dawn, you'll be coming around almost constantly. That'll make it much easier for him to provide you with an obvious solution—you and Dawn can both move in with him permanently. Problem solved."

Teeny's scenario took her by complete surprise. "You think that's what he's really angling for?"

"What do *you* think?"

"Listen, friend to friend?" he said, then seeing her nod, continued. "Move slowly with the Reverend. Nothing draws you in faster than a puzzle or an unanswered question. If you like the guy, that's one thing, but curiosity may not be healthy in this case. That guy has a seriously heavy past. You may be better off never knowing what he did before he took up the ministry."

Ella nodded somberly. Teeny was right. But now that she knew this much, she'd never be able to let it rest. "Makes perfect sense. Too bad I'm so lousy taking advice."

It was dark by the time they drove down the street in the old Farmington neighborhood where Ben Richardson's modest three-bedroom home was located. The streets were quiet and the house lights, for the most part, were off.

"Richardson works the day shift, so it's possible he bowed out of the poker game early. His car could be in the garage," Justine said. "Want to go up and knock?"

"Yeah, but wait a sec," Ella said, checking out the street. A few cars were parked at the curb, but in every case there was already a full driveway. "That car—the four-door sedan parked across the street and two houses down from Richardson's. There's a big guy inside, slumped down. He's got the side mirror angled so he can see across the street and behind him—like a stakeout."

Justine watched through the rearview mirror as they continued down the street. "I see him, behind the steering wheel. How do you want to handle it?"

"Drive around the corner, then I'll double back on foot. It could just be a guy pulled over using his cell phone. Let's try to figure out what's going on first."

"We could be stirring up a hornet's nest, partner. Without backup . . ."

"We can handle it if we tread carefully and keep in contact with each other. I want to avoid calling in for backup now since the situation could be perfectly harmless, and it'll tell way too many people what we're doing," she said. As soon as they'd driven around the corner, Justine stopped the car and Ella stepped out.

Moving through the darkest nighttime shadows was second nature to Ella. She'd been doing this as far back as she could remember. Childhood games of hide-and-seek with her brother Clifford had taught her how to be a good tracker and rely on her senses to guide her. Right now, her intuition was telling her that she wasn't facing a crisis situation. Yet, whoever was watching Richardson's house was doing that for a reason, and she intended to find out what was going on.

Ella moved toward the car, positioning herself so she'd be coming up directly behind the vehicle. He wouldn't be able to see out of the rearview mirror without shifting and sitting up and, if he did, she'd see it happening and be ready.

As she came within twenty feet of the car, the door opened and a man stepped out. The fact that the dome light didn't come on told her he was a pro. She froze, watching his hands for a weapon, ready to duck to the right, screening herself with his car.

He turned and looked right at her, as if he could see her easily despite the surrounding darkness and silently motioned her to approach. Ella recognized the CID man immediately. Neil Carson was staking out Richardson's house. "I'll save you some time," he said. "He's still not home. I came directly here after your partner called."

"Why are you here?" she whispered, quickly getting into his car.

"I wanted to question Richardson first."

"This is *my* case. I think it's time we—" Ella felt her phone vibrate. "Wait. I need to notify my partner."

After Ella assured Justine that she was all right, Justine gave her some puzzling news.

"I've just heard from Dispatch," Justine said. "The duty officer got an anonymous call from someone who sounded like a kid and he claimed that there was a vehicle in an irrigation ditch several miles from the crime scene."

"Has anyone verified that yet?"

"Yeah. Dispatch sent a unit right away."

"My guess is that the tip came from the Many Devils, and it's Jimmy's rental car," Ella said.

"We'll find out soon enough."

Ella closed the phone and turned to Carson. "I've got another lead I need to check out." She decided not to share the information with him until she'd personally verified that they'd really found Jimmy's car.

"Go ahead, Investigator Clah. I'm going to stay put. If he shows, you can have a shot at him after I'm through."

Ella debated whether or not to tell Carson about the poker game then decided against it. There'd be time for all that later. "You and I have to talk. Soon," she added with emphasis.

"Noted," he said with a nod.

Justine was pulling up as Ella stepped out of the car. They were underway again in seconds. "You've got a location?" Ella asked.

Justine nodded. "I've also called Neskahi and Tache and asked them to meet us there."

"Good."

"Have you ever wondered what it would be like to work a job that had regular hours?" Justine mused as they sped down the highway.

"We'd be bored stiff," Ella answered with a tiny smile. "I don't think sameness suits us, partner."

A half hour later, they were walking along the ditch bank northwest of Shiprock a quarter mile from the river. The crime scene unit was there, and lights had been set up.

As soon as photos had been taken of the submerged vehicle, Ella waved to the tow-truck driver. He started the winch, and the sedan, connected via a cable to its tow hook, rolled up the bank onto the service road atop the levee. Ella watched as hundreds of gallons of foul-smelling water flowed from the vehicle through the broken front-door windows. Smaller amounts trickled through the half dozen or more bullet holes on the driver's side, particularly the door, leaving little doubt that it was Jimmy Blacksheep's rental. The condition of the vehicle confirmed what had happened to the car and Jimmy.

Ella watched, hoping that they'd have some answers soon—connections and physical evidence that would pull the fragmented picture together and bring the resolution they all needed. As the water drained, something large and frighteningly familiar descended from where it had been trapped atop the interior roof of the sedan, coming to rest on the backseat.

FIFTEEN

✖ ✖ ✖

Now we know why they dumped the car," Ella said, ignoring the stench and studying the rotting corpse. It was still wallowing faceup in the dirty water that covered the seat cushion.

Water and dead flesh were adversaries. The body was bloated and discolored—the stuff of nightmares—a caricature of a human drawn by death. There were also crawdads and scavenger fish in the ditches, and some had paid the rental vehicle a dinner call.

Ella glanced at Justine, who'd turned away after seeing what was left of the victim's face. "Call Carolyn," Ella said. "The M.E. needs to be here."

Neskahi got close enough to open the passenger-side door, which was slightly higher due to the position of the tow hook and therefore easier to open. Most of the water still inside came flowing out onto the dirt road, filling a long tire rut. This was one way to make sure that anything washing out of the vehicle remained at the scene, rather than flowing back down the embankment and then being carried downstream.

"Wish there was a way to drain the ditch," Neskahi said, standing back to keep his feet as dry as possible.

"Best we can do is check the gates downstream and see if any-thing got washed out of the vehicle and caught against one of the screens," Ella answered. "At least you managed to keep whatever settled to the floorboards by dumping the last foot of water onto the road."

"Looks like the guy in the car was shot, several times," Tache said. "He was probably dead when they dumped the car. Any idea who he is?"

"The dead soldier was supposedly traveling alone, so I have no idea who this person was." Ella stepped in closer with a flashlight to check out the distorted face but it didn't help. "Maybe the soldier took this guy out. We know he fought back."

"I think I recognize the vic," Justine said, her flashlight on the body.

Ella didn't ask for a name as the man who'd operated the tow truck came over to unhook his cable from the wrench. Even modernists hated calling a murder victim by name at a crime scene. "Good. We need to run what we've got. Ask Blalock to get some background info for us on this guy. He can speed up the process."

"The victim traded in stolen weapons," Justine told her. "Nothing fancy or heavy duty, just hunting rifles and pistols. He had an operation where you could order what you wanted and he'd get it for you—that is, until he got busted."

The M.O. triggered her memory. "I didn't work that case, but I remember it. Big Ed insisted on handling it himself. His nephew had bought a revolver off this idiot and nearly got killed. The weapon had been reassembled with a hair trigger and a round went off when he picked up the gun. Nearly shot himself in the leg."

She nodded. "The suspect got off on a technicality—the search warrant was thrown out," Justine said, handing Ella a piece of paper with the man's name—Herbert Edsitty, "but Big Ed continued to keep an eye on him—unofficially, of course. Word went down that if he started doing business on our turf again, we were to do whatever it took to bust him." Justine lowered her voice. "If what I heard is true, Big Ed also hired Teeny out of his own pocket to tail the suspect and keep him apprised of his activities."

Ella nodded slowly. Big Ed's nephews were like the sons he'd never had. But she hadn't known about the arrangement between Teeny and Big Ed.

"Now we have a connection between illegal weapons and the incident that resulted in Blacksheep's death," Ella said softly. "Unfortunately this also places Big Ed and Teeny right in the middle of our investigation."

"As suspects? You're not serious," Justine said softly.

"Don't write it up in a report yet. We don't want to go official on this. But we'll need to verify where Teeny and Big Ed were at the time this guy was killed. Not for our own benefit. We both know neither man is responsible. But we have to cover those bases in case somebody's attorney brings it up later on," Ella said. Teeny's record for violence wouldn't do either much good if a defense lawyer managed to discover Teeny's interest in the dead man.

Soon the vehicle had drained enough for them to search the interior. As they went over the bullet-riddled sedan, working around the body without moving it and coping with the smell the best they could, Justine extracted a round from one of the armrests in the backseat. "I won't know until I measure this in the lab, but I think this came from an AK-47. It's military ball ammunition."

Ella nodded. "Notice the damage to the dashboard and driver's area, even the steering wheel. Whoever shot Jimmy moved in close to finish him off, and they didn't waste ammo."

"Yeah, but who fired the AK—was it at Jimmy, and was it just bad luck not finding 7.62 bullets in his body? I know an assault rifle has quite a bit more penetrating power, but still . . ." Justine said.

"Check out the backseat. Those look like impact marks in the floorboard and seat," Ella said, aiming at the points of interest with her light.

"But the driver was in the front seat."

"Maybe these bullets were intended for the guy in there now, and the AK was used on him?" Ella suggested.

"A falling out among the killers?"

"We know Jimmy shot back. If he hit this guy, and the others couldn't risk a trip to the doctor, maybe they finished him off themselves, and this is why he's in here now."

Justine nodded. "Makes sense. So, if the ME recovers both AK rounds and bullets fired from Jimmy's weapon from the vic's body, we'll know both sides contributed to this man's death."

"What's that?" Ella pointed toward a brassy object on the seat close to the body.

"I'll get it," Justine said. Wearing the two layers of latex gloves used by Navajo cops, she reached in and brought out the object. "Ugh, I nearly touched him . . . it."

"Short case with a shoulder, about eight-millimeters. From an AK-47, right?" Ella said.

Justine nodded, turning the case in her hand so she could see the markings at the base of the brass around the primer. "Arabic, and, from the triangle in the headstamp, it's Iraqi."

"Less of a surprise than if we'd found it on day one. The connection with Iraq and Jimmy's unit just keeps getting stronger. Let's see what else we can find."

Ella worked alongside the crime scene team, and they found several shell casings for a nine-millimeter handgun on the floor of the vehicle, most in the front-seat area. Her assumption was that these had been ejected from Jimmy's weapon as he returned fire. She was still searching the interior for trace evidence when a bleary-eyed Carolyn Roanhorse showed up.

Giving Ella a sharp look, she muttered, "Don't you guys ever sleep?" Not waiting for an answer, she looked at the body, now on the backseat of the vehicle. "That's where you found the body?"

"It may have been elsewhere in the vehicle the past few days, but it ended up there when we drained out the water. Nobody's touched it," Ella confirmed. "Justine thinks she knows who it was, but until we get fingerprints . . ."

Carolyn nodded. "I'll do what I can here, then I'll be needing help moving the victim out of the car."

Ella thought of poor Neskahi. "We're particularly interested in any slugs you recover. Could you give me a call if you find more than one caliber round in the vic?"

"I'll let you know soon as I can," Carolyn said. "But it won't be before morning, probably."

Ella went to find Justine, who'd gone downstream to check the ditch for anything that may have washed from the vehicle. "I'm going to take the car and wake a few people up. Can you catch a ride back with Neskahi or Tache?"

"You bet." Justine wrote a few things into her notebook, then tore the page out and handed it to Ella. "This is where the victim hung out—it's that hole-in-the-wall coffee shop across from the high school."

"Thanks."

Ella, driving down the highway a short time later, called Big Ed at home on her cell phone. "Chief, I have a problem that won't wait till morning."

"Then come over. Claire is in Albuquerque visiting her sister, so don't worry about being quiet."

Claire, the chief's wife, had been lonely since her sister had moved away to the city. It was no secret that she frequently went to visit her—an arrangement that was almost guaranteed to put the chief in a foul mood—almost as foul as when Claire's sister came to visit at their home.

Ella arrived a short time later at the modest ranch-style home and was greeted by the chief's large shaggy dog. "Hey, Felonius," she said, petting him, then walking up to the door. The porch light was on as was the light in the living room.

Big Ed, in flannel shirt, jeans, and worn moccasins, let them both in. "Come in quickly. It's too cold out tonight for these old bones. The mutt heard a coyote howling, and just *had* to go out and see for himself." He waved her to the couch. "This have to do with finding the Blacksheep rental? I got a call from Dispatch earlier."

Ella nodded, then filled him in about Edsitty.

"That walking piece of crap is still busting my chops, this time from beyond the grave," Big Ed muttered. "Herb swore that someday he'd make my life as difficult as I'd made his. I know you need my whereabouts considering the history I had with the victim, but, fortunately I've got a verifiable alibi for the morning in question. I met with the tribal chairman that day in the Totah's private dining room. On my way over, at around five-thirty in the morning, I filled up the gas tank on my truck and paid with a credit card. I got to the Totah at around six—early so I could go over my notes. Merilyn Baca was working the tables that morning and spilled coffee on my financial report. I embarrassed the hell out of her, so I'm sure she'll remember."

Ella smiled, relieved. "I hope Teeny has an alibi that's as solid as yours."

"Whatever it is, we both know it won't lead to bad news. The important thing to remember is that you've got a clear lead that establishes a link between Jimmy's death and the guns and gunrunners, especially with the Iraqi ammo expended. But here's what I don't get. If the gunrunners wanted Jimmy dead, why didn't they just kill him while he was overseas? He would have ended up as one more casualty, the details lost in the fog of war. Killing him here put him into an individual spotlight."

"Maybe they didn't know what side of the fence he was on until he returned. Then they found out about the story he'd written. We suspect it was in two parts and I wasn't the only one he mailed it to. In the end, he may have trusted the wrong person," Ella said, reminding him of what they'd learned. "The way I figure it, Jimmy must have kept a copy for himself, too, so the killers may have wanted that as much as they wanted to take him out."

"Then break that code, and find out why they considered it worth killing for."

"I'm doing my best," Ella said.

Ella left the chief's home, relieved to know that his alibi was as ironclad as it could get. She'd still have to verify it later, but she didn't expect any problems. Yet one thought niggled at the back of her mind. If Big Ed really had been involved in the victim's death, he would have made sure his alibi was unimpeachable.

Ella stopped by Teeny's office next, not expecting to find him, and not surprised when that turned out to be the case. Ella then went directly to his home, just off the reservation and not far from the old power plant. As she pulled up in his driveway, Ella knew that the well-lit perimeter meant that her approach was being monitored. Just then her cell phone rang. It was Teeny.

"Saw you driving up. Come in," he invited.

Ella was inside his sparsely furnished, technically enhanced home a moment later. Near as she could tell, Teeny had been playing computer games. "Don't you ever sleep?"

"I only need about four hours' sack time. Comes from my days on the force. What brought you out—so late—early?" he asked, never one for idle chitchat.

"We found Herbert Edsitty's body," she said, and described the circumstances.

"You heard that I'd been tailing him, off and on, right?"

She nodded. "I have to clear you from my list of suspects—for the record. So tell me the whole story."

"Herbert was walking garbage," Teeny said. "He bought and sold guns of all makes and types—ripping off everyone he did business with, I might add. His specialty was doing business at gun shows, where he and his clients could weasel around the gun laws. But a few months ago, he suddenly decided to shut down his operation. Since I'd been leaning on him, I hoped that I was the main reason for that fortunate turn of events. I was really pleased with myself, until I started hearing some odd stories about Herbert getting into the import-export business. That news came courtesy of Philden Jackson, who owns the gas station next door to Herbert's shop."

"Did you get anything more, like maybe what kind of merchandise Herbert was supposed to be dealing?"

"I tried, but Herbert suddenly dropped out of sight. Guess we know where he went, don't we?"

"Okay, bottom line. Where were you the morning Herbert got killed? I'm guessing he was killed the same day as Jimmy. The car disappeared immediately, and Herbert was inside at the time."

Teeny paused before answering her. "You mean a case can be made that I was following Herbert and let Jimmy get shot before moving in and taking out Herbert," he said, constructing events thoughtfully as he'd done a trillion times during his days on the force. "Then I covered the whole thing up by dumping the car and Herbert—but not Jimmy too? Come on, Ella. Does that make sense to you on any level?"

"No, but I don't believe you're guilty anyway. I know you too well. What I'm hoping is that we can prove Jimmy killed Herbert, or at least was the first one to shoot him, because Herbert was one of the carjackers. The rest will be fuzzy until the bullet evidence is clear. I'm guessing that Jimmy had decided to go to the authorities about their gunrunning operation and they sent Herbert and somebody else to stop him and make the whole op look like just one more carjacking. If I'm right, the evidence will bear me out and we can get back on track."

"I appreciate your trust in me, Ella. I may beat the crap out of some lowlife, but I won't set myself up as judge and jury, and you know that." He paused. "You really have to know where I was that morning?"

She nodded. "Around seven, just in case it comes up."

He paused for a long moment. "I was with Jayne," he said at last.

"Jane? Jane who?" Ella asked, confused, then stared at him in surprise. "Jayne with a 'Y,' as in Justine's sister?"

He gave her a sheepish smile. "She and I ... well, we kinda hooked up. We've been seeing each other. It started as a no-strings-attached deal, but I think we've got something. This isn't just another checkmark in my black book, if you get my meaning."

Ella stared at him, dumbfounded. Out of all the things he could have said, she'd never expected this. She wondered if Justine knew.

Almost as if he'd read her mind, he added, "Nobody knows—particularly her family. Jayne wanted to see how things went before she told them about us. She said that her mother has been hoping she'd get married, and makes her life miserable every time she goes out with someone. She's barely out the door with a guy and her mother's hearing wedding bells."

"Are *you* hearing wedding bells?"

He leaned back in his chair and looked at her seriously. "I've never thought of myself as the marrying kind, Ella. Once, a long time ago, I met someone I thought I might like as a wife, but things didn't work out," he said.

Although he spared her any longing looks, Ella knew he'd meant her. "And now?" she pressed, sensing what he'd left unspoken.

"Living alone—and someday dying alone—isn't what I want for myself. The world is made for couples, Ella. You need someone to share the day with, as well as the night. You might drive each other crazy from time to time—Jayne's a real girly girl, you know—but she adds something to my life that wasn't there before. I look forward to having dinner with her, or just being around her. We can talk about almost anything."

Ella knew Jayne well enough to believe she'd be an adventure for any future husband. As the news sank in, she came to the conclusion that spring had come early to the reservation. Ella thought of Ford, then of herself and Dawn. Maybe when fall came once again, and the birds and the bees got some quiet time, sanity would return.

"Kinda weird, huh?" Teeny asked, almost as if asking for her blessing.

Ella gave him a gentle smile. "I think it's terrific, Teeny. And I understand exactly how you feel. I don't want to bring another person into my life. It's complicated enough as is. But, without someone, it can get . . ." she paused, fumbling for the right word.

"Lonely?"

"Yeah—but it's a special kind of loneliness. I have a lot of people in my life, so I'm seldom alone. But there's a corner of your heart that stays empty when you're not in love. After a while, that emptiness becomes a part of you," she said, then added, "Eventually, you start to wonder if you even know how to fill it anymore."

Teeny nodded somberly. "I hear you. You teach yourself not to care too deeply because, if you do, someone can come along and cut your heart out. Then, after a while, you take the easy route and stop letting anyone get close."

"Yeah, like that," Ella said.

"Jayne reminds me of all the things life's taught me to forget." He paused then added, "Is that how you feel about the Reverend . . . Tome, not Campbell."

Ella laughed out loud. "At the moment, the most I can say about Ford is that he interests me, and I'm starting to enjoy his company."

"He's got to be less boring than most of the . . . generic . . . men in your life," he said with a grin.

Although he hadn't said so, Ella knew he meant Kevin. To Teeny, and many current and former police officers, five minutes with an attorney was four and a half minutes too long. "Ford intrigues me, I'll admit that. But as for anything else coming of it . . ." she said and shrugged. "Who knows? You can like the first part of a movie, but it's the last reel that sells you one way or the other."

"Just watch your step with that guy, Ella. Something about his background is . . . off-center."

"Yeah, I hear you." Ella stood up. "I'd better be on my way. I've got to check in with my people and see what we've got that's new and will move the case forward. Looks like I won't be going home again tonight."

She'd nearly made it back to the cruiser when her cell phone rang. It was Blalock. "I've got some interesting news for you. ATF processed the weapons they confiscated at the raid last night. Apparently some of them still have traces of U.S.-military-type solvents—formulations that meet the military's specifications and are used by field units. Stuff from the motor pool."

"Ben Richardson," she said almost immediately. "He said something to the effect that he had to keep everything clean so it would run."

"Funny you should mention him. I checked the customer list of that gun shop we raided. Turns out Ben Richardson was one of their more frequent customers before shipping overseas. He always paid cash, according to the books. Richardson also bought an expensive rifle after he got back."

"The CID man, Neil Carson, is staking out Richardson's place. I'm going to check in with him."

"Keep me posted. If anything goes down, I want in."

Working on little sleep came easily to her, and Ella was completely alert when she met up with Carson a half hour later in Farmington. The soldier was still in his vehicle, keeping a low profile. After alerting him of her presence by making a pass around the block, Ella came down the sidewalk and slipped into the passenger's seat noiselessly.

Carson looked as if he hadn't moved a muscle. After a stakeout of this length, she and Justine would have been squirrelly, praying for some action. But Carson appeared alert, yet at ease, despite the tedious wait.

"Do you need to take a break?" Ella asked, noting there was no sign of a coffee mug or thermos bottle. Too much coffee on a stakeout could create all kinds of problems, she knew from experience.

"No, my job's here. I can stick it out as long as it takes."

"He still hasn't come home?" Ella asked.

"No. He doesn't have a girlfriend—at least not a regular. I checked into his activities before I ever got into town, so I expect he'll show after he's done playing poker and drinking with his buddies."

Ella was impressed that Carson knew of Richardson's schedule. She quickly updated him on the discovery of Jimmy Blacksheep's rental, the body inside, and the news that Richardson had done business with the gun shop.

"It's possible that Jimmy Blacksheep's killers know we found that rental," Ella said. "If Richardson was part of that operation, he may be running scared."

"Maybe, but he hasn't bolted yet."

"How do you know?"

Carson cocked his head at the rearview mirror and Ella saw approaching headlights.

The car pulled into the driveway and they both saw Richardson get out. He was alone, and didn't appear to have drunk enough for the booze to affect his stride.

"We can go in together now and question him," Carson said.

"How about a change of tactics?" Ella suggested. "We've given him and the others something to worry about. If he's got any evidence in that house, he's going to try and get rid of it fast. The type of things we're looking for—guns, ammunition, metal preservatives, solvents—aren't easily disposable. He can't flush the solvent down the drain without eating up his pipes or leaving chemical traces, for example, and the guns are too hot to market now. So I'm betting he'll try to move the stuff, maybe bury it someplace, and I'd like to catch him doing that. Since night's the perfect time for sneaking around, we might get lucky."

"We'll give him a few minutes to settle in, then I'm moving up close and taking a look inside," he said.

"Sounds good. Just remember he's probably well armed. Don't get yourself shot."

Carson brought out a low-light scope and started to watch the house. Ella called Blalock, but before she even finished, Carson called her attention to the side door. "Something's happening."

SIXTEEN

✖ ✖ ✖

"Hang on, Dwayne," Ella said, setting the phone down. Carson handed her the light-intensifying device and she looked where the CID man was pointing.

"He's got a post-hole digger," she noted, handing the scope back to Carson. As they watched, Richardson went to the alley behind his home, walked several feet, then began to dig in the hard ground. It was obvious he was working slowly to avoid making excessive noise.

"We don't have anything yet. Let him work," Carson said. "Let's see what he's going to put in there. My guess is he's not digging for fishing worms."

"Agreed," Ella said, then updated Blalock, who assured her he was on his way over, already in the neighborhood.

Ella glanced over at Carson. "Agent Blalock's going to join us soon," she said. "He's been working the carjacking case with us."

"I know who he is," Carson said, then gestured ahead. "Looks like Richardson's made good progress since he got past the hard surface."

There was a mound of dirt beside the hole. Richardson set the post-hole digger down, looked around the alley, then went back into his home. A few minutes later, Richardson came out the door struggling with the weight of two large metal containers. He placed one down, carried the remaining container over by the hole, then pried the lid off.

"We have to stop him before he dumps what he's got into those holes," Ella whispered.

"It could be anything. What if it's cooking oil?" he countered.

"Covert lard dumping after midnight?"

"You're right. Let's go." Carson was out of the vehicle in a heartbeat.

Ella bolted after the CID man, but before they got within fifty feet of Richardson, he looked up, saw them coming, and sprinted toward his home. Carson suddenly shot forward with incredible speed and intercepted him. By the time Ella caught up, Carson already had Richardson on the ground, facedown.

Hearing footsteps rushing up behind her, Ella spun around, reaching for her pistol at the same time. She relaxed a second later, seeing Blalock hurrying toward them, out of breath.

"Carson, you're in great shape," Blalock commented. "I didn't think anyone could cover that distance so fast."

"When was the last time you had to advance under enemy fire, FB-Eyes?" Carson said, hauling Richardson to his feet after Ella cuffed him.

"Was that yesterday, or the day before, Ella?" Blalock shot back, glancing at her.

"Oh, yeah. Forgot about that." Carson almost smiled.

Blalock pried off the lid on the closest container, then jerked back after taking a sniff.

"It's just parts-cleaning solvent I'd had sitting around for too long. I wasn't sure how to dispose of it, okay?" Richardson said. "I ran because you were coming at me in the dark. Wouldn't you have done the same?"

Blalock stared at him, expressionless. "So what do you think—would an analysis of this stuff detect gunpowder residue and oils manufactured in places like, say, Iraq?"

"Even if it did, that wouldn't prove anything," Richardson argued.

"It would if some of that solvent formula turned out to be current U.S. Army issue—the same stuff used by your unit in Iraq. The military has its own specs, different than commercial stuff."

"Let's search his garage," Ella suggested.

"I have rights. You need a search warrant for that," Richardson countered.

"Yeah, you're right. Good thing that these days I can get one over the phone, search now, then show the paperwork to you later," Blalock said.

"Of course, you might consider cooperating," Ella said. "If you give us enough, you might be able to avoid the death penalty, or a thirty-year prison vacation. But if you plan on helping us out, you'd better do that before we go search the garage."

He said nothing for a long moment, then finally nodded. "Yeah, okay. I'll tell you what I know—which isn't much, by the way. All I did was follow orders."

"From whom?" Carson snapped.

"Jimmy. Jimmy Blacksheep. He'd tell me where to pick up the weapons. They'd be in storage containers and ammo boxes stashed around our company's base, usually field stripped to save space. I don't know how they got shipped back to the States. After I got back home I was contacted via e-mail and told where to make the pickups. My job was to clean and reassemble the weapons and grind down some of the serial numbers and markings."

"Who's e-mailing you?" Ella asked. "It couldn't have been Jimmy. They don't have computers where he's at now."

"Don't know. Don't want to know. Didn't ask," Richardson said. "That's what got Jimmy dead—he asked too many questions. I didn't want to end up like him."

"How many people in your company are involved?" Carson asked bruskly. "Or was it just your platoon?"

"Man, you deaf? I said I don't know, and I didn't want to

know. I suppose it has to be people in our unit who live in this area. But I don't know who."

Ella looked at him for a long time. "A Navajo man was killed on the Navajo Nation. We have evidence that links you to that event, and that means the crime falls under our jurisdiction and the FBI's. The Army will be all over you as well. From where I stand, Ben, your future doesn't look so hot. So we're going to take you to jail, and on the way, you might want to think of new and inventive ways to cooperate. Life, as you've known it, is now over."

Blalock and Carson pulled an all-nighter questioning Richardson, who was locked up in Shiprock to keep him away from the Farmington officers in his Guard unit. Ella quit sometime after five in the morning, too tired to even think, and went home, desperate for a few hours of sleep.

Shortly after nine in the morning, sounds of life right outside her window forced her awake. Although her daughter was trying to be quiet, Dawn loved Rose's old mutt. Two loved her as well, and, between his occasional barks and her giggles, on top of the pony's whinnies, Ella realized that additional sleep was not in the cards this morning.

With a martyred groan, she got out of bed, showered, and dressed, ready for a quick breakfast. After that, she'd have to go back to the station. More than anything she wished she could have taken the weekend off. She really needed time to spend with her daughter, particularly with Kevin vying for additional custody. But the investigation was approaching a critical stage and she had to wrap up the case before the Army took away her remaining suspects.

About twenty minutes later, Ella walked outside, a half-eaten breakfast burrito in her hand. Seeing her, Dawn came running over.

"Mom, can I spend the night at Daddy's? He said I could."

"Why do you want to go over there?"

"The new bed! It's really cool. And he said I could ask Beth Ann over."

"Whoa. Slow down. The bed? What bed?"

"It's a bunk bed, Mom! Daddy bought it so I can ask my friends to sleep over anytime I want. And he said that this weekend I could get a puppy, too! He would keep it at his house, so Two wouldn't get jealous."

In a supreme act of willpower, Ella forced herself to take a deep breath. "You and I agreed weeks ago that I'd buy the bunk bed you wanted *if* you raised your English grade on your next report card."

Dawn looked down at her shoes. "Daddy said it was okay, because it would be at his house, not here. And my grades *have* come up! But my next report card won't be out for weeks!"

Ella sat down on the back step, and gestured for Dawn to join her. It was cold outside, but her daughter was dressed warmly, and this was one conversation she wanted to have away from Rose.

"Your father wants you to see his home as yours, too. He buys you things so you can be comfortable there. But I also love you, and your place is with me," Ella said gently.

"And with him, too. He said so."

Ella said nothing for a long moment. She wouldn't bind her daughter to her with bribes, nor would she turn her child into the center of a tug-of-war between the adults in her life.

"I'm working a case right now, pumpkin, so go ahead and sleep at your dad's if you want. But you won't be able to come back until Monday. Your *shimasání* will make her own plans if you're not here. She has a wedding to think about."

"So I can go? Really?" Dawn asked, her voice rising with excitement.

"Yes, I think it's a good idea all the way around. Your father needs to know what it's like to have active children around his house. You, your friend, the puppy . . . I think you'll all be learning about each other and that's a good thing," Ella said, trying not to smile at the prospect. Kevin had no idea what he was getting into, but it was high time he learned.

"Your dad will have to set up his own rules about who'll feed the puppy, who takes him out, cleans up after him, when you do your homework, and so on."

"Daddy doesn't have rules," Dawn said.

"Okay," Ella said. Just thinking what lay in store for Kevin this weekend brightened her mood considerably.

"Do I still have to keep my grades up?"

"Yes, that's one of *my* rules. Nothing's changed here, except that since you already have bunk beds, there's no reason for me to buy them, too."

"Then can I have something else?"

"What do you want?"

"Animal puzzles!"

"Puzzles?" Ella asked, pleased to discover this new similarity between them.

"They're on a Game Boy, so they start up new each time you press a button. Then you have to find the animals that are hidden in the jungle. I'm really good at it!"

"Okay," Ella said with a nod. This she could deal with. "But you'll have to honor our original deal. Your grades have to come up from a C average to a B."

"Okay, Mom," Dawn said, then hearing the phone ring, ran past Ella and hurried into the house, Two at her heels.

Dawn was growing up too quickly. The knowledge filled Ella with mixed emotions. Half of her wanted to hold on tight and never let go—but that wasn't what Dawn needed. Hearing her daughter on the phone, she tried to picture Dawn as a teenager, then shuddered. One step at a time.

Ella finished the rest of her burrito in three large bites, but as she was walking toward her police cruiser, Rose came out the kitchen door to join her.

"I was in the laundry room and heard what you told your daughter," she said softly. "I think your instincts were right."

"Mom, Kevin doesn't have the remotest idea of what it's like to be the single parent of an active kid. Let her stay there for a few days—with a new puppy and her friend—while he tries to get some work done. I may even insist that he take her for a week. Let him cook and handle things by himself. And do her laundry, too."

"He'll just hire Boots, you know," Rose said sourly.

"Not for another week or so. Boots just left to spend some time in Albuquerque, remember?"

Rose laughed. "What a wonderful day this is turning out to be."

Ella arrived at the station twenty minutes later. One look at Blalock, slumped in a chair just outside the interview room, told her he hadn't gotten any sleep.

"How did it go?" she asked him, handing him the cup of coffee she'd just picked up from the vending machine.

"I'll let Carson brief you. The man's a machine. He's still at it. Exhaustion's not in his vocabulary."

"He's in his late twenties—or early thirties, tops. At his age, I could go two or three days without sleep, too," Ella said with a grin. "But all things considered, maybe I should have stayed and lent you two a hand."

"It wouldn't have made any difference. I got a call from the Bureau ordering me to let Carson take point shortly after you left. They're more worried about the guns—and an out-of-control group of soldiers—than the death of Jimmy Blacksheep. I kept looking in on him and took over a few times but, as of two minutes ago, he was still at it."

Just then Carson knocked on the door. It couldn't be opened from the inside, so Ella did the honors, and the big man stepped outside, closing the door behind him. Surprisingly, Carson didn't look either bleary-eyed or tired. Ella didn't even see the beginnings of a beard on him, which made her suspect that he'd shaved recently. As she looked at his clothing, she came to the conclusion he'd changed as well. He was still wearing dark slacks, and a white shirt, but they didn't look crumpled.

She motioned him toward an empty chair, but he stood beside her instead. "When did you have time to shave and clean up?" she muttered, glancing at Blalock, then back at Carson.

"I keep a kit in my vehicle, along with a change of clothes. Military expects it." He looked at Blalock. "We're all done here. Why don't you get some sack time, then come back?"

Blalock threw back his shoulders and rolled his head to get the kinks out of his neck. "I'm fine. Fill us in on what you've got," he said.

Ella knew that Blalock was wiped, but she also knew that he would have thrown himself through the one-way glass before admitting that to Carson.

"Richardson is still sticking to his story about not knowing the identities of the others in the theft ring, but he suspects the unit's imbedded photographer played a big part. The guy, a civilian, would apparently disappear for days at a time, and none of them ever knew where he went."

"Did you get his name?"

"Martin Zamora, a freelance journalist. CID is checking his background as we speak, and will try to locate him."

"I'll put it through our records, too," Blalock said, then stood. "I'll be in touch. I'm going home to clean up, then I'll be back."

Ella watched Dwayne as he walked down the hall. Blalock gave the Bureau one hundred and ten percent and, even though he was close to retirement, he never cut corners. "He's a good man. Even better in a fight," Ella told Carson, recalling how FB-Eyes had taken a bullet meant for her several years ago, and still walked with a limp because of it.

"Sharp, too."

"My turn to have a go at Richardson," Ella said.

"Okay. Let's get to it," Carson said, cocking his head toward the room with their prisoner.

"No, let me try it alone for a while. Men act differently around other men—macho crap—and are more prone to keep their guard up. Right now he's got to be exhausted, and if I keep it low key, he might loosen up and give me something."

"I think I've already gotten everything he's going to say, but knock yourself out."

Ella went inside and sat down across the table from Ben Richardson. There was an empty foam cup. "You want a refill? Coffee, or water?"

The question surprised him. "CID through with me?"

"For now, I think."

His shoulders sagged as the tension washed out of his body. "When's chow served in this joint?" he asked with a thin smile.

"You'll be getting something to eat after they take you back to your holding cell. When we're done, Ben."

He leaned back in his chair. "So now what?" he asked, his gaze never wavering from hers.

"That's pretty much up in the air. You've been with us over-night, failed to show up for work at your police department job, so your pals are probably wondering where you are. If they manage to find out you're here, they're going to assume you cooperated—maybe even sought us out. I really wouldn't want to be in your shoes, Ben," Ella said simply, meaning it.

Maybe it was because her tone of voice had made it clear that she was simply stating a fact, not passing judgment, that the seriousness of the situation hit him hard. She could see it on his face.

"I'm going to need police protection," he said, leaning forward. "If you turn me over to the Army, the guys I worked with will know about it, and they'll find a way to kill me. Believe it."

"Protective custody for more than a day or two is the domain of the FBI, not the tribal police," Ella said slowly. "And, just so you know, they'll need more than what you've given them so far to make it worth their while. If you don't have any actual names to trade, or pertinent information that'll lead to a conviction, you've got zip, as far as they're concerned. We'll let you go, and you'll be on your own."

Richardson thought about it a moment, then swallowed hard. "I have something to trade."

"Like what?" Ella said skeptically.

He hesitated. After about ten seconds, Ella stood up as if getting ready to leave.

"Just listen to me for a minute, okay?" he asked. "I'm thinking."

She sat back down and waited a full minute. "Okay. What have you got?"

"I knew from the beginning that I'd have to watch my own back. So I did a little extra bookkeeping—insurance, kind of. I kept a record of all the weapons I handled, cleaned, assembled. I took photos—or if you prefer—visual souvenirs."

"Where are they?" Ella asked, trying to sound unimpressed.

"Do we have a deal?" Richardson pressed.

"I'll talk to the Feds for you. Let me see what I can do," she said, then stood and knocked on the door.

Carson let her out, but didn't speak until the door was closed again. "Smooth. But who'll handle protective custody? This guy can't just disappear, you know. If he does, the others will scramble to get rid of the evidence like he was doing, or more likely, head for Mexico."

"We need to put someone in place with him at his home. He can call in sick and we'll stick to him like white on rice. But I don't expect any problems. He knows that if he tips someone else off, he'll have to take all the heat himself, including the murder of Jimmy Blacksheep. But just to stay on the safe side and make sure he plays nice, we'll monitor his e-mails, his phone calls, any deliveries. The works."

"That sounds like my responsibility. I'll do the babysitting," Carson announced.

"I was thinking you'd like the job. If a cop goes bad, other cops like to come in and clean up the mess. Same with the Army, right?"

Carson nodded. "But let him stew for a while before we answer him. Like we're wondering if we can get a better deal from someone else in his unit."

"My thoughts exactly. So, why don't you come with me to my office? There's something you need to see," Ella said, leading the way. Once there, she waved him to a chair. "I received this from Private Blacksheep after his death," she said, showing him a copy of Jimmy's story. "We backtracked. He mailed it the day before he headed home from El Paso, and apparently, sent another package to his brother on the Farmington police force at the same time. The brother, Samuel, denies getting any mail from his brother. So either he never got it, or Samuel's lying."

Carson read it over quickly. "Looks incomplete—and cryptic in a mishmash folklore way. Why wasn't I shown this before?"

"Would it have done any good?" Ella countered.

He shook his head. "Only thing I can assume is that it's some kind of user-generated coded message. Why else send it to you?"

"Our thoughts as well," she answered, giving him more details of what they suspected, a brief explanation of why she believed that part of the message was missing, and their attempts to break the code. "Until recently, I wasn't sure who to trust or how far-reaching this arms smuggling operation was. So it wasn't just a matter of letting you in on what was going on. I was worried about the chain of command you have to follow. If senior officers in the unit are involved, and other units as well, we might have tipped them off."

"But now that you've reduced the list of suspects to local members of the company, things are clearer," he concluded.

"Exactly. But we need more than this to bring charges, and what the tribe wants is the killer or killers."

"I understand. Let me know if Reverend Tome, or anyone else

breaks the code. Insider intel would come in handy trying to bust this gang—lead us to the physical evidence."

"Give me a half hour to round up my team. Together we'll see if we can break this code once and for all."

After Carson left, Justine came into her office and Ella briefed her. "Blalock will focus—pardon the pun—on the photographer, Martin Zamora. In the meantime, I'd like the rest of our team here ASAP. I want to brainstorm and see if any of them might have some ideas."

As Justine left, Ella called Ford. "Can you come over as soon as possible? Bring anything you've got, ideas, doubts, solutions, guesses. I need to bring you up to speed on what we've learned. That might give you some new insights on Jimmy's story."

She'd just hung up when Carson knocked lightly on her door frame. "I was out in the hall and happened to hear you talking. I know you trust your team, but you're relying on this Reverend Tome a great deal. What have you got to convince me he's as trust-worthy as you think?"

"Not a whole lot. Mostly my instincts," Ella said, just as Justine came in.

"Let me do a more thorough check on Tome—first name Bilford, correct?" Carson asked.

"If you're running him down, you're going to encounter some firewalls," Justine warned.

"Humm. Sounds like a challenge," he said, and walked down the hall and outside.

"He's going to his car. You think he's got a wireless laptop?" Justine asked, envy dripping from each syllable.

It was no secret that she'd wanted one for a long time, but the department's budget was strained and there was no way her request would be honored anytime soon. "It's probably one of those five-thousand-dollar Department of Defense jobs," Ella said. "His budget comes from the Pentagon, not Window Rock."

The meeting was switched to Big Ed's office—at his request.

Ella was walking in that direction when Carson caught up to her. "Reverend Tome has more clearance left over from his old career than you and I put together."

A dozen or so questions popped instantly in her mind, but there was no time for her to comment as they walked into Big Ed's office. Blalock was there, looking physically tired but still mentally alert. Carson, of course, looked as if staying up all night was just another drill. Justine, Tache, and Neskahi were also there, eager and ready.

Big Ed nodded to Ella. "Take it."

Everybody had met everyone else, so Ella got started without preamble. "I wanted everyone in on this because we're running out of time. We need to solve this investigation before most of our suspects leave the country."

Ella introduced Ford to the others, most who'd met him casually already or knew he was a local preacher, and explained what Reverend Tome had been doing. "What I'm hoping is that by letting all of you in on this, we can work together to decode what Jimmy was trying to tell us."

Ford knew all about presence—an effective tool for any preacher. He glanced around the room, meeting everyone's gaze, then glanced down at his notes. His voice didn't exactly boom, but his speaking cadence commanded and his audience listened to every word. "The real problem with this . . . unfinished story is that it's a code within a code—or actually several codes. At first I thought it was more akin to a parable, but that's not it. Mourning Dove, a character in Navajo creation stories, is the narrator—a creature said to carry messages, and Jimmy is really writing about events he saw or heard about while in Iraq. We read about the Dark Ones—Trickster, Gopher, Gray Wolf, and Stripes—bartering for umbrellas—an absurdity for animals in the desert—from non-Navajo, apparently humans, called Walpole, Mountbatten, and others. Mourning Dove says these Dark Ones also buy gumdrops, shoes, and finally, nails."

Ella nodded. She had her own idea about the items bought, and recent events had only served to support that notion. But maybe Ford had more.

Reverend Tome continued. "The people they obtain these objects from have a combination of familiar and unfamiliar names, such as Walpole, Weigel, Mountbatten, and Chopra."

"The last two are well-known names, but Walpole and Weigel certainly don't ring a bell," Blalock said.

Ford nodded. "On page four Mourning Dove gathers his courage. Hearing the song of his soul he decides to follow his own lead. This entails even greater danger to him but, ultimately, Mourning Dove hopes it'll free him. They all get ready to go home, with umbrellas, gumdrops, shoes, and nails . . . but the story ends. . . ."

"That certainly doesn't tell us much," Carson said.

"I'd thought about the items bought, wondering if they represented something else, like guns," Ella said. "But you'd have to know what kind of guns the nails represented—or maybe the nails were just ammunition? And what about the gumdrops? Grenades? If that's what Jimmy had in mind, it certainly isn't obvious or conclusive. Or am I trying too hard to make a Codetalker kind of connection out of this?"

Reverend Tome smiled. "Many old, simple codes substitute letters or words for something else entirely, or just use ordinary words and have a system where you pick out one predetermined letter in a string of words and that forms the intended message. Anyone ever write notes in school, and have the message concealed in, say, the third letter of each word?"

"Anagrams . . ." Ella muttered thoughtfully and looked down at what she'd written in her notes. "Wow. I never thought it would be this simple. Umbrellas, gumdrops, shoes, and nails. If you rearrange those so that gumdrops come first, then take the first letter of each, you get the word 'guns'. That was what the characters were buying, right?"

SEVENTEEN

✖ ✖ ✖

But we've already reached that conclusion, haven't we?" Justine said. "And how do we know that was the intended message?"

"Sung, gnus, nusg? It has to be guns. Very simple code, once we think about it, and have the knowledge of subsequent events," Blalock said. "Do you suppose he picked gumdrops, so we'd know to put it first? It's the only food item in the items bought, so it's different from the others."

"Okay," Ella said. "Now what about the famous and not-so-famous names?"

"This is where it gets interesting," Ford added. "Lord Mountbatten was a famous British war leader, and the best known Chopra is the self-help guru. Walpole and Weigel drew a blank so I tried a Google search on Walpole, and one of the first hits I got revealed that someone named Walpole was the victim of a highwayman. Recalling that Lord Mountbatten was killed by an IRA terrorist bomb, I had a possible connection. Both had been crime victims. When I searched the other names, adding a crime variable, I learned that Chopra had been the victim of a blackmail plot, and Weigel is the name of a person who'd been kidnapped. And Google's also where I found out who Bula and Konik were. These are nicknames for men who were casualties of a Polish Mafia hit."

"Okay, that links with the two men from the Guard unit who died overseas. So what Jimmy was giving us here are descriptions of the methods the Dark Ones used to obtain guns," Ella said. "With that in mind, I believe more than ever that characters like Trickster, Gray Wolf, and the others link directly to the suspects, men in Jimmy's unit. But I still can't figure out how Jimmy expects us to make an ID—not unless, like Jimmy, you happen to know what the soldiers did overseas and can link that to their namesakes in the story. I was hoping that we could brainstorm and compare the qualities of each animal in the story to specific suspects, and see if we can make a tentative ID that way."

"Trickster might be the imbedded photographer, Zamora," Justine said. "From what we already know this doesn't seem too far a stretch. By naming him 'Trickster,' Mourning Dove may have been alluding to the fact that he presented himself as one thing—a photographer—and, in reality, was nothing more than a thief."

"Zamora was sent home after the MPs searched his luggage on his way back to his imbedded unit in Iraq and found that he had thousands of dollars in cash," Carson said. "He came up with a lot of explanations, but none of them rang true."

"I've got an update on Zamora," Blalock said. "He died in a one-car accident on a mountain road in southern Colorado the same day Jimmy did. The local sheriff said that it looked like he'd been drinking, but a blood alcohol test showed that he was well within the limit."

"Maybe more pinpoint evidence, like whether Zamora is Trickster, is on the half of the story that disappeared—the part we believe originally went to Samuel Blacksheep," Ella suggested.

"I might be able to look over the unit records and see if any of the crimes Jimmy alluded to, like the blackmail or the kidnapping, turned up on any form within their platoon's day-to-day operations," Carson said. "Certainly a Mountbatten kind of action, a terrorist bombing of an authority figure, would be listed. If we can link a suspect to an incident like that maybe we can start identifying the other players, too."

"We need to identify the leader of the operation. Who would you all say is the focal point of the story?" Neskahi asked.

"Trickster went his own way, so my guess is that it has to be Gray Wolf, Stripes, or Gopher," Ella said.

"Gopher seems too passive to be a leader, and Stripes, who is that? A skunk?" Justine asked.

"Gray Wolf would be my guess," Ralph Tache suggested.

"Stripes could be a sergeant. You know, stripes on his sleeve," Ella said, thinking out loud.

"But a captain and a lieutenant wear bars which could be referred to as stripes by a non-career soldier or a civilian," Carson pointed out.

"There's still no hint of a resolution in the story—it was as if the writer was telling us that the battle was an ongoing one and Mourning Dove didn't know how it would end," Big Ed said. He'd been silent until now, taking notes, not wanting to intrude his authority into the discussion. "I suppose the resolution could be in the second part, but judging from the overall tone, I doubt it."

"But we're all in agreement that guns were stolen overseas to be resold here at home for a handsome profit," Justine said. "The motive is clear as well—Jimmy was killed because he knew too much and was on his way home to reveal the story, hopefully with a lot more details of the events alluded to in here."

"If we've got a dirty cop involved, who's to say that the operation stops with weapons from Iraq? Maybe weapons confiscated in a raid—those that normally get taken off-site and blown up as a way of destroying them—aren't being destroyed after all," Big Ed suggested. "Or maybe evidence that should be locked up is turning up missing, jeopardizing future cases."

"There're a lot of possibilities," Ella said. "But the heart of our investigation is Jimmy's murder."

Big Ed looked around the room. "We've got a long list of suspects but, as I see it, the key player—if he's clean—is Samuel Blacksheep. He knew Jimmy better than anyone else. He might be able to break the code—or may even have the remaining part of the story and has been keeping it from us." He looked at Blalock. "Can you check his bank accounts, and things of that nature?"

"I'll see what I can do," Blalock said.

"Samuel's investigating on his own, Chief. And though he may have that last part of his brother's story, I don't think he knows about the part sent to me," Ella said.

"We need more evidence to tie the guilty to the crimes," Big Ed said flatly. "Let me see what I can do through the Farmington PD's back door. What about the body we found in the rental?"

"I questioned his known associates and they claim that the victim had started a new business. He was playing with the big boys and that got him dead," Tache said.

"No other prints except Blacksheep's were found on the vehicle, inside or out. The deceased was dumped onto the backseat, then shot with the assault weapon as he lay there, judging from the damage to the seat, which corresponds to several wounds on his torso," Justine added. "He wasn't killed by Jimmy Blacksheep, that's pretty certain, though Jimmy probably shot him at least once. There was one nine-millimeter slug recovered from his thigh which happens to have been fired from the same gun that put the round in the sign where Jimmy's body was found. From the angle, that round had to have come from the sedan," Justine concluded.

After they left Big Ed's office, a heavy silence fell over the group. Somehow, they had to narrow down the field and sort out the innocent from the guilty.

As Carson left to make the necessary arrangements regarding Richardson, Justine caught up with Ella in her office. "We just got a call from one of the Many Devils. He didn't identify himself, but I took the call and think it was Tony. He says that he suspects that the carjackers are going to be on the watch for targets on the stretch of highway south of sixty-four between Farmington and Kirtland."

"The isolated stretch a lot of power-plant workers take?"

Justine nodded.

"When?"

"He said soon, and that they seemed to be casing the traffic flow for early evening, after the go-home rush has ended."

"We thought they'd be changing their M.O. When did the call come in?"

"I took it less than a minute ago when I stopped by to check phone messages," Justine answered. "But it's not on our turf, you know."

"Yeah, but most of the vehicles on that route are driven by Navajos, and it's within a stones' throw of the Rez. It's our informant, so I'm sure we can get in on this. Let's get with the Farmington PD and sheriff's people who are working with us on these crimes and set up a sting. The carjackers like pickups, so let's see what we can get from the closest Farmington dealer. Hopefully one of the same models they've taken before, but not the most common. We don't want to make it look like a trap."

"I'll get that ball rolling with a call to Sheriff Taylor," she said, and walked out of the room.

The day went by quickly. Carson left with Richardson, and her team focused on processing the evidence and getting the details of tonight's operation worked out. Knowing she wouldn't be home until late the next morning, Ella stopped by the house at around dinnertime. To her surprise, Dawn was back.

Dawn met her at the door, giving her a big hug. "What are you doing home?" Ella asked.

Rose came in. "Her father had to drop her off. He had an unexpected meeting with some tribal officials," she said with a trace of a smile.

Ella didn't comment.

"But Daddy will pick me back up after. Beth Ann's coming over tonight, too!"

It was all they could do to calm Dawn down so she'd sit still long enough to have dinner with them. Even before they finished, Dawn asked to be excused and, a second later, Ella heard her on the phone. Ella and Rose continued eating in silence for a while. Then Rose finally spoke.

"*Bizaadii* and I will be married next Saturday. We won't be sending out invitations or making it a big thing. We'll have the wedding at my son's hogan and start the ceremony at sundown according to custom. That way, when we leave, darkness will cover us with peace."

Ella smiled. "You're a romantic at heart, Mom," she said, all sorts of opposing emotions clashing inside her. "I'm glad you're happy," she said. "But the date you've set doesn't give us a lot of time to make plans. Do you have a dress? You can borrow one of mine. I have a few fancy ones I've never worn."

"Thanks, daughter, but I'll be sticking with something a little more traditional. Maybe you could wear a dress yourself. Its been a while since I've seen *you* in one."

"They don't go with my job. But they still fit—I hope. You can help me pick out one when the time comes."

"It's a deal. Just don't worry, the important things are taken care of. Unless you make other arrangements, your daughter will stay with me until you can pick her up at night—or stay over if you work until morning," Rose said. "Oh, and one last thing I nearly forgot to mention. Your brother has consented to conduct the wedding ceremony. Everything will be done the Navajo way."

Ella nodded, remembering her father and his Christian ceremonies and rituals. But now, her mother had come into her own. No longer a young woman, she was at peace with herself and the Navajo traditions she loved.

"You understand," Rose said, reading Ella's expression. "It *is* my time."

Hearing a car horn, Dawn suddenly ran back into the kitchen. "There's Dad! Can I go?"

"Sure," Ella said with a nod, barely managing to give her squirmy kid a hug and a kiss before she dashed out the front door, backpack in hand.

Ella went to the window and saw her daughter get into her father's BMW. Kevin didn't drive his pickup much, though with the roads around the Rez—or lack of them—pickups were infinitely more practical.

Rose came up beside her. "Don't worry, things will work out for you. Just don't stand between her and her father. He's just starting to figure out that no matter how well you plan things, when you have a child there's bound to be a certain amount of chaos."

"He doesn't like chaos," Ella replied, smiling.

"He's got some hard lessons ahead. Your daughter likes all the presents he's been giving her but, pretty soon, she'll start taking advantage and he'll see it. Then he'll have to lay down some rules, and reality will set in. Your daughter loves you and, more important, she needs you. She looks to you to define herself."

Ella left for work shortly afterward and, as she glanced back at her home receding in the rearview mirror, her chest constricted. Someday soon, she'd be coming back to an empty house—her mother gone, and possibly even her daughter. When she'd been younger, she'd valued her time alone and her privacy a great deal—never wanting either to end. She'd loved not being responsible for anyone or anything but herself. But, over the years, she'd discovered that her family—Rose and Dawn—completed her in a way nothing else ever could. But life was about change, and she felt things shifting all around her, adjusting to a new order, even as the fading view of Sacred Mountain traveled across her window into the night.

Ella arrived at the station about twenty minutes later. As she walked into the lobby, Big Ed poked his head out of his office door and motioned for her to join him.

"Shorty," he said, closing the door, "I've spoken to certain people at the Farmington Police Department. Samuel and his brother had many disagreements—including that trouble over the woman they both wanted—but Samuel has been looking into his brother's death pretty much around the clock. There's some dirt in that PD, more so among those who served with the National Guard, and he knows it. But, from what I've been told, Samuel Blacksheep is clean—one of the good guys."

"It looks like both brothers took to swimming against the tide," she said thoughtfully.

"Yeah—two different sets of trouble—one's already proven deadly. And I got a call about a half hour ago from the Army. They want us to turn the entire case over to them."

"A request from Carson?"

"No, in fact, I was told that he felt that it was being played right. I'm betting it's politics. The National Guard leadership, especially at the state level, is worried about the bad press. We're going to find out things that'll make 'em look bad and give all the good soldiers a black eye as well."

"Unless we continue to play this out, none of us will get anywhere and these men will get away with murder."

"Then get me something concrete, Shorty, to convince them we'll be able to close this fast. I need it by the end of the day tomorrow. No later."

"I'll do my best," she said. "If our trap works, we'll have more of the carjackers in custody tonight. And, with luck, we may be able to close them down permanently."

Ella met with her team minutes later. The county and the Farmington PD had insisted on their own decoy at the east end of the road, but at the west end, closest to the Rez, Justine would be the bait.

"This'll be the first move the 'jackers have made since we almost busted them. The press is still writing about the police failures concerning the recent 'crime wave,' though it's finally off the front page. Expect the perps to be wary of a trap even though they'll be hitting around dark instead of dawn," Ella reminded them. Then looking directly at Justine, she added, "Don't take any chances, don't show them a gun, and don't resist until you've got the upper hand because we're closing in. If it means losing the truck for a while, okay. There aren't any good roads out of there that won't be covered and we've got two GPS's installed, one for them to find." Ella paused, then added, "Are you sure you don't want to switch places with me?"

Justine shook her head. "You've got a kid, I don't. I'm shorter, younger, and look like an easy mark."

"You saying I look old?" Ella said.

"No way, boss," Justine said with a grin. "But you make better backup than I do 'cause you're more accurate with a rifle—particularly now," she said, looking down at the missing joint from her right hand, a reminder of another case they'd worked in the past.

"Got your vest?"

"You bet," Justine said, then checked the duty nine-millimeter semiauto she carried at her waist. It would be hidden by her jacket.

"Remember their tactics and watch your rearview mirror for their second vehicle," Ella said, suiting up with her own ballistic vest, then heading out the door.

Tache, Neskahi, and Blalock were going to be set up in three likely locations along the road, watching with infrared scopes. If the carjackers hit even close to their turf tonight, there was no way they'd be able to escape this time.

Less than forty-five minutes later, Ella waited on top of a bluff overlooking the highway, just below the crest and to the side of a large rock. Below her was the best place to set up a phony break-down, according to Justine, who'd scouted out the entire stretch and picked the surveillance points. Even though it was getting dark, Ella didn't want to risk presenting a silhouette to anyone looking up at that spot. She had a Remington bolt action three-o'-eight with a night scope, so she'd be able to see details. Justine was already in position. She'd make the run from the power plant toward Farmington, hoping to draw them in.

Hours passed, but nothing happened. Justine drove east until she reached Farmington, then circled around on the northern road and returned to the power plant via the western route. Then she cruised the isolated stretch again.

Everyone else kept an eye on the road for other vehicles stopping to set up a trap, or otherwise fitting the profile of the carjackers' M.O. Justine pulled to the side of the road a few times, ostensibly to check her tires, but no one came near her or the truck she was driving.

Around midnight, the road saw a short burst of heavy traffic from the evening shift leaving the power plant and the graveyard people going to the facility. Justine waited at the power plant for the traffic to thin again, knowing the carjackers weren't likely to strike when the road was well traveled.

Once the traffic lightened again, Ella contacted Justine on the radio. "How you doing, partner?"

"Tired—and bored."

"Bad combo, so fight it and stay sharp. Way I see it, either our informant was mistaken, or they've decided to wait until it's closer to dawn, imitating law-enforcement raid tactics and catching people when they're really sleepy. Don't let your guard down."

"I bought about a dozen candy bars at the power plant snack bar. That'll help keep me wide-eyed for a spell."

Ella laughed. "Yeah, that'll do it."

They stayed in position until five-thirty in the morning. Soon the reservation would begin to stir awake and some early day-shift people would be hitting the road.

Nothing had gone down—not for any of the PDs countywide. Ella thought of the report she'd be making to Big Ed, and tried not to cringe. "Make this run, Justine, then let's pack it in," she said, contacting her and the rest of her team on the radio. "When we're done, get a few hours of sleep, people, then meet me back at the station at nine."

She heard the groans, then the ten-fours as she walked down the hill toward her vehicle, hidden in an arroyo from the road, to take a new position. Justine passed by, toward Farmington and suddenly a tribal unit appeared on her tail, hitting the siren and turning on the emergency lights.

"Who in the . . ." Ella said, groaning, then reached for her radio. No Navajo units were supposed to be in the area except for those driven by her own team, and the call letters on the cruiser ahead didn't look familiar. Normally, she wouldn't have interfered, but none of her people needed to be pulled over now—they'd already gone beyond the call of duty as far as she was concerned. And this was off the Rez, barely, anyway.

"Three-three-three Baker, this is SI Unit One. Channel six," Ella said, trying to open communications directly with the patrol officer. After multiple tries, she switched over to dispatch.

"Whatcha got, SI-One?" Dispatch answered.

"I need to raise three-three-three Baker." The abrupt silence from Dispatch tipped her off. Something was wrong.

"SI-One," Dispatch said after a pause, "that unit is missing. Disappeared from the service garage lot last night. You can't raise it because the unit's radio was removed for replacement."

"That unit is pulling over my partner. This is now a ten-eighty-three," she said, using the ten code for officer needs help.

Ella immediately switched frequencies to call Justine directly, but it was too late. Her partner had already pulled over to the shoulder, and was getting out of the truck.

EIGHTEEN

— ✖ ✖ ✖ —

Ella scrambled to get everyone back in position, and to watch for the backup vehicle employed by the carjackers. She was second to the end in their stakeout locations running from east to west, so Blalock was still between Justine and Farmington. Farther west were Tache and Neskahi. With FPD and county units working locations east and north, they could all converge on Justine's location.

But Ella was closest. She climbed into her unit and pulled out onto the highway, closing in from the west without any emergency lights or siren. Switching on her searchlight, she illuminated the scene just as the bogus officer pulled a pistol on Justine. In an instant, Justine fought back. Blocking the pistol to the side, she doubled her assailant up with one well-placed kick. Stepping inside his reach, Justine grabbed his wrist and threw him to the ground with a judo move. By then the assailant's gun was in her hand.

Ella, seeing that Justine had the upper hand, slowed her approach and searched ahead and behind for the second vehicle. They always had a lookout and, by now, that person was probably on the alert.

Ella directed her headlight beyond Justine, farther down the road. A van was approaching from the east, about a hundred yards away, and was slowing. She aimed the searchlight away, not wanting to blind the driver, who might be an innocent passerby, then hit the switch on her emergency lights.

The van slowed, pulled over to the driver's left to stop, then suddenly accelerated and shot past Ella's vehicle. Out of the corner of her eye Ella noted the driver—a short-haired blonde woman.

"Get 'em! I'm fine," Justine's voice came over the radio.

Ella was well schooled in pursuit driving, and with a practiced combination of brakes and steering, slid to a stop, reversing directions at the same time. Putting pedal to the metal, she raced after the fleeing van, one hand on the radio mike. Glancing out the window, she noted as she passed the two stationary vehicles that Justine had the perp on the ground and was applying handcuffs.

"Ralph, green van coming your way. Block the road. Joe, come east to back up Ralph," Ella spoke over the tactical frequency.

"Ten-four," Tache called.

"Backup on the way, Ralph," Neskahi's voice came in loud and strong.

Ella had no trouble keeping up with the old van, a tired-looking Dodge with a wired-on bumper. The highway was good, nearly empty of traffic, and she knew there were no side roads offering an escape. Sirens on, she inched closer, passing through a section of road that had been cut through a hillside. She fought the sudden wave of claustrophobia created by the darkness above and the illusion of passing through a tunnel. Keeping her thoughts focused on the target vehicle, she slowed, backing off just a bit. Ralph Tache's roadblock was only a quarter of a mile ahead, and she didn't want to ram the van.

Suddenly the van started to skid to the left, tires smoking as the driver braked hard after having spotting the police car ahead in the middle of the road. A tire blew.

Ella slowed, watching helplessly as the van tipped over onto the driver's side, sliding along the asphalt with a terrible screech.

Ralph dove in the opposite direction as the van continued sideways off the road, barely missing the police unit before it dropped into an arroyo. The van struck the opposite bank with such a crunch that Ella felt it, despite being a hundred yards away in her own car. It flipped end-over-end like a football before finally disintegrating into a rocky hillside. A heartbeat later the van's gas tank exploded, engulfing the vehicle in flames that spewed out in every direction.

Ella slid to a stop just in front of Ralph's car. Ralph was already racing up the road toward the van with a fire extinguisher, so she called it in as she ran.

It took a while to locate the driver within a wall of flames, still buckled in her seat, but Ralph couldn't get close enough to use the extinguisher. Unable to think of a more horrifying death, Ella prayed that the crash had instantly killed the driver.

Justine pulled up two minutes later, her suspect in the back of the extended-cab truck. He was in his mid-thirties and Navajo, and seemed in shock. He stared wide-eyed at the flaming wreck, his face paler than was natural. Ella noted his uniform, up close, was a khaki fake that Justine would have spotted and reacted to instantly.

"Good work," Ella told Justine. "Nobody else in that squad car?"

Justine shook her head. "Just the cop clone—Fermin Dodge—according to his real driver's license. He faked me out until I got a look at his phony uniform. But I caught him by surprise when I fought back. Maybe we'll finally have a perp who'll lead us to the others." She then raised her voice so the prisoner could hear. "This guy will also be standing trial for the murder of Jimmy Blacksheep."

Dodge sat up as if he'd been jolted by a cattle prod. "Murder?" he called out to them. "No way. That wasn't me—us. We heard all about that, but it was some other guys. Talk to the people we stole from. We didn't even start carrying guns until after that soldier got killed. It wasn't us."

Ella glanced at Justine. "Please tell me that you read him his rights."

"Of course. Twice. I've got it on tape."

"Good," Ella answered, then climbed into the front seat, sat down, and turned to face the prisoner. "If you and your carjacking buddies didn't kill that soldier, Fermin, then who did?"

"Probably some copycat who wanted us to take the blame. But it wasn't one of our guys. We only steal junkers to set up the marks, and our targets are always newer-model pickups and trucks, not cheap rental cars. Check your records."

"You sure about that?" Ella asked.

He nodded, then leaned back in his seat and shook his head. "That's all I'm saying until I see a lawyer."

"You realize that we caught you red-handed," Ella said. "In that phony uniform, in a stolen police car, with two police officers as the main witnesses, you don't have a prayer in court. But if you're willing to cooperate, we'll make you a one-time offer and get some of the charges reduced. You're still going down, but it's up to you for how long—a few years or a couple dozen."

His eyes remained glued on the fiery wreck. "Felice always said she'd never go to jail," Dodge said softly, then lapsed into silence.

"We're missing one," Ella told Justine softly. "The gang usually works in teams of three."

Justine nodded but didn't comment.

Ella looked at Fermin. "So where's the third member of your team? Was somebody else in that van?"

"It was just the two of us," he said, his tone and gaze revealing nothing else.

The M.E. was called, and Tache and Neskahi were left behind to process the scene of the accident, while Justine headed back to the station with the suspect. Blalock, who'd arrived from the east, followed Justine down the highway, and Ella joined them a short time later after briefing the county deputies.

When Ella arrived at the station, Dodge's attorney had already joined his client and Justine and Blalock were questioning him. The station's duty officer was watching from the outside, but left when Ella nodded. Then Blalock knocked, and Ella let him out of the interrogation room. "How long have you been out here?" he asked.

"Just arrived. What does Dodge have to say?"

"For what it's worth, Ella, I don't think he's our killer. According to him, he spent the night with the deceased, Felice Maples, and was in bed with her until midmorning the day Jimmy Blacksheep was killed. It's totally unverifiable from that standpoint, but he said that the woman's neighbor saw him shortly before seven because he had to get up and yell at her dog, who'd been barking nonstop. I've got the address." Blalock looked at her. "For my money, he's telling the truth."

Justine came out next, and, after a few words to verify she'd made no further progress, Ella handed her Felice's neighbor's address. "See if you can get Farmington PD to check this out."

As Justine walked off, Ella led Blalock back to her office. "We may have a third carjacker to track down, and even if these two were alone, there are probably others. I'm getting our suspect's phone records and will try to backtrack on his contacts, friends, et cetera. We'll be processing the stolen cruiser shortly, too. Maybe that'll give us some more prints to work with."

"All good," Blalock said. "And on what's looking more and more like a case totally unrelated to the carjackings, I spoke to Neil Carson when I first got to the station. He said that Richardson received an e-mail request sometime after midnight to make a drop-off. He's got several ex-Iraqi assault rifles that are already cleared of markings and stashed in a rental self-storage place. Carson's beginning to think that Richardson may have been telling the truth—he has no direct contact with the others. But he still believes the man knows who he worked with in Iraq."

"Looks like we have another stakeout coming. Anything on a drop-off time or location? Or a trace on the e-mail?"

"Not yet. I've got somebody from the Bureau trying to back-track the e-mail and nail down a user, but nothing so far. Until then, we have to wait for the next e-mail," he said, then added, "I've spent twenty-five years in the Bureau. And the waiting part never gets easier."

Ella didn't get home until 8 A.M. and went straight to bed. The sun streaming in between the part in her curtains woke her up at ten in the morning. Getting her bearings, she noticed that Two was lying at the foot of the bed, sleeping. His soft snoring was the only sound that marred the all-encompassing silence. That atypical stillness pressed down on her as she showered and dressed. She missed hearing Rose's and Dawn's voices. Laughter and love defined the spirit of their household. If this oppressive, near-total absence of sound was what lay ahead of her, with Dawn at her father's half the time and Rose gone, she wasn't sure how she'd cope.

The emptiness of the house disturbed her. As she passed the phone on the counter on her way to the kitchen, she almost stopped to call her daughter, then changed her mind.

Once they started talking, it would be impossible to say no when Dawn asked her to stop by. Kevin was probably going bananas right now as well, and she didn't want a confrontation in front of her daughter. Then, there was the time factor. Ella had to get back to work soon.

Tearing her hand away, she went to get herself a breakfast bar. It tasted like cardboard and sawdust in comparison to her mom's breakfast burritos, but she wasn't hungry anyway, just in need of a few calories. Ella fixed herself a cup of instant coffee, then placed a bowl of kibbles on Two's rug. The dog picked at his food, not much more interested in eating than she was.

She'd miss the old boy when he moved away. Maybe her mom

would bring him with her when she visited. Certainly, she'd give him a hug and a walk whenever she dropped by her mother's new home.

The ringing of the phone made her jump, and Ella hurried over to answer it. It wouldn't be the station—they'd use the cell. But maybe it was Rose.

To her surprise, she heard Kevin's voice at the other end. "What are *you* doing home at this hour?" he said.

"Good morning to you, too." She could hear the squeals and laughter coming from Dawn and her friend as they played. Ella felt her heart tighten at the sound.

"You usually don't spend much time around home when there's a case this big on your desk. I've heard all about it from my tribal contacts."

"I just caught a few hours of sleep, and, actually, I was about to head out again."

"Can I speak to Rose?" he asked.

"She's not here," she said. "Mom and Herman are off planning their wedding. It's coming up this weekend, and they've got a ton of arrangements to make even though they've both decided to keep it small."

"You know if she'll be back soon?"

Ella knew desperation when she heard it. Then there was a klunk as Kevin dropped the phone and yelled, "No, the puppy *cannot* come inside my office. It's off-limits. Why don't you two go outside and play for a while?" He came back on. "Sorry. The puppy is a hit, but he's not housebroken. So far he's chewed my shoelaces and carried two socks into the kitchen while I was making breakfast."

Ella smiled.

"The reason I'm calling is that I need to run over to the tribal office, but I don't want to take the girls along. I was hoping that Rose . . ."

"Sorry. Like I said, she's not here," Ella repeated, glad for the first time this morning that Rose wasn't home. "And I have to go back to the station right now. Good luck. I know you can deal with these last-minute problems without my help."

"And how will *you* handle them without Rose?"

She chuckled. "Nice try, counselor. Find your own answers."

"I'm in a bind, Ella."

"In that case, it looks like you're going to have to take Dawn and Beth Ann with you," Ella said, unable to suppress a tiny smile. "Or maybe you can get Beth Ann's mom to help you," she added, not totally without sympathy.

"She's gone to Gallup for the day on business and I can't reach her."

"I suggest you lay down some rules for the girls, then take them with you to your office. Don't worry, you'll do fine."

She heard Kevin mutter something incomprehensible, then, with a curt good-bye, he hung up.

Ella laughed as she placed the phone down. She was in a far better mood now. Whether he'd realized it or not, he'd already started to lay down some rules. More rules would follow; any good lawyer could think of a hundred right off the bat. Before long Kevin would learn that keeping a home office full time with a kid around wasn't as simple as he'd believed. Up to now, he'd only scheduled fun weekends—and everything had revolved around Dawn. But, now, he was seeing what it would be like to have her around when he had work to do. It would be hard for all his theories about child-rearing to survive in the face of that reality.

Ella was two minutes away from the station when her cell phone rang. "I've found some prints in the stolen cruiser," Justine said. "We've sorted out those of our own people and are trying to ID the rest. We also confirmed the ID of the dead woman, Felice Maples, and tracked the suspects' phone records and found a lot of calls made to an old riding school in Waterflow just north of the Rez, and several from Ms. Maples to a man from Farmington who happens to be a locksmith."

Justine paused for a moment, apparently looking at her notes, then continued. "The locksmith's name is Burt Greenwood. One of the Farmington PD's unmarked units has Greenwood staked out, and followed him to the riding school about an hour ago. The county and Farmington SWAT teams want to move in as quickly as possible, and Sergeant Sanders recommended that our team take part in the raid since we broke the case. He's back on the team, bumping Samuel Blacksheep, apparently."

"Why am I not surprised? Get ready, and give Blalock a heads-up." Ella slowed, then turned her vehicle into the station parking lot.

"He's here," Justine said. "We're just waiting for you now."

Ella walked through the doors, cell phone still in hand, then seeing Justine standing in the hall, closed it up. "Ready to roll?"

"We all are," Blalock said, stepping out from Justine's office. "Here's a vest. You might need it."

They met with the Farmington SWAT and Sergeant Sanders less than twenty minutes later beside the highway, a quarter mile from the riding academy, which was hidden from the road by an orchard. Sanders had been given tactical command of the operation. Both SWAT teams were moving into position on foot, and everyone, including Ella's team, had been given radio headsets and black raid jackets for ID purposes.

"The riding academy has been closed for several months, but someone's still doing business there, judging from the vehicle tracks. We called the company that manages the property, and they said it had been rented out as a storage facility," Sanders said.

"That indoor riding arena could house several dozen pickups," Ella said, "and a chop shop."

Sanders nodded. "The big building, like a hangar, is sheet metal and steel with a dirt floor. No interior rooms, just a big overhead garage-type door at the west end, and a standard metal door halfway down the south wall. There's another building, cinder block, on the south side, facing the access road, but it's tiny by comparison. It houses a bathroom and the business office. If we get any resistance, it'll probably be from inside the big building, where there's bound to be more cover for the perps, depending on how many vehicles are still inside. Our surveillance team has already spotted four men in there, and three vehicles are parked outside by the overhead door. The smaller structure has only one south-facing window and a steel door facing west, so anyone in there can be quickly isolated."

"How come you know the place so well?" Justine asked.

"My daughter took riding lessons here for a while . . . before my divorce. My wife got custody."

Ella heard regret and sadness in his voice as he'd spoken of his family. She wondered how any parent made it through the day knowing they wouldn't be coming home to their child. "Divorces and cops—they go together, don't they?"

"Yeah," he muttered, but before he could say anything else, a call over the radio brought his thoughts back to the present. "Okay. Both teams are in position," he told Ella after he finished the transmission. "FPD SWAT will make a move on the smaller building, approaching from the east side. While they're clearing the small building, we'll hit the big structure with county SWAT. As soon as they block the overhead door with their vehicle we'll enter the south door of the hangar. Once we're inside and can determine the layout, I'll call out the assignment for each team. By then, the office building should be secure, and FPD can back us up, coming in as a third team, if necessary."

"SWAT snipers covering the doors, right?" Ella asked.

"One from the orchard, and the second across the field on the north side of the main building. No one's getting away today."

It took five more minutes for Ella, Sanders, and her people to move in from the west inside the county SWAT vehicle, a step van much like a delivery truck except for the armed officers crowded inside.

They bounced over the soft ground, then stopped with a lurch. Three heavily armored deputies, one of them carrying a bag containing explosive charges, jumped out of the rear, followed by Sanders and Ella.

Her back against the cool metal west wall of the hangar, Ella waited, her pistol out, for the next step of the operation. She could hear shouts inside, and wondered how well armed the perps were. The walls of the building might stop or slow down a pistol bullet, but not one from a rifle.

Sanders gave the signal, and one of the deputies stepped around the corner, brought a bullhorn up, and called for those inside to come out with their hands up. There was silence for a long moment, then several shots rang out, forcing the officer with the mike to duck back as more than one round penetrated the door and whistled across the perimeter.

"Okay, it's going down," Sanders said, scrambling forward in a crouch toward the corner of the building.

There was a loud crunch, shouting, then someone in the direction of the small office yelled, "Clear."

"Okay. Blow the door," Sanders whispered.

Standing away from the wall but still out of the line of sight from the south door of the hangar, Ella could see FPD SWAT officers crouched behind the walls of the block building, their weapons covering the three county men as they quickly worked, attaching a charge around the latch of the metal door.

The operation took about fifteen seconds, then all three men sprinted back around the corner. Ella could see the short fuse burning before she ducked back. "Fire in the hole," the third man to turn the corner yelled.

Five seconds later, there was a loud, hollow metallic bang and a small cloud of black smoke.

"Execute!" Sanders ordered, and the SWAT men inched around the corner. Sanders and Ella followed, the rest of her team close behind, their weapons ready.

The door had been blown open, and a smoking, jagged hole was all that remained of the knob and latch. Heavy gunfire erupted from inside the old arena, striking the metal door frame and whistling out across the grounds.

Everyone hugged the wall as the covering SWAT team returned fire from the adjacent building. There was a pause, then Sanders tapped one of the deputies on the shoulder. "Two flash-bangs," he whispered.

The deputy brought out one of the light-and-noise grenades, designed to stun an assailant, then showed it to the deputy next to him. In five seconds, both deputies were ready.

"Now," he whispered harshly, and the two grenades went into the hanger together.

Everyone outside looked away, Ella included. Even with her eyes closed, she saw the flash, and the concussion made her ears hurt. Three seconds later, they went in.

NINETEEN

———— ✖ ✖ ✖ ————

The explosions had stirred up the earthen floor, and it was like running through a horse-manure scented duststorm. Ella spotted a bullet-riddled pickup just ten feet away to her left, and ran for its cover. The SWAT officers and Sanders, Team One, had gone to the right, seeking the concealment and protection of a second pickup.

Gunfire filled the big metal enclosure, but at least the dirt floor deadened any echoes. Ella, at the tailgate now, peeked over the top to get a clearer picture of the tactical situation and make sure the bed was empty. Judging from the dozen or more bullet holes in the cab door, nobody inside was likely to still be functional.

"Clah, secure the west end, then advance east down the north row of vehicles. My team will advance east down the south row. We'll cover each other's open flank."

"Ten-four," Ella replied, knowing everyone with a working headset knew the plan now. The dust was beginning to settle a bit, and she could see the entire length of the building. Across the sandy surface of the former riding arena were about twelve pickups in three loose rows, all facing the west end and far enough apart that they took up most of the interior. At the east end were four other vehicles, two of them SUVs, plus two half-stripped pickups. Two long folding tables, a metal framework with chains and pulleys, and boxes of tools were in the area of the stripped vehicles. The bad guys were somewhere out there, maybe as close as the other side of the truck she was hugging.

Ella felt a presence to her right, and noted the arrival of Justine and Blalock, who were using the engine block for protection. "The bad guys could be behind any vehicle, so we have to clear each one, and keep an eye behind us in case we miss someone," Ella whispered, pressing the button that kept her words from being picked up via her throat mike and transmitted to the radio headphones they were all wearing.

"There's one we don't have to worry about." Justine pointed to a leg that was sticking out from behind a white Ford 150 just ahead.

Ella ducked down and saw a man lying faceup, blood on his chest. He'd probably been hit in one of the original volleys from outside.

"Cover and advance?" Blalock suggested. Ella noted he was equipped with his duty pistol rather than a submachine gun.

She nodded. "I'll go first."

Ella moved around the rear of the truck, took a quick look, then sprinted north toward the white Ford, watching for someone to pop their head around a fender or above the bed. She doubted anyone would be dumb enough to take a position inside a cab, where they could be easily trapped.

Crouching beside the front fender, she looked down the line of vehicles toward the east. A perp was down on the dirt about fifty feet away, groaning and holding his thigh. He had his hands up, obviously surrendering to someone she couldn't see from her angle, someone from Sanders's team.

She took aim, watching, then heard either Justine or Blalock coming up. It was Blalock, who inched around the back of the vehicle, then took a covering position. Justine came next.

There was a burst of gunfire at the northeast corner, then it stopped. Deciding on her next move, Ella was about to slip to the next vehicle when a call suddenly came over her radio. "Clah, is that you at the west end, center, behind the white Ford?"

"Yeah," Ella whispered back.

"Can you give me some cover fire? We got caught crossing the open flank. My backup went down and I'm alone against the north wall, close to the center, under a red Dodge. Somebody has me pinned down," Sanders said.

Ella looked over at Justine and Blalock, who nodded. "Hang tight. I'm coming. When I get there, crawl to the west toward me."

"Hurry," Sanders said, his voice hard.

"Once I start to move, shoot into the northeast corner. Try to pin them down," she whispered to Justine and Blalock, who'd also picked up the radio call.

"Why you? There are a half dozen of us in here," Justine whispered, shutting down her call button to keep her words off the radio net.

"Yeah, why?" Ella responded, also blocking the call.

"We'll cover *you*," Blalock whispered. "Sanders is up to something."

Ella nodded, then sprinted around Blalock and Justine, took a quick look to the east, then zigzagged across the clear space between the second and third rows. Justine and Blalock had already opened fire, so anyone aiming for her would be taking a risk showing themselves. Ella reached the end truck, a green Chevy, diving to the ground beside the rear tire. The north wall was just to her left. She couldn't see any legs, so maybe the other side of the truck was clear as well. The red Dodge was the third one down, so she'd have to work her way past two other vehicles, hopefully without encountering a perp.

Inching around to the tailgate, she pulled the lever and jerked the tailgate down, her pistol ready. Nobody was lying on the bed. Pistol forward, she took a quick look around the vehicle. It looked clear to the end, but that didn't mean somebody wasn't between the trucks.

In a crouch, she moved toward the front end of the driver's side, hugging the Chevy. Suddenly a bullet struck the side mirror, sending glass flying. Jumping up onto the running board, she tried to hug the door. She saw a black sleeve, then heard a bullet thump against the west wall of the building and a simultaneous shot.

Getting as low as possible, she reached down for her radio. "Sanders, it's me, Clah. Stop shooting!"

"It's not me, it's one of the perps at the east end behind one of the SUVs," he said. "Move to the other side of the truck and work your way down."

She reversed her direction, chased by another bullet as she went back around the tail end of the Chevy. She waved to Justine and Blalock, who could see her now, and inched down the row, hoping that all the vehicles south of her had been cleared.

Getting to the front of the Chevy, she saw movement at the east end, beside one of the wrecks, and dove to the ground just in time as a bullet struck the Chevy's headlight.

Ella grabbed her radio again. "Justine, there's a shooter behind one of the wrecks. Can you return fire?"

"Ella, the angle is wrong. Stay put until we move north one more row."

"Sanders, where are you?" Ella called.

Sand kicked up just to her left, and there was a thud in a tire behind her as two more shots went off, and she rolled out into view of the perp beside the wreck. He raised up, and quickly ducked back as gunfire from her and her team struck the engine block of the stripped vehicle he was using for cover.

Ella cursed. The last two bullets that had nearly struck her had come from where Sanders had supposedly been, not the northeast corner. He'd set her up, then tried to take her out himself when the perp behind the wreck had missed. But he'd missed as well, and she wouldn't be able to prove a thing.

With a muttered curse, she focused on her next move. Her

immediate concern was getting out of this alive. "Third team com-ing in, center row," Ella heard over the radio. Her chances were getting better. There would be more firepower now that FPD was reinforcing the assault. She looked beneath the row of trucks, and saw the red Dodge. No Sanders. Knowing he couldn't rush her with Justine and Blalock keeping watch up high, she ejected her spent clip and slipped in another.

Adrenaline pumped in her bloodstream as she thought of Dawn. The fear that she might not live to see her child again filled her with determination. Jumping up onto the bed of the truck in front of her, she looked around the cab toward the Dodge to the east. Sanders was either hiding behind the front of the vehicle or underneath. Either way, he couldn't take another shot at her with-out poking his head up.

Ella decided to take the top route. Hoping Justine and Blalock were in a position to cover her, she jumped onto the top of the pickup, ran down the hood, and dove into the bed of the Dodge. Looking into the cab of the truck through the back window, just in case, she saw a red-shirted man in front by the hood, aiming a pistol straight at her.

Before she could move, two shots rang out and the man fell. Ella dropped down to her knees and looked to her left. Samuel Blacksheep had come up the north wall behind her, then taken the perp out when he raised up. "Yeah, I know, Clah. Officially, I'm not on the operation anymore. But I've got my reasons for ignor-ing orders."

"Whatever they were, I'm glad you showed up," she said, climbing out on his side onto the ground. "I'm going after that second guy behind the wreck at the east wall. Will you cover me?"

He nodded. "Go."

Ella slipped around to the front of the Dodge, glanced down at the dead man, then sprinted east. The man back there tried to look up, but covering fire from behind her forced him back down. Ella dove to the ground, aimed her pistol under the derelict vehicle, and stared right into the man's face. "Don't shoot!" he yelled. "I quit."

Samuel was the first to arrive, and he went around the back to cuff the man as Ella stood. "Good hunting. And we have someone left to question," he said.

Ella took a look around, and all she could see were SWAT members and her approaching team. "You saved my neck, Samuel."

"I came in behind your team and saw you working up the line. You were doing just fine without me until that last shooter showed up. He must have moved around a lot, because those bullets that kicked up right beside you couldn't have come from his last position."

"Maybe it was friendly fire," she said. But she knew better. Sanders, wherever he was now, was going to remain in her crosshairs.

Two hours later, Justine and Ella were still at the scene, helping the county and Farmington PD process the evidence despite being out of their jurisdiction. As expected, all but two of the vehicles were stolen, cooling off before being moved out of the area. Those two that were being stripped had their most valuable parts already boxed up, ready to sell.

As she and Justine were looking at the list of vehicles and their serial numbers, Blalock walked over and motioned them away from the stolen parts storage location.

"We've got a problem," Blalock said, keeping his voice low. "I saw the round you suggested we look for in that tire, one of those that barely missed you. The first thing the FPD tech that dug it out said was, 'Hey, that's one of ours', meaning a nine-millimeter one hundred-twenty-four-grain Gold Dot hollow point—department issue. None of the perps were using those rounds in their weapons, based on what's been recovered so far."

"Were any of the perps wearing black jackets or shirts?" Justine asked. "Ella said that some of the shots coming at her came from a man with a black top."

Blalock shook his head. "The prisoner, and the five that went down were all wearing other colors. One of the dead perps was wearing a brown long-sleeved T-shirt, but he was taken out early in the firefight behind the first row of trucks."

Ella remembered seeing him. The facts were clear to her, now, and the implication pointed toward Sanders and the weapons-smuggling operation. "Sanders," Ella said flatly. "Where is he?"

"Outside, talking to his captain and Sheriff Taylor."

"You all heard the radio traffic, and it was recorded over the network. I was supposed to rescue Sanders, but suddenly he 'disappeared' and I started taking fire. I think he tried to set me up."

Blalock nodded slowly. "I'm interested to read how he explains all this in his debrief and the action report. Sheriff Taylor will get custody of the evidence, so we don't have to worry about Sanders tampering with the bullets and audio, but, since we're outside the Rez and dealing with possible corruption, I'm going to get some federal people, maybe ATF, to start watching Sanders."

Although no one had heard him approach, Samuel stepped around from behind one of the trucks, just five feet away. "That's a good idea. He was a solid partner before shipping overseas. But lately he's been working against me. Jimmy apparently sent me an express-mail package, but I never got it. The only reason I discovered it at all is that a couple of days ago I ran into the department secretary and she happened to mention a package from Jimmy that Sergeant Sanders had accepted on my behalf. It came on the day my brother died. I'd moved recently, and my mail was being forwarded to the station. I asked Sanders about it, but he claimed that our secretary was mistaken—it was to him from a relative also named Jimmy."

Samuel looked around, then motioned them closer, and spoke softly. "So I decided to search his office today when he was out and see for myself. The desk locks are easy to pick. Inside, I found what looked like the last part of a kid's story Jimmy had written. I recognized my brother's handwriting right away. He was a wannabe writer, remember? The tale didn't make much sense with the first four pages missing, but what caught my attention was that it didn't read like one of Jimmy's stories. It looked more like some kind of code using a mix of Navajo names I recognized and some others I wasn't sure about. I made a copy, and put the original back so Sanders wouldn't know I'd seen it."

Samuel shook his head, his face grim. "But the bottom line is that Sanders lied to me, and he stole something my brother had intended me to have. Maybe Sanders was the one who took the stories from Jimmy's house, too. I'm not sure what went on overseas, but if it has to do with those stolen weapons I've been hearing about, and Jimmy's dead because of it, Sanders is involved."

"Maybe now's the time to tell you about the first half of Jimmy's story," Ella said. "He sent me pages one to four but I haven't exactly been ready to share—until now. But first, let's catch the bad guys," Ella added.

Ella was at the county jail waiting outside the interview room where the perp she and Samuel had captured was being questioned by representatives from several agencies. As she waited, she got Big Ed on her cell phone.

The car-theft gang had been struck a mortal blow, and the investigation regarding Jimmy Blacksheep's murder had led to at least two viable suspects. These events had taken some pressure off Big Ed, and he had an upbeat tone for a change. "I just got a call from the Bureau. They'd been checking the gunrunning suspects' bank accounts for suspicious activity and there's more money in them than can be explained by their salaries, though my guess is that most of their take is in cash," he informed her.

"Based on black-market gun sales, their estimated profits could go up as high as half a million."

Ella whistled low. "We've got Richardson and Sanders in the hot seat. We'll keep pushing."

"Do that."

Ella closed the phone and filled in Blalock, who was keeping his back to the wall—figurative and literally. "Have you checked with Neil Carson?" she asked.

"Yes. Apparently, that e-mail Richardson got was backtracked by the techs to Kent Miller, who was Jimmy's sergeant. He's one of Carson's short-list suspects in the 'accidental' deaths of those two soldiers in Jimmy's unit over in Iraq, the ones we think Jimmy called Konik and Bula."

"Miller? We've been trying to find him for a week. He was supposed to be roaming around fishing spots and unavailable."

"Well, he's surfaced now, and Carson has a location. Based on the computer used to send the e-mail, Miller's in an older section of Farmington at his brother's home. The brother's a gunsmith, wouldn't you know. Carson wants to nail Miller before Sanders or anyone else can warn him, or Miller has a chance to destroy any evidence he might still have in his possession."

"I think Carson's right about that," Ella said.

"The big guy also gave me a serious heads-up. Calvin Sanders and Miller were first on the scene in Iraq when those two soldiers died, so it could have been staged."

Justine came up to her a moment later. "Bad news. Sanders didn't report to his police chief after he left the riding academy. His own PD is worried that he might have been ambushed by another carjacker after he left the scene. They have officers out looking for him."

"They don't have a clue. He's probably making a run for it," Ella said.

"Or warning the men Richardson's supposed to meet," Blalock suggested.

"We better move fast, or we'll lose them," Ella said.

"Who do you want to trust at this point? Where do we go for backup?" Blalock asked.

Ella considered it for a moment. "ATF. They and you will provide the jurisdiction. We'll also take Samuel with us, and ask Big Ed to find trustworthy backup for us in FPD. But we can't wait. While they're getting our backup together, we'll have to roll."

"Agreed," Blalock said.

As they hurried outside to their units, Ella recalled the two recent firefights she'd been thrown into. The suspects might not go down easy this time either, especially if Sanders was among them. But Navajo blood had been spilled, and balance needed to be restored.

TWENTY
————— ✖ ✖ ✖ —————

Ella, crouched low near the front grille of her vehicle, stared through binoculars at the wood-framed white house sitting on a gentle sloping hill. They'd ordered the perps to come out, but their response had been a swift and deadly burst of automatic gunfire that had sent everyone diving for cover and shattered the windows on Blalock's car, which had been parked across the street closest to the house.

"They're armed to the teeth in there. But why on earth are they fighting? It's broad daylight and there's no way out," Justine called in over the radio.

Justine, Officer Blacksheep, and two ATF men were covering the rear and one side of the house, which was essentially surrounded now, and they were all on the same tactical frequency. "The house is alone up there, surrounded by a big, open lawn and a cliff on the left nobody could climb up without mountain gear," Justine added. "If they try to make a run for their cars, they won't get ten steps."

"I'll tell you why they're going to fight it out," Carson said, speaking into his radio. Leaving Richardson in jail, the CID man had insisted on taking part in the operation and had arrived at the same time as Ella and the others. "They're facing life or a firing squad for their crimes while in the military, then civil charges as well, including homicide. Men who've just come back from combat often have a tough time adjusting. Adrenaline gets in your blood when you live on the edge for months at a time. Going out in a blaze—fast and hard—might appeal to them a lot more than life in prison."

Once again Blalock brought up the bullhorn and ordered them to come out. They all flattened again as a renewed burst of fire peppered Blalock's vehicle in response.

Samuel and Blalock scrambled away from it, using the vehicle as a screen until they reached Ella's car.

"Come on up and play," someone yelled from the house.

Ella didn't recognize the voice—maybe it was Miller or his brother. An uneasy silence settled over the area once again. Ella glanced at Blalock. "We'll have to wait them out. In fifteen more minutes, we should have enough backup and firepower to come up with a plan."

"Sanders and Miller are both cowboys. I spoke with their company commander, and these guys were always proactive, pushing for action. If you don't go after them, they're going to come out for us," Carson said. "You've got to understand their mind-set. They *want* something to happen."

"Better to have a good defense than a weak offense. These guys are packing more firepower than we are right now, but if they come out firing, we should still be able to pick them off. If they wait us out, then *we'll* have the manpower to force a surrender. Either way we win," Ella said.

Blalock gave her an approving nod. "Sounds right," he said softly.

"One thing we need to take into consideration is that we have no idea what's in the basement," Justine said. "That makes them a possible danger to the surrounding community. For all we know, they collected bombs and plan to blow up the block."

"They've been doing this for the money, and the adventure. If they decide to commit suicide, my guess is that they'll do it in a firefight, not in a sudden blast," Ella said. "Either way, we're not in a position to stop them from doing anything inside at the moment. Two of us need to move back across the street and take up positions at either end of the Bureau car so they won't be able to use it as a screen. Then all we need to do is sit tight and stay sharp. We'll lessen casualties that way," Ella answered. "Worst-case scenario, we use tear gas or set fire to the house."

Carson glanced at Ella and nodded. "Sound strategy with our limited resources. In the military we call it aggressive defense. You force the other guy to attack you."

"Let's see how it works out before we issue any commendations," Ella answered somberly. She'd seen too many operations go wrong in the blink of an eye to count her victories before they were earned. "Meanwhile, let's make sure they can't drive away in those vehicles." Ella raised her pistol, took careful aim, and shot out the right front tire of the car closest to the house.

"Now I'm having fun," Carson said, shooting out the front tire of the second vehicle, an SUV. "Now let's you and me go use FB-Eyes's car for cover," he added, glancing at Ella.

Minutes passed slowly but Carson's words about looking for action and spoiling for a fight stayed in her mind. She understood wanting to avoid the boring sameness of a routine life. That's why she hated administrative duties. It was in situations like these—where death waited in the sidelines—that she felt most alive. Danger helped her appreciate everything in her life more.

She thought of her daughter. The love she felt for Dawn went so deep it had become part of each heartbeat and every breath she took. Dawn was the only reason she'd ever consider going back to Kevin. She'd often thought of giving in to his frequent suggestions that she leave the field and marry him. But the day she did that, she knew she'd lose a vital piece of herself.

Her work defined her. She restored order. She made sure that good and evil were kept in balance so that harmony could prevail.

This is who she was and that was the legacy she wanted to leave for her daughter.

Suddenly the men inside opened fire, and they were forced to duck. The door burst open, and a man wearing heavy body armor came out blazing away with an assault rifle. Then, out came a second and third man, also wielding what looked like AK assault rifles.

Ella recalled the raid in Albuquerque, wishing she had a high-powered rifle in her hands right now. Her team fired back, scoring hits, but all three men remained on their feet, their body armor making it impossible to achieve penetration. The shotgun and nine-millimeter rounds from their handguns would knock the suspects back a step, but all they'd do was flinch, then continue firing.

"Go for the head and legs," Blalock yelled from his position behind and to the left of her.

"Volley on the first guy!" Ella shouted, ducking down below the bumper and aiming at the thighs of the attacker closest to them now.

Everyone fired, and several shots struck the shooter in the legs. He went down, screaming, losing his weapon and writhing on the grass.

The two men remaining hesitated, then the second, short one emptied his clip into the pavement in front of Blalock's car. Ella and Carson rolled behind the tires, and Blalock, taking fire as well, dove backward onto the grass, using the curb for protection. The shooters, having forced Ella and the two men with her to dive for cover, turned and fired from their hips as they jogged toward Justine and the AFT agents, who were behind two vehicles.

"They're after a car!" Carson yelled.

Justine, Officer Blacksheep, and the ATF men opened fire on the second shooter, who had stopped to reload. He took hits then, first dropping the magazine, then the automatic weapon.

"Help me, Sanders!" the wounded man yelled, pulling a pistol from his belt and staggering on toward Justine.

"Get him," Justine yelled. A shotgun blast from an AFT agent struck the pistol wielder's vest, but he trembled, shook it off, and kept coming.

Ella slipped in another clip, stood up and used the hood as a rest, then took aim for a head shot. But Sanders opened fire with his assault rifle, sending Justine diving away as a bullet clipped her shoulder. Rolling away from the car and behind a tree, Justine continued to fire at the advancing men as bark chipped off the trunk.

Feeling the heat and protection of the badger fetish she wore around her neck, Ella gathered her courage and squeezed the trigger. The man with the pistol stumbled, falling forward onto the grass.

Everyone opened fire on the remaining man, Sanders, who suddenly realized he was alone and in the open. The volley continued, and his body jerked like a marionette as several shots hit his vest.

"I quit, I quit!" he said, dropping his weapon like it was on fire, then throwing up his arms.

"Give us a reason," Blalock muttered as he jogged forward along with the others, all their weapons still on Sanders.

Ella looked over at Justine, who was on her feet now.

"I'll live," her cousin said, her hand pressed over a bloody spot on her upper arm. "A clean exit, two holes for the price of one." An ATF agent was already bringing a first-aid kit from his car.

The man Ella had shot in the head was dead, and the first man that had gone down, Miller, was bleeding badly but would probably live. Sanders had been hit at least three times in the arms and legs, and he and Miller were being given first-aid when backup and the EMTs arrived.

Ella and the others who'd first surrounded the house stood back as FPD SWAT searched the house. The bomb squad was right behind them, but found no active explosive devices.

Carson stood beside Ella as they watched the EMTs treat

Justine's messy but minor wound and the injured men were loaded into an ambulance.

"Those men are the exception rather than the rule," Carson said somberly. "Our troops are second to none—they're men and women of honor who fight for their country. But every profession has its bad seeds. Like law enforcement."

"You're right. Greed is there in every walk of life."

"Let's see what they've been hiding inside," Blalock said, brushing dust off his jacket, then scowling at a grass stain that had probably ruined his trousers. "The bomb squad just gave us the all-clear."

Ella was first inside, but as they passed through a small foyer into the living room, she didn't see anything out of the ordinary. "They were in the basement when we got here. Where are the stairs?"

Justine, who'd agreed to go to the hospital *after* checking out the house, walked ahead into the kitchen. "In here," she said, stepping into view and motioning them toward an open utility closet with a washer and dryer and a half-open door at the end. A light was on somewhere below, and she could see stairs.

Ella glanced at Blalock. "Lead the way, broad-shouldered one."

"Heck no, ladies first. Besides, if the bomb guys missed something, your young reflexes are much better than mine."

"Your chivalry brings a lump to my throat."

"You made my day, Clah. Now quit stalling." Blalock waved his hand, signaling for her to go ahead.

Ella went down the narrow flight of stairs carefully, holding onto the small rail on the right, her weapon in her left hand now, ready. There was no such thing as too much caution in sites like these, and she'd seen enough action for today. With luck, things would go smoothly, but she wasn't counting on anything.

Downstairs, on the rough plank floor, were racks made of un-finished pine holding at least a hundred weapons—pistols, rifles, assault rifles, curved, fancy knifes, and semiautomatics—and a big plastic tub half full of rings, earrings, necklaces, and gold watches that she suspected would sell for many thousands of dollars. She didn't know one piece of jewelry from another, but she knew the name Tag Heuer, and recognized that many of the pieces were from the last century or earlier, probably antiques looted from the Middle East.

Samuel, who'd been the last in line coming down the stairs, walked around the room slowly, taking it all in. "I thought that once we found my brother's killers, I'd feel better—that it would stop hurting. But nothing's changed."

His grief touched her deeply as she recalled her father's brutal murder—the event that had brought her back to the reservation—and the pain her family had endured. "I can tell you one thing—life doesn't end," she said softly. "Your brother is . . . someplace else now," Ella said, her voice barely above a whisper. "A happier, safer place. I _know_."

"I heard about your accident. Were you really . . . dead?" Samuel asked, his tone matching hers.

She nodded. "The essence of who we are continues. I can't prove it to you—but I know what I saw."

He nodded once. "Thanks. I've heard all that from preachers and the department chaplain, but it's different coming from you. The religious people . . . well, they kinda have to believe that, but people like us don't. We're cynics . . . cops."

"Speaking of ministers, why don't you come back with me to Shiprock and bring that copy you made of the coded story your brother sent you? Reverend Bilford Tome has been looking at the pages I received from your brother and trying to help us figure out the hidden message. We found our own answers the hard way, but if we all put our heads together maybe we can finally fill in the gaps." Looking back at Blalock, Ella added, "You, too, Dwayne, if you're interested."

"Yeah, I am."

In response to Ella's glance including him in the invitation,

Carson shook his head. "I'll take a pass. I've got all I need here to proceed with the CID case. If you get more details on how they moved the stuff, I'd like to know. I'll certainly need it for court. But right now, I'm going to concentrate on our prisoners."

Forty minutes later they met in Big Ed's office. Reverend Tome was present and anxious to examine the remaining pages. Samuel read the part of Jimmy's story that Ella had received while the others read over the segment Samuel had discovered in Sanders's desk—pages five and six.

Once everyone was up to date, Ella spoke. "What Jimmy sent Samuel is pretty straightforward, talking about a time for balancing the good and bad, with the Dark Ones being sent to judgment. I can now guess at some of the IDs in the story, but I think Samuel can fill in a lot for us because he knew Jimmy best."

Samuel nodded and began. "In my half of the story Gray Wolf is also known as *naat'á yázhí*, which means 'little chief.' I remember my uncle Marvin, who went by that nickname. He was a sergeant in the Marine Corps, so Gray Wolf is undoubtedly Sergeant Kent Miller."

"I agree with your logic," Ford said, smiling. "Neil Carson can probably confirm that from the unit records, correlating them with what Gray Wolf does in Jimmy's tale."

Everyone else nodded.

"Gopher is also known as *dinédííl*, which means 'stockily built man.' A friend of our father's went by that name. He was a mechanic, so I think Jimmy was telling me that Gopher was Richardson," Samuel added.

Justine jumped in. "Jimmy said that Trickster's other name was *bi'disziih*. That means 'one who turned up missing.' Can that be the photographer, Zamora? He was forced out of the unit and turned up dead the same day Jimmy was killed. My guess is that one of the suspects ran him off the road, maybe Miller."

"That sounds right. How about Stripes, who was also known as *hastiiltsoii*," Ella asked Samuel. "Another family connection?"

Samuel thought about it for a moment. "It means 'yellow man' . . . we used that term when my brother and I played cowboys and Indians and, of course, the Indians were the good guys. The bad guys, the cavalry, were led by a lieutenant with a yellow stripe on each shoulder of his uniform. He had yellow stripes on his pants as well. We got that from a TV series we watched."

"That makes Stripes the code name for Calvin Sanders, who was Jimmy's lieutenant. It all fits," Big Ed interjected.

"Like a glove," Ella added.

"From everyone else's smugness, I guess you've already figured out what those names like Walpole and Mountbatten mean," Samuel said. "Would somebody fill me in?"

Ella explained how Jimmy had apparently used a computer search to find character names associated with certain crimes to indicate, indirectly, what the corrupt soldiers were doing to get guns from the Iraqis. "Of course we need to clarify all this, and make sure it matches with what the other soldiers report, and the unit records and history. That's where Neil Carson's help will be needed. And I heard from the officer who accompanied Miller to the hospital that he wants to testify and avoid the death penalty. He claims Sanders was responsible for killing Jimmy and Herbert Edsitty. Zamora is another issue at this point, but I doubt his death was really an accident."

"If I'd known about the packet Jimmy sent me and the one sent to you, we could have broken the code days ago," Samuel said.

"It's finished now. That's the important thing," Ella said. "Jimmy's writing career may have been shorter than he planned, but it certainly had an impact. He's saved even more lives now that most of those guns will never reach the streets."

Big Ed received a call, and after a few words, put the caller on the speaker. "Warrant Officer Carson of CID would like to fill you in on some details. Go ahead, Carson."

"I've got information that may clear up a few more details. It appears that Calvin Sanders and the men in his platoon, including those in Jimmy's section, stayed at a home of a wealthy Iraqi for a few weeks. The owners had been killed in an air raid. That's where they found that stash of jewelry, and it gave them an idea. Eventually, they branched out to weapons smuggling. Two soldiers who were involved initially got cold feet after several months and an 'accident' was arranged for them. The group's operational objective was to amass enough cash overseas to get their dreams off the ground once they got back. Richardson, Zamora, Sanders, and Miller were the only ones associated with the military who were involved in the actual crimes and smuggling. We already know about their civilian contacts here in the States. They were the ones who received and processed most of the smuggled weapons."

"Neil, Miller's agreed to testify against Sanders," Ella told him. "Let's hope he makes it through surgery."

"No honor among thieves. Thanks for the info. Good working with you and your team, Investigator Clah," Carson said, and hung up.

"Between the physical evidence and the testimony from Richardson and Miller, it looks like the operation is going to be shut down for good," Ella said, sitting back in her chair.

Big Ed looked around the group and nodded in approval. "Good job, officers. Go home. Take some time off. You all deserve it. You too, Reverend, if you can get permission from The Boss."

The rest of the week passed quickly. When at last the wedding day arrived, Rose was calmer than Ella, who couldn't make herself sit down for more than a few seconds at a time. Maybe it was the long, deep purple pleated skirt and silver concha belt Ella was wearing instead of her comfortable slacks.

She rarely wore a traditional outfit like this—the last time had been at her brother's wedding years ago.

Dawn, who was beside her now, was dressed in similar fashion, and, like Ella, had her hair in a traditional *tsiiyeel*, the signature knot for Navajos. The style symbolized keeping good thoughts and knowledge stored away.

After one of the longest days in Ella's life, sundown finally approached. Although, traditionally, Herman would have arrived on his horse, and his saddle carried to the hogan by the bride's family, these were modern times, and concessions had to be made. Herman drove up in his shiny, polished, and freshly waxed pickup, and Ella and Dawn took his saddle from the back and carried it into the ceremonial hogan.

"And this shows that he'll never leave *Shimasání*, right, Mom?" Dawn whispered excitedly, then seeing Ella nod, added, "It's *so* cool, Mom."

"The wedding basket she'll carry represents the home and symbolizes Navajo wisdom," Ella reminded Dawn. "The cornmeal mush we've been cooking all day will go in it. Corn is life to the Navajo and white corn, in particular, represents the East. That's where everything new is born."

"I want a wedding like this someday," Dawn said quite seriously. "There're lots of special meanings and rules and things to remember, but that's what makes it so . . . cool. Why did *Shimasání* choose Uncle's hogan for the wedding?"

"Normally, with young brides, the wedding would have taken place at the house of the bride's mom, but in this case, your grandmother thought having it here would be perfect."

They left the saddle inside the hogan. Back outside, they nodded to Michael and Philip Cloud, Kevin, and Lena Clani, her mom's Plant Watcher friend, all who were waiting outside for the wedding to begin. Ella and Dawn hurried over to her brother's house. Inside, Rose was dressed in a white charmeuse long-sleeved blouse and a full, pleated white skirt. The shawl draped over her shoulders was woven in an intricate blanket design using vivid earthtones that matched her deerskin moccasins. A beautiful turquoise squash blossom, cuff bracelet, and ring—gifts from Rose's own mother many years ago—completed her wedding attire.

"Mom, you look spectacular," Ella said, barely able to speak at the moment.

Rose beamed. "I'm much too old for all this fuss," she said, though clearly pleased by her daughter's words.

Dawn, who'd been looking out the window, rushed back. "The sun has set. It's time! It's time! He's going inside the hogan with his family!"

Rose smiled. "And I thought I was the one who was impatient."

Ella poured the white cornmeal mush into the basket, then handed her mother a fire-poker stick. Ella turned and gave Clifford's wife, Loretta, the Navajo jug filled with water, and the gourd. Then Dawn and Loretta lined up quickly, Clifford joined them, and they began the procession to the hogan.

Taking a deep breath and giving Ella a smile, Rose pulled aside the shawl covering the entrance to the hogan and entered. Shawls, which signified to all that a wedding was taking place, were draped on the interior log walls as well. Scarcely noticing them, Rose walked clockwise around the fireplace and sat to Herman's right. Placing the basket down on the sand, she and the others waited as Clifford said a blessing over the cornmeal mush, then sprinkled pollen over it.

Rose took water from the gourd and washed her hands, then washed Herman's. After she finished, Herman did the same for her. "This washes away our pasts," Rose said softly. "Today, we begin a new life."

Careful not to move the basket, which would bring bad luck, Herman took a pinch of cornmeal from the east side of the basket and fed it to Rose, then Rose did the same for him. Following the customs of The People with meticulous care, they fed each other from the other cardinal points, south, west, and north, then from the center, until the mush had all been eaten.

Once the basket was empty, the ceremony was complete. They were now man and wife. Since Herman's mother was no longer alive, Rose chose to give the basket to Ella. "The next wedding is yours," Rose whispered.

Ella smiled. Her mother—the perpetual optimist.

As the feast began, Loretta brought in large platters of food, and everyone ate to bursting. Normally, after the meal, the elders would have given the young couple advice, but because Herman and Rose *were* the elders, only Lena had anything to say.

She cleared her throat and the hogan fell silent. "You are both my lifetime friends, so you've been listening to my advice for years, whether you've taken it or not. All I have to say is that you should continue to respect and love each other."

Herman nodded and Rose blinked away tears that had formed in her eyes despite a wide smile.

Ella looked at her mother and at Herman, glad to see them both looking so happy, then stood up. "May your lives be blessed and companionship and love guide your paths. And may you both walk together in beauty," Ella said.

Rose wiped the tears from her face. "The Holy People have blessed us all today."

Herman smiled. "Two families have come together. There is beauty all around us."

As Loretta began passing out the small bags of food, customary gifts for the guests, Ella walked away from the group, needing a few minutes alone. She'd promised to take Dawn for that long trail ride tomorrow morning, and she was hoping to find a way of getting Dawn home early so they could grab some sleep tonight. She was staring silently at the blanket of stars above her when she heard footsteps. Turning her head, she saw Kevin had come to join her.

"Our daughter looks beautiful tonight, as does her mother," he said quietly.

Ella smiled, recalling similar words from her father so long ago at her own small wedding. "You know, we really do need to share Dawn, Kev. We both add to her life and she needs us to be strong parents—not just two adults she can play against each other to get whatever she wants."

"I know, and we'll work something out, I promise. It's not a competition—it's parenthood."

As Kevin walked away, Ella remained on the fringe of the gathering, watching the celebration. Marriage affirmed the future—one filled with hope. It was a completion, a bringing together of two sides, male and female, and the restoration of the *hozhq*—balance and harmony.

Yet, as it often was, one change would open the way for others and, soon, new possibilities would come her way, too. As the breeze touched Ella's face, she remembered her mother telling her that Wind whispered secrets. A smile on her lips, Ella stood tall and listened.

Look for

TURQUOISE GIRL

(0-765-31715-X)

AIMÉE AND DAVID THURLO'S
EXCITING NEW ELLA CLAH NOVEL,
NOW AVAILABLE FROM FORGE.

Ella and Justine have been summoned to the scene of
a homicide.

Special Investigator Ella Clah of the Navajo Tribal Police missed her daughter Dawn with all her soul. Years ago, the prospect of moving in with two other women—both police officers—would have seemed perfect. No one would complain about the crazy hours or the dreadful toll taken by the pressures of a law enforcement career. But those days were gone. Now, living away from Dawn, her eight-year-old daughter, made her throat tighten up and her chest feel constricted.

Dawn had chosen to stay with her father until the renovations on their home were completed. All in all, it was a very practical arrangement, but Ella still worried. It was part of being a mom. With luck, the next few weeks would fly by.

The construction was necessary—there had been so many changes in her family's life this past year. Her mother, Rose, was now married to Herman Cloud. The couple had decided to build an addition to Rose's home so their extended family could stay together. Unfortunately, while the renovations were being done, the family was scattered all over the Rez.

"Yo, partner?" Justine Goodluck called as she half dragged and half pulled Ella's duffel bag out of the SUV. "What do you have in here—adobes?"

Emily Marquez, Justine's roommate, laughed. Emily, a San

Juan county deputy who worked outside Rez borders, was tall, blonde, and had clear blue eyes. "Let me take it."

"Go for it."

Emily barely managed to keep the duffel from falling to the ground. "Ugh, Justine's right! Are you stealing cinder blocks from your mom's construction site?"

"Okay, let's double-team this one," Ella said, laughing as she grabbed hold of one of the hand grips. "I've got half a library in there. I've been trying to read up on something."

"Near-death experiences?" Justine asked on a hunch, jogging ahead to open the door for them.

"Mostly," Ella answered as she and Emily manhandled the bag into the house.

Justine led the way to the bedroom Ella had used once before. "I've turned this into a permanent guest room. At the far end of the hall is our office. There are fresh towels in the bathroom."

"Thanks," Ella said and began unpacking the big suitcase she'd placed on the bed. The first thing she set out on the night stand was a photo of Dawn with Wind, her pony. Before she was able to remove more than a few articles of clothing, Justine's pager—and Ella's—went off.

Ella called in. Hanging up a moment later, she said, "We've got to roll, partner. We've got a 10-72." As they raced toward the highway in their unmarked tribal vehicle, Ella gave Justine the details. "Trouble's going down at the access road to the new power plant construction site. They were scheduled to move in heavy equipment to begin digging foundations for the main reactor building, but a group of diehards are blocking access to the site."

"Is there another way in?" Justine asked.

Ella shook her head. "Not unless the construction company put in another road we don't know about. I remember from our earlier visits that there's a fence on both sides. The place is pretty easy to seal off, and what the protestors haven't blocked with vehicles, they're covering with manpower."

The small nuclear power plant, first proposed by a mostly Navajo consortium called NEED, had already cleared years of paperwork. But tensions appeared to be escalating once more now that construction was finally under way.

As they approached the turnoff, Ella saw that a fire had been set in the middle of the graveled road about fifty feet from the east bound lanes of the highway. Beyond that fire, between the construction workers and their vehicles, were the protestors.

Just beyond the chained and locked metal gate were four warmly dressed Navajo men holding signs whose messages she recognized from earlier incidents. 'Protect our holy places', read one, and the other held big letters, NO NEED, which referred to the Navajos Opposed to the Navajo Electrical Energy Development project. Outside the gate were a half dozen workers, standing beside a loader, two dump trucks, and a big bladed caterpillar atop its transport semi and trailer.

As Ella got out of the SUV, she felt as well as heard the deep throated pounding of drums somewhere up ahead. She saw two more protesters on their knees beside the fire, beating the drums in a steady tattoo.

"You come at night like cowards," one of the protestors yelled. He was standing just out of reach beyond the gate, shouting through a bullhorn.

"That's Benjamin Harvey. He was arrested last time for disorderly conduct. He's trying to goad someone into starting a fight," Ella said quietly. "Call for backup. It'll make it easier on everyone if we can outnumber them."

Ella walked up to the heavy metal gate, her eyes alert for possible weapons. Standing at the edge of the glow from the fire, away from the other protesters, was a seventh Navajo in a low-billed cap filming everything with a video camera.

Ella turned as someone from the construction company, wearing a gray company shirt, walked up to join her. The man, his name tag identified him as Stover, was a tall, light-skinned Anglo.

His expression suggested he was barely restraining his temper. Ella moved back her jacket, showing him her badge which was clipped to her belt. Her pistol was also there, holstered. "I'm Investigator Clah. My partner is Officer Goodluck. Bring me up to speed."

"I chose this time to bring in our equipment because it would avoid traffic tie-ups on the main highway. I had also hoped to avoid any more protesters. With actual construction about to begin, I figured—"

Another tribal police unit pulled up, emergency lights on. Ella knew from the number on the patrol cruiser that it was Officer Michael Cloud, one of Herman Cloud's twin nephews. Her new stepfather was related to two of the best patrol officers in the department. Michael Cloud was an excellent officer with a cool head, just the person she wanted as backup.

As Michael got out of his unit, one of the construction workers used a pair of bolt cutters to snap the chain the protestors had used to lock the gate. The second it opened, another employee slipped through with a fire extinguisher and ran toward the fire. The drums stopped as the drummers hurried to block the way, but the man with the bolt cutters joined his ally, waving the heavy tool at the closest protestor, snapping the jaws. The workers outside the fence shouted encouragement and began moving toward the gate.

Ella knew she had to intervene before the two groups met or the situation would spiral out of control. "Keep them outside the fence," she yelled to Michael as she and Justine raced through the gate.

When the man with the fire extinguisher tried to douse the fire, one of the protestors broke the stick holding his sign over the worker's hard hat, then tore the extinguisher from his hands. Without skipping a beat, the Navajo man ran to the gate and tossed the extinguisher into the windshield of the company's pickup.

Ella took advantage of the distraction to grab the bolt cutters from the other worker's hands. Justine went after the Navajo who had thrown the fire extinguisher. The protestor ran into the darkness.

Officer Cloud had closed the gate and was blocking the way with his body. "Touch the gate, and you'll get an eyeful of Mace," he said, the canister in his hand.

The redheaded security guard joined Michael, a container of pepper spray in his hand. "Ya'll back off!"

"Benjamin Harvey!" Ella shouted, trying to find him among the remaining demonstrators, who'd moved forward to defend the drummers.

"Yeah, I know. We're under arrest!" Benjamin stepped forward, holding out his hands, palms up. "Cuff me. But the *Diné* will be back!" he announced, turning toward the man with the camera. Unfortunately the man had disappeared, and Benjamin frowned, upset that his big moment wasn't being recorded for posterity.

"You've made your point, people," Ella said to the demonstrators. "Go home now, or spend the night in jail."

In the distance, she heard the sound of a motorcycle racing off. The perp Justine was chasing must have hidden his transportation elsewhere in the dark.

"What about my windshield?" the Anglo named Stover asked, coming up to the gate, then stopping as Officer Cloud turned in his direction.

"One problem at a time, sir," Ella responded, her eyes searching in the direction Justine had gone. Then her cell phone rang.

Motioning with her head, Ella gestured for the two construction workers to step back outside the gate, and, as the first one passed, she handed him the bolt cutters.

"Yeah?" she said into the mouthpiece of her cell, still looking for Justine.

"One of our officers called in a 10-58, Priority One," the Dispatcher said, giving Ella the address and the details. "We've also contacted Agent Blalock of the FBI, but he's in transit down from Colorado. Your crime scene unit and the ME will meet you on site. Officer Marianna Talk is there now."

Ella took a breath. A 10-58 was a report of a dead body, and Priority One designated it as a murder victim.

It was going to be one of those nights. Justine returned, alone.

"The vandal got away. Had a motorcycle stashed in an arroyo. I was able to ID the plate, though. I also called in a description of the perp, and they're running down the tag already."

Ella turned to Michael. "I just received a 10-58 call. Once you get some backup, we're leaving."

"It looks like we've got things covered here. Go ahead." Michael pointed with his lips toward the highway.

Ella looked past him to see that Officer Philip Cloud, Michael's twin, had just stepped out of his unit and was walking toward the crowd. Sergeant Joe Neskahi was with him.

"The body's in the apartment just behind the Morning Stop," Ella said as she and Justine drove toward the new crime scene.

"They fix a decent breakfast burrito. Stan Brewster, an Anglo, runs it."

"We don't have an ID on the victim, but the first officer on the scene was the rookie Marianna Talk. She comes from a Traditionalist family so she won't want names mentioned if at all possible," Ella said. "Just a heads-up." Although tribal police officers adapted to the demands of the job, some habits were too deeply ingrained. "Apparently Marianna responded to an anonymous tip."

"Will Agent Blalock meet us there?" Justine asked.

Ella shook her head. "He's in transit from Colorado, so we'll be working the scene on our own."

The law dictated that the FBI had to be involved in felony investigations because if prosecution followed, the case would be handled in federal court.

"What about Ralph?" Justine said.

"He'll meet us there. And so will Carolyn," Ella said, referring to the tribe's ME.

Justine pulled into the small parking lot in front of the Morning Stop Café. The officer at the scene had cordoned off the area with police tape.

Ella got out first, and went directly to meet Officer Talk, who was standing just outside the tape perimeter. Officer Talk was barely five foot two, and that height was enhanced by the boots she was wearing. Although she was standing guard like a professional, protecting the crime scene, Ella saw the slight tremor in her hands as she raised the yellow tape to let Ella pass beneath.

"I don't have much to give you, Investigator," she said, avoiding using Ella's name. "I responded to an anonymous tip that came through Dispatch at twenty-two-fifteen. A man reported a break-in at this location and claimed he'd heard a woman screaming. The call has already been traced to the pay phone just down the highway at the Quick Stop. I was dispatched Code Three Priority One and promised backup as soon as possible."

Ella sensed that Marianna Talk was fighting hard to keep a tight lid on her emotions. Ella was willing this was her first Code Three—emergency—and Priority One—homicide—call. Marianna's upbringing as a Navajo told her that staying near a corpse was dangerous, yet her duty as an officer demanded the opposite.

"When I arrived on scene, it was quiet," she said in an unnatural but steady voice as Justine headed for the apartment, camera in hand. "I checked the café and then went around to the other building. I saw that the door had been forced. Inside it's a mess and the body . . . well, once you go inside, the sounds reported by the witness who made the call will make a lot of sense."

"Did you touch anything?"

"No, ma'am. I left everything as it was and came out here to secure the scene."

"Excellent. You've done a good job, Officer."

Ella stepped carefully into the apartment, pulling on latex gloves—two pairs—as she did. The extra set of gloves would insure she didn't touch anything that had come into contact with the dead. Not that she was a Traditionalist, but some teachings went too deep to ignore. The practice of wearing two sets of gloves was one followed by most of the officers in the force and, in particular, those in her Crime Scene Unit.

Justine, who'd been taking photos around the entrance, followed Ella inside, carrying an evidence kit and her camera. The place had been tossed and, judging from the blood splattered all around including the floral patterned wallpaper, Ella suspected the victim hadn't gone down easily.

After doing a preliminary walk-through, she called back to Justine. "Body's in the bedroom. From the wounds and the blood splatter it appears the vic was knocked into the wall mirror during the fight."

Ella focused on the victim, studying the way the killer had posed the body. He'd arranged the dead woman in a kneeling position against the side of the bed, as if in prayer. Her hair was a bit damp. A *jish*, a medicine bundle filled with pollen and soil, had been tied to one of her wrists and a closed Bible had been placed on the bed in front of her. A handwritten note lay on top of the book.

"Bathtub's full," Justine said. "The water is bloody, and there is a lot of spillage on the floor. Maybe a forced baptism—after at least some of the cuts were inflicted?"

Ella focused on the immediate area around the body. The waste basket against the wall was full of bloody paper towels.

Streaks on the carpet made it clear it hadn't just been the perp's intention to clean himself—some of the paper towels had been used to mop up blood and water from the carpet.

Ella moved to the side of the bed to take a better look at the victim's face. "I know—knew her," she said feeling as if someone had just knocked the wind out of her.

Though her nose had been broken, and possibly some facial bones as well, Ella recognized Valerie Tso. Her daughter Boots—Jennifer—was Dawn's babysitter. Deep cuts and bruises covered her naked arms. She'd been dressed in Sunday best. The clothes were clean and undamaged, which told Ella that Valerie had been dressed after her death.

Blocking the emotions running through her, Ella looked for defensive wounds on the body—torn fingernails and bruises on her hands. She was surprised to find only a few cuts on the woman's palms and fingers, perhaps from trying to rise off a floor littered with broken glass. Finally, she examined the note that had been left on top of the Bible.

She could read it without having to touch it. "'The Lord has made all things for himself: yea, even the wicked for the day of evil. Proverbs 16:4.' Bag and tag this, partner. Maybe the killer left us more than he intended."

Justine placed the note in a transparent evidence pouch, then held it up and studied it for a moment. "What the heck is it supposed to mean? God made the wicked for a reason?"

"I'm sure there are numerous interpretations. Maybe the perp was using scripture to justify his own actions."

Ella saw dried blood on the broken mirror and on the pieces of glass that lay scattered on the floor. Streaks showed where the killer had pushed some of the pieces out of the clean zone, probably with his foot. There was even some blood splattered on the ceiling. "Maybe the blood's not all hers. She may have taken a chunk out of her killer," Ella said, then took a deep, steadying breath.

"Hey, you okay?" Justine asked.

Ella nodded. "According to what I've heard, mostly from my mother, the victim worked here at the diner and got free rent. She was just starting to get her life together again and was hoping to patch things up with her daughter."

"Your mother's best friend is the victim's mother, isn't she?" Justine asked.

Ella nodded. "And my mother will be right beside the victim's family, demanding answers, when she finds out what happened. This won't be just another case. It hit too close to home. This one's personal." Valerie Tso's life had ended, but Ella's work was just beginning.

Forge

Award-winning authors
Compelling stories

. . . .

Please join us at the website
below for more information
about this author and other great
Forge selections, and to sign up for
our monthly newsletter!

. . . . www.tor-forge.com . . . .

CPSIA information can be obtained at www.ICGtesting.com
Printed in the USA
LVOW13s1612190514

386428LV00001B/165/P